Demon Unleashed

Part Two in the Day-Walker Saga

―――――――

By Elle Brice

Demon Unleashed
Copyright © 2015 by Madison Brice

All rights reserved. No part of this book may be reproduced or transmitted in any form or by any means without written permission from the author.

ISBN **978-1511493918**

Printed in USA by Create Space
Cover design by James, GoOnWrite.com

Acknowledgements

For my mom, who is my number one cheerleader.

Table of Contents

Acknowledgements 3
Prologue 5
Chapter 1 7
Chapter 2 27
Chapter 3 40
Chapter 4 61
Chapter 5 83
Chapter 6 117
Chapter 7 144
Chapter 8 163
Chapter 9 179
Chapter 10 193
Chapter 11 213
Chapter 12 233
Chapter 13 250
Chapter 14 270
Chapter 15 297
Chapter 16 323
Chapter 17 344
Chapter 18 361
Chapter 19 376
Chapter 20 393
Chapter 21 409
Chapter 22 422
Epilogue 426

Prologue

The Las Vegas air was dry and hot, much like the Judean Desert. There was serenity in the wild that couldn't be found anywhere else. Here, there was sin; murder, debauchery, lust. It reeked of it. Maximus could smell it the moment he'd arrived. One of the downsides of being in his position.

He wandered the dimly-lit streets, waiting for the pull to lead him toward those he was looking for. The pull was the most inconvenient side effect of his power. No matter where he went, he could feel it, gnawing at his soul. The more secluded he was, the stronger the pull. He never responded to it unless it was absolutely necessary.

After living as a recluse in Judea for the past four hundred years, mingling with other human beings was almost foreign. He preferred the company of snakes and birds. They didn't talk back. He cringed at the sound of chatter from those he passed by. The smooth walkway was the only part of the city he didn't mind. The harsh sand and rocks had been uncomfortable against his feet.

The pull grew stronger as he continued to walk. There were only two in the whole world whose pulls he felt more than any other. And he could feel them both at once. The connection was so overwhelming that he could barely think. He had to get to them before he would lose his mind

He found himself walking towards an apartment complex on the edge of town. Whoever he was sensing had to be there. The will to go inside was too powerful to ignore. He got closer and closer until he was across the street. He was about to head for the door when he heard someone coming. He hid behind a tree as a young man came out and started a car parked on the side of the building. He seemed frantic, or worried about something. Maximus could tell he was immortal by the scent of his blood.

And he was undeniably drawn to him. He had to be one of the four and the others were not far from there. He could feel them. What mattered to him was that their blood be contained. Those searching for it could not get to them or else Lucian would live.

Instead of going inside, he decided to remain outside and wait for them to make another appearance. He wasn't going to speak with them.

He only wanted to keep an eye on them. He had someone among them who was tasked with keeping Lucian from rising a second time. His appointed one had succeeded in the past and Maximus trusted that they would not fail.

Chapter One

I don't know how long I drifted in and out of consciousness. Time became nonexistent and all that I could perceive was the terrible pain shooting through my body. Sometimes it was sharp and sometimes it was dull. Sometimes it lingered and sometimes it came and went.

Every now and then I would hear shouting as well. I could distinguish one voice, but another was unrecognizable. I couldn't tell if it was a woman or just a man with a high-pitched voice.

"We have to do it," one person said. Was that the strange woman?

"We're not surgeons. What if something goes wrong?"

That last voice sounded like Mark. It couldn't be Mark, he was dead. I saw his body. Then again, Aaron sounded very similar to him. My hearing was probably just warbled.

"She's going to die! If you won't do it, then I will."

Following that last phrase, I felt something slicing into me. I'd been able to endure the pain before, but this was excruciating. I could feel whatever was cutting me, sinking at least two inches into my skin. It hurt so bad that I couldn't even hold back the yell that escaped my throat.

"Stop, that's enough!" I heard someone shout. I still couldn't tell if it was Aaron or someone else.

"I already got four out," the higher voice said. "There's only three left. Do you want me to help her or not?"

There was a long pause before the other person finally said, "Finish it. But at least give her something for the pain. You must have something."

Not long after I felt a prick in my right arm and the voices became more warbled than ever. But what I did like was that the pain finally stopped. I felt ten times lighter and I fell into a deep sleep. I hadn't slept like this since before I turned. I didn't think tranquilizers could affect me, though I didn't really care about whether or not that was so. All that mattered was that I felt no more pain.

I woke up feeling disoriented and my vision was blurred. My head pounded, my ears throbbing loudly, so I tried to sit up. I was underneath a blanket pulled up all the way to my shoulders. The flowered pattern jumped out at my eyes. As I began to see more clearly, I realized that I was in my hotel room. I pushed myself up into a sitting position and an excruciating pain shot through my body. I looked down at my tattered shirt then lifted it up to see three bullet holes in my abdomen.

The memories of what had happened that night came flooding back to me, and I began to sob. I'd heard as Samil's follower put a bullet in Mark's head then let Matthew stab my mother. They'd taken Robin, leaving Kevin and me to die in our backyard. But I'd survived. I felt like death, but I was alive.

I forced myself out from under the covers, the pain nearly

immobilizing me, and stood up. As far as I knew, I was alone, but I wasn't sure how I'd gotten there. I hoped that Kevin was okay and that Gallard had somehow discerned from my message that I was in trouble. I didn't want to be alone in my grief. I'd been alone when David had died. David; my real father. The sobs overtook me once more and I buried my face in a pillow. It hurt to cry, but I couldn't stop. With each convulsion, my body would be overwhelmed with agony.

When I was finally able to gain composure, I searched the room for my phone. I wasn't sure who I planned on calling, but I needed to talk to someone. I found it on the table next to the TV and was about to dial a number when someone opened the bathroom door. I dropped the phone and ran to the corner of the room, preparing myself in case I needed to fight. I was terrified, especially since I'd been unconscious, but when I saw who it was, my fear subsided.

"Kevin!" I said, relieved that he was okay. I hugged him, but when he hugged me back, he squeezed me so hard that it hurt. I winced and he pulled back.

"I'm sorry. I need to work on that," he said. I frowned in confusion.

"Work on what?" I asked. Before he could answer, Aaron came out of the bathroom as well. I went over and hugged him, and he returned it, only gentler than Kevin had.

"I'm so glad that you're awake," Aaron said. "For a while there, we thought we'd lost you. Your skin healed over the bullets and I had to reopen the wounds to get them out."

"So that was you? What about the woman?"

"W...woman?" Aaron was stuttering a bit. "There was no woman. Just Kevin and me."

I was so sure I'd heard a woman. I just chalked it off as hallucinations due to blood loss. So many things had happened in such a short time that it was possible that I'd imagined things.

"How did I get here?" I asked. I glanced at the clock to check the time. It was almost two in the morning. About six hours had passed since the horrible event. It could have been six years, and I still would have been as distraught.

"Kevin called me after it happened. I told him to get you out of there before the police came and he put you in mom's car. He nearly wrecked because of the blood loss and I found him passed out on the side of the road. We brought you here afterwards. Your friends from Vegas will be here soon as well."

Gallard was coming. That seemed to make everything better and I was eager to see him again. He always knew just how to make me feel better when I was hurting. He'd gotten me through David's death, and I desperately needed him now.

A familiar scent reached my nose and I inhaled deeper to see if I wasn't imagining it. I smelled blood and it was coming from somewhere in the room. I walked passed Aaron, trying to find the source of the smell and I stopped in front of the bathroom then opened the door.

"Lela, don't go in there!" Aaron shouted. He'd been too

late. I already saw what he was trying to hide. Inside the bathtub was not one, not two, but three bodies; one woman and two men. They were completely drained of blood and their limbs were distorted from being thrown in awkwardly.

"What the hell is this?" I asked, shouting at Aaron. "Are you insane? You can't bring victims into the hotel; someone is going to find them!" He came up beside me and slammed the door shut. I glared at him, waiting impatiently for an explanation.

"I'm sorry, I must have missed the part where you were in charge of what I do," he said. "Just because you've been a vampire four years longer than I have doesn't make you the expert on victim disposal."

"Screw you, Aaron! You know that this is an irresponsible thing to do!"

"He needed to feed, all right!"

"Who needed to feed?"

He looked away and I followed his gaze to Kevin. It instantly dawned on me; the comment he'd made earlier about needing to work on his hug had been about his not knowing how to control his strength; his new vampire strength.

"No, please tell me you didn't..." I said to Aaron, the tears starting to stream once more.

"I had to, Lela. Samil killed mom and dad, and there's nothing to stop him from killing Kevin as well. He had an unfair advantage, so I gave him the ability to defend himself."

This couldn't be happening. I'd left to keep my family

away from this mess, and now not only was Aaron a vampire but Kevin as well. I felt like I'd failed them.

"Kevin, did he force you to do this?" I asked. He shook his head.

"He suggested it, but I agreed. We talked it over for a while, weighing the pros and cons. I concluded that there were more pros. Mom and dad are gone, and you, Aaron, and Robin are the only family I have left. Yes, I am sacrificing ever having a normal life again, but at least I'll be with the people I love."

I wrapped my arms around his waist, burying my head into his chest and he held me, less tightly this time. I cried as I listened to the hollowness of his chest; a reminder that his heart would never beat again. My baby brother was now a monster like me.

Though I didn't want to be alone, I needed some time to think. I'd been hit with too much at once; my parents' murder, Robin's abduction, Kevin's transformation. I was going to go crazy if I stayed in the hotel a moment longer.

I found my suitcase next to the sink and began digging in it for some clean clothes. The first thing my hand touched was the blue, t-length dress that Gallard had given me for my birthday. I wanted to wear it for when he arrived, so I pulled it out along with a pair of white socks and my dark-blue vans.

I reluctantly entered the bathroom, dreading the need for me to pull the bodies out of the tub so I could use the shower. I detached myself from them, keeping my eyes away from their faces as I gently laid them on the floor. The blood smelled good, but knowing Kevin's newfound hunger, there was probably none left to drink.

I stripped down then turned on the water, waiting for it to get hot before getting in. almost instantly, the water turned dark red from my blood that had been caked onto my skin. As I washed off, I counted all of my wounds with the tips of my fingers. I found four on my front and three on my back. They were healing slower than usual and looked horrible. I could only imagine what shape my internal organs were. I had to have suffered from some internal bleeding.

I finished showering once the water ran clear, wrapped a towel around me, and then stepped out. It was difficult maneuvering around the bodies since the bathroom was so small. I quickly pulled on my clothes prior to running a brush through my hair and went out of the bathroom then grabbed my phone and room key from the dresser.

"I'm going out. I need blood," I told my brothers.

"Are you sure it's a good idea for you to be alone?" Kevin asked.

"I'll be fine. Samil wouldn't come after me twice in one night."

"Let her go, Kevin. She is the expert after all," Aaron sneered. I flipped him off then blew Kevin a kiss before walking out the door. I was afraid if I didn't leave then, I would end up pummeling Aaron. His immortality had corrupted him in ways I never knew were possible. The kind, loving, and level-headed brother that I'd grown up with was gone, and in his place was an unreasonable jerk. One thing I couldn't deny was that he had saved my life. If he hadn't come when he had and gotten the bullets out, I probably would have died.

I exited the hotel, making my way down the street. It was a little after one, but the traffic was still heavy. There were tons of cars driving up and down the road and I would occasionally run into small groups of people walking on the sidewalk. I looked both ways before crossing to the other side of the street, searching for anyone that was alone. Most of the people I came across were in pairs or threes, and I didn't want to make a scene, so I kept going.

I found a string of night clubs and watched as partiers went in and out. I found one with some Spanish name, and since it looked pretty busy, I decided to go in. The bouncer didn't even card me; he just smiled and moved out of the way so I could enter. The inside was decorated in tons of neon lights and Latin music blared from the speakers. The dance floor was filled with couples, all of whom were doing elaborate dance moves that I could only dream of performing. I felt like I was in a *Step Up* sequel, replacing street dancing with Samba and Salsa.

Eventually, I made my way through the crowd and began to sway as I looked for a potential blood donor. I wasn't sure how I would approach the situation. I thought about what Lydian would do if she were in my shoes. She was an expert at flirting, and if I was going to get any attention, I would have to channel her somehow.

I swayed in the same spot for about ten minutes before someone turned me around. It was a man with very tan skin and a black, silk v-neck. His hair was gleaming with tonic, and he smelled like a Hollister store.

"I hope you don't mind my saying, but it is painful to watch you," he said with a thick Spanish accent.

"That bad, huh?" I asked. He nodded then put his hand in the middle of my back, pulling me closer to him. I winced since my back was still sore, but didn't let it show on my face.

"Let me teach you. By the end of the night, you will be a professional," he said.

He spent the next half hour teaching me some fancy moves. It took me a while to pick them up, but I managed to learn a small portion of a routine. I didn't really want to dance; I was only complying so that I could get closer with him. The sooner he warmed up to me, the sooner I could feed.

My hunger began to grow, so I sped things up a bit.

"Wanna get out of here?" I asked, trying to be as flirty as possible.

"What did you have in mind?" he asked.

I took his hand and pulled him through the crowd of people. I'd spotted a room blocked off with a curtain earlier and figured it would be a discreet spot to feed on him. I peeked through the curtain to make sure there was no on behind it, and to my relief, there wasn't. We went inside and I pulled the curtain shut. Before I turned around, he moved my hair away from my neck and started kissing it. I grimaced, not liking it at all. I was willing to flirt, but I refused to go any further than that. This was way outside of my comfort zone, and I needed to put an end to it.

I turned to face him then bit down on his neck. He yelled, but I wasn't worried that someone would hear; the music was too loud. I wasn't as strong as I usually was, but I was still stronger than him. He tried to fight me off but failed, and I kept drinking until his heart stopped. I lay his body on the couch in a reclined position so it would look like he was just sleeping then left the room. I made my way through the dancers, out the door, then back onto the sidewalk.

My body was coursing with adrenaline, and I wanted to feed more. The one man's blood hadn't satisfied me, so I continued down the street to look for another victim. By then, there were less people out walking, broadening my chances of catching someone alone.

I saw two thuggish looking men walking my way. I didn't care that it would be difficult getting the both of them; all I cared about was their blood and how much I wanted it. I approached them and started a conversation. It didn't take long before I was able to coax them into the alley. They were a bit sleazy, so I wasn't surprised that I'd charmed them so quickly. They probably would have followed me if I had large warts on my face.

I waited until we were further into the alley before I attacked the first guy. His friend tried to run off, but when I finished with the first, I ran after him, catching up about a block away then finished him off as well. I became consumed with the high that came with hunting. This was one of the reasons why I'd been grateful when we'd switched to living off of blood bags. It was easy to get addicted to the feeling of power I would get from taking a life. This was the part of me that I'd fought so hard to suppress. I needed to stop before I would go too far.

After I hid the second man's body underneath some trash bags, I started heading back to the hotel. I felt horrible about what I'd done, but it was the only way I could feed. I didn't have any hospital connections like I did in Las Vegas.

I blocked out my feelings of guilt as I ran down the sidewalk. I had to slow down after a while since my feet hurt from slamming the pavement so hard. Even after feeding so much, my body was still weakened from the gunshots. I couldn't figure out why I wasn't as resilient as I used to be. I'd recovered from being shot by Matthew only moments after drinking blood, but this time, I was healing a lot slower.

By the time I reached the hotel, I was exhausted. I wanted nothing more than to lie back down and sleep until I was better. I took the room key out of my shoe, where I'd stored my phone as well and stuck it in the door slot, pulling it out quickly. The light remained red, so I repeated the action again and again. The fourth try didn't work either, so I threw the card on the ground and swore.

"Now that's something I've never heard before," a voice said. I turned around to see Gallard standing behind me and I threw my arms around him, melting into his embrace. He kissed my forehead, his lips lingering for a moment then pulled back.

"Hey, you're wearing the dress," he said. "Do you like it?"

"Like it? I *love* it. It was nice surprise. Thank you."

He smiled and caressed my cheek with his finger. "Are you healing all right? Kevin told me what happened; that you were shot multiple times."

"I'm better than I was. I'm not healing as quickly as I'd like to, but I'm getting there."

He pulled me into another hug and sighed.

"When you stopped answering my questions over the phone, you about gave me a heart attack. I was going crazy thinking about what could have happened to you. How are you holding up? Kevin told me everything."

"I'm devastated. I finally make things right with my parents and then they were taken away. And my poor siblings. Kevin and Robin saw everything. Their parents were stolen from them and I feel responsible. If I hadn't come back Samil might have—"

"It isn't your fault. Samil always knew where your family was. He could have killed them at any time, but he chose to do it in front of you because he's a psychopath."

We went inside and walked towards the elevator. He pushed the button, and while we waited for the doors to open I asked,

"Where are Lydian and Jordan?"

"They're out feeding. The flight was only four hours, but Jordan was eager to eat. They should be here soon."

We got to my floor and I led the way to the room. There was a maid coming out of the one next to mine, pushing a cart of towels. I smiled at her as she walked by to be polite, but as soon as she walked passed me, I caught her scent. I whipped my head in her direction, using every ounce of self control I had to not attack her.

I didn't realize how hard I was squeezing Gallard's hand until he mentioned it. He was about to unlock the door when he was stopped by my intense grip.

"Are you okay? You seem tense," he said. I eased up on my grip, but I trembled as my will to remain calm lessened by the second.

"Yeah, I'm fine," I lied. He gave me a look and I knew that I wasn't fooling him. He took my face in his hands and studied it. I probably had crazy eyes, and there was no hiding that.

"You're shaking like crazy, what's going on?" he asked. I turned away from him and looked at the woman. She was halfway down the hall and about to go into another room. I became wild with hunger and I couldn't fight it any longer. I rushed towards the maid, nearly at full speed. She screamed as I closed in on her, but Gallard stopped me, pushing me against the wall.

"Lela, you can't do this!" he said. "Just breathe! I know you can control yourself."

I tried to push him away, but he was stronger. He pinned me to the wall so that I couldn't move my arms. I struggled; keeping my eye on the woman as I failed about, but there was no way I could escape from his grip.

Almost as suddenly as my hunger intensified, it began to wane and was replaced by nausea. He lessened his grip and I used his arms to steady myself.

"I'm so sorry," I said to the frightened woman.

Gallard gave me a look of concern before putting his arm around me, walking us back to the room. He unlocked it then we went inside. I was surprised to find the room empty. I opened the bathroom door and relief washed over me when I saw that the bodies were gone. My brothers must have been out disposing of them. How they managed to sneak four bodies out of the room was a mystery to me; not one that I particularly wanted to know.

My stomach began to turn, this time crawling up my throat, and I had to run to the toilet. I vomited just after I lifted the lid, and my stomach contracted as it pushed out nearly three liters of blood. Gallard graciously held back my hair and flushed the toilet whenever it got too full.

I was in the middle of throwing up for the third time when the door to the room opened and my brothers, Lydian, and Jordan walked in. I wanted to close the bathroom door to hide what was going on, but my loud retching would have given it away.

"Uh oh, someone is prego," Lydian, said smirking.

"Gallard, you know they have protection in the twenty-first century, right?"

"Lydian, shut up," he said harshly. I had never heard Gallard snap at her like that before, but I was glad that he did; she was taking things too far. If I wasn't feeling so terrible, I would have punched her in the throat.

The group went further into the room and I got up from the floor. I rinsed out my mouth in the sink. After I dried my face with a towel, I turned to find everyone staring at me. I set the towel on the counter, walking slowly towards Gallard and standing next to them.

"What? What's with the stares?" I asked.

"Lela, you just threw up," Gallard said. "Vampires don't get sick, nor do they have problems keeping blood down."

He was right; something was wrong with me. The slow healing, the insatiable hunger; all of it was unnatural for me. I hadn't been sick since long before I'd turned, and now I was displaying odd symptoms.

"Samil must have done something else besides just shooting you. Do you remember him injecting you with anything or giving you anything to drink?" he asked.

"He forced her to drink my blood," Kevin said. "He cut me and drained some in a flask then forced it down her throat."

My eyes shifted in thought. I'd forgotten all about it. I remembered everything except for that. The memory of how Kevin's blood had tasted became all too clear. I hadn't felt as satisfied as I had when I'd fed on it. I hated myself for enjoying it since he could have died from blood loss.

"How much did he give her?" Gallard asked.

"I'm pretty sure he filled the flask. It was a six ouncer, if I'm guessing right."

Gallard sighed, resting his hands on the back of his neck and turned around.

"Samil said something about a gift and how I didn't deserve immortality," I recalled."What did he mean?"

"He meant that he was curing your immortality; you're going to be mortal again, Lela."

I let out a soft laugh, though I wasn't finding it humorous. I wanted this to be a joke; this was beyond what I could imagine.

"No, I can't! This can't be happening; not right now" I said, panic stricken. "How is that possible?"

"There was a time when people would turn and slaughter their entire families. To keep that from happening, something was done to make sure that such tragedies wouldn't happen again. From then on, any vampire that feeds on someone related to them by blood will lose their immortality. Some would feed on their descendants because they were tired of living forever, but what they didn't know was that that once they turn human, they age rapidly until they die," Gallard explained.

"So I'm going to die?" I asked, even more terrified than before. Gallard gently grabbed my shoulders.

"No, you should be fine. The only ones that would happen to are the immortals that have been alive longer than a normal human lifespan. You only turned four years ago, so you should age at a normal rate."

This was a bit comforting, but I still wasn't thrilled with my new fate. If I was human, that meant that I wouldn't be able to defend myself against Samil and his followers. He'd done it on purpose because he knew that I was stronger than him, and I was easiest to get to. Now, there would only be two day-walkers for him to go after.

"How long do I have?" I asked, breaking the silence.

No one had spoken a word in over five minutes. Nobody knew what to say in a situation like this. By standards, I should have been thrilled. Becoming human again would mean that I didn't have to hide who I was or ever kill anyone for a life source.

"I'm not sure. I've never known anyone that this happened to," he said.

I thought back to what my mother had revealed to me not two nights before; how David had been my real father and that he'd somehow cured himself so that they could be together. But he hadn't aged rapidly; he'd remained the same age. If he was supposed to have died upon being cured, how had he stayed young for the past twenty years? I had so many questions and the only person who could answer them was dead.

"I do," I replied. "It happened to David."

Confusion swept through the group and I gave them a brief summary of everything my mother had told me about David, the affair, and how he was my real father. They all had a hard time believing my story at first, but considering all the crazy things we'd experienced, it wasn't all that far-fetched. My mother would have had nothing to gain by lying, and her knowledge of the vampire world had been astonishing; she couldn't have made it up.

"There's more," I said, suddenly remembering my conversation with the gypsy. I never told Gallard the whole story, and I doubted he said anything to Lydian and Jordan. "I ran into the woman who gave me the vampire blood at the circus, and she told me why Samil wants us so badly."

"Are you serious?" Lydian asked. "You should have told us that first; we're dying to know!"

"I'm sorry, my memory is hazy; everything is coming back in weird spurts. Anyway, she told me that he's trying to resurrect Lucian Christophe. She finally told me who he was. He's another day-walker that was killed to stop him from wreaking havoc in sixteenth century London. Apparently, the killer drained Lucian's blood and it was separated into four jars. They were given to us over the past two-hundred years to keep anyone from obtaining them and bringing him back."

"You're saying that you, Lydian, David and I all walk in the day because we drank this Lucian's blood?" Gallard asked.

"It explains why we were all drawn to each other. The gypsy said that Lucian's spirit wants to be unified in any possible way; that's why you felt those pulls. When David turned, you were drawn to him and when I was born, the direction of the pull changed since I was born with Lucian's blood. You said that the pull stopped shortly after we met, and then we were drawn to Texas where Lydian was."

"How does Samil plan to use us to bring this Lucian character back?" Lydian asked.

The answer was heartbreaking to reveal. I didn't want to tell them that possibly a few of us would die if Samil ever managed to capture us. I couldn't imagine losing more people that I cared about; it would be too much to bear.

"The gypsy said that...that he has to drain our blood back into Lucian's body," I replied.

"The blood from all four of us?" Gallard asked. I shook my head.

"He only needs two of us...so that means two of us will have to die if Lucian is to successfully be resurrected."

The room went silent. There wasn't much anyone could say in response to this. It's not like any of us were going to rush in to volunteer in case we failed to escape from Samil. I didn't want to throw anyone under the bus either.

"Well, I'm not going to stick around for that," Lydian said. "I didn't become a vampire so I could be used as some sacrifice."

"Thanks, Lydian; we appreciate you offering us up for the slaughter," I said.

"I didn't say you two should be the ones, I'm saying that I'm not going to put up with this. If you two were smart, you would high tale it out of here too!"

"We've been running for four years, Lydian. I'm done running and I'm ready to start fighting," I said.

"Really? And just how do you plan on fighting Samil?" She stood up from her chair and walked up to me. "Face it; you're turning back into a mortal. The only thing you'll be fighting is the pain while Samil cuts you open and drains you, and as your cold, bloodless body hits the floor, you will realize that I was right."

Her words actually hurt. The way she was talking sounded like she'd already given up; on me, and on everything. But I couldn't let her get to me. If I started having that attitude, we were bound to lose. I may have been losing my ability to defend myself, but I wasn't going let it keep me from fighting back. My sister needed my help, and I was determined not to let her down.

Chapter Two

I spent the next few days adjusting to my transition. It was a slow and very uncomfortable process. I could neither eat food nor drink blood, so I was constantly starving. My friends had sort of moved into my house for the time being, but I didn't mind. I wanted them with me. Their presence helped me forget everything that was going on.

When the police finally questioned us, my brothers told them that they'd been out of town the night our parents were killed and that I'd only arrived after hearing about it. The facts didn't really match up well, yet there was no suspicion that we'd been there or weren't telling the whole truth, but that didn't stop the police from constantly showing up to ask more questions.

My aunt Evelyn, Mark's sister, and her husband Jeff flew in from Texas for the funeral almost a week later. By then, there were several fliers all over town advertising Robin's kidnapping, and not a single lead. I wasn't expecting there to be any. Samil had disappeared and we wouldn't see him until he contacted us again. I tried not to think about her too much. I didn't want to imagine what horrible situations she was in or if Samil was treating her cruelly.

I was the only one of my siblings who could go out during the day, so I had to lie to my aunt and uncle, telling them that my brother's were too grief stricken to attend the funeral; that they wouldn't have real closure until the men responsible were found. I at least wanted Gallard to come, but he was still a fugitive and couldn't risk being recognized in case the police were there, so I had to go alone.

The service was held at my old church and almost the entire congregation was there. My family had attended that church as far back as my great grandmother, so my parent's death was a huge hit for everyone. One of the priests ushered me and my relatives to the front row and we sat down. It felt weird to be in a different spot after sitting in the same pew for so long, let alone being at church at all for the first time in four years. It was close to Christmas, so everything was decorated for the holiday.

Several people stood up to say touching things about my parents. The thought of getting up in front of everyone to speak terrified me, so I let my aunt read what I wanted to say for me. I felt like a coward, but I was too much of an emotional wreck to try and give a speech.

By the time we'd driven to the cemetery for the wake, I was ready to go home, though I'd agreed to host a reception at the house. I didn't mind, but being at the house would be better than out in the cemetery or the church.

The priest's message went on and on, and I could barely contain my impatience. I felt uncomfortable in my own skin, and the fact that I was intensely hungry didn't help matters either. People probably thought that I was just overcome with grief when

I hurried to the car almost directly after the priest stopped speaking, but I was eager to leave. I shut the car door then rubbed my face with my hands. I wanted it to be over so I could focus on getting my sister back. Only then would I be able to properly grieve my parents' deaths.

My aunt and uncle got into the car not longer after I did. I sat up to face them and forced a smile.

"Are you all right, Lela?" my aunt asked. She looked younger than I remembered. I knew she was fairly younger than Mark, but I never noticed their difference in age until now. She couldn't be more than thirty or thirty five.

"Yeah, I'm just tired. It's been a long couple of weeks," I said.

Jeff started the car then pulled out of the cemetery. I looked out the window while we drove back to the house. They were leaving town the next day, and I felt bad for wishing they would leave sooner, but my friends, brothers, and I couldn't begin our search for Robin until they were gone. They'd tried to insist on staying longer to help out with the investigation, but Aaron somehow managed to convince them that we would be fine. I loved them, but their being around was somewhat inconvenient.

We pulled up to the house and we got out of the car. Jordan said that he would take care of everything, which surprised me. He was such a sweetheart and Evelyn tried to get him to let the two of us help him, but he insisted on doing everything alone. I decided to trust that he would get everything done in time. If he could trick Samil into thinking he was Gallard, he could put together a funeral reception.

The three of us walked into the house and admired the work he'd done. He'd gotten all the chairs we used for our barbeques and set them up so that there were several places to sit and he'd rearranged the furniture as well. I hoped that my brothers had helped out, or else I would have felt bad for him doing all of this work

Some of the shelves had been cleared out and replaced by tables, which were covered in trays of different foods, like vegetables and deli meat. Another had my mother's punch bowl and it was filled with an orange drink with sorbet floating in it. To the left were clear disposable cups as well as paper ones and the pot was filled with fresh coffee.

I found Jordan in the kitchen cutting rolls in half for small sandwiches and I stood next to him to see what else he'd been working on.

"Jordan, you are amazing," I said. "Where did you get your incredible party planning skills?"

"It's a secret." He smiled at me as he continued with the bread. "How was the service?"

"It was good. A lot of people came and they said some really nice things." I turned on the sink so I could wash my hands and help out. I needed to do something besides watch. I then grabbed some of the bread and began slicing it. "You didn't have to do all of this, you know. We could have had this catered or something."

"No, I wanted to do this. You were there for me when I was sick and I wanted to return the favor. Besides, I understand that you're having a hard time with all of this. I went through the same thing when I was a few years younger than you."

I looked up at him. I knew that he'd said his grandparents died when he was young and that his parents died a few years later, but he never told me how they'd died. I'd assumed it was a car accident or something like that.

"What do you mean?" I asked.

"When I was sixteen, my parents were murdered. They think they caught the guy, but he claimed innocence until the day he was executed. I didn't have any living relatives, so I emancipated myself and continued running the farm."

I suddenly felt compelled to hug him and he hugged me back. We'd always gotten along, but we never really had anything in common until now. Knowing that he understood what I was dealing with comforted me. I knew this would bring us closer than before.

My aunt Evelyn came into the kitchen and he stopped hugging me to continue with the sandwiches.

"Do you know where your brothers are?" she asked me.

"They're upstairs getting ready," Jordan said. "They've been helping me all day so I gave them a break."

The guests began to arrive about fifteen minutes later. Everything had been set up on time and now all I had to do was entertain, shake hands, and be a good hostess. My brothers made sure to stay in areas away from the windows because my aunt had opened the curtains to let in more light. People probably thought their behavior was odd, but only due to their grief.

Having this many people in the house at once began to stress me out. I still hadn't developed an appetite, so I sipped on some punch to keep myself occupied. Most of the guests had spent the past hour asking me questions, like where I'd been for the past four years and what compelled me to come back. All of my parents' friends had kept up to date on my runaway and were very interested to know my story.

Lydian came over and sat in the chair next to me. Apparently, Jordan had sent her to the store since she kept butchering the food arrangements and had just returned with more soda for the punch. For once she wasn't wearing something tight or low cut. She had on a black jumpsuit with matching sandals that had rhinestones on the straps.

"Gallard wants to know how you're doing," she said.

"You saw him?"

"No, but he texted me. He would have asked you himself, but he didn't want to text you during the service."

Gallard had been gone for the past week. He'd made a trip up to Orlando to see if any of Bodoway's customers knew anything about Lucian Christophe. He'd gotten even more protective of me after he learned I was turning mortal again. I
missed him and anticipated when he would return.

I was going to ask her if she knew how his search was going when I noticed a man standing by himself near the door. He'd scared me at first because I thought for a second that it was Mark, but the longer I looked at him I saw that he was both taller and had straighter, darker hair. His eye color was different as well. Still, it was almost like a ghost was in my house.

I stood up and made my way towards him. He wasn't talking with anyone and I wondered if I was the only one who noticed his resemblance to Mark. I half expected him to run away when I approached him, but he only looked at me, giving a light smile.

"Hello," he said. His accent was unexpected. It was like a mixture of English and Italian. "You must be Mark's daughter."

"One of them," I shook his hand and his touch was cold. Colder than mine. "I'm Lela."

"It's a pleasure to meet you, Lela. I'm Solomon Schaech. I'm an acquaintance of your father's."

I quickly took my hand back, staring at him in shock. Though he'd given a different last name, I knew this was the man that Samil was looking for; the one who had killed Lucian and his family and he was standing in my house. How had he found out about my parent's death? Why, after almost twenty years of silence had he decided to reveal himself?

"You're the one Samil wants," I said, my voice quiet so no one could hear. "You have Lucian's body."

His expression became panicked and he began to back

away from me.

"This was a mistake. I shouldn't have come, I apologize."

He hurried to the door and opened it, exiting quickly. I followed after him, trying to keep up, but I wasn't as fast as I used to be. I couldn't let him leave; not if he could help me get Robin back and save my friends from being killed.

"Wait! I need to know why you came here!" I shouted after him. "You have to help us! If Samil—"

"He can't know where I am. Lucian's body must stay hidden. I needed to know you and your brothers were safe and you are, so I must go. I'm sorry, but I can't help you."

He ran off at a speed too quick for my weakened eyes and I stood on the front lawn, taking in the strange encounter. The only person in the whole world who could have helped us not only refused to be of assistance, but he'd disappeared without explaining himself. If he wasn't going to help, I wanted him to at least tell me why he'd sent my family money all these years.

I spent the rest of the day mulling over what had just happened. I would have to tell the others once the company was gone. Solomon Sharmentino had finally given a face to his name and as I'd suspected, he was a day-walker. Had he drunk Lucian's blood too, or was he something else? Samil probably wanted to know the same thing and I was determined to find out before he did.

The last guest left around four o'clock and all that was left was my aunt and uncle. They, along with Lydian and my brothers cleaned up the house in less than a half hour and put all the extra food into plastic containers. Our fridge was getting full since people had been bringing casseroles almost every other day. I felt bad for wasting them, but no one could eat them.

I walked my aunt and uncle to the car after we finished cleaning. I could tell my aunt had developed a fondness of Jordan, especially because of his generous favor of setting up. She even hugged him goodbye before they went out the door.

"You guys should stay," I said. "We have a ton of food you could eat for dinner."

"We would love to, but we're getting tired, so we're going back to the hotel. We'll stop by in the morning before we head to the airport," my uncle said. I leaned down and hugged my aunt through the window.

"Thank you guys for everything. I'll see you tomorrow."

"Of course, sweetheart. We love you!" she said.

"Love you too." I waved as they drove off then trudged into the house.

When I closed the door behind me, I leaned against it, sliding down until I was on the floor. My body felt like it weighed twice as much and I no longer wanted to move. Still, I forced myself to stand back up and go upstairs to the bathroom. The door was open, and I was glad that it was free. Lydian always seemed to be in the bathroom, and I was lucky to find it vacant if I needed it.

I closed the door then pulled my black dress off. It was itchy, and I'd settled for it because I didn't feel like trying on a bunch of dresses since I was only going to wear it once. It was strapless, so I'd had to buy a special bra to go with it. The entire outfit was annoying me, and I couldn't wait to get into more comfortable clothes.

I saw movement in the corner of my eye and jumped. Jordan stepped out of the shower wearing only a towel.

"Jordan!" I shrieked, scrambling for my dress to cover up. "What are you doing in here?"

"I took a shower," he said, laughing as he turning around to give me privacy. "I thought you were Lydian, she was just in here."

I cringed, trying not to picture Lydian and Jordan in the shower. I was even more annoyed that she'd left the door open, allowing for anyone to walk in thinking they were alone.

I quickly pulled the dress back on then started to leave when I turned around.

"Oh, uh…I was wondering. Since Samil knows about you and all, you don't have to dress like Gallard anymore. I can cut your hair if you want."

"Why, are you afraid you'll become attracted to me because I look like him?"

I rolled my eyes. "No! I just want to return the favor for what you did today."

"You don't have to pay me back. But I would like to cut my hair. Whenever you're free let me know."

The door flew open and Lydian stood outside the bathroom

in the doorway.

"Trying to sneak a peek at my man again?" she asked with mischief in her voice. I rolled my eyes then pushed passed her. My shower would have to wait until later, after some thorough scrubbing. I would have to bleach everything before I would ever use the shower again.

I changed into some shorts and a t-shirt. My hair had been curled earlier that day, but now it was as flat as it had been when I woke up. I tied it back in a pony tail as I walked back downstairs.

Aaron was in the kitchen talking with Kevin in hushed tones, but they stopped talking the second I joined them. I stood next to Kevin by the island then hoisted myself up onto the counter.

"What's with the hush-hush conversation?" I asked.

"Nothing," Aaron said. "We were just talking about how we hated missing the service."

"I would say that it was touching and gave me closure, but that would be a lie. Our parents were just ripped away from us and our sister was taken hostage. None of this is going to be okay until Samil and his followers are stopped."

They both nodded in agreement. I was glad that my brothers were with me, even if I was still furious at Aaron for turning Kevin, but it was hard to stay mad at him in the face of tragedy. We'd all lost people very dear to us.

"Oh, I forgot to tell you. Curtis is stopping by later," Aaron said. "He wanted to go to the funeral, but he couldn't get off work in time to drive into town."

"Curtis? Wow, that's a name I haven't heard in a while. What's he been up to?"

"He's an orthodontic assistant. He got a job at some fancy orthodontist firm and now he makes a killing putting braces on people."

So, Curtis had a successful career. I was happy for him. Both he and my brother were both academically driven, and I knew that he would end up with a great job. I wished that Aaron had followed in his footsteps and stayed in med school. Maybe he wouldn't have gotten tangled up this crazy life if he'd just done what he'd set out to do.

Lydian and Jordan came into the kitchen and sat on the stools on the other side of the island.

"What are we going to do now?" Lydian asked. "I'm bored, and I'm starting to get cabin fever."

"We're having company later," I said. "He's a family friend, but you don't have to stick around. You and Jordan can go out and do whatever."

"Are you going to come on to him while he's in a towel too?" she jeered.

I ignored her comment. I wasn't in the mood for arguing with her. She was one to talk, since she'd been in more relationships in a month than Taylor Swift had in her lifetime. Jordan may have been her soul mate, but she'd still gone out with him while she was dating another guy. Not to mention she'd stolen him from me when I was dancing with him first.

"Down, kitty," Jordan said. "She didn't know I was in the shower."

"Whatever, she has magnified hearing. She could have heard you all the way outside."

"Actually, Lydian; I didn't hear him. In case you've forgotten, my abilities aren't what they used to be. I'm weaker, and that means my hearing is not as good as it was."

"Excuses, excuses," she said, dragging Jordan out of the room.

I was glad when she left the room. I was looking forward to Curtis' visit because I needed someone human around for once.

I cooked myself a steak to medium rare then took it into the living room to eat while I watched the news. Lately, I couldn't keep anything down accept for undercooked meat. It was the one food that lingered between blood and human sustenance. It wasn't the most appetizing meal, but I made it edible by adding seasoning or sauce.

Almost every news channel had a snippet about my parents' murder and sister's disappearance; her cute picture flashing on the screen. I'd only just met her a few weeks ago, but I'd grown attached quickly. She was my baby sister, and I would give my life for her. The thought of Samil keeping her locked in some cage, barely feeding her anything often kept me up at night.

Chapter Three

My eyes flew open when I heard a knock at the door. I'd unintentionally fallen asleep and the news had turned into an episode of *America's Funniest Home Videos*. I shut the TV off while I rubbed my eyes and stretched before getting up to answer it. I peeked through the peephole then opened the door.

"Curtis, hi!" I said.

"Lela Sharmentino, is that you? You're all grown up!"

We hugged and I let him in. "When Aaron told me that you were back, I couldn't believe it."

Aaron and Kevin joined us from the kitchen and greeted Curtis as well. I went back into the living room and everyone followed me and I curled up in the chair next to the TV. It had been so long since the four of us had hung out.

"How's the job?' Aaron asked.

"It's great! I never would have thought that I would enjoy putting braces on thirteen year olds all day, but I love it."

I studied him while he talked with Aaron. He was dressed like a businessman with his light-blue button up and khaki slacks. His hair was longer than I remembered and he'd gotten rid of his chin-strap beard. Despite his new look, he still reminded me of Justin Timberlake.

"Did the three of you stop going outside?" he asked.

"You're all looking a little pale. And why do you all have black hair?"

"We've been cooped up in the house lately," Aaron explained. "We haven't really felt like going anywhere. As for the hair...it's an old Italian mourning ritual thing."

That was the dumbest excuse Aaron had ever come up with in all our years of lying. An Italian mourning ritual? Of all the things he could have said. It was obvious by the look on Curtis' face that he wasn't buying it.

"Uh huh...what about the investigation? Are there any leads?" he asked, his voice softening in concern.

"None," Kevin said. "The police have been doubtful that they're going to find Robin ever since we reached the forty-eight hour mark. She's been gone for ten days, and no one knows anything."

"But we still have hope," I chimed in. "She's out there somewhere, and we're going to get her back."

Lydian and Jordan came into the living room from the basement. She was dressed in a white, strapless top and a blue skirt that stopped mid-thigh and hung longer in the back. She looked more like herself than she had in her black clothes.

"Curtis, these are my friends Lydian and Jordan. Guys, this is Aaron's good friend Curtis."

The three of them shook hands.

"Where you guys headed?" Curtis asked.

"We're bored. We're going to find a night club," Lydian

said. "You're all welcome to join us."

"I'll go!" Kevin said. I gave him a look but he ignored it. "I'm bored too, and I'm tired of being at home."

"Go change then. We'll be outside," Lydian said. Kevin left the room and went upstairs. I looked at Aaron to see if he was going to protest, but he said nothing. I didn't like the idea of my baby brother partying with Lydian, even if he was seventeen.

"Well, I guess it's just going to be the three of us then," I said. "How about I make dinner?"

"Are you sure? I don't want to make you cook for me," Curtis said.

"We have like five casseroles that family friends have dropped by. I could heat one up in the oven and it would only take a few minutes."

I went into the kitchen and took out all of the options. One was a broccoli dish with cauliflower and cheese while another was a potato bake. The other two looked like vegetarian lasagnas, and I decided the potato one looked the most appetizing. I removed the plastic wrap then set the oven on low.

I'd just put the casserole in when Aaron came into the kitchen. He had his phone in his hand had it pressed to his shoulder as if to keep the caller from hearing out conversation.

"Hey, plans have changed, the group is going to meet Gallard to talk about some new information."

"Now? What about dinner, and Curtis?"

"We should be back in an hour. I told him that the police

need to talk to me at the station. Could you entertain him until I get home?"

I sighed as I set my spoon on the stove. I was getting left behind a lot lately, and I didn't like it. Just because I was weaker didn't mean I couldn't help chase leads. I was tired of being last to know things.

"Sure, just hurry back, okay."

He smiled then started to walk out of the room when I stopped him.

"Wait, is Gallard on the phone?" I asked.

"Uh, yeah, you wanna talk to him?"

"If you wouldn't mind. I'll make it quick."

He handed the phone to me. "I'll come back for it in five minutes."

Once Aaron had left, I cradled it with my shoulder while I looked for some meat to eat with the casserole.

"Hey, old man, how's it going?"

"Frustrating. For being such a notorious immortal, not many people have ever heard of Lucian Christophe."

I suddenly remembered what had happened earlier that day. We'd been busy cleaning and resting after the reception that I'd forgotten to mention to the others about Solomon being at the house.

"You're never going to believe this, but Solomon Sharmentino showed up at my house today," I told him.

"So I've heard. Apparently, Samil has eyes on your house.

They were ordered to watch in case he decided to pay his respects then they left to report. What was Solomon like, did you talk to him?"

"Yeah, he was friendly at first. But after I mentioned Lucian's name, he couldn't leave fast enough. I never even had the chance to ask him questions."

"So, he's a day-walker like us?"

"Appears so. And here we thought you, me and Lydian were the only ones left. I doubt he's dangerous, though. He came to pay his respects to my family, so he must be a decent person. Then again, he did slaughter Lucian's entire family. I just wish he'd stuck around longer to help us out."

"I knew I should have stayed. This whole trip has been very unproductive." He grew quiet for a moment then spoke again. "Enough about this mission. How did the funeral go?"

"It was almost surreal. I never imagined going to my own parents' funeral. Not so soon in life anyway. I wasn't as emotional as I thought I would be either. I think I cried so much these past couple of days that my tear-ducts are dried up."

"I wish I could have been there. I miss my girl."

I smiled. He always knew how to make me feel better, even with just a simple phrase.

"I miss you too," I replied. Aaron came back into the kitchen and my heart sank. I wasn't ready for the conversation to be over. "I'll see you soon. Be safe."

"Will do, take care." He hung up then I handed the phone

to Aaron.

After Aaron left with the rest of the group, and Curtis sat in the kitchen as I finished cooking the meat. I felt bad that everyone had left only an hour after he'd arrived, but he'd always been a laid back guy and probably didn't mind.

"How is Gabby doing these days?" I asked. Gabby and I were never really close, but she would usually come over to hang out if her brother did. She'd dated Aaron for a few months when she was in ninth grade and he in eleventh, but they'd decided to just stay friends. They'd kept things civil for Curtis' sake, and were able to spend time together without it being awkward.

"She's doing great. She's finishing up art school in New York. She's engaged too."

"No way, that's so exciting! What about you? Do you have anyone special in your life?"

"Not lately. I've been busy with school and now my job. How about you?"

I didn't know how to answer that. My feelings for Gallard were very complicated and while I'd tired to ignore them, they weren't going away as I'd hoped they would. We were just friends, though. And I really wanted to keep it that way at all possible.

"No, I'm riding solo these days," I finally replied. I scooped the steaks out of the pan and onto a plate. He got out of his seat and leaned against the counter next to the stove.

"Remember that party Aaron had here all those years ago?" he asked. I laughed as I thought about it.

"I remember you almost throwing up on me. I cleaned it up real good though. My parents never even suspected that there was once vomit on their carpet."

"That was definitely not one of my shining moments. I'm just glad that your brother saw that and not what happened before."

There was no way he could be talking about what had happened between us. He'd told me that he couldn't remember anything from the party because of how much he'd drunk that night. If he'd lied, then our conversation was about to be very awkward. I hadn't thought about that night in so long and now it was all coming back.

"You didn't think I'd forgotten that amazing kiss, did you?" he continued.

"Oh please, it wasn't *that* great." I suddenly wished that Kevin hadn't gone with the rest of the group. I'd been okay with keeping Curtis company, but now that I knew he hadn't forgotten the party like he'd said, it was awkward to be around him. "You told me at the circus that you'd forgotten everything that night."

"Well, I lied. When I asked you if anything happened, it was a rhetorical question. I wanted to see if you were still into me."

"If I was still into *you*? If I can recall, you were the one who freaked out when you found out I was fourteen."

I started getting out silverware and plates, eager for the conversation to change.

"So, you *were* interested?" he asked.

"Maybe for a second, but I was *really* drunk. I just got caught up in the moment."

"I wasn't interested for a just a second. I didn't get over you," he said, smiling.

I wasn't falling for it. I'd seen this move before. Lydian had used the same line after she'd broken up with her boyfriend Elijah and needed him to take her as a date to some party. Even if Curtis was serious, I'd become an expert at deflecting any flirting from my practice with Gallard. And I wasn't going to let another mortal guy fall for me when I knew my secret life would scare him away.

"The food's ready," I said, changing the subject. "What would you like to drink?" I opened the fridge and looked around. "We have...nothing. The guests must have drunk all the punch." I closed it then went into the living room. There was still a ton of alcohol in the liquor cabinet. "We have scotch...or if you're feeling classy; red wine."

"Scotch sounds good," he shouted from the kitchen. I took it out, trying to be gentle as I carried it. It was the scotch Mark had drunk the night he was killed and had some sentimental value to me. I twisted the lid off then filled his glass at two fingers.

"You having any?" he asked. I put towels on the island then set the hot casserole dish on top.

"Nah, I haven't had a drop since that night."

I heard the front door open and I braced myself to see who it was. Ever since Matthew had broken in, I found myself jumping every time someone came in the door from the front. I hated that he'd caused me to live in fear, but at the same time, I had to be prepared for whenever he decided to return.

My tension went away when I saw that it was only Jordan. He'd returned alone and I was curious to know why this was so.

"Hey, what brought you back?" I asked.

"Gallard didn't want you here alone," he explained.

"Who's Gallard?" Curtis asked. I figured he wasn't all that informed on my kidnapping case, so I decided to tell him the truth, somewhat.

"Jordan's younger brother. Hey, Jordan, why don't you join us? There's plenty of food."

He nodded then took a seat next to Curtis. I got out another plate for him and they began serving themselves food. I pitied Jordan for having to stomach the food, but it would seem weird if he didn't eat. I stood across from them, taking a bite every now and then. It tasted better than I'd anticipated. This was another sign that my mortality was just around the corner.

"So, Jordan, what do you do?" Curtis asked.

"I ran the family farm up until a few years ago. I was going through intense chemotherapy and I had to sell it since I was too sick to keep up with everything. I'm in remission now, so I'm trying to find another profession."

"I thought being Lydian's boyfriend was a profession in and of itself," I joked. Jordan laughed as he played with his food.

"Lydian is a handful," he said, grinning to himself. "But I love her. I just wish that she wouldn't worry so much that I'm not as into the relationship as she is."

I squeezed his hand then continued eating my food. He was right; Lydian was very defensive when it came to Jordan. She knew that I had feelings for Gallard, yet she would give me an icy stare if I even so much as looked at Jordan. If anything, I was envious of their relationship. I wanted what they had, but I was too scared to try and have that for myself.

We finished eating and Curtis helped me clean the kitchen. I was glad that Jordan stuck around so he wouldn't try to continue our conversation from earlier. I put the last plate into the dishwasher then turned it on.

"I should go," Curtis said. "I worked all day before I drove out here, and I'm exhausted. I'm going to head over and crash at my parent's place."

"Okay. I'm sorry that Aaron had to run out like that. This investigation is so crazy."

"Yeah, I understand. I don't mind Aaron not being here; your company is just as enjoyable."

I hugged him before he went out the door. It had been nice having a non-vampire to talk to for a bit, but it was hard to lie about everything. Involving him in our dangerous situation would only put him at risk for becoming a target.

After he left I went back into the kitchen to talk to Jordan. I wanted to know if he'd gotten to hear any of the information that Gallard had found before he came back to the house.

"What was it that Gallard wanted to talk to you guys

about?" I asked.

"Matthew contacted him. He passed on a message from Samil. He knows that your relative was in town and said that if we know what's good for us, we won't try to get to the body first."

"Oh please," I scoffed. "Solomon never told us where he's hiding it. And even if he did, does Samil really think we wouldn't jump at the chance to find it first? He'd be an idiot to assume we'd sit back and let him do his dirty work."

"He's just finding a reason to threaten us. He's a sadist. He finds more enjoyment in watching us squirm than actually inflicting harm. He knows he can't hurt your sister because we would stop cooperating."

Except that he did inflict harm. He murdered my parents, and I'm sure that he enjoyed doing it. I hated this entire dance of Samil threatening us, only to go silent for a long period of time and then come back out of nowhere either threatening us some more or doing something terrible.

"Hey, why don't I cut your hair now?" I asked. "It's not like we have anything else to do."

"Yeah sure."

I hurried upstairs and got a towel and the scissors before going back down. As I walked, I wondered if maybe I could make a profession out of this. I wasn't super talented, but I'd never had any complaints. Cutting and styling hair was definitely more rewarding than cleaning toilets.

Jordan sat on the bench and I draped the towel over his

shoulders before beginning. He said he was fine with me cutting it the way he'd had it before, so I did my best to recreate the style. The more I cut, the less he looked like Gallard's doppelganger. I had to admit, Jordan did look better with shorter hair, though.

"Can I ask you something?" I said.

"Sorry, but I'm taken."

"That's not what I was going to ask." I laughed. "It has to do with Lydian. Why is she so…jealous lately? I can't even look at you with her getting all up in my grill."

"You're not the only one who's noticed that. I asked her about it before and she explained why." He paused for a moment then continued. "It's because she's intimidated by you."

I stopped cutting his hair for a second.

"She's intimidated by *me*? Why? She's the one who is confident and outgoing. She even dresses way better than me."

"She is that way because she feels like she has to try. You're tall, athletic…beautiful." He'd hesitated before saying that last word. "She's afraid that I'm going to leave her for you since Gallard hasn't made a move. And it didn't help either that I tried to kiss you as a joke. That was my fault. But I love her more than anything and I wish I could make her insecurities go away."

This was eye opening to me. I would have never thought in a million years that Lydian felt that way. If only I'd known, I would have talked to her about it. I'd always been envious of her and her ability to be so confident when it came to going after what she wanted, and this whole time she'd been envious of me.

I finished cutting his hair just as I heard the front door open again and the two of us went out to see who it was. The others had come back and to my surprise, Gallard was with them. He looked tired, but his eyes lit up when he saw me.

"It's good to have you back," I said. I gave him a quick squeeze around the waist before the whole group went into the living room to talk.

"I'm fairly confident that Samil will be ready to make a deal with us soon," Gallard explained to me once we were all sitting. "I'm not sure how at the moment, but we'll have to try and find Solomon if we want to get close enough to get Robin back. If not, we'll pretend to cooperate and—"

"Which of us are going to pretend to cooperate then?" Lydian asked, interrupting him.

"You and me," he said.

Lydian quickly shook her head. The look in her eyes was terrifying, like she was about to run off and disappear any second. Lydian always tried to look tough and confidant on the outside, but I knew on the inside she was scared out of her mind when it came to Samil.

"That's bull, do I even get a say?" she asked. If it had been any other circumstance, I would have been annoyed by her uncooperative attitude, but I had a sudden urge to stand up for her.

"I agree with Lydian," I said. "I want to be the other person. Robin should be retrieved by someone that she knows."

"If you were stronger, I would let you," Gallard said.

"Unfortunately, you're not. There's no way I'm letting you get anywhere near Samil. Not after what he did to you."

I stared at him for a while then turned to the others and asked, "Could you give us a minute?"

Lydian grabbed Jordan's hand and pulled him off the couch with her.

"Gladly. *I* still want to go dancing," she said. Aaron and Kevin stood up also and I remained silent until I heard the front door close, ensuring that we were alone.

"Gallard, I know you want to protect me, but I can't think about my safety. I have to think about Robin's. She's probably terrified enough as it is, and if you and Lydian show up and try to get her to leave, she's not going to trust you."

"As much as I hate to agree with Lydian, she was right when she said you would be as good as dead. Samil reversed your immortality so that you would be an easy target; he'll kill you before you tried to escape with Robin."

"So you would rather me stay behind and what, knit, while the two of you go off and get *yourselves* killed?"

"Better me than you. You're human now. I want to make sure that you are safe from any more harm that comes with association with immortals."

"What about my brothers? They're vampires too, are they going to have to stay away from me as well?"

He looked down and my heart lurched. Had I been correct? They couldn't leave me, not after everything that had happened. If they did, I would be left alone to take care of Robin all by myself. I wasn't ready to have that kind of role, especially to a child who had just been through as much as she had.

"They've been talking about it, and they've hinted that they might take off when this is over. They know too many people here, and their friends are going to start getting suspicious when they stop coming out during the day. They're thinking of you as well, Lela. When you turned, you left so that they would be safe from all of this, and they want to do the same for you in return."

I hated that they were right; what they planned to do was no different from what I'd done. If I tried to make them feel guilty for leaving, there would be no way to justify my argument. It would be hypocritical of me if I tried to make them stay.

It would have been different if they were day-walkers like I had been. They couldn't blend in with society as easily, making it almost impossible for them to stay in one place for very long. They would be able to visit me every now and then, but they could forget about seeing Curtis or our aunt and uncle ever again. If they were going to leave, I wasn't looking forward to not having them in my life as much as I used to.

I didn't want Gallard to leave either. I didn't want to be left alone, even if it was a good idea to keep Robin unexposed to more strangeness. Unlike my brothers, he could stick around without anyone being suspicious about what he was. He'd been the one stable thing in my life for years, and I didn't want to lose that.

"Are you going leave me too?" I asked. He pulled me closer

to him and I rested my head on his shoulder.

"Are you kidding me? I'm not going anywhere. You're stuck with me, Miss Sharmentino. I'll be around until you're eighty and drooling over your oatmeal in a nursing home."

I smiled, not because of the joke, but because he was sticking around.

As he stroked my hair, I started thinking about my strange situation. He'd said that I was turning back because I'd drunk Kevin's blood and it was the result of some ancient rule. I wanted to know more about it. I wanted to understand what was going on. There was still quite a bit about the immortal world that I didn't know. Other than the basic rules of what we could and couldn't do, I was completely clueless. Where did we come from? How did it all begin?

"What else do you know about our history? Do you know who created our kind?"

"I never told you that story?" He asked. I shook my head.

"You kind of just said, 'We drink blood, we turn into bats, we won't die,' and then pushed me out of the nest."

He laughed. "Well since we have time, I might as well tell you. I had the same questions when I first turned. Bodoway's tribe had legends of their own, but they only went as far back as the twelve hundreds. Even then, the legends were merely of sightings and strange occurrences. So, to learn more information, I left the colonies with Bodoway as my companion and searched for someone who had the real story. I would go into how I obtained the story and where I went to find it, but that would be long, boring, and irrelevant. I am going to skip that part so you won't fall asleep.

"It's been told that the one who created our kind was born close to the time of Christ. He was associated with the Apostle Paul and well known throughout the country as a healer and for raising the dead. But apparently he wanted more power and the only one who would give it to him was the Devil.

"After he was imbued with a stronger gift, he was able to raise the dead and keep them alive forever, thus creating the first immortals. They were said to be ravenous and out of control. Back then, everyone lived with their families under one roof. Put a new vampire under that house and you have a slaughter on your hands.

"Anyway, this man realized that they were too wild, so he used his devilish power to curse them so that they would be discouraged from feeding on their families. He made it so their blood took away their immortality. But that wasn't the only problem. When the vampires weren't feeding on the people, they were...uh...copulating."

I interrupted him by laughing. His word choice was too comical to take with a straight face.

"Copulating? Seriously? Gallard, I'm nineteen, not nine. You can say they were having sex."

"Maybe I like the word copulating better. Back to the point. Not only were they—"

"Fornicating."

"They were also procreating. And though the children

weren't feeding on blood like their parents, this man wanted to put a stop to it. But he noticed that the ones created by these monsters were weaker and more...dead for lack of a better word. They could go in the sun but they couldn't have children and the ones created by these weaker ones couldn't do either of those things. So basically he killed the strongest of his creations and what was left was the kind of immortal that your brothers and Samil are. Well...except for us of course."

This was a very intriguing back story. We were the result of a man who wanted to help people but lost himself to greed. Like the rest of us, he was just a normal man who was sucked into something bigger than himself until it got out of hand.

"So he basically just created a bunch of blood sucking tramps and before he could stop it, they spread out all over the world?"

"Blood sucking tramps? Sounds like David's description of me."

I laughed again. "I almost forgot about that! Oh, David. His being my father explains so much. Why he was so protective and leery when it came to you and me. I miss him so much."

"There's something I need to tell you," he said. "I would have mentioned it sooner, but I wanted to tell you in person."

Curious, I sat up to face him. His tone had turned somewhat excited.

"When I was talking to Matthew, he let something slip after I asked about Robin. He said that she wasn't hurt and that they had someone taking care of her."

"Who?" I asked, even more curious than ever.

"He said that it was David. Lela I think he's alive."

My brain was having trouble processing this. I was so used to bad news that it was like good news couldn't even register in my mind.

"What do you mean he's alive?"

"When Matthew realized that he'd given away a secret, he hung up. I'd threatened him, saying that if any harm came to her, he would regret it and his exact words were, 'Relax, David's taking care of the kid,' and when I asked what he meant, I heard a click then the dial tone."

"But how? Matthew shot him; he died in my arms! I—" I began to babble, shocked by everything I was hearing. How had David survived when I'd been so sure that he was dead when I'd left him for the ambulance? Had I been so ignorant as to not check to see if he was still alive?

"If Samil has him, and David was one of the four that drank Lucian's blood, then that means he just wants *me* now," Gallard continued. "You told me before that he'll only use me for this ritual, so Lydian can rest assured that she won't be killed. And you can too."

"No. It can't come to that. I won't let you die on me, old man." I sighed then thought about the good news. It was so exciting that I could barely wrap my head around it. "David is alive; that means…my real father is still alive!" I said, tears of joy stinging my eyes.

"We'll get him back, Lela; him and Robin both. I'll do everything in my power to make sure that happens."

I fell asleep while leaning against him. We'd talked for a few hours until exhaustion took over. It was getting harder and harder to stay awake for long periods of time, and I was running out of energy quicker than usual. With the funeral, Solomon's appearance, and the news that David might still be alive, I was at my limit for the day. I'd probably fallen asleep mid-sentence.

I had odd dreams as I slept. They were so real that I could feel everything around me. Sometimes, I would be somewhere cold; my entire body wracking from the chill. It was how I'd imagined the ice bath that Kevin had been in when he had scarlet fever as a child. Then, without warning, I would switch to being hot, not in the unbearable sense, but enough to be uncomfortable.

A tingling began in my fingers and toes, almost like they were regaining circulation. I hadn't felt this sensation in a long time, and it startled me at first. My head pounded as if it were starving for oxygen until the need for air overpowered all the other sensations, forcing me to wake up.

"What's the matter?" Gallard whispered to me.

"I can't breathe," I said, sitting up. I cringed as my lungs burned for air and he gently massaged my back.

"This must be the last part of your transition. It shouldn't last too long if it's anything like the initial transformation."

I waited and waited for the pain to stop, and it seemed to never end. But I'd felt worse pain than this; anything hurt less than being shot. If I could survive that, I could get through the next few minutes.

When my lungs finally expanded, I took in a huge gulp of air. After years of just breathing by habit instead of for necessity, it felt strange to use my lungs properly. Not long after, my heart started beating and the feeling of warmth returned; my body had risen from room temperature to a normal ninety-eight point seven.

The jarring effects of the experience subsided quickly and I returned to my original position, resting my head against Gallard's chest. He kissed the top of my head as I fell asleep once more.

Chapter Four

"Do you really want to wake her up? She looks so peaceful."

These were the words that brought me back to the real world. I opened my eyes to find that I was still lying on the couch next to Gallard. He'd stayed with me all night, even into the early hours of the morning.

"Oh look, she's awake!" I heard Aaron say. I sat up, stretching and letting my vision adjust. I was startled a bit when I became aware of my heart beat, but relaxed when I remembered why it was so. "Good morning, blondie," Aaron continued.

"Blondie? What do you mean?" I asked, yawning.

"Your hair is back to normal, well almost."

I grabbed a chunk of my hair and inspected it. He was right; I was blonde again, save for the black tips. My hair had gone from black to blonde in less than ten hours.

"So, why did you want me to wake up?"

"I invited Evelyn, Jeff, and Curtis over. They wanted to see us again before leaving town, and I suggested that they come over for breakfast."

"When are they coming?"

"Ten minutes."

"Are you serious?"

Gallard and I both stood up from the couch and I ran up

the stairs to get in a quick shower and change.

Lydian was in the bathroom, as usual, putting on makeup. When she didn't take the hint to leave, I just stripped down and jumped into the shower. I didn't have time to try and coax her out.

"Hey, you're blonde!" she shouted above the running water.

"Yup, appears so," I replied. I was scrubbing as quickly as possible, trying to put conditioner in my hair while shaving at the same time. I cut my leg and let out a groan.

"I can smell you," she said. "Never thought you would end up on the opposite end of the food chain, did you?"

I finished rinsing then turned the water off. I grabbed a towel from the rack, wrapping it around myself as I stepped out of the tub. I pulled my blow-dryer from underneath the sink and started drying my hair. I did so until it was just slightly damp since I didn't have much time and ran out of the bathroom into my room.

It was hard finding any pants that weren't sweats since I hadn't done laundry in forever. My old clothes were still in the closet, but hardly any of them fit. My hips were slightly bigger since I'd matured over the past four and a half years, so there was no way my jeans would button. I settled for some black capris that I'd worn three days before and a slightly dressy pink tank top.

As I bumbled down the stairs, I ran into Gallard at the bottom. He'd changed into the ripped jeans that I loved and a grey, long-sleeve shirt with the sleeves pushed up to his elbows. He smelled good too.

"Are you sticking around?" I asked.

"Why, do you not want me to?" he asked, giving me the same grin that made me feel as though I were melting. My heart skipped a beat and started to get warm. I could have kissed him right then and there, but I didn't. I would have to learn to control my emotions now that they could be shown through my change in body temperature.

"I always want you around," I assured him. He leaned against the railing and folded his arms.

"Actually, Jordan, Lydian, and I planned to hide out in the basement."

"Or, you could stay and meet my family and Curtis. I'm sure they'll like you. Everybody likes you. Besides, I need you to protect me from Curtis."

He raised an eyebrow. "Why is that?"

"I'll explain later, but maybe if you're there, he won't flirt with me."

"Right. He's the one you made out with at that party. I remember you told me once. So you want me there to make it look like he has competition?"

When he put it that way, it sounded horrible. I didn't want it to seem like I had several guys making a play for me; I just wanted Curtis to back off and see me as a friend.

"Maybe you should just stay in the basement," I suggested.

"And miss out on the chance to meet this Curtis character that's infatuated with you? No way, Miss Sharmentino. You've piqued my interest."

"Well, at least I don't have to worry about my aunt and uncle recognizing you. Your hair is different than the one in your mug shot and you shaved."

"Or, I could impersonate Jordan. That would be interesting to try."

Lydian came down the stairs behind me and smirked.

"You can't pull off being Jordan. He's got about ten pounds of muscle on you. They'd figure it out in a heartbeat."

"Lydian, your optimism is inspiring," I jabbed.

We parted and I went into the kitchen to see what Aaron was making. I'd never seen him cook and hoped that he wasn't planning to serve Eggo waffles and microwaved bacon. I was relieved when I saw that Jordan was at the stove. Aaron was scrambling twenty eggs in a mixing bowl.

"I'm probably making too much, but I'm kind of enjoying this whole cooking thing; I haven't done it in a while," Jordan said as he added a tenth pancake to a large stack. It all smelled so good. For the first time, food sounded appetizing.

"It's great, Jordan; you've outdone yourself again," I said. "I'm glad someone around here knows how to cook besides Gallard and me."

"You cut my hair, so I thought I'd—"

"Return the favor? Jordan, you really don't have to. If we keep doing stuff for each other, we're going to end up repaying each other for the rest of our lives."

"That won't be too long. So I have...seventy years of favors? Maybe sixty, since you're so prone to dangerous situations."

"Haha, very funny."

Kevin got out seven plates and I helped him set the table. I'd had to dust it first since it hadn't been used in ages. It looked like new once I was finished. We normally wouldn't have done so much preparing, but we wanted everything to look normal; like a bunch of humans lived there and not immortals.

"So...what is it like to eat food? You know...as a vampire?" Kevin asked. I cringed at the memory. The best way to describe that experience was chewing on cotton balls soaked in water.

"It isn't pleasant. I'm not exaggerating when I tell you it's disgusting, so when you do eat, try not to let it show."

"It can't be as bad as my cravings for blood. Gallard has been helping me, but I have to admit that it took every ounce of self control not to bite Curtis last night."

"Now you understand why I had to leave. I didn't want to lose control with you or anyone in our family." I paused for a moment. "Sit next to me at brunch okay? If you start to feel like you're going to lose control, at least you'll bite me and not Curtis or our aunt and uncle."

"I can't bite you. If I did, I would be mortal and useless like you." He smiled and nudged me.

"You're a real comedian, Kev."

I put a napkin in each place then set up the glasses. I was looking forward to having breakfast with my relatives since I hadn't shared a family meal in years. Drinking blood bags on the couch didn't really count as a family dinner, and it was refreshing to not have to hide what I was anymore.

The dining table had been a wedding gift to my parents and was large enough to seat twelve people. Apparently, someone assumed that they'd planned to imitate the *Cheaper by the Dozen*. Catholic families were usually big, but the Sharmentinos weren't ones to follow the norm. Considering this, it now seemed somewhat poetic that my brothers and I had gotten involved with immortals. We were far from normal, at least my brothers were.

Jeff and Evelyn arrived first. I had to answer the door because my brothers would have caught fire the second it opened. I'd already had to extinguish Kevin twice after he'd forgotten about his new weakness and walked outside. They weren't close calls, but it was scary enough to keep him from continuing to make the mistake of exposing himself to the sun.

"You went back to your natural color," my aunt said. "I like it so much better."

"Me too."

I hugged both of them then lead them into the dining room. Everyone accept for Gallard and my brothers had already adjourned to the basement so I introduced them to him. I was glad that he was going to join us. He was just as much of my family as my real family was.

Curtis showed up five minutes later, and I introduced him to Gallard. Curtis gave him a friendly greeting and I was relieved he didn't act jealous or anything. I wasn't able to fully relax until everyone was sitting at the table and eating.

"Curtis, it's good to see you again," my aunt said. "You've come a long way from the boy who set off stink bombs at our Fourth of July parties."

"Yes I have, Evelyn," he said. "Too bad we can't say the same thing about Aaron."

"I've changed!" Aaron said defending himself. "I'm just taking some time off from college. Med school will always be there when I'm ready to go back."

"What about you, Kevin?" my uncle asked. "You excited to graduate next year?"

I nervously shoved a huge bite of pancake into my mouth as I waited to hear what he had to say. Kevin couldn't finish school now that the sunlight was an issue, so he would have to find another means of completing his education.

"Actually, I'm thinking of skipping senior year and just getting my GED."

"Really, why?" my aunt asked.

"I'd like to do some traveling, that is, after Robin is found."

I could tell that my aunt and uncle wanted to protest but were choosing not to. Everyone on Mark's side of the family had attended college. Even my mother went, though she didn't obtain anything more than an associate's degree. She'd chosen to be a stay-at-home mom instead. My brothers and I were breaking the college streak, and if Mark were still alive, he would not be pleased.

I took another nervous bite and swallowed quickly. I was going to take another one when Gallard reached over and gave my knee a reassuring touch. For a second we made eye contact and he started to move his hand when I put mine over it to show him that I was okay with the gesture. My eyes found his again and he smiled at me, causing my heart to beat faster.

"Gallard, tell us, did you go to college?" my aunt asked. We both moved our hands and I went back to eating. It was difficult recovering from our little moment and I hoped that I wasn't turning red.

"Yes, I did. I have a degree in business," he answered.

"You should convince Lela to go. She's a great runner; she could get in on a track scholarship."

"I don't know. Have you seen her wrestle? She's a monster," he said, winking at me.

My brothers started laughing and I knew that they had turned what he'd said into a dirty joke. I felt my cheeks grow hot and I swallowed my food only to replace it with another bite of eggs.

My aunt and uncle didn't seem to get the joke because they just let out confused chuckles and continued eating. Curtis' expression, on the other hand, showed that he knew exactly what they were laughing at. I had to find some way to change the conversation before it was too late to recover.

"I may not be in college, but at least I'm not a stripper like your brother's girlfriend," I teased, nudging Gallard. My brothers let out a long *oh* as if to cheer on my witty comeback.

I then stood up to put my plate in the sink. I was stuffed since I'd been feeding my face out of anxiety. So far, no one suspected that something was amiss with my brothers. I needed a second to recover from the embarrassment. It was bad enough with Lydian spouting out innuendo, and I definitely didn't need it from my brothers.

As I rinsed my plate off, I thought about what Kevin had said he planned to do after this was all over. The way he'd talked made it sound like he was definitely thinking about leaving Miami. I wondered if Aaron would sell the house since it had been left to him. I wouldn't want to live in it by myself; it was too big. The house may have had sentimental value, but it would be of better use to a bigger family.

When the family lawyer had come to discuss the will, I'd learned that my parents had left me fifty grand, which I would receive every year for the rest of my life. This money was all from Solomon Sharmentino, and I had no idea what I would do with that much money. I was used to living a paycheck to paycheck life, and now I was sitting on a large sum and even more to come. I'd never dreamed of being that fortunate, but now that I could afford almost anything, I was at a loss for what I would invest in.

But the money was the least of my worries. I'd put that on the back burner to think about on a later date; there were more important things. For now, I wanted to enjoy what little time I had left under the same roof with my family, so I was going to focus on

Robin.

"You're deep in thought," Curtis said, entering the kitchen with his plate.

"Yeah, I guess so. How long have I been in here?"

"Long enough for me to come looking for you. Are you okay?"

I put the stopper in the sink, squirting some soap around before turning on the water.

"I will be. It's tough, but I've survived this far."

He grew silent and we listened to the sound of the conversation in the dining room before he spoke again.

"So…what's with you and Gallard?" he asked, somewhat with enmity. I shut the water off then turned around.

"What do you mean?" I asked as innocently as possible. I didn't like to play dumb, but I was too nervous to do otherwise.

"It's so obvious that the two of you are more than friends."

"Gallard and I *are* friends."

"I don't buy that. You're different when you're around him; you seem happier. It shows in your eyes how you feel."

I waited a minute to reply to him. I had to choose my words carefully instead of speaking based on how I felt at the moment. I also had to take into account that Gallard could possibly be listening to our conversation.

"He's done so much for me these past few years. He's the most selfless, kind, and loving person that I know. I couldn't ask for a better friend."

Aaron entered the kitchen before Curtis could reply. I knew that he wasn't going to let this go, but at least I could have more time to come up with a way to end his suspicion for good.

"Jeff and Evelyn have to go. Their plane leaves in forty-five minutes," Aaron said. I walked passed Curtis, giving him a look that said *we'll talk later* and went back into the dining room.

I joined my brothers in saying goodbye to our aunt and uncle. I would be able to see them again, but Kevin and Aaron wouldn't, so the parting was somewhat bittersweet for them. I tried to fight the tears while I watched Kevin gingerly hug his relatives.

As they were about to walk out the door, my uncle waved me over and whispered, "Lela, try to get that little brother of yours give his education a second thought, okay."

"Will do, Uncle Jeff. I'll see you," I said, giving him one last squeeze. I watched the two of them walk down the driveway and get into their car. I was the only one who could stand on the porch, so I went back inside, not wanting to be out there alone.

To my delight, Curtis and Aaron did some more catching up in the living room, so Gallard and I were able to sneak into the basement to see Jordan and Lydian. I got to the bottom of the stairs and the lights were off, but the TV was going.

"You guys better be fully clothed down here," I said, preparing to cover my eyes if needed. Jordan got up from the couch and paused the movie.

"Lydian isn't here. She sneaked out about a half an hour ago. I'm not sure where she went, though."

Gallard and I sat next to him on the couch and he pressed play again. He'd been watching *Terminator 2*, and it was almost over. I pretended to watch the movie as I listened to them talk in French. I found it amusing when they did that and sometimes they would mingle their language with English. Jordan liked to call it Frenglish, so we stuck with it.

Eventually, I would have to go back upstairs and face Curtis again, but I wasn't ready just yet. I'd been wrong; immortal company was less stressful than human company. At least it was now. Even if I wasn't one of them anymore, I was forever linked to them because I'd been a part of their world for just a blink of an eye.

The movie ended and the three of us sat in the darkness as the credits rolled. I tried to strain my ears to hear the conversation upstairs, but I no longer had the ability to stretch my hearing that far. It would take some getting used to.

I heard the door at the top of the stairs open and the three of us turned to see who was coming down. The light turned on and I squinted my eyes as they adjusted to the brightness.

"Hey, Kev. What's up?" I asked.

"Curtis is driving back to Tampa. He wants to say goodbye."

I got up from the couch and followed my brother up the stairs. I was surprisingly winded when I got to the top, and I felt pathetic. My heart was pounding and I felt lethargic, probably from the huge meal that I'd just eaten. By the time I got to the front door, I had to catch my breath, all from just walking up a flight of stairs.

I would have to start running again and get back in shape.

"Hey," Curtis said upon meeting my gaze. "Can we talk for a minute?"

I nodded then we both went outside onto the porch. We took a seat next to each other on the porch swing and I held my breath as I waited for whatever he was going to say.

"I wanted to apologize," he said. "I was out of line earlier. Your personal relationships are none of my business and I shouldn't have told you I was still into you either. Dropping all of that on you while you're going through a hard time probably stressed you out."

"I suppose I can forgive you for old-time's sake," I said pretentiously. He smiled.

"I'm glad. I would hate to leave if we were at odds."

I could never imagine being mad at Curtis. In a way, he was like Tyler, minus the old fashioned ways. I'd really missed him, despite our somewhat awkward parting. I had to admit that for a short time after I'd left, I wondered what would have happened if I'd never turned and stayed around. Would we have ended up together, or would we have remained friends who happened to make out one time?

I cleared my throat before replying, "Were you serious when you said that you never got over me?"

"I was...but that isn't why I wanted to talk to you."

Now I was even more nervous. Whatever he was going to say couldn't be something I wanted to hear.

"Your brothers informed me that they're going to be leaving very soon and Aaron plans to put the house up for sale. He mentioned that you don't plan on going with them, so I asked if—" he paused and I began to slightly perspire. This conversation was heading in a weird direction. "I asked if he would mind if I asked you to come with me to Tampa after they leave."

I stared at him for a moment then laughed out loud. He was basically asking me to move in with him like it was the old days when women would be forced to find a husband in the event of their parents dying. It was comical; I couldn't help but laugh.

"Are you serious? Why would I do that? I have an apartment in Vegas."

"Do you really want to spend the rest of your life in the gambling capital of America cleaning toilets?" he asked.

"I wouldn't be alone there. I have my friends and I have...Gallard."

His expression turned disappointed and he looked down. "Do you love him?"

The last time I'd been asked this question, it had been in relation to Tyler. I had loved him and after he rejected me, the subject of love became sensitive for me. I didn't trust that phrase anymore, unless it was from my family or friends. In the romantic sense, I didn't think I could ever say that I loved someone ever again.

"I care about him. He's my best friend and I trust him with my life. But that's as far as it goes."

This felt like such a lie. I knew deep down that I felt more than that for Gallard, but I would never say it out loud. I would have to settle for the occasional flirting and not let it go beyond that.

"I don't buy that," he said. "Anyway, I think it's time that you move on from the past and come here where you can build a better life for yourself."

"Move on with *you*?"

"You don't have to move *on* with me, I'm asking if you'll move *in* with me. I just bought a new house, and I need another person to sign the lease. I figured if you could sign it, you could stay there as well. You wouldn't have to have a job; you could focus on working with the police to find your sister."

This crazy idea couldn't have been something he'd just thought up. I sensed that the others had something to do with it. I was no longer physically able to help them take down Samil, and now they planned to leave me behind and they were using Curtis to hide their secret schemes.

I would be better off, though. My friends and brothers were going to be leaving and I would have no one; accept for Curtis. I would be safer as well since Samil's group was somewhere off in London and not sticking around to spy on us. He knew about the apartment in Vegas as well as where my parent's house was. If I moved to Tampa, he wouldn't have a clue where I was.

I also thought of Gallard. If I spent some time away from him, maybe I could take the time to deal with what I was feeling and try to get rid of my attraction to him. But Gallard and I were bonded for life, no matter what kind of relationship we had. We would be friends for the duration of my recently shortened lifespan. He'd done so much for me, and I owed it to him to do anything I could to protect myself so that it wouldn't be in vain.

"How long before the lease needs to be signed?" I asked. His eyes brightened with excitement.

"I have until next Friday. That will give you a week to decide and I'll drop by that Thursday. You can give me your answer then."

I wasn't really sure what I was going to do, but I was glad that I had some time to think. Even after Curtis drove off, I stayed on the porch to weigh all of my options. Moving to Tampa would be my best option if I wanted to stay off the radar. I didn't know how long I would be there, though, or what I would do with all my free time. I had enough money that I wouldn't need to work, but I couldn't picture myself as a homebody.

I never finished the conversation I'd started with Gallard the night before, but my gut feeling was that he was absolutely not going to let me tag along. I was frustrated by this, but I didn't want to be irrational. I'd been told by both him and Lydian that I was basically useless; not in those exact words, but that was what I'd interpreted.

I went back inside feeling more conflicted than ever and shuffled around the house, trying to see what everyone was up to. Lydian still wasn't back, so it was pretty quiet. I found everyone in the kitchen and my brothers had just finished doing all the dishes.

I felt bad that I hadn't been there to help, so I began to dry the ones that were on the counter.

"Whose idea was it for me to move in with Curtis?" I asked. Kevin and Aaron looked at each other and pretended to be oblivious, so I looked at Gallard and Jordan to see if they would be more honest.

"This is the first I've heard of this," Gallard said. "Did he ask you to move in?"

By the sound of his voice, I sensed a hint of jealousy. I'd heard this same tone when he'd seen my engagement ring almost a year ago. It was subtle, but I'd noticed it. I would have addressed it if I weren't still annoyed about my brothers plotting behind my back.

"Yes, he did. He never said it, but I have this inkling that he wasn't the one to come up with this crazy idea." I stared hard at my brothers. Aaron turned on the dishwasher before answering.

"I admit it. It was my idea. I wanted to make sure that someone was looking out for you while we're gone. Curtis is my best friend, and I can trust him to keep you safe."

"He's an orthodontist; how can he protect me?" I asked. "Is he going to attack Samil with his drill bit? Give him a root canal?"

"He took karate, remember?"

"You both did, and neither of you made it passed the yellow belt." I paused for a minute. "Was this really the best thing you came up with; having me shack up with Curtis?"

Everyone laughed except for me. They wouldn't be

laughing if one of them were in my shoes.

"It's only going to be for a few months," Aaron assured. "He doesn't need you to live there forever; he mostly just needs another lease signer. And if you do decide to take him up on his offer, you don't have to go right away." He smiled then looked at Kevin. "Or...you could always stay with Sharon Lockfield. I'm sure she'd love to have your company."

I let out an exasperated breath. There was no way I could live with her. Not after I'd stolen her bat and she'd dated Mark. Not to mention her cheating on Mark with Aaron. I couldn't put my finger on it, but while I thought she was very nice, she seemed off to me, and not in a Lydian sort of way. Lydian I liked because her eccentricities were lovable, but Sharon acted like she was hiding something.

I didn't want to try and come up with a decision at that moment, so I went out into the backyard by the pool.

I hadn't been able to go to that part of the house since the night my parents were killed. The crime scene people had made sure that there was no evidence that a murder had been committed, but that didn't stop the horrific images from creeping into my mind as I looked around. My backyard was no longer my backyard; it was the place where my mother and Mark each drew their last breaths.

I dragged my feet through the grass as I walked towards the pool. It hadn't been cleaned in a while since there were some leaves floating at the surface. I sat cross-legged at the edge and closed my eyes. I remembered how I'd sat in that exact spot the last night I'd been at the house before leaving. Our pool had always been the place I would go whenever I wanted to do some deep thinking. For once, I wanted to just clear my mind and focus on the sound of the water rippling from the slight breeze.

In those quiet moments, I thought maybe being mortal again wouldn't be so bad. I'd missed being able to properly enjoy the warmth of Miami; the relaxing rays of the sun; the pleasure of a tall glass of ice water on a hot day. The only part I missed about being a vampire was my ability to defend myself. I could walk down an alley without worrying that someone was going to mug me, and now I was as helpless as any other young woman.

I sensed that someone was standing next to me and I flinched as I opened my eyes. I used to be able to hear someone coming from far away, but my hearing was normal.

"Did I scare you?" Lydian asked. I nodded and she sat down, putting her feet in the water. Her demeanor was different than it had been the day before. She was more relaxed.

"Where were you all morning?"

"I had to run an important errand. I didn't mean to take so long, though."

"You chose to run an errand when you had Jordan all to yourself in our basement? I'm shocked!"

She nudged me and I nudged her back. When she pushed me again, I elbowed her as hard as I could in the ribs, knowing it wouldn't hurt her. She laughed at me.

"You're so weak. I don't think I'll ever get used to this," she said. I smiled at her. She was a lot more pleasant to be around than she had been earlier. I liked the fun and spontaneous Lydian, not the jealous and angsty Lydian.

"While you're out here, I need some advice," I said. I figured she would be a good person to talk to about the whole moving in with Curtis thing. Unlike my brothers and Gallard, she wasn't worried about protecting me, which was nice. She would give me a straightforward answer, without any personal interest.

"If you're going to ask if you should profess your love to Gallard and kiss him like he's never been kissed before, then I say go for it."

I rolled my eyes. "No, that's not what I was going to ask."

"Damn. What advice do you need then?"

I took my shoes off and joined her in swishing my feet in the water. It was colder than I expected, but I got used to it after a few minutes.

"If you had the chance to be safe; to go into hiding and escape from any danger, would you do that? Or would you rather fight knowing that the possibility that you could die in the process is very high?"

"Hmm…I think I would rather hide. It's not cowardly to try and protect yourself if there's no chance you'd survive. Why would you fight if you were going to die? You're not good to Robin dead, you're just…dead."

This was the most logical answer I'd come across so far. I

wasn't sure if I agreed with the whole saving myself part of it, but she was right; what good would I be if I were dead? Robin would lose another family member; I would have made an unnecessary risk and ended my life abruptly. But could I live with myself if I didn't even try to help? It was my sister and David who were in danger. I wanted to be there with my brothers to help get them back.

"My brothers want me to go into hiding while they handle Samil. They suggested that I move in with Curtis over in Tampa."

"Their plan is have you shack up with their friend?" she asked with a shocked tone.

"That's what I said! It's utterly ridiculous."

We stopped speaking for a bit, something unusual for Lydian. She always had something to say.

"What does you-know-who have to say about that?" she asked, breaking the silence.

Before I could answer, someone came up behind us and said, "I think it's a good idea."

Gallard sat next to me and Lydian replied, "Eavesdrop much?"

"I promise I wasn't eavesdropping, I just heard the last couple of sentences."

I hoped that he was telling the truth. I would probably die if he'd heard what Lydian had said about me professing my love and kissing him. I decided to ignore that possibility and ask his opinion on the matter. This was his last chance to speak up before I would decide to go with my brother's plan. If there was any indignation that he didn't want me to do it, I would change my mind.

"You really think it's a good idea to live with Curtis?" I asked.

"I would rather you live with him for a few months than live by yourself in Vegas. Like your brother said; it would be temporary. After Samil is dealt with, you can go wherever you want. Go live in New Zealand, or Spain."

"But he likes me," I said, pouting. "What if he gets the wrong impression if I move in?"

"Then you better invite me to your wedding," Gallard replied. I groaned in disgust, but he continued, "Not only that, but I expect you to name one of your twelve kids after me as well."

"*Twelve* kids?" Lydian asked. "She's a girl, not a bunny!"

This conversation was getting awkward so we changed the topic. I had taken all the advice everyone had given me to heart and was able to come to a conclusion. I would comply and move in with Curtis. Staying in Florida was the safest choice for me and though it would be hard, I would have to trust my friends and siblings to save my sister.

Chapter Five

The plan was that I would move to Tampa two days after New Years. Curtis was going to spend the holiday with his parents and I would ride home with him afterwards. At first I thought it was weird moving somewhere without any luggage or other household items, but I was reminded that I had money to buy new things with like a bed, sheets, and other furniture that goes in a bedroom.

Everything at IKEA was on sale because of the holidays, so Lydian forced me to spend an entire day there picking out dressers and nightstands. I'd seen the apartment the day I signed the lease, and I had plenty of room to work with. Despite the huge space, I chose to get a twin-size bed so that I could have more room for other things, like a desk or chairs. I went with the color schemes of blue and silver, to Lydian's chagrin. She'd tried to convince me to go with black and red, but I wanted something more cheerful.

I had all of my things shipped to the house a week before Christmas, and I was excited to decorate my new room. My old room was so blah since we hadn't been allowed to paint, so I was ready for a change of scenery besides white walls and a nasty, flowered bedspread I'd gotten for cheap.

To my surprise, my brothers and friends agreed to go to the Christmas Eve service at our church. It was in the evening, so there was really no excuse for why my brothers couldn't go. They even dressed up; accept for Gallard and Jordan who didn't have any nicer clothes. Lydian had to borrow a more appropriate outfit since everything she owned was either for going to a club or working out. There was really no in-between for her.

Christmas day was spent sitting in the living room watching classic Christmas movies. Jordan, wanting to break out his inner chef again, made me a Cornish hen, mashed potatoes with gravy, and a personal-sized pumpkin pie. I tried to insist that he not cook for me, but there was no stopping him.

What was even more surprising was that Lydian didn't act jealous about it. In fact, she'd almost completely stopped with the jealous comments all together. I was glad, more so for Jordan's sake. It would be easier for him if he didn't have to work so hard to prove his devotion to her. I would miss both of them a lot and I hoped that after everything was over, they would stay together.

New Years rolled around sooner than I thought it would. Lydian somehow convinced my brothers to join her and Jordan at some big event going on in town, but I couldn't go because I'd gotten sick a few days after Christmas. I had a fever and sore throat, which left me somewhat bedridden. I was feeling a little better, but not enough to go out.

Gallard didn't want to leave me alone, so he stayed in with me. I'd been cooped up in my parents' room since they had a TV and we decided to watch the ball drop. Gallard even made me beef stew using his mother's recipe. I felt so pathetic having the D'Aubigne men cooking for me all the time, but they'd kept insisting on it. It was hard to say no them.

"You know, I saw the very first New Year's Rockin' Eve," Gallard said. "Dick Clark was a funny guy."

"I'm so jealous. You have all these cool stories to tell and I'm going to have none. What did I experience? Facebook. Justin Bieber, and…the first black president? I suppose I could brag about my shark wrestling. But they'll probably just think I'm crazy and drug me up, leaving me to babble to myself in a corner."

"Don't talk like that. Nobody is going to drug you. Not if I have anything to do with it."

He probably didn't know that I noticed, but whenever the subject of my mortality came up, he became slightly sad. I'd thought he would be happy that I was able to be normal. But no matter how many times he said it, he couldn't hide from me the regret in his voice.

"Don't be sad," I said, touching his shoulder. "Who knows, maybe Lucian's blood will keep me alive longer like it did with David."

"You're right. And if not, I'll sooner take care of you myself if I find out you're being drugged."

"*You* take care of *me*? What if we both get Alzheimer's and forget to give each other our meds and we'll both scare each other, thinking the other person is an intruder. Considering we'll still be living together in Vegas with Jordan and Lydian."

He laughed then took the thermometer out of the drawer. My fever had gotten pretty high the night before and I had to practically beg him not to take me to the emergency room. He finally gave in, but we made a deal that if I didn't get down to at least ninety-nine, he was going to take me to the hospital.

"Oh look! It's ninety-seven. I told you it would go down," I said once I'd taken my temperature.

"Thank the lord. I couldn't leave you here, knowing that you were sick. Maybe we should wait it out. You shouldn't travel while you're still feeling bad. You might relapse."

"I should be fine by Friday. But there is one thing you can do. How about a shoulder rub?"

"I suppose. Since everyone thinks I can't my hands off of you. I might as well."

"You can't keep your hands off me? Which one of the two said that?"

"Lydian of course. Jordan isn't that straightforward."

"Did you know that she insinuated that we share a tooth brush?"

"That's disgusting! I wouldn't share a tooth brush with my own brother." He sighed. "To hell with what Lydian thinks, right? She's the one who practically lives in Jordan's lap."

"Do D'Aubignes have comfortable laps or something?"

Without another word he tugged me closer to him so that I was sitting in his lap then began massaging my shoulders as we watched Taylor Swift begin singing.

"I'm going to miss this," I said.

"The massages? If you want, I could give Curtis a crash

course before you leave. I learned from the best."

"No, weirdo, hanging out with you. How often do we get to hang out without Lydian and Jordan popping up at every corner to make some nasty comment?"

"Not enough. Which is why you should go out with Curtis. Maybe the crude jokes will stop."

I rolled my eyes. Why was he always joking about me and Curtis getting together? Especially since he was the one flirting with me every chance he got. I couldn't keep up with what was going on in his head.

"You should give him a chance," Gallard said. "I think he'll stick around, depending on whether or not you decide to tell him everything."

"You said that last time with Tyler and look what happened. No more dating advice for you, Mr. I haven't had a date in five hundred years."

"Ouch! It hasn't been five hundred years. I took Hilary out one time."

"After I told you to. And you took her to Starbucks. That's hardly a date."

We stopped talking and paid attention to the concert for a while, but Gallard's massage was feeling extra good for some reason and I found myself closing my eyes and getting lost in his touch. He must have sensed what was going on because his touch became less firm and he gently rubbed my back, moving his hands in a circular motion that gave me goose bumps. My mother used to do this to Kevin when he was a baby to help him fall asleep and I suddenly realized why it worked so well. I swiftly removed my sweater so I could feel it better and he resumed with the massage as soon as it was off. I still had the feeling I wasn't getting the full effect.

"You know, it feels better when...when you—" I couldn't even get the words out. I was glad that we were usually on the same page because he then said, "On the skin? You're so demanding, Miss Sharmentino." His tone was playful so I wasn't worried that he was bothered.

But as soon as his cold hands slid up the back of my shirt, I wondered what the heck I was doing. What *we* were doing. I was supposed to be avoiding this kind of thing and yet here I was encouraging it. The whole thing where he'd touched my leg at brunch was one thing, but sitting here on my parents' bed while he massaged my back was another. I knew I should have put a stop it then, but at the same time I didn't want to.

My trance slightly broke when I noticed that there was fifteen seconds left of the countdown. We watched as Ryan Seacrest got to five then four, three, two; and then everybody in Times Square cheered and the traditional song began to play.

"Happy New Year, Lela," Gallard said. He then surprised me with a light kiss on my cheek. I don't know if it was unintentional or on purpose, but his lips brushed the corner of my mouth, causing my heart rate to quicken.

What was even more shocking was that he didn't stop there.

He kissed my cheek closer to my ear and then my jaw, finally ending at my neck. But he didn't kiss me where I really wanted him to, and I was too scared to make the first move. Instead, not wanting the moment to end, I just let him continue brushing his lips against my neck.

Before I knew it we were lying down with me on my back and him on top of me. He was kissing my neck more intensely then his lips made a trail down lower, finding their way to my collarbone. He pulled my shirt down over my shoulder and kissed that too while he began caressing my leg. I had my arms around his waist, holding him against me.

I loved the way he smelled; like a mixture of rain and peppermint. For the next ten minutes, I focused only on him and the fact that I didn't want him to stop touching me.

"Que mes baisers soient les mots d'amour que je ne te dis pas," he whispered.

I didn't even ask for a translation. Whatever he'd said, it made me even more enamored by him. I didn't usually behave like this. I'd never done anything like this with Tyler, save for the night he proposed. Even before that, we never got too carried away.

I started unbuttoning his shirt and oddly enough, he didn't try to stop me. This was a side to him I'd never seen before as well as a new side to myself.

"Gallard," I whispered. He stopped what he was doing and looked into my eyes.

"I..." I continued, slightly stuttering. "I lov —"

What stopped me from my sudden burst of honesty was the front door bursting open and Jordan shouting, "Happy New Year!"

Gallard quickly moved away from me and I sat up, positioning myself on one end of the bed, under the covers while he was on the other. He re-buttoned his shirt quicker than I'd ever seen a person do it then casually folded his arms. It made me wonder what would have happened if the others hadn't come back. How far would we have taken things? What scared me more was the fact that for a moment I didn't care how far we went.

"You missed a great party," Lydian said as she came up with Jordan. "Some guy tried to roofie me. You should have seen the look on his face when he—" she suddenly stopped speaking. "Are we…interrupting something?"

I groaned inwardly. I was stupid to think that we could pretend nothing was going on. Normally, Gallard and I would sit close to each other whenever we spent time together, and Lydian probably knew this. It was even odder that we were so far apart. She was bound to notice something.

"Yeah, you're cutting into the Taylor Swift concert!" Gallard said with a playful tone. "Where's Kevin and Aaron?"

I hadn't noticed my brothers weren't with the two of them. I wasn't worried, though. If there was any danger, they wouldn't have been in such a good mood.

"Aaron went off with some woman and Kevin is upstairs. Who would have thought Aaron had a chick on the side."

"I need to make a quick run up to Orlando," Gallard said as

he stood up. "Want to join me, Jordan?"

"Sure, I'll go." Jordan then glanced at me then back at Gallard. "I always like a good road trip with my old and feeble uncle."

The two men went downstairs and Lydian plopped into Gallard's spot and changed the channel to some stupid adult cartoon. Normally, I would have been annoyed, but I was still reeling from what had just happened. I could barely process a single thought, let alone form a coherent sentence.

"So…did you two have fun…watching the ball drop?"

The way she said that sounded almost provocative and I instantly knew that there was innuendo behind it.

"Yes. It was a nice quiet night. We just needed some one-on-one time before we part ways. We don't get it that much these days."

She rolled her eyes. "Oh, come on! I know you two weren't in here watching the Taylor Swift concert. You are going to tell me or I am going to put you in head lock until you talk!"

"I told you, we watched the concert and then the count down."

She threw her arm around my neck and began squeezing. It wasn't hard enough to inflict damage, but it still hurt nonetheless.

"Hey! You're killing the sick girl!" I shouted. She let go then returned to her original position, smiling with victory. Lydian was always so pushy that I couldn't pretend around her like I did Gallard. "I guess I'll tell you before you maim me again. We were watching TV for a while then we…fooled around."

"Finally! I knew you two would hook up eventually, it had to—" She sat up and leaned really close to me. "Lela, is that a hicky?"

"No way!" I got up and ran into the bathroom, flinging on the light. She was right; I did have one. So much for sneaking around.

"Damn," Lydian said after leaning against the doorframe. "D'Aubigne Senior is bolder than I thought."

"This is just great. I was going to pretend this night never happened and now there's evidence."

"Pretend it didn't happen? That's not what you need to do. You need to tell him how you feel!"

"I started to…but, I can't." I kept staring at the mark on my neck, hoping it would somehow disappear if I wished hard enough. "I told you, I'm done with relationships. Maybe fooling around with him was what I needed. Like a drug fix or something. I got my hit, and now I can move on."

Lydian looked like she was confused. Why should she be? She was the one who serial dated several guys before settling down with Jordan. Why would she care if I just hooked up with Gallard one time and moved on?

"No, he's not a fix. You're in love; messy, complicated, passionate love. You two were made for each other and you both are making the rest of us crazy with this back and forth flirting. I know you said Tyler hurt you or whatever, but Gallard isn't Tyler.

He's stuck by you through everything and he hasn't bailed yet. What more could you ask for?"

Nothing. She was right; he was the only guy I wanted, but the last guy I wanted to lose. At least if we were friends, I could ensure neither of us would get hurt. We excelled at being friends. I was closer to him than anyone and shared everything; my worries and fears. But there was one thing I couldn't be honest about and it would have been so much easier if he would speak up first.

The afternoon I was to leave, I helped Gallard clean the pool. The real estate agent wanted to start showing the house as soon as possible, so we'd spent all of our free time packing it up and getting it ready. It was officially on the market, and all that had to be done was putting up the for sale sign. Aaron planned to hire someone to do it for him while everyone was away. It was weird thinking about someone else living in our house. I'd lived there since I was born, and soon it would belong to someone else.

Gallard sat next to me on the porch when we were done and I rested my head on his shoulder. Despite what had happened on New Years, he'd acted as if it never happened. If he wasn't going to be weird about it then I wasn't either. It was easier to forget since Lydian helped me use make up to cover the mark. I probably would have died if he knew about it and that he was responsible.

Regardless of the awkwardness, I wasn't ready for him to go away for a month, or possibly longer. We'd looked through Mark's old check stubs that he'd saved from Solomon and found that most were sent from London, England. The group decided to start there because they wanted to try and find Solomon against Samil's warning. It was a risky move, but if they didn't take risks, they would be letting Samil win without a fight.

I felt lightheaded again like I had the day after my parents' funeral. I attributed it to leftovers from my recent illness and decided to ignore it. I was tired as well even though I'd taken a nap. My human weaknesses were hard to get used to, but I did my best to grin and bear them since I was stuck that way for good.

"When is Curtis going to be here?" Gallard asked, putting an arm around my shoulder.

"Around three; his family always gets super drunk on New Years, so he wanted to take an extra day recover from his hangover."

"We're leaving too, as soon as the sun sets. We're flying to the UK, but not by plane. We'd get there a lot sooner if we went by flock, for lack of a better word. That way we won't have to deal with security and passports."

"You guys better be safe. I'm expecting you back here, and I don't want it to be for another funeral."

"We'll do our best." His expression turned serious and he shifted in his seat so that he was looking into my eyes. "In return, I need you to promise me something."

"Anything, you name it."

"Promise me that you will stay human. Don't try to find someone to turn you so that you can help. You've probably never thought about it, but I just want to make sure that you never do. I was serious when I said that I want you to have a normal life. And staying human is the only way you can truly achieve that."

I hadn't thought of that idea, but I wasn't expecting that to be his request. Some part of me wished that he would ask me to wait for him. That was an irrational thought since his leaving was supposed to help me get over him. At the same time, I was curious about how he really felt. The flirting had been innocent up until two nights before, and I knew why I was holding back, but I didn't know why he was.

But instead of being bold and asking him all of these questions, what came out was, "I promise."

"With that said, I wanted to talk about New Years."

Here it was. We'd avoided talking about it for two days and now he was bringing it up. He never brought up our almost kiss the night we met Jordan or the almost kiss that happened later on. Why would he bring up New Years?

"What about it?" I asked hesitantly.

"What I...what happened was...intense at best." He cleared his throat before continuing. "I don't want to leave without apologizing."

He was apologizing? This was even worse than asking to forget it ever happened. What if I was wrong about his having feelings and only fooled around with me to see what it was like; to clear up what we were both probably curious about. Still, I wished that he could have really kissed me to clear everything up for good.

"You don't have to be sorry. Unless...you didn't want it to

happen." I looked into his eyes. "Did you?"

"Lela...you're my closest friend. I care about you more than anyone and I think that my leaving is a good thing. We're uh...getting too dependent on each other. More me than you and—"

"Gallard, please answer my question. Do you feel like New Years was a mistake...or not?"

Gallard opened his mouth to speak but was interrupted when Aaron shouted "Curtis is here!"

We both stood up and I went inside to say goodbye to everyone. I hugged my brothers first, but it was harder saying goodbye to Kevin. I'd told Aaron earlier that I was putting him in charge of watching out for him. Kevin was still very new and developing his strength, so he was the weakest of the group. I hugged Jordan as well, with Lydian's permission-she'd rolled her eyes when I'd asked- and then I playfully punched her in the arm. Our relationship wasn't of the hugging sort, so I had to show that I cared in other ways.

I noticed that Gallard was talking to Curtis about something. Probably going into protective mode and leaving him with a list of instructions on keeping me alive. It wasn't like Curtis could do much. If Samil showed up, we would both be dead in a second.

Gallard finished talking to him then handed me my small travel bag, giving me a firm but gentle hug.

"*Je t'aime,*" he mumbled in my ear. I slightly shuddered, but recollected myself quickly.

"Care to translate?" I asked. He rested his forehead against mine and replied, "Be safe."

I broke from the embrace and reluctantly walked out to Curtis' car. I had a feeling that they were going to be okay. I didn't know why, but I just knew. This comforting thought was what helped me get into the car and allow Curtis to drive me away.

Tampa was a four hour drive away, and I actually enjoyed the trip. Curtis wasn't flirty or weird, so we were able to have normal conversation the entire way. I forgot for those four hours that I was supposed to be worrying about my brothers and friends; and Robin and David. If I was going to keep my sanity, I would have to try and not spend my time worrying about everyone. I worried enough for ten people.

"What were you and Gallard talking about?" I asked.

"Nothing much. He asked me to take extra good care of you." Curtis smiled. "You know, he's actually not that bad of a guy. In fact, he's pretty normal. When you told me you lived together in Vegas, I automatically assumed he was shady."

I laughed. "Gallard is the least shady guy out there. He doesn't even have a tattoo. He works in a night club, but he doesn't drink or smoke. He appears intimidating because of his size, but once you get to know him, you find he has this way about him that makes you feel comfortable."

"Yeah I can see that." He paused for a moment. "The only weird thing is that he barely ate anything. I don't think I remember him taking a bite."

"He doesn't like his brother's cooking," I joked. Curtis chuckled and after that didn't say anything more about it.

It was dark by the time we got to the house. We had to park on the street since the house was next to a main road. It was a nice neighborhood, though so we wouldn't have to worry about vandals. Music was radiating from the house next to us, probably from a party. Curtis told me that most of the people who lived in the neighborhood were college students so I was to expect to hear a lot of noise on the weekends. I didn't mind; party sounds were better than the blaring of *Bridezillas* re-runs from the neighbors in Las Vegas.

Curtis unlocked the door and we went inside. It looked creepy in the dark so I turned on the light. All the furniture was set up in the living room, complete with the TV and entertainment center. He'd done a lot of work unpacking the house. It was decorated very nicely; almost too nice for a bachelor.

"In case you're wondering, my mom picked the furniture," he said.

"Oh okay, I was going to say…"

"If it were up to me, I would have just gotten a couch and some chairs from the Goodwill, but she wouldn't have it."

I went towards the back where my bedroom was. I thought that I was going to have to sleep with just my sheets and the mattress, but I was surprised to find that my bed had already been assembled and the mattress was on top. All I would need to do was put the comforter and pillows on.

I left the room to find Curtis and ask him about it.

"Who set up my bed?" I asked.

"Matthew did. I paid him fifty bucks."

I froze and my heart began to race. I shook with fear and I had to steady myself with the door frame. There was a time when Matthew's name would only invoke rage and hate, but now it had me terrified.

"Matthew who?" I demanded. "What did he look like, where did you meet him?"

Curtis frowned in confusion. "It's Matthew Walker; my Uncle Mitch's son. He wanted to earn some extra cash so I asked him to help out since I've been so busy."

I sat at the table in the dining room and covered my face with my hands. Relief swept over me, and I suddenly felt silly for being so paranoid. Curtis took a seat next to me and I looked up.

"Aaron never told me what exactly happened to you when you disappeared, but whatever you went through, you can talk to me about it...if you want," he said.

I almost told him everything right then and there; how my friends and family were all vampires and that my sister wasn't taken by thugs, but was being held hostage so that two of us would participate in a ritual to bring an old vampire back to life. It would have been absurd to dump all of this on him and shake his peaceful and normal life.

"I'm not quite ready to talk yet...someday maybe, but not

now," I said. "Thanks for offering to listen, though."

He nodded then got up to go to his room and I did the same. I wanted to sleep. I was extremely tired, and worn out from the drive. Lately, my energy had been lacking, so I was looking forward to sleeping in.

I found the box with my bedding and unenthusiastically put everything together to make my bed able to be slept upon. The blue comforter was slick and shiny on the outside but warm and fuzzy underneath. I only put on the fitted sheet since I hated the hassle of having to re-tuck the other one. It was too warm to have so many covers on the bed anyway.

I slipped into the first pair of pajamas I could find, though they were miss-matched, and crawled under the blanket. I shot a quick glance at the clock before shutting my eyes for good. It was eight, so the others had probably left already. I wasn't just guessing; I could sense it. Somehow, even though I was human, I could feel Gallard and Lydian getting further and further away from me, and I was being left behind with nothing but the ache from the strong pull of the separation.

• • •

I groaned as another drop of light-blue paint plopped on top of my hair. I put the roller back in the paint tray and ripped a paper towel off the roll to try and wipe it out. A little over a month had passed and I was already tired of the plain, white walls, so I took on the project of painting them.

    I was trying to be artsy with an attempt to make two large triangles on the ceiling by painting half of it grey and half of it blue, but it wasn't going so well. I'd never painted walls before, so I didn't know all the tips to keeping the paint from dripping. Curtis offered to help, but I insisted on doing it myself. I wanted to prove that I could do something on my own, yet I was failing in the process.

    When I cleaned most of the paint off, I grabbed all of my supplies, climbing down the ladder in a slow fashion. I'd already gotten most of it on my clothes. I couldn't afford to waste it by dumping it all over the floor. Actually, I could have, but just the same, didn't want to waste any good paint. I'd almost put too much confidence in myself by not laying a drop cloth on the carpet, but my gut feeling told me to use it as a precaution. I had been smart to do so.

    The second my foot hit the floor, I became light headed, almost to the point of falling over. I held on for dear life to the tray as my equilibrium restored to normal and I set it down before going into the kitchen. I'd been blaming my recent lightheadedness over the past few weeks on my not completely getting over the flu. I was getting annoyed because this was too long to still be sick.

    Lela, a voice said.

    I stopped walking and looked around. I could have sworn that I heard a voice, and it sounded familiar. My neighbors below often yelled at each other and sometimes Curtis and I would eavesdrop. This was different, though.

I shrugged it off as someone who had walked by then I opened the bread bag to take out a few slices. A sandwich didn't sound that appetizing, but I wasn't in the mood for cooking. I wanted to get the ceiling done before dinner time. I threw together a turkey sandwich with a bit of mayo and lettuce and ate it as I went back into my room. I ate half it before I even got to the door, so I picked up where I left off and began the difficult process of painting the rest of the ceiling.

I finished shortly before Curtis came home from work. I was in the middle of cleaning up when he poked his head into my room.

"Wow, you've been busy," he said, admiring the room. All four walls were painted blue and grey, alternating between colors. The triangle was a bit off, but I wasn't extremely detail orientated. I could live with it.

"Yeah, I've worked almost non-stop all morning and afternoon."

"You've been painting for two days straight. You should take a break. Come out with me tonight. The group is meeting at the Hub for drinks."

I'd accompanied Curtis to most of his social functions since I moved there. At first, I was afraid that when put in the situation, I wouldn't have anything exciting to talk about. Most of the things in my life worth bringing up weren't exactly appropriate to talk about with new acquaintances. I doubted anyone else had been shot twice, broke someone out of jail, or had an immortal enemy out to sacrifice them. I had absolutely nothing in common with regular people. But somehow, I managed to get along with his circle of friends. I even hung out with a few of them one on one, which I was proud of myself for.

"I can't go drinking, I'm nineteen."

"I'm a regular, I can get you in," he said without missing a beat.

I continued cleaning the room as I thought about it. It seemed like every time I went to a bar or club something weird would happen. Perhaps it had something to do with the company I kept. I concluded that as long as I hung around humans, I would be drama free, at least in the fatal sense. Plus I could change my predicament of not having anything human to talk about. The more practice the better.

"What time are you going?" I finally asked.

"In a half hour."

"All right, I'll change," I said. He gave me a weird look and I asked, "What?"

"You might want to shower too…unless you want to go with blue paint in your hair."

I'd forgotten that I was covered in paint. I hurried into the bathroom down the hall and scrubbed as quickly as I could to get all the paint off. Some of it was a losing battle, but I completely cleaned it out of my hair.

Once I was clean, I changed into the navy dress that I loved so much. I hadn't worn it since the night my parents died, and I wanted to wear it again, especially because of who it was from. Wearing it was like having him with me in a way. I didn't have time to dry my hair completely, so I French braided it, tying the rest into a low messy bun.

"Ready to go?" Curtis asked as I stepped into the living room. I nodded and we went out to the car.

I walked into the bar a few paces behind him. He'd been able to get me in as he'd promised, but I didn't plan on drinking…too much. I didn't want to come off as snobby, so I decided to just order something and take a few sips.

"Curtis, Lela; hey!" one of his friend said. It was Martin, a coworker of his. The rest of the group, which consisted of two women and two men all together, were people I'd met before as well, except for the one man sitting on the right side of the table.

"Lela, this is Andre, Delia's boyfriend," Curtis said.

I shook his hand and sat down on the chair next to Curtis'. The bartender took our orders and I asked for whatever Curtis was having, which turned out to be a scotch on the rocks. Probably a manly drink, but I figured if I sipped it delicately it wouldn't seem so masculine.

What was wrong with me? I wasn't usually this timid, boring person. I needed to loosen up for a change. I spent the past four years worrying about everything and everyone and now I finally was in a safe place. There was no danger and my friends were going to bring my sister back to me.

"Could I change my order?" I asked as the waiter passed by.

"Sure, what would you like?"

I thought for a moment. Sometimes Lydian would drag Jordan to Gallard's night club and since I spent a lot of time watching him mix drinks. I tried to remember some of them.

"How about a Cosmopolitan? With…a little extra lime?"

"Coming right up."

I already felt more at ease. I didn't know why I was so leery about alcohol. I probably reacted badly to it when I was fourteen because I wasn't use to it. I wouldn't make the same mistake this time.

"So, Lela; did you finish painting your room?" Delia asked me. She was a nice woman who always wore skirts every time I saw her. I liked her because she actually paid attention when I talked to her and acted genuinely interested in other people's lives.

"Yes, I finished it today. It's not perfect, but I think it looks all right."

"Are we still on for our run this weekend?" Sarah asked. She was the other friend at the table whom I'd gotten closer to. She was a runner like me and we'd started running together after I'd mentioned wanting to get back in shape.

"Definitely. I can already feel the results."

This was a lie. I'd thought running was going to help with my lightheadedness and lack of energy, but instead I was so winded after our runs that I had to sleep for the rest of the day.

While I listened to the murmur of voices, I happened to notice that Andre was hardly participating in any of the discussions and spent most of the time just stirring his drink. I didn't want to come off as a gawker, so I occasionally glanced in his direction to try and figure out what was up with him. He had curly black hair and dark blue eyes, which had a fake appearance to them. They had to be contacts; no one had blue eyes of that shade naturally. It was mentioned earlier that Andre was a new boyfriend of Delia's, so Curtis must not have known him that well. I waved off my suspicion as paranoia and decided to ignore his odd behavior.

You turned out well. You are beautiful, the voice said.

I looked up to see if someone at the table had spoken, but they were all involved in conversation. I'd thought the voice calling my name had been a trick of my mind, but now I was sure. The voice from my past was back after four years of silence.

Where have you been? I asked, feeling slightly crazy. It had been amusing when I was younger, but now that I was an adult, it was strange speaking to a voice in my head.

I could not hear you after you turned. It has been lonely without you, Lela.

It's nice to know you're still creepy. Not.

It is not nice to know that you still keep company with Curtis. Is he still trying to steal your virtue?

As I was conversing with the newly returned voice, I suddenly felt extremely light-headed as I had earlier that day. I reached over and took one of the deep fried zucchini and ate it. It had been a while since I ate the sandwich, so that was probably the reason I felt bad.

"Are you all right, Lela? You look like you're going to be sick," Curtis said. I must have looked as bad as I felt if he'd pointed it out. I wanted to lie and say that I was fine, but I couldn't; I was miserable.

"Yeah, something came onto me all of a sudden. I think I'll head home."

I stood up and was about to say goodbye before leaving when Curtis stood up as well.

"I could take you. I've had enough of these guys anyway," he said, chuckling.

"We don't want you around either, Curtis, get out if here!" Martin said in a jocular tone.

"I'm sorry to leave so soon," I apologized, "It was great seeing you guys again. And it was nice meeting you, Andre." To myself, I said, *Andre with the fake blue eyes.*

"Same here," Sarah said. To Curtis she said, "Go home and take care of your friend. I'll see you this weekend, Lela."

We said goodbye to the rest of the group then drove back home. I felt bad that he had to leave his friends, but he kept insisting that he didn't mind. I didn't remember mortality being this hard. I'd been a relatively healthy person before, now I was weak and sickly.

"Do you need anything from the drug store; some medicine or something?" he asked. I shook my head. I wasn't sure what I would take for the nausea. Maybe drinking soda water would help or maybe antacids, both of which I had at the house.

"I think I just ate too much," I said, trying to abate his concern.

"You hardly even touched any of the food," he recalled. "You barely touched your drink either."

"It's nice to know you pay attention to my eating habits," I said, slightly harsher than I meant to. I immediately felt bad about it. "I'm sorry, that was rude. My illness is making me cranky."

He grew silent as we continued down the road. I wanted him to talk more so that I could focus on what he was saying instead of the nausea that was overwhelming me.

"Are you," his voice faltered almost to a whisper. "Do you think you might be pregnant?"

"What?" I asked in utter shock. I was speechless. His assumption was so out there that I almost found it comical. I stared at him, waiting for him to show any sign that he was joking. But his expression remained serious, even a bit worried.

He got you pregnant! I knew it! You should never have trusted him! The voice said.

No, he didn't get me pregnant! You are so presumptuous, you know that? Now be quiet, you're starting to bother me again.

"Gallard told me that you were sick for the last two weeks before I came. You've been tired and weird lately. You don't eat very much either." Curtis stopped talking when he pulled up to the stop light then spoke again. "Did Gallard get you pregnant? Is that why it was hard to convince you to move out of his apartment?"

Who is Gallard? How many men do you have in your life?

Shut. Up!

"No, Curtis. Nobody got me pregnant. I just feel sick is all."

"You should go to the doctor. Aaron wouldn't forgive me if he came back and found out you were sick."

"I don't think that's necessary, it's nothing Theraflu can't cure."

I hated doctors. I avoided them at all costs. The thought of getting poked and examined was enough for me to shut down the idea.

"I'll drop you off at the walk-in clinic before I go to work," he said firmly.

I realized at this point there was no changing his mind. It was for the best, though. Something was wrong with me and I needed to know what so that I could feel well again. The worst it could be was a stomach virus of some sort. It would explain the nausea and why I felt so tired all the time. I was still in the mindset that I was immortal and I wasn't. I needed to accept that it was time to start taking care of myself.

As I sat in the waiting room at the clinic, I distracted myself with a *Better Homes and Gardens* magazine. The other people there were either coughing, wearing masks, or had tubes in their noses. I wanted to just walk out, but the constant nausea reminded me of why I was there. A looming sense of dread crawled up my spine with each tick of the clock. I wanted to know what was wrong, but I also wanted to be oblivious.

"Lela Sharmentino," a voice called. I waited a second before standing up. The room spun a bit as I followed her to the back and I dreaded it because I knew I would have to be weighed. I'd lost a few pounds since I'd last checked. I wasn't underweight, though, so I wasn't concerned by it. The nurse then led me to a room and I went inside, sitting at the chair next to the examination table.

She did the normal procedures of taking my temperature and blood pressure before she began asking me questions.

"Your temperature is low. This can be due to a number of things like stress or emotional trauma; have you experienced either of these?"

"I was shot a while back…and my parents were killed."

Your parents were killed? The voice asked. *When did this happen?*

Wow, your concern almost sounded genuine!

"I'm sorry to hear that," the nurse said. "I'm sure in time as you heal from these experiences, your temperature should be back to normal. Just keep an eye on it to make sure it doesn't get too low, all right?"

I nodded and she wrote something on her notepad. Afterwards, she asked me why I was there and I went on to explain the dizziness, the fatigue, and lack of appetite. When she asked how long ago I'd been shot, I said two months. The scars were still pretty new. My shift back to mortality had stopped the wounds from healing completely.

She finished with her procedural questions, assuring me that the doctor would be in shortly then left the room.

I was glad that the doctor was female as well. She was middle aged and very thin with smile lines around her mouth. She instantly made me feel comfortable about talking to her.

"Hello, I'm Doctor Helen Cadbury. How are you today?"

"I've been better."

I tapped my foot as I waited for her to ask more questions. I was anxious to get the appointment over with.

"It says here that you were shot some time ago, where was your injury?"

I wanted to say everywhere, but that would have been a drastic confession.

"My shoulder," I replied.

"So how long have you been having these symptoms?"

"About a month now. It started with my getting short-winded from very light activity and escalated to feeling dizzy almost all the time. I had the flu around New Years, and I've never felt the same after. I feel nauseous most of the time as well."

She had me get up on the examination table and lift my shirt.

"Is there any chance that you're pregnant?" she asked.

I sighed. There was that word again. I found it sad that doctors had to ask that of nearly every young woman who went in for stomach pain.

"No, there isn't," I said.

"Just the same, I'd like to do a urine test. But I'm thinking that the dizziness you're feeling has something to do with your iron levels, so I'd like to do a blood test as well."

I did each test that she'd needed. The results of the blood analysis would take a while to get, so I returned home to wait twenty-four hours for the diagnosis. I had nothing to do and a lot of time to fill, so I sat on the couch and read *The Fellowship of the Ring*. It was long and would take me a while to finish, a convenient way to pass the time.

As I read, I wondered what could be wrong. My family didn't have any history of serious illnesses and I'd maintained a healthy diet after I'd turned. I began to worry even more. My hands starting sweating as I held onto the book, my fingers sticking to the pages. I set it down; wiping my hands on my pants then checked my phone. I hadn't heard from anyone since they'd left, and they seemed to have dropped off the radar. I still felt the pull, sometimes so strongly that I would wake up in the middle of the night. I didn't mind it though. It was how I knew that Gallard and Lydian were still alive, possibly David as well.

When Curtis came home, he insisted that we have take-out so that I could rest. We usually switched off who cooked every other night, and tonight was supposed to be my night. I wasn't hungry but forced myself to eat the chow mein to appear as if I were fine. I told him about the blood tests, but didn't elaborate. Whatever was wrong, I would deal with it on my own.

The next day, as I walked back into the clinic, I was a complete nervous wreck. I had chills and my equilibrium was so bad that I could barely stand up straight. I was good at pretending to be okay since no one had needed to give me a wheelchair yet.

I was called in once more, this time skipping the normal procedures and just going straight to the examining room. While I waited for the doctor, I fiddled with a seam on the hem of my shirt. I didn't normally have nervous habits, but this was a new situation for me. My heart was pounding so hard that I was afraid someone would hear it in the next room.

The doctor finally came in and I stopped fiddling so I could give her my complete attention.

"How are you feeling today?" she asked, her tone somber and sympathetic.

"Honestly? I'm worse. I feel like I'm in a maze of circus mirrors whenever I walk."

She looked down then started shuffling through some papers. The feeling of dread returned and I worried that I wouldn't like what she was going to tell me. I get bad news all the time. I should have been used to it by now.

"Lela, we found something in your blood test. Something that's very serious."

I swallowed hard but kept my eyes on her. There was a chance that if I made any movements I would burst into tears.

"Do you have any family members in town? Siblings; an aunt or uncle?" she asked. I shook my head.

"No one in town," I replied. "I'm living with a friend, but he's at work right now."

"Would you like to call him in?"

"No, I can...I'll talk to him later."

She looked through her papers one more time before setting them on the desk and folded her hands in her lap.

"The results from the tests show that you may have some form of Leukemia. We would have to do a biopsy to confirm this, but...I'm fairly certain the results are conclusive. Your liver and your kidneys are in very poor shape. You also have an extreme case of anemia, which I believe to be the cause of your dizzy spells. I would prescribe you some iron pills for that, but the deficiency is so severe that it would take more than just pills to correct it."

She stopped speaking, so I started asking questions.

"What would you have me do then?"

When she sighed, I knew that it wasn't good.

"In all my years of practice, I've never seen anything like this. I've never seen cancer work this way before. It's spreading at an unusual rate. All of your major organs are starting to shut down, and since I don't know what kind of Leukemia yet, I don't know how to treat it. I would have to do more tests, and that would take some time, but for now, it might be best that you check into a cancer treatment center."

These were the most uncomforting words that anyone could hear from a doctor. I was critically ill, and she had no clue how to help me. My hands trembled as I hung onto the armrests of the chair. I still had one more question, one that I was sure that if she knew anything at all, she would have an answer to it.

"Am I dying?" I asked. Instead of answering me, she

avoided my question with more options.

"There are specialists in town that I highly recommend you see that deal with kidney and liver failure. And there are amazing cancer treatment facilities available. They've been able to prolong the lives of many patients, some even up to five years. Of course, you would have to be put on the waiting list for transplants, and that could take a while, unless you can find someone in your family that's a match."

"Am I dying?" I asked again. I wanted a straight answer. Not options, not treatments; an answer.

"Yes, Lela. I'm afraid that you are," she said.

My fear was suddenly gone. What was left was an overwhelming sense of hopelessness. Samil had been wrong; his making me mortal wasn't a gift; it was a death sentence. He should have just killed me along with my parents. It would have been better to die instantly than slowly, wondering when I was going to run out of time.

"Um...you said that taking an iron supplement might help. With the dizziness, I mean."

"Somewhat—"

"I'd like to get a prescription. I don't think I'll go to the hospital, so if I could take something to feel a little better, that would be nice."

I probably should have checked into a hospital after I left, but I didn't see the use. They couldn't help me; no one could. My illness was caused by something supernatural, and I could only be cured by something supernatural.

But I couldn't cure myself. I'd made a promise to Gallard that I would stay human. He'd never broken a promise to me, and I was determined to keep mine. That meant that there was no option of finding someone to turn me and stop my inevitable death. I'd tasted my family's blood, and whether it was forced or not, the rules still applied. I would suffer the consequences; consequences that were put into motion thousands of years ago, and there was nothing I could do to escape it.

Chapter Six

I stood at the counter peeling potatoes for the beef stew. I had my iPod going, and I hummed along as I cooked. Curtis was going to be home soon, and I had no intention of giving him my bad news. I knew he would call Aaron if he found out, and I didn't want anyone, especially my brothers, to know of my illness. Nothing could distract them from finding Robin right now.

I dropped the last potato into the boiling water then began chopping up some carrots just as I heard the front door open. My heart raced as I thought of what I was going to tell him. At least I wasn't feeling as dizzy as before. The iron pills were extremely helpful, though I probably was taking more than I should.

"How's the patient?" he asked as he walked into the kitchen.

"I'm fine," I sort of lied. "Doctor said it's another bout of the flu. I'm on antibiotics."

"That's a relief," he said. I continued cutting the carrots and he asked, "Would you like some help?"

"If you want to. I still need to sauté some onions and cut the meat."

"Let me do the meat. I'll go change real fast."

He left the kitchen and I dumped the carrots in with the potatoes. I was relieved that he'd believed my story. At least I could stall for a while. Eventually, I wouldn't be able to get up and around anymore, but until then, he had to think that I was healthy.

He came back, wearing jeans and a t-shirt and took the chuck roast out of the package. I stirred the onions and garlic as I watched him cut it up, smiling to myself as I thought about how much we must have look like a married couple cooking dinner together.

"Have you heard from your brothers at all?" he asked.

"No. They're kind of off the radar right now."

"You'd think they would have stayed in town in case they find your sister sometime soon. Where did they go again?"

Gallard had told me they were going to England, but I doubted they were still there after a month. None of them had contacted me since they'd gotten there, so for all I knew they could be in Antarctica or Russia trying to find Solomon.

"Who knows? They don't talk to me anymore."

"That's too bad that you couldn't go with them. I love having you here, but being left behind isn't fun."

"Yeah, being left behind blows. Karma's a bitch."

Curtis let out a hearty laugh and I chuckled.

"Yes…yes it is," he replied, returning his attention back to the meat. "If I hadn't been an idiot by keeping my mouth shut, maybe we would have been together."

I stopped stirring for a second then continued.

"I don't think that's karma," I speculated.

He glanced at me as he cut the meat then flinched as he accidently sliced his finger. On instinct, I backed away from him and held my breath. I didn't want to lose control with him. I couldn't hurt him.

"What's wrong? Are you afraid of blood?"

"Somewhat," I said without breathing. "I'll get you a Band Aid."

I hurried away then found the bathroom. I grabbed some disinfectant as well as some cotton balls and the box of water-proof bandages. Holding my breath had caused me to be dizzy again, so before I returned to the kitchen, I popped a couple of iron pills.

I found Curtis pressing a paper towel to his finger and I held my breath once more. His finger stopped bleeding which was good. I didn't want to have to take him to the clinic and risk running into Dr. Cadbury again. She was still calling me to try and convince me to seek treatment.

"I didn't know blood made you squeamish," Curtis said as I doctored his wound. "Wasn't *Jaws* your favorite movie when you were six?"

Somehow, this conversation reminded me of something. I wasn't a vampire anymore and I didn't have to be careful around blood. I'd forgotten because I was so used to controlling my hunger. With that in mind, I took in a deep breath and found that I didn't smell anything but the food cooking on the stove.

"Yeah, I'm not afraid of blood...it's just that I've seen a lot of it lately and it brings back bad memories." I wrapped the Band-

Aid around his finger then smiled. "There. I think I got all the shrapnel out. You'll live."

"You're good at this. I think you were the one who took care of me when I cut my knee on that glass back in fifth grade."

"Did I? I almost forgot about that. I guess it's from taking care of Kevin for so long."

"That's what I like about you. You're so...caring and nurturing when it comes to others. I would cut myself any day if it meant you could take care of me."

He leaned closer and before I knew it, his lips brushed mine. I thought about pulling back, but at the same time, he was acting as the perfect distraction; from Gallard, from my illness; everything. After all, Gallard did joke about my being with Curtis. He practically told me to go out with him and he wasn't rushing to be honest about his feelings so I was only doing what he suggested.

I set down the spoon and held onto Curtis as we continued to kiss and I had to admit that it was way better than the first time. What ruined the moment for me was that the longer I kissed him, the more I couldn't shake the wish that I was kissing Gallard instead. This wasn't fair to Curtis, so I pulled back before I would get myself in too deep.

"I'm...I'm sorry, that shouldn't have happened," I said. "I can't do this."

"Because of Gallard," Curtis stated. He moved away, giving me my space back and leaned against the counter. "I could take care of you. I know you don't love me, but I can assure you that with me, you'll never feel rejected. You wouldn't have to worry about whether or not I care about you. I would tell you every day just to make sure you know."

A tear fell from my eye, and I wiped it away. Tyler had said almost the same thing when he proposed and I'd believed him. That was before he knew what I was and our three happy years came to a horrible and heartbreaking end.

"Curtis, if you knew what I was; the things I've done. You wouldn't say that."

"How do you know? Lela I've known you since we were kids. I practically grew up at your house and I know you. You're a good person and nothing can change that."

I set the spoon down then turned to look at him. I hadn't talked about Tyler with anyone in a very long time, but now that more time had passed, it was easier. I needed Curtis to understand where I was coming from, why he couldn't get too close to me, besides the fact that I had feelings for someone else.

"Let me tell you a story," I said. "A girl met this guy when she was young and she didn't think she wanted to date, but this boy was special. He was kind and funny and treated her like most girls only dream of being treated by their boyfriend. One date to a dance turned into three years of a serious relationship. When they were eighteen, the boy told the girl that he loved her and proposed to her. She loved him too, but she had secrets; secrets that were both dangerous and frightening. So to prove that she loved him, she told him all of her secrets. The boy couldn't deal and then he bailed, leaving the ring behind."

"Was...was this girl you?"

I hesitated before nodding. "I've had time to heal, but I would be lying if I said it didn't leave scars. Besides Gallard, I've never told anyone my secrets. They're too much for people to handle and I learned that the hard way."

He didn't speak again until we'd finished eating. It was one of the most awkward meals I'd ever had in my life, and I'd had some pretty weird dinners. The stew was good, though. I was worried that I would botch it since I'd been distracted during most of the preparation. The highlight of my evening was that I'd blocked out the sickness for a few hours.

"So what are these dangerous and frightening secrets you told him?" he asked.

"How do I know you won't bail too?" I asked, half serious.

"Look, how about I don't promise you anything? That way, it's an open question and no one can be let down."

I definitely wasn't going to tell him the entire story. He wasn't ready to hear all of it, and I wasn't sure I ever wanted him to. I would have to give a censored version, kind of like what I'd told Tyler.

"Gallard and I...we got tangled up in a dangerous crowd. We tried to hide from them and a friend of ours was killed. We got away eventually, and we've been living in Las Vegas to lay low. It's a pretty bad situation. Several laws were broken, people were killed. It's very ugly." I poked at a potato chunk with my fork.

"Curtis, I've changed so much that I don't even recognize myself. If you knew some of the things I've done, you would be disgusted."

"Did you O.D on heroin?" he asked with a straight face. I raised an eyebrow, unsure of how to respond. I couldn't tell if he was being sarcastic or serious.

"Where did you come up with that assumption?"

"Because that's what I did."

I almost choked on my food. I was shocked by this. Curtis didn't seem like the type of guy to do drugs. Then again, I probably didn't seem like the type of girl to murder people, and I'd done it…more times than I could count.

"When did this happen?" I asked, suddenly very concerned.

"A year after you went missing. Aaron and I experimented with Heroin in high school, but I started using it regularly after graduation. I overdosed at a party, and your dad paid for my rehab. That's the main reason why I'm looking out for you. I wanted to return the favor for everything he did for me."

"Mark did that? That was generous of him, did he ask for a payback?"

He shook his head. "I basically owe him my life. If I hadn't been able to go to rehab, I would probably be dead right now. I cleaned up my act and focused on college after I got out. I won't go near that stuff anymore, and the strongest thing I take is Nyquil." He took a bite of food and I did as well. There wasn't really anything to say. "Your turn; what's the worst thing you've ever done?" His mood had lightening a bit.

Of everything that I'd done, I couldn't pick the worst. From the jogger in the street, to the woman at the gym, they all seemed equally has horrible. I'd numbed myself for so long to keep from being overwhelmed with the guilt so that I could do what was necessary. Now I could finally be normal again.

"I killed someone," I said in a tone that was somewhat sarcastic.

"Whatever. You cried when Aaron euthanized your sick gold fish. You couldn't take a human life."

"Maybe we should save this for another day."

"I'm going to hold you to that." He set his fork down. "In the mean time, I have a suggestion, or proposition. Whatever you want to call it."

"O...kay. What's this mysterious proposition?"

"Go on a date with me. I know you like some other guy and the one from your past broke your heart, but I think you should give me a chance. Maybe in time you'll grow to trust me with whatever secrets you have and you'll see that relationships aren't so bad."

"It wouldn't end well, Curtis. I don't want to hurt you. You mean too much to me."

He sighed then pushed his food around on his plate. He didn't look like he'd given up, but that his wheels were turning. A date with Curtis? That would be crazy. I wasn't trying to get rid of my feelings for Gallard so I could find someone else.

"What if there were no strings attached?" he asked.

I laughed. "You mean friends with benefits?"

"No, I mean...no promises or expectations. I like spending time with you and...I do like you. And if when the police find your sister and your brothers get back and you still feel the same way, I'll back off. No harm, no foul."

I didn't know what I thought of this idea. I knew I would still feel the same way and I didn't want to lead him on when the situation was doomed. I decided to give it some thought and talk more about it in the morning.

That night, I mulled over everything that happened that day as I tried to fall asleep. Curtis' offer sounded tempting. Even though I'd kissed him, I didn't feel a spark or any real emotion. That didn't mean I hadn't enjoyed it. But if he could somehow soothe the ache in my heart that came from my loving Gallard, how could I pass it up?

At the same time, I didn't want to be that girl; the girl who settled for a guy because it was convenient or beneficial. I didn't need a guy in my life, no matter how much I occasionally envied Lydian and Jordan. I was fine being alone. Right?

That's when I had an idea. I needed to clear up any mixed signals that I'd been getting from Gallard over the past year. He'd conveniently been let off the hook from answering my question when Curtis came to pick me up, so if I called him, I could finally know the truth.

I dialed his number then nervously held the phone to my

ear. I didn't know what I would say or how I would go about it. I just knew that it needed to be done or else I wouldn't be able to make a decision.

My heart sank when it went to voicemail and after the beep sounded I began to speak.

"Hey old man, it's me. The blonde who wrestles sharks. Anyway I called because...well, I miss you." That was an understatement. "Scratch that, I *really* miss you. This would be so much easier if you'd answered the phone so I'll have to settle for a message." I took a deep breath before continuing. "You never answered my question about New Years. I know it's been a month and I should get over it. But I can't. I need to know if you feel something for me beyond friendship. Because if you don't then...I'll take your advice. I'll give Curtis a chance and I'll wait expectantly for you to return with my sister and David.

"But...if you do have feelings for me, I need you to tell me. I don't care if it's by phone or if you fly here to see me. However you decide I would like to know by Friday. That's four days from now so you have time to think.

"If I don't hear from you, I'll take it as your answer. And I promise I won't be mad or anything. You'll always be my best friend no matter what. Take care of yourself, okay? And tell everyone I miss them. Bye."

When I hung up, I was an emotional mess. I couldn't believe I left that message and what made me even more frustrated was that I hadn't even had the courage to say I loved him. What right did I have to demand an answer when I hadn't even been honest myself? I was tempted to call again and leave a second message, but by then I'd lost all my courage and cried myself to sleep.

That night, I had a horrible nightmare. It started with me walking through a forest full of apple trees, all covered in blossoms. The ground was white from the fallen petals and I was wearing a lavender dress. The atmosphere was serene and I inhaled the lovely scent of the air. I felt at peace here, and I never wanted to leave.

A small laughter caught my attention and I turned my head in time to see a little girl with curly blonde hair run behind one of the trees. I instantly knew it was Robin, so I darted after her. I rounded the tree and groaned when I found she wasn't there. The laughter sounded again and I caught sight of her just as she'd disappeared at the end of the path.

As I ran after her, the forest began to darken and the blossoms died, turning brown and ugly. That's when I noticed the ground had become somewhat damp. Reluctantly, I looked down and saw that I was standing in a puddle of blood. I tried to move away from it, but I slipped and fell, getting blood all over the dress and on my hands. I got up and continued down the path, following the blood trail.

When I got to the end something shiny caught my eye on the ground. I went for it and bent down, picking up the item and saw that it was the titanium and apple wood ring I'd given to Gallard. Why was it here? Why wasn't he wearing it?

I grew sick with fear as I walked forward then stopped as

soon as I saw the horrific scene. I saw my brothers, Lydian, David, and Gallard lying dead on a stone altar, their throats slashed and their eyes blank. I tried to scream, but no sound would come out. I rushed to them stopping in front of the altar and wept for them.

What drew my attention from them was the feel of a small hand wrapping around mine and I looked down to see Robin standing next to me, her hair framing her face and she was dressed in all white.

"Don't be sad, Lela," she said. "You still have us."

"Us?" I asked, my voice cracking from grief. That was when I noticed there was another man standing to Robin's left, holding her other hand. He was average in height, about an inch taller than me and somewhat thin. His skin was alabaster and his hair a deep red. But it was his eyes that captured my attention the most. They were a blue unlike any I'd ever seen. Almost alien-like.

"Yes, Lela," he said. "You still have us."

I awoke, scrambling to find the lamp switch and I turned it on. I sensed that someone was in my room, and I looked around to make sure I wasn't still dreaming. I crawled out of my bed, nearly stumbling, to check in my closet and under the bed. The man's presence had been so vivid that I could still feel his piercing eyes.

Did you like that? The voice asked.

What the hell? That was you?

Maybe. It was your dream. I merely inserted myself in it.

This was so surreal. He'd never done anything like this before, nor had he ever shown me his face. Now that I knew what he looked like, the voice became even more frightening. It used to be comforting to me, but now it was menacing.

That is what you get for kissing Curtis, he continued. *I do not want you kissing him or any man.*

Stop talking to me. I don't like the creepy dreams or the creepy things you say. Go away!

Unable to sleep any longer, I changed into some denim shorts and a t-shirt, tugging on some socks and sneakers last before exiting my room. I needed some fresh air, to shake off the disturbing nightmare and clear my head. I grabbed my key that was hanging in the kitchen as well as my debit card, which I stuck in my back pocket, then locked up upon leaving the house.

I didn't have a set destination, so I headed towards town. We lived near a drug store, two restaurants, and some sleazy, twenty-four hour bar. Of the five places, the last seemed like the best option.

I opened the door, expecting the place to be less crowded since it was a Tuesday, but there was an average amount of people there. Mostly men playing pool with scantily-dressed women cheering from the sides. I sat down on a stool at the very end.

"What'll it be?" the bartender asked. I looked passed him at all the bottles on the shelf. It wasn't the best idea to have alcohol considering my liver was shot, but I needed something to get the edge off; to possibly silence the voice.

"How about a suicide?"

You are drinking again? The voice asked. *Did you not learn from the first time?*

"How about some ID?" the bartender asked, folding his arms and glaring.

"I have money, how much do you want to forget about ID?"

His mouth twitched and I waited for his answer. This wasn't my usual behavior, and I was acting slightly out of character. Taking risks wasn't really my thing, yet here I was at a bar, bribing a man so that I could do some underage drinking.

"Fifty bucks a shot; no more, no less," he grunted. I nodded then he began mixing my drink. He slid the glass over to me and I downed it. It burned my throat, but I didn't react to it. I signaled that I wanted another and he refilled it.

I saw movement in the corner of my eye and turned to see a woman and a man go into the men's room. I wrinkled my nose, not wanting to think about what they were possibly doing in there and downed the second shot. I wanted another, but I didn't want to end up staggering home or passing out along the way, so I just ordered water.

A few moments later, I saw the same man walk out of the men's room, only this time he was alone. We exchanged glances for a second and I realized that I knew who he was.

"Andre?" I asked.

"Hey, you're Curtis' friend, Lena was it?"

"Lela. You're the last person I'd think to see here."

He sat next to me, resting his feet on the bars underneath his stool. He looked different tonight; his eyes weren't royal blue anymore. My instinct had been right; he was immortal. He'd probably just finished feeding before we ran into each other.

"What brings you to this dive so late at night?" he asked.

"I couldn't sleep."

"Me neither. This is my go-to place whenever I'm up at night."

I was conflicted about revealing that I knew his identity. If he was hostile, he might drag me out of there and kill me in order to silence me. There were very few vampires I trusted, if not any outside of my group. But since I was taking a few risks tonight, I figured one more wouldn't hurt.

"Aren't you up every night, though?" I asked, somewhat cockily.

What are you doing? The voice asked. *You are provoking an immortal with no one to protect you!*

I'm going to die anyway. Who cares?

"What do you mean?" Andre asked.

"You probably don't sleep much; immortals rarely do. It takes a lot to wear them out."

I waited for him to lash out at me, but he didn't. He just gave me a horrific stare.

"How did you know?" he asked.

"Your eyes gave you away. At first, I thought you were just wearing colored contacts for fun, but you never touched your drink the other night. I had my suspicions, and now I know why."

The bartender asked if I wanted more water, and Andre

ordered me a martini, which he offered to pay for.

"You know about immortals," he speculated. "How?"

"Believe it or not, I used to be one," I replied as I took a sip of the martini. It didn't taste any better than the suicide shot, but I drank it anyway so it wouldn't go to waste.

"Get out! Why are you human now?"

I looked at him, waiting to see if he would figure it out. I had no idea how old he was, so it was possible that he wasn't informed in all of the rules.

"Oh...I know what happened," he said. "You fed on a family member, didn't you?"

I nodded. "It wasn't my choice, though. I was forced into it. Not that it matters. I'm riding the mortal boat now."

"That's a shame. I don't know what I would do if that happened to me. I guess I should be grateful that all my family died fifty years ago." He swiveled the stool around so that he could rest his elbows on the counter. "Does Curtis know what you are, or what you used to be?"

"No, and I hope that he never does. I'm taking this secret to my grave, which won't be long from now."

He scoffed and shook his head. "Don't tell me that mortality is so miserable that you're going to take your life."

"No, my illness is doing that for me," I replied, downing the rest of the martini. "One of the few perks of turning back is that your body becomes your own enemy. I'll be dead in a matter of weeks."

A sympathetic look crossed his face. I didn't want his pity; I didn't know why I'd mentioned it in the first place. It was easier to talk to him than to someone I cared about.

"Is there a way to stop it?" he asked. I opened my mouth to reply, but he spoke first. "Come with me." He slid off the stool. I threw two fifties and he laid down ten on the counter and started walking out of the bar. Curious, I followed him until we were outside. The air was cooler since it was late January, and I wished that I'd thought to bring a jacket.

He walked at a quick pace, so I had to jog to keep up. We continued down the street until we were in the shadier part of the area then he slowed down, stepping into one of the alleyways. I did the same and found him leaning against the building. A bad feeling formed in my gut, and I could have kicked myself for being so foolish. I'd forgotten, yet again, that I wasn't immortal and I'd just followed one into a dark corner, far away from screaming distance.

"You said that there was no cure," he stated.

"Yes...and?"

"I happen to know that there is, and I brought you here to prove you wrong."

He put his wrist to his mouth and bit down, hard enough to draw blood then started walking towards me. It struck me why he'd taken me to such a secluded place. I began to back up as he got closer and closer.

"No...don't. It's not...I don't want this," I stammered. He

stopped a few feet away from me.

"Why not? It will save your life."

"I've chosen to die, and I'm asking you to respect that," I replied, suddenly growing angry. I turned to leave, but he grabbed my arm, jerking me closer to him.

"Just let me help you! It will be over soon; but you know that already, don't you?"

He held his wrist to my mouth and I pressed my lips together, determined to keep blood from getting in. I pushed his hand away, but he forced it on me, his blood smearing on my cheek.

"Stop, I can't do this; I made a promise!" I pleaded. He loosened his grip on my arm and I yanked it back, stepping further away from him in case he tried anything else. I wiped the blood off of my face with my hand.

"You love someone, don't you?" he asked. By then, I wasn't in the mood for anymore chit-chat. He'd almost forced me to turn, and was no longer on my good list. "That's pretty cruel for someone to ask you to promise to stay human when you're dying."

If he cared, he would not have left you here to die, the voice said. *Shut up.*

"He doesn't know," I said, keeping my eyes cast down. "He left before I found out."

"So you became mortal and he ditched you. Doesn't sound like a nice guy."

"It wasn't like that, he's...busy." This was a lame answer, but I wasn't about to launch into my group's agenda to a total stranger.

"He's busy? That means he's far away from here, am I correct?"

Run, the voice commanded

Like I could out run him.

Lela, do as I say. Run!

Without another word, I took off down the street. I didn't get far before I ran out of breathe and I no longer had the energy to run. The street lights seemed to dance before my eyes. I felt someone yank me off the street, and Andre shoved me against the wall.

"Sorry things had to end this way, Lela. Don't take it personally; I'm just thirsty," he said. He bared his fangs then bit my neck. I yelled because of the pain, growing even more lightheaded than I was before. This was the first time I'd ever been bitten by a vampire and it was extremely painful.

Suddenly he stopped and I watched as he spit my blood out onto the sidewalk.

"Ugh, you taste horrible!" he said, gagging. "But I can't have you running off and telling Delia about me."

He started throttling me when a group of people started heading our way. He waited a moment, but when it was clear they weren't leaving anytime soon he let go of me.

"Looks like tonight is your lucky night. Speak of this to anyone, and I'll kill Delia and maybe even Curtis too. Don't think I won't."

He disappeared into the night and I was left to find my way home. I was still bleeding, but not as badly as before. I would have to take up wearing scarves to keep Curtis from seeing the wounds.

I found my way back to the house and quietly let myself in. It was about four in the morning, so there was still about three hours before Curtis would wake up. I hung up my keys then tiptoed into the bathroom.

I regretted turning on the light because I could clearly see how bad my wound was. The bite mark was very deep and it ached whenever I tried to turn my head. I gritted my teeth as I began to dab disinfectant on it. It stung horribly, but I didn't yell. I then put a pad of gauze on it then returned to my room.

Later that morning, I got up as soon as I heard Curtis moving around the house and I tied a scarf around my neck before throwing a hoody over my head then went to greet him He always got up extra early so he could take his time and enjoy his breakfast.

"Good morning," I said in the most cheerful voice I could muster.

"You're in a good mood," he said. "Are you feeling better?"

"Oh yeah, much better." I winced as I leaned against the counter and found one of the several bruises that I knew were forming. "Why don't I make you breakfast?"

"You already patched me up yesterday. I should be making *you* breakfast."

Before he could protest, I got out the bacon, hash browns, and eggs then started cooking. Everything that happened the night before felt like one crazy dream; Curtis' proposition, my ultimatum for Gallard, the horrible nightmare, the vampire at the bar. That's when I realized it wasn't a dream. I had made that phone call to Gallard. He hadn't called me back yet, but he still had a few more days.

"So I thought about what you asked," I said as I turned the hash browns. "Could I give you an answer this weekend?"

He looked up, suddenly looking as cheerful as I was pretending to be. I couldn't believe I was doing this; agreeing to this idea. Still, I needed some form of distraction from my worrying about Robin. The previous night's dream reminded me that just because Samil wasn't around causing problems didn't mean he wasn't out there, skulking. And poor Robin was most definitely terrified.

"Sure, I can live with that." Curtis smiled then relaxed in his chair. "I do have a few questions though."

I took the pan off the stove then started with the eggs. "What kind of questions?"

"Well, for one. Am I allowed to kiss you?"

I laughed. "Curtis, you're making this sound like a contract. You said you wanted to go out with me and I said I'd think about it. But I will promise you that it will be one way or another. I refuse to be friends with benefits. It will either work out or it won't."

"Okay. We're on the...same...page." His speech suddenly grew choppy and I turned to see why. He was staring at me strangely.

"What is it?"

"Lela, your neck is bleeding!"

I quickly ran to the bathroom, tugging off the sweatshirt as I did and then the scarf. He was right; my wound from the night before had bled through the gauze as well as the scarf and jacket. It had to be because my blood was so thin. The iron pills weren't working like they should.

I peeled the gauze away then tore off a couple sheets of paper towels, pressing them to the bite. Why did I have to be so stupid and go into the alley with that vampire? The voice was right. I'd been an idiot for provoking him and now I was suffering the consequences.

I looked up and saw that Curtis was standing behind me. I'd forgotten I was only wearing a camisole underneath my sweatshirt, so all of my injuries, old and new, were visible. The bullet wounds hadn't completely healed yet, so they probably looked horrible. And the bruises on my arms from the night before were black and blue.

"Who did this to you?" Curtis asked with an angry tone. I tried to hurry out of there and avoid the conversation but he put his arm up and blocked my way.

"No one did this to me," I lied. "I bruise easily."

"And your neck just happens to be cut by walking into a door right? Please don't lie to me Lela. Some of the wounds on your back have been there for a while. Someone hurt you and I want to know who it was."

I looked down at the floor. I'd been found out, and there was no hiding the truth now. The question was how much I was going to tell him.

"A few months ago, I was shot by the same men who killed my parents. I barely survived, but I recovered." I tried with difficulty not to fall apart. "But they found out where my family lived and they went after them to get to me."

"My God," Curtis whispered. "And they took Robin. Why?"

"Leverage. They know Gallard would do anything for me, so they're keeping her until he gives them what they want. That's where he is right now; trying to find a way to get her back."

Curtis pulled me into a hug and I started weeping. He didn't ask me anymore questions, but I still felt obligated to be a little more honest. He'd been so good to me and deserved to know about my illness.

"I'm afraid there's more," I said, now that I had stopped sobbing. "I lied about my having a stomach virus. It turns out that I'm terminally ill. Apparently I have been for quite some time, but I didn't know it."

"Lela! I don't believe this! You're already going through enough and now you have to deal with illness?" He sounded like he was going to cry himself. "What is it? Is it cancer?"

I nodded. "The doctors aren't sure what kind. All they know is that my body is dying, and there's no way to stop it, not even with transplants or treatment."

"Do your brothers know about this?"

I didn't want to lie so instead I chose not to answer. He could make whatever assumption that he wanted.

Curtis ended up calling in sick and we spent the rest of the day relaxing and watching a *Friday the Thirteenth* marathon. This probably wasn't the date he had in mind, but we had fun nonetheless. He didn't bring up my illness once and I was able to forget about it for the rest of the day. All the while, I checked my phone every hour to see if Gallard had called or at least texted. If I couldn't clear up everything with him, I at least needed to let him know about my condition so he could pass it on to the others.

By the time we got to *Jason X* it was nearly ten o'clock and we still had to see the remake as well as *Jason vs. Freddy.* They were starting to get somewhat repetitive so Curtis and I talked while we watched. We'd ordered Italian and it was some of the best spaghetti I'd had in a long while.

"I think it's funny that the virgins always live," I pointed out about the movies.

"Really? I never noticed that. I guess if we were in the movie, we would die."

"Excuse me? I am daisy fresh, son. This girl would live through to the sequel."

Well, that's a relief, the voice said.

You're making me uncomfortable. Please keep your weird comments to yourself.

"I'm sorry," Curtis said. "I just thought...you said you were in a serious relationship back when."

"Not serious enough." I didn't like where this conversation was going, so I changed it. "You know who else would die? Aaron."

Curtis and I both laughed. I would describe Aaron as the male version of Lydian. Girls always thought he was so amazing and he did too. If only they knew the real Aaron, they would see they were wasting their time. Aaron was more into himself than anything.

"He would kill me if I told you this, but I think you would find it funny," Curtis said.

"Do tell. I love having stuff to hang over his head. He owes me for something he did a year ago."

"What did he do?"

I shook my head. "No, no! You have to go first. Knowledge comes at a price."

"Okay. So back in November, he spent Thanksgiving with your dad and Sharon Lockfield and apparently when your dad was in Miami picking up Kevin and Robin, Aaron slept with Sharon."

"So it is true! Kevin told me, but I thought Aaron was just pulling his leg. Did my dad find out?"

"Oh he found out all right. Aaron and he got in a yelling match and I nearly had to keep them from getting physical. Did I mention I was there? I forget. Anyway we went to my place that night and he left not long after. I didn't see him again until I came to visit last month."

As gross as this story was, I couldn't help but feel sorry for

Mark. He'd already been cheated on once by my mother and then Sharon cheated with his own son. That had to hurt. I hated cheating, no matter what the purpose, which was why I was worried when Lydian started seeing Jordan. I didn't want her to hurt him. He was like my brother.

"Curtis...do you know about my mom's affair?"

He nodded hesitantly.

"Aaron told me after you left. Your parents always seemed so happy, I couldn't believe it."

"Yeah...looks can fool you."

"Your turn. What did Aaron do that he owes you?"

I decided to be honest...mostly. I couldn't tell him the whole story, but the basics would suffice.

"He found me in Texas almost a year ago. I asked him not to tell my parents because I wasn't ready to come home, but he broke his promise. He called the cops on Gallard and we had to leave town. That's why I was living in Vegas."

"Jerk move. After you took the fall for the broken lamp, the hamster getting out, and not to mention you covering for him when he was hooking up with his girlfriend in the basement."

"Right? He owes me a dozen favors. I've decided I'm done doing them for him."

"Older brothers can be the worst."

I often forgot that Curtis had an older brother; Riley. He was so much older than Curtis, so he wasn't around much. From what I saw of him, he had no ambition and often bummed off his parents for money. He had this surfer dude look that most girls probably liked, but he never impressed me.

Curtis held up his glass of Scotch and clinked against my glass of Dr. Pepper. "Here's to being the middle children. May it suck less as we grow older."

I laughed then took a drink. I forgot about being sick in those few hours and I hoped that Curtis would continue to keep my spirits high while I got through it.

Chapter Seven

Wednesday came and then Thursday. I still hadn't heard from Gallard and I was beginning to get worried. But I didn't know what I was worried about, exactly. Was I worried that he didn't feel the way I did, or that I would have to give Curtis my answer? I still didn't know what I was going to tell him.

To distract myself I decided to go grocery shopping. For some reason, the two of us forgot to go for almost two and a half weeks until we realized the only thing edible in our fridge was a cucumber. Since I had nothing else to do, I told Curtis I would take care of it. I didn't mind. It was better than sitting on the couch with my phone.

I finished getting the food then moved over to the other side of the store to get soap and other bathroom necessities. While I was over there, I happened across the medicine section and out of curiosity, started looking for some over-the-counter iron pills. I'd only filled my prescription that Monday and I'd already run out. There was no way Doctor Cadbury would refill it in the same week, so I had to rely on the low grade stuff.

I was reading the back of one bottle when a nearby conversation caught my attention. I wasn't usually an eavesdropper when it came to everyday chit-chat, but something about what they were talking about was so interesting that I couldn't tune them out.

"Did you hear about those murders that happened yesterday?" one teenage kid asked his friend.

"I did! And it happened one block away from me. My mom freaked and she's insisting that I call her before I leave school and work to come home."

"What psychopath decapitates someone? The weird thing is, they can't figure out what was used."

"What's even weirder is that the bodies already looked like they'd been decomposing for weeks when they'd only been reported missing two days prior. The police think that there's a serial killer in Florida and that these murders are linked to the Sharmentino case."

When I heard my last name, I froze. I'd nonchalantly pushed my cart closer to the two guys and pretended to be interested in some antacids. They thought my family's deaths were the work of a serial killer? I knew it wasn't true because Samil was nowhere near Florida. Or at least I hoped he wasn't.

"It does fit the M.O.," the second kid continued. "A husband and wife killed in their home. No fingerprints or evidence left behind. This guy knows what he's doing."

"Oh please, everyone knows that the daughter did it. She takes off for years then conveniently returns the same day her parents are killed?"

"That is kind of fishy. I heard a lot about her case in the news. Didn't she join some gypsy coven? She probably killed her parents for the money and sacrificed her sister in some satanic ritual."

A lump formed in my throat and I had to get out of there. I couldn't listen to this any longer. If these random teenagers thought that about me, did everyone? Did the police think that I was responsible? It was already bad enough that I still blamed myself for Samil coming after my family.

"Excuse me, miss?" someone said. I turned and saw that I'd stopped my cart next to a samples stand.

"Huh?" I asked, my mind still on all these paranoid theories.

"Would you like to try our new product? Trojan Delight? We have six samples and if you decide you like it, you can buy the whole pack for only five ninety-five."

"No thanks I'm not interested."

"Are you sure? It's a good deal! A Valentine's Day special. After next week, they'll be selling for eight ninety—"

"Yeah, sure," I said, grabbing a handful and tossing them into the cart. I didn't really want them, I just wanted to get out of there and I didn't want to listen to all the good deals he had. The whole Déjà vu and worry about my sister and my illness was beginning to be too much. I had to get out of there.

I got back to the house and began putting away the groceries while I fought back the tears. It didn't help that I felt awful and I was so sore from being beat up that all I wanted was to pop some sleeping pills and forget the rest of the world.

A gypsy coven? Really? That idea must have stemmed from Mark telling the police about my meeting with the gypsy at the circus. How could people think I would kill my parents for money? I'd never been a violent person in the past, nor was I a wild child that often got in trouble. And I would never hurt my sister. How could they say those horrible things?

This whole thing was stupid. Why was I worrying about my relationship problems when my parents were in the ground and my baby sister was probably locked up somewhere being treated horribly while she waited for someone to come rescue her? I shouldn't even be thinking about whether or not someone cared about me because she was more important.

My eyes wandered over to the cupboard next to the microwave and I remembered that Curtis kept a bottle of Scotch in there. I needed something to distract me. Curtis was always great, but he wasn't there at that moment and wouldn't be for another three hours.

Without giving it another thought, I took it out of the cupboard and poured some into a glass. I didn't sip it delicately as I had at the bar, but chugged it instead. The sooner the affects could start, the better.

I was on my third glass when someone knocked on the door. This was perfect. I was well on my way to becoming very wasted and now I had company. I stumbled as I hurried to put the scotch away then popped a piece of gum into my mouth from the miscellaneous drawer. Gum would help with my breath, but it wouldn't hide the fact that I was tanked.

I opened the door and as soon as I saw the person, I started giggling like an idiot. It was a priest and he was all dressed in his black robes and white collar. He had brown hair and brown eyes. He appeared to be around forty years old. What was a priest doing on my porch? He couldn't have come at a worst time.

"Good afternoon," he said. He had an Italian accent. "I am Father Frederick. I'm here to see Lela Sharmentino. Are you she?"

"The one and only!" I tried to fight back another laugh as I moved so he could come into the house. He smiled at me politely then took a seat on the couch. I tried to sit in the chair across from him and nearly missed.

"So, Father. What brings you to my humble abode?" I asked, trying to sound as sober as possible.

"I came as a favor to Cardinal Solomon. He's worried about you and wanted to see how you're doing."

Solomon was worried about me? Since when did he care? He was the one who refused to help, even after I'd begged him to stay. If he'd stuck around, we could have worked against Samil to help my father and sister. Solomon was the one person in the world who knew where Lucian Christophe's body was.

Do not listen to him. Priests are liars and will only betray you. Solomon cares for no one but himself.

Wait, how do you know Solomon?

"How did he even find me?" I asked. "There are six people in the entire world who know I'm here."

"Miss Sharmentino—"

"Lela." That was Gallard's name for me and for some reason having someone else call me that resurfaced the reasons I was drunk in the first place.

"Lela, Solomon has the knack of knowing where to find people if he needs to. He knows that you are in danger and I promise you that I am the only one besides him that knows you are here."

He cannot protect you, Lela, the voice said. *He promised that before and now she's-*

What the hell are you talking about? Go away, I can't deal with you right now.

Somehow, the priest's words were comforting. That didn't change the fact that I was still mad at Solomon. If he was so concerned, why didn't he check on me himself? He'd cared enough to pay his respects at my parents' funeral. In fact, I was mad that no one had called me this past month. Most of all, I wanted to pulverize Matthew then do the same to Samil.

"And what does Solomon plan to do about my imminent danger?" I asked.

"He wants you to meet him in London. He can protect you there until you're safe again."

"I'm safe here," I said firmly. "It's been a month and Samil hasn't come after me. Besides, there's only one thing I want from Solomon and unless he gives it to me, I don't want his help."

Father Frederick folded his hands and looked at the floor. I felt bad for snapping, but I wasn't in the mood for being pleasant. My sister and father's life depended on one small bit of information that Solomon had and if he didn't give it to me, then I wasn't going to listen to him.

"I will let him know that you feel that way," Father Frederick said, breaking the silence. He then reached in his robes before handing me a card. "This is his mailing address and phone number. If you change your mind, just call him and he'll come for you as soon as possible."

I thanked him and tried my best not to stagger as I walked him to the door. He looked disappointed and I felt sorry for him. He'd come all this way out of the kindness of his heart to try and help me and I'd turned him down. Even after he left, I stood in the entryway and read the card he gave me. This was the only link of information I had to Solomon. I wondered if my friends would benefit from this.

I took out my cell phone and looked for Aaron's number while I refilled my glass with Scotch. If Gallard wasn't going to answer, then maybe he would. Kevin still didn't have a cell phone, so I only had three other people I could call.

"*Heeeeey*," I said, slurring my words. "This is the third time I've called. Are you guys avoiding me? Whatever. I called *becaaaause* I have some information. Solomon sent someone to try and convince me to go to London *aaaand*...I have an address. Maybe you could use it to find him." I read it off for him, struggling to speak. "Anyway. I *looooove* you and tell Kevin I miss him."

As soon as I hung up I checked to see which number I'd called. I screamed in shock when I realized whose it was; Jordan's. Somehow I'd clicked on his name instead of my brothers. I then flopped on the couch. I'd just left my first drunk message and it was to Jordan. I was feeling more and more embarrassed by the moment.

Curtis came home at the same time he always did and I woke up when the door opened. I hadn't realized that I'd passed out for several hours, and I felt horrible. The dizziness on top of a hangover and bruising was unbearable.

"Did you work a have nice at day?" I asked. I then wished I hadn't said anything. I still spoke with a slur I'd given myself away.

"Lela, are you drunk?" He said while chuckling.

"No!" I massaged my throbbing temples. "Yes."

"Well, I know exactly what will help. Lay down and I'll get you some water."

I wanted to protest, but I was afraid that I would throw up if I tried to speak, so I took his advice and lay down again. I felt like a terrible friend. He'd just spent his whole day working and now he had to take care of me.

When he came back he sat next to me and I took slow sips of water. Here we were again. Back in the same place we were before I'd left. And back then, I'd promised myself I wouldn't get this drunk again. It was official. I was going downhill and I could only continue to roll.

"What brought this on?" Curtis asked.

"It sounded like a good idea. I was wrong."

He chuckled. "Yeah I've been there." He grew silent for a moment. "Lela...why did you buy a bunch of condoms?"

I'd forgotten about the samples I'd taken. It wasn't exactly a planned thing, and now I was stuck with them. I might have tossed them in with the bread. One embarrassing situation after the next.

"They were free. The guy wouldn't stop talking until I took some."

"I see."

I looked at his face, wondering why he'd gotten quiet.

"Wait...you didn't think I got them for us did you?"

Now he was red from embarrassment.

"Maybe for a second." I laughed and he rolled his eyes. "I see now that you wouldn't have purchased such items and thrown them in with our bacon."

I laughed even harder and then he started laughing with me. Curtis' little misunderstanding had been just the thing to cheer me up. He made me feel better than any alcohol.

"I think one of them was banana flavored," I said. "That sounds...unappetizing."

"Yuck! No wonder they were free. Trojan Delight indeed." He gazed at me and smiled. "If only I didn't have to wait until this weekend to know your answer."

Instinctively, I looked at my phone that was sitting on the

table. I doubted that I was going to hear from Gallard or anyone for that matter. It was so sad that Solomon, the very man who my friends were looking for, was the only person to contact me.

I was about to speak when a searing pain shot through my stomach. I thought that it was the alcohol, but it shouldn't hurt my stomach. The pain was growing worse and worse until I could no longer hold in a yell.

"Lela what's wrong?" Curtis asked.

"It hurts! My stomach, it hurts!"

Without another word, he lifted me up and rushed out the door. The pain continued to increase, but I did my best to endure it. I took in even breaths to brace myself against the pain as Curtis drove me to the hospital. What a perfect way end to a mostly horrible day.

I didn't even listen as the doctor asked me questions. I felt silly being wheeled down the hall on a stretcher, but there was no way I could walk. I didn't start paying attention until I felt my body grow cold. I heard everyone around me start shouting and then something was forced down my throat. The disgusting liquid made me nauseous and I threw up on instinct. That was when I realized they'd wanted me to do this. I threw up two more times before I felt a prick in my arm and after, drowsiness overtook me.

The pain was gone, for now. So I took this opportunity to sleep. For the first time in weeks, I was completely at peace. There was no pain, no worry; just the still quiet along with a soothing, steady beeping noise. I didn't even have any nightmares and whatever drugs I was on silenced the voice.

I felt rested and better than I had in the past days. I even felt the urge to wake myself up and look around. My vision took a few moments to adjust and when it did I was in a bright room with white walls and grey ceiling tile, the smell of ammonia filling my senses. I turned to my right to see a machine with a heart monitor and other contraptions.

Once I was fully awake, I sat up, finding myself constricted by a tube going up my nose and another stuck into my left arm. I was hooked to an IV drip. I saw that I was alone in the room, so I looked for the nurse-call button and pressed it. I must have been on some pain medication because all my aches were nonexistent.

The door opened and a short, balding doctor with glasses came in.

"Hello, Lela. How are you feeling?" he asked.

"How do you know my name?"

"Your friend brought you in. You don't remember?" He checked my monitors and the IV. "You gave us quite a scare last night. Your heart stopped twice and you went into anaphylactic shock after we gave you an iron injection."

I was glad that I'd been unconscious for all of that. I was tired of being sick, injured, or all of the above. My body had been through so much over the past month, and things were only getting worse.

"When can I go home?" I asked. The doctor chuckled, which

annoyed me.

"You, young lady, aren't going anywhere. The stomach pain you were experiencing; that was from an iron overdose. Not to mention your kidneys are in very poor shape and your white blood cell count is unlike any I've ever seen."

"How long have I been asleep?"

"You've been in and out of consciousness for almost four days. We've been doing everything we can to get you stable and since you're awake, we feel we're making progress."

"Progress? Does that mean I'm getting better?"

The doctor's mouth twitched and he looked down at his papers, slowly sifting through them. I couldn't tell if he was really reading them or if he was avoiding my question.

"We may be able to prolong your life…but I'm afraid the extensity of your illness is beyond what we can save."

I knew it was dumb to have any hope. What could modern medicine do for a three thousand year old curse? At least I was in a better mood than the day before…or more accurately four days ago.

That's when I remembered. I'd asked Gallard to call me on Friday and it was way past that day. More importantly, I needed to make sure he and the rest of the group got my information about Solomon's address in London.

"Well, I'm sure you would prefer better company than me," the doctor said. "I'll let your father know you're awake."

I sat up straighter.

"Wait my father? That isn't funny, my father is dead."

The doctor grew silent.

"Then...who is the man in the waiting room?"

"Probably some creep. Is my friend Curtis here?"

"I'm afraid he left this morning. Would you not like to see the man? If you don't believe he's your father, we won't permit him in here."

I thought for a moment. Whoever this person was, their company would probably be better than a doctor giving me depressing news about my condition. I wondered if it was Solomon. I'd thought he wasn't going to come unless I wrote to him.

"No...let him in. I want to know who it is."

The doctor left and my heart began to pound. I had no idea who to expect to come through my door. There was no way Mark survived. I'd seen his body; he'd been shot in the head and drained of blood. Not to mention that I'd gone to his funeral.

When the door opened a tall man with chocolate brown hair stepped in. He had a full beard with hints of grey and beautiful blue eyes. Whoever this guy was, he definitely wasn't a doctor. Could he be the weirdo who claimed to be my dad? And how long had he been here?

"Okay, what's your angle?" I asked, folding my arms. He stared at me for a moment then slowly sat down as if he were confused.

"My angle? What do you mean?"

"You told the doctor you're my father? Well, considering

one of them is dead and my real one is supposed to be, but possibly isn't and is most likely far away from here, you can't be. What do you want? Are you here to pretend to know me so you can play the dutiful father and take care of me while I'm sick so you can score my money?"

He raised an eyebrow then laughed. For some reason his laugh was very familiar but I couldn't remember where I'd heard it before. I didn't know why he was laughing. It was a fairly rational assumption.

"You've always had a weird sense of humor, Lela," he said. "I'm glad that hasn't changed."

I stared at him for the longest time, trying to register in my mind what was happening. He couldn't be here; it was impossible. Gallard said that he'd had suspicions, but they weren't validated until now.

"David?" I asked, slightly terrified.

"Yes, Lela, it's me."

He moved closer and I put my arms around him, holding him tight for the first time in almost a year. I was so happy that I couldn't find the words. My biological father was alive and finally back with me.

After I finally let him go, he moved his chair closer so we could talk. He told me that Curtis was at work and that he'd devotedly spent his nights in my room while I slept. I wasn't surprised, and I wished I could see him. I probably gave him a major scare.

"How did you know about my being your real father?" David asked.

"My mom told me the night before she was killed. After I told her that you were dead, she reacted in a way that puzzled me. She was devastated and I wanted to know why. She told me about the affair and how you used to be immortal."

A morose expression crossed his face and I took his hand in mine. He must have been distraught when he learned that the woman he loved had been murdered by Samil's followers. He'd waited twenty years for her and now she was gone forever. I couldn't imagine how that felt.

"I would have killed Matthew myself if I were stronger. I planned to return to her after all this was over, but he stole her from me; from us."

I gave him a moment to compose himself. He was angry and I didn't blame him. I was too.

"How did you survive?" I asked. "I watched you die, and yet you're here."

"I lost a lot of blood from the gunshot wound. I passed out and woke up in the hospital two days later. Samil showed up soon after. Originally, he wanted to torture me into giving away your location, but I told him about my previously being a day-walker. I made him promise that if I was a donor, he would leave you out of it."

"What did you do to convince him to let you see me again?"

"I'm sworn to secrecy. I can't tell you where he is or what

he's planning, and in return I get three days. If I'm not back by Thursday, he's going to kill Robin then use the two of us for his ritual."

I leaned back against the bed and grinded my teeth in frustration. I didn't think it was possible to hate Samil even more, but I did. I hated that he could still threaten us and I hated that he was still calling the shots.

"How is Robin? Is she okay?" I asked.

David nodded. "She's all right. She's scared, but I'm doing my best to keep her distracted. She's so much like how you were at four." He leaned forward and rested his hands on the bed. "Lela, I came back because I found out you'd turned mortal, just like I had. Samil didn't tell me until recently, and I needed to see you before it was too late."

"You knew that I was dying?"

"Obviously you do too, but I'm here to tell you that you can stop it."

This was great news. Everything seemed to be getting better and better; Robin was okay, David was alive, and I could finally get well again.

Do not tell me you are talking to yet another man, the voice said. *I did not know you were so popular.*

He's my dad, okay! Lay off already. You're acting like a jealous boyfriend and it's weird.

I thought you said your father was killed.

News flash; I have two!

"Lela, you're spacing out on me, are you okay?" David asked.

Since I didn't have to worry about him thinking I was crazy, I decided to be honest. I told him about how I used to hear a voice and how it had started speaking to me again. I was relieved that I finally had someone to talk to about these things who understood what I was going through.

"That's so odd," he said. "After I changed back, along with the rapid aging, I heard a voice as well. I realize now that it stopped around the same time you were born. The voice was what told me how to stop my situation. After that, I was able to get better."

"Okay, so then what would you have me do? What is this miracle cure that will stop my tragic and premature death?"

"You need blood. I'll help you in any way that I can, but you need it to restore your body back to health."

I didn't speak for a while, hoping that he was kidding. This was the big cure? I had to go back to depending on blood? I was supposed to be living a normal life as a normal woman who had a normal diet. Now I had to drink blood?

"You're kidding right? I have to drink blood again?"

"I know it's not the most exciting thing in the world, but it will help. And you won't need to drink it that often. Four ounces a week or so would be enough. And the rest of the time, you can eat food."

I didn't know why I was being such a sourpuss about it. I had to rely on blood again, so what? If it meant I had more time, then I should have been happy. What I needed was a major attitude adjustment and to stop having a pity party. If this was the only way to get better, and I was willing to try it.

"I suppose I can live with that. How long will I live, exactly?"

"However long you want. If in a hundred years you decide you want to let nature take its course, then all you have to do is stop drinking blood. This way, you're only semi-immortal."

"And why didn't *you* let nature take its course?"

He smiled. "Because I loved my girls too much. And if this whole thing ends happily, I plan to stick around as long as you want me to."

"You're such a sap. What did you do this whole time anyway, read *Jane Eyre*?"

"What did you do, come up with more ways to insult my taste in books?" He laughed. "So do you have any preferences for how you'll get blood?"

I thought for a moment. I definitely wasn't going to take a life, and I didn't want to feed off of a willing person either. Drinking a blood bag was my only option, but I had no access to any. Not in town anyway.

"Can we go to Orlando?" I asked. "Gallard owns a blood bar there and his friend is the manager. He can sell us a decent ration."

"Why don't I just sneak you some from here?"

"Because I'd like to see Bodoway anyway. And I don't want

to be hooked up to these tubes anymore."

"All right, Orlando it is. Now let's get you there before you get any worse."

Chapter Eight

It wasn't easy convincing the doctors to let me leave, but legally they couldn't keep me there. I then asked them to tell Curtis that I was out of town and that I'd be back later that night. I knew he would be worried and probably freak out, but I couldn't call him now.

I changed into some comfortable clothes that Curtis had packed for me. David then rented a car since neither of us wanted to prolong the trip by taking a bus. Orlando was only one hour away. I let David drive since I was tired. My energy was still lacking and the drugs were wearing off.

"Curtis seems to really care about you," David said. "Does Gallard know about him?"

"Yeah, he knows. Gallard practically signed the lease for me when I told him Curtis asked me to move in. He wanted me to be safe."

David drummed his fingers on the steering wheel. He used to do that whenever he was thinking about something, and it was somewhat endearing that he still did it. After all, only nine months had passed. He'd changed on the outside, but he was the same David that I knew and loved.

My lungs began to feel like they were full of fluid and my breathing was labored. I did my best to appear as if I was fine. I was getting good at acting like nothing was wrong. But I was freezing cold despite the warm weather, so I turned on the heater. I put my fingers in front of the vents and David touched my cheek with the back of his hand.

"You're freezing, Lela!" he said. He removed his jacket with one hand while keeping the other on the steering wheel and gave it to me. I put it on, zipping it up to the very top then put my hands back by the heater.

"Can you believe everything that's happened? Almost five years ago, I was at home. I had my family, some friends, and I was on the track team." A humorless laugh escaped my lips. "Now both my brothers are vampires, my best friend is one as well, my biological father used to be a vampire, and is now a mortal who can stay alive longer by drinking blood. If I'd done an essay on where I saw myself in five years, this definitely wouldn't be on my list."

"I feel responsible for everything that's happened to you."

"Why, because you gave me half of your DNA? That doesn't mean you're responsible for *everything*."

"Actually, I am. When I went searching for a way to reverse my immortality, I ran into this strange woman. She was young, maybe about your age, and she wasn't going to help me until I mentioned your mother. For some reason she was fixated on the fact that her last name was Sharmentino, and that was when she told me how to cure myself, but she said it would come at a price.

"When I learned that I was dying, I realized what she meant. Anyway, it was because I mentioned the Sharmentino name that she sought you out. It was too much of a coincidence that you were turned afterwards."

"She gave me Lucian's last bottle of blood because she thought I was a Sharmentino?" I asked. What was even more puzzling was why she was interested in my family's name. The Sharmentinos weren't anybody special; they'd just descended from a rich Italian family. As far as I knew, we didn't have any enemies, other than Samil of course. Unless Solomon had conjured up his own enemies.

I thought back to the night before I turned. There had been a strange woman at Aaron's party, and she'd left after having a very cryptic conversation with me. I'd been positive that she was the one who left the flier for the circus. Could she be the same one that helped David?

"I tried to find her again after your mother ended things with me, but never saw her again. I don't think she's a threat to us. If she was working with Samil, she wouldn't have given you Lucian's blood."

"Maybe we have someone on our side that just hasn't come forward yet," I said. "Even though I'm not too happy that I got roped into this, it's a comforting thought that we may have a common enemy with this mysterious woman."

I shivered then looked down at my hands. My fingernails were starting to turn purple; most likely from the lack of oxygen. I was getting colder, and it was even harder to breathe. The fluid in my lungs was building to the point where I could feel it flowing with each breath I took.

"Could we stop at a gas station? I need something for the pain."

David nodded. We'd passed a sign that indicated we were five miles from Fort Pierce, and there was a Sunoco gas station there.

I coughed and my lungs felt like they were on fire. The fluid seemed to loosen up, though, so that was a relief. We were only about two hours from Orlando, and I told myself that I would survive.

We pulled into the parking lot of the gas station, parking as close as we could to the door. David had to practically hold my arm as I walked in to keep me from falling. I paced the aisles, searching for what I needed, but my vision was blurred.

Eventually, I gave up on finding the right section since I was so overwhelmed with sickness and exhaustion. I knew that my body couldn't take anymore. The reality that I was dying finally hit me. I'd been so cavalier about it, but only because I'd thought that I had more time.

David pulled me close to him and I held onto him, doing my best to stay conscious.

"You're going to be okay, sweetheart," he said. "Just another twenty minutes and we'll get you healthy again."

I pulled back and he gently rubbed my arm then kissed the top of my head.

"Go back to the car, I'll find it for you."

I nodded then obeyed, shuffling out the door. It was weird having David act paternal towards me. I'd always seen him as my friend, and he'd treated me as such. He'd completely switched roles, and it was as if he'd been my father for years.

When I got into my seat, I pulled my phone out of my pocket and thumbed through my contacts. I couldn't decide who I was going to call, or think of who would be the most likely to answer. I'd called three people in my group and none of them had answered. It was a lost cause, but at this point I was desperate.

I clicked on Gallard's number and put the phone to my ear. It rang twice, which meant that it wasn't off. It went to voicemail and I smiled as I listened to his greeting. The phone beeped and I was suddenly at a loss for words. Nothing I thought of could emulate how I was feeling.

This was goodbye. I knew there was no way I was going to last for another twenty minutes in the car. I was stupid to insist on waiting instead of getting blood at the hospital. This was it. And I had no idea how I was going to say everything that I wanted to in a single voicemail.

The automatic recording informed me that my message, or rather my silent message, had been recorded and rattled off the options. I hung up just as David got back into the car.

"I got you some water as well," he said. I thanked him and took the pills and drink. "Who did you call?"

"I need one last favor," I said once I'd washed down two of the pain relievers. I coughed and my lungs burned once more. "If I don't make it, I need you to tell my brothers that I love them; that they need to get Robin back and take care of her."

"Lela, don't—"

"Wait!" I said interrupting him. "I also need you to tell Lydian that she was a great friend, even though she drove me up the wall most of the time. And tell her that I said to not worry about Jordan leaving her because he loves her.

"And last, but not least, I need you tell Gallard not to blame himself because I was only keeping my promise to him by staying human. I couldn't have lived more in forty years than I did for the four years that I was his friend."

"You're going to tell that to them yourself. Just hang on for a little while longer. You're going to make it!"

I began to cough again, this time more violently and I covered my mouth with my hands. When I removed them, I saw that they were covered in blood.

"David," I said, in a trembling voice. I tried to speak again, but I started coughing once more, this time more blood coming out. I felt the car accelerate, causing me to slightly slam against the seat. I looked down at my hands and saw that my skin was turning blue. Fluid filled my lungs, but I didn't have the energy to cough it up. I was drowning in my own blood. It wasn't how I expected it to happen.

David drove fast and faster, yelling things at me, but I couldn't understand what he was saying. I closed my eyes, pressing my forehead against the window. My memory jumped back to the day my brothers and I had gone to the circus. I reminisced on the great time that we had up until I'd gone into the gypsy's tent. It then went to the night Gallard took me to the blood bar and after that to the first time I met my little sister and that morning when I'd been reunited with David again. These were the moments that I cherished most in life.

The car stopped and shortly after, David opened my door and lifted me out of the seat. By then, his voice was nothing but a bunch of distorted sounds. He carried me a little ways, using one of his foot to push open the door.

A few moments passed then I felt him lay me on something soft. He left my side and I waited, either for death to finally come or for some relief; either would have been better than how I was feeling. The blood filled my lungs to the point where my body forced itself to cough it up.

I became oblivious to the passage of time. It could have been an hour, or a minute; I wasn't sure. The only thing I could focus on was pain in my head from my brain dying due to lack of oxygen. I couldn't decide which was the most unbearable, the ache in my lungs, or the throbbing pain in my head.

I forced myself to open my eyes and I froze in horror at what I saw. The redheaded man was standing next to me, almost two feet away. His hair seemed even redder under the fluorescent light. I hadn't seen him that clearly in my first dream since it was dark, but now I could make out his features. He looked confused, like he didn't know where he was or what was going on. I wanted to get up and run away, but I couldn't move. I was paralyzed with fear.

"What do you want?" I asked, finding the strength to speak. He touched my face with his finger, tracing my features until he got to my lips.

I can feel you. How is this possible?

"I...don't know. Who are you?"

You do not know? The answer has been in front of you this entire time. Why do you think I despise the Sharmentino family so much?

At that moment, I finally realized who he was. I'd thought he was just a figment of my imagination; a voice that I'd been forced to live with. But his words had given me a revelation about his identity.

"Lucian," I snarled. "This whole time it was you?"

I am afraid so. Tis a relief that you finally know my name.

I heard David return, and I glanced in his direction. He probably couldn't see Lucian, so if I continued to talk to him, he would think that I was suffering from hallucinations.

"Drink this," David said. I felt something press against my lips. I used every bit of energy that I had left to reach my hand up and feel what it was. A cup; plastic I assumed.

You are more like me than I realized.

"In what way?"

When I was alive, I grew ill if I did not feed. I nearly died as a teen until I realized what I needed.

"Lela, who are you talking to?" David asked, looking around the room. "Do you see someone?"

"I...see him."

I nearly dropped the cup, but David caught it in time. He tilted it until I felt the warm liquid spill into my mouth. I couldn't differentiate which blood that I tasted was mine or what David had given me to drink. I swallowed it all until it stopped flowing. Once it was gone, I noticed that Lucian's appearance began to fade until he was completely gone.

You must help me, Lela. I need to live again.

How would that be possible?

Find my body. Solomon knows, he must. I will give you something in return.

A surge of energy filled my body and I tensed up from the strange sensation. I could feel the blood as it healed each internal organ. My heart began to beat normally, the circulation slowly returning to all of my limbs. I could breathe again, and my head stopped hurting as the oxygen returned. The throbbing pain lessened almost instantaneously until it was gone completely. I felt alive; I was normal again.

I sat up from the small bed I was lying on and looked over at David. His relieved expression was enough for me to know what he was thinking. I planted my feet on the ground and stood up, expecting the pain and dizziness to return. But it never did. Three minutes passed, then five; I was still healthy.

"How do you feel?" he asked me in a hushed tone.

"Like myself," I replied. "I feel...stronger."

He took the cup from my hand and threw it in the trash. I

didn't want to ask where he'd gotten the blood. It was probably best that I didn't know.

"You are stronger," he said. "I'm not sure why, but I think it has something to do with Lucian's blood. Even though we're human, it still gives us strength. We're not as strong as vampires, but we're stronger than the average human." He took my hand and led me towards the door. "We need to get out of here. This isn't a hospital, and someone's going to notice that you're covered in blood."

We left through a side door of the building, which I learned was a homeless shelter, and hurried to the car. I buckled in just as he pulled out of the parking lot, speeding down the road. Once we got back on the freeway, he continued to accelerate.

"David, you can slow down," I assured him. "I'm okay, now. You don't have to rush."

"I'm sorry; I just…you almost died back there."

"That's the story of my life, David; it wasn't the first time I've been on the brink of death."

"Lela, please don't joke. If I hadn't gotten blood to you in time, you would have been gone. My little girl would have died."

I took his hand in mine and he stopped talking. He was right. I'd almost died, and somehow, I was okay with that. I'd had such a defeatist attitude about the whole thing, but when the moment actually came, I hadn't wanted to go.

Now that I had the chance to reflect on everything that had just happened, I was angry at myself. Furious even. I'd been sitting around, self destructing, and drowning my sorrows in alcohol. At that moment, my brothers and friends were off trying to fight for a good cause while I'd been here wallowing in self pity.

But I wasn't that girl anymore; the pathetic, and hopeless person that I'd become was gone. I was myself again; the girl who'd wrestled a shark, the girl who'd won her first fight with another vampire, the girl who despite being shot up twice and falling ill with a supernatural sickness, was still alive. When I'd been human- or a normal one anyway-I hadn't been as pessimistic, and I shouldn't have been now.

I couldn't sit back and wait any longer. If I was putting myself in danger then that's what it was going to take. Samil wasn't going to go down without me being there to see it. I was going to find my group and help them stop Samil for good, get Robin back, release David from Samil's bondage and Gallard from his harassment.

Gallard had made me promise to stay human, but he hadn't made me promise not to follow them and help. I was stronger now, in body and spirit. I wasn't going to go through what I just had again. If I could stay alive, I wanted to for as long as I could, even if it meant having to drink blood.

"You're right," I said. "I can't die; I have to stop Samil. And I'm going to make sure that you get your life back."

"What are you talking about? Does this have to do with what happened back there? Did you see Lucian?"

I didn't answer his last question. I wasn't quite ready to talk about what I'd seen.

"I'm going to talk to Bodoway in Orlando. He can probably tell me where Gallard is, and I'm going to help him take down Samil."

David shook his head. "No, absolutely not. He'll kill you!"

"That's a risk I'm willing to take. At least I will die fighting for something and not because I was sick or something lame like that."

"While I'm happy that you're better, I'm not thrilled that you're going off on a suicide mission. You may be stronger now that you're drinking blood, but that doesn't mean you can fight Samil and have a winning chance. If that were so, I would have killed him long ago."

I took off the jacket and my sweater as well since I was starting to get hot. The two had soaked up most of the blood but hadn't protected my shirt. There was a huge, red stain about the size of a grapefruit on the front.

"Not to sound like a rebellious teenager, but you can't really tell me what to do. Samil is expecting you back on Thursday, and after that, you'll no longer have the power to stop me."

David chuckled. "Oh really? What makes you think I won't stop you before I leave?"

"Well, I could always knock you out and steal your car again," I said, flashing a seditious smile. I chuckled at the memory of that night. I couldn't believe it when I'd knocked him unconscious. It wasn't something that I was used to. I was just glad that I hadn't seriously hurt him. I'd felt bad then, but now it was just funny.

"Just so we're clear. I *let* you knock me out."

"Whatever! I creamed you, and you know it."

As we drove through town, I started devising a plan for what I could do with my newfound connection to Lucian. I could communicate with him and this might be helpful when it came to getting my sister back, if we could put our differences aside and stop with the back and forth banter.

David had gone through somewhat of the same thing as I had before discovering that blood could heal him, but he never mentioned actually seeing Lucian. He'd heard his voice, but it never revealed to him who he was. This meant that, as far as I knew, I had been the first person of the four who drank his blood that he showed himself to. Why he chose me, I had no idea. Maybe because I'd been the one closest to dying. The reason didn't matter to me, though. I wanted to use this to my advantage.

The idea came to me when we stopped at a diner for dinner. It was insane, dangerous, and I would probably risk my life in the process, but I was willing to take a leap to save my sister. I wanted to keep it to myself, but I felt obligated to talk about it with David first.

I changed into some clean clothes then ordered scrambled eggs, hash browns, sausage, plus a side of two pancakes. I was starving since I hadn't eaten anything that wasn't from a tube in days. I devoured the sausage and hash browns in less than fifteen minutes then started with the eggs and pancakes. The look on David's face as he watched me eat was priceless. I probably looked like an animal.

"You're hungry," he said as he ate his country-fried steak. I nodded as I took another bite of pancake. I couldn't remember the last time I'd eaten that much food. It was like I had the munchies after getting high. "So are you going to tell me what happened earlier today?"

I stopped chewing then swallowed the bite of food. What I was about to tell him was bound to freak him out, and he would most likely freak out even more when he found out what I planned to do.

"While you were getting me blood, I saw Lucian," I said. David's eyes widened and he set his fork down. "It was almost as if he were in the room with me. I could even feel it when he touched me."

"Wait, he touched you? That creep was touching you?"

I ignored his grilling and continued. "It gets even weirder. He's the voice I've been hearing my whole life. I think I can use this connection to stop Samil."

David's angry stare hadn't softened, so my explanation hadn't calmed him as I'd hoped. Now that I was thinking about it again for the first time since before we'd arrived in Orlando, I was getting a bit freaked out myself. But I couldn't get scared now. If I flaked now, the plan would be ruined.

"I have an idea for how we can get Samil to let you and

Robin go," I said. "Lucian can communicate with me and I with him." I studied David's face to see how he was reacting, and he hadn't moved so I kept explaining my plan. "I was thinking that if I could somehow get Lucian to tell us where his body is, we could find it and use it as leverage. Samil has been searching for his body for years; he's bound to make a deal with us!"

"And how exactly do you plan to convince him?" David asked.

"Well...I wouldn't go as far as saying we were friends, more like frienemies." I thought some more. "He said he wants to help."

"He wants to help. And you believe this psycho?"

Did he just call me a psycho?

Don't listen to him, he's in dad mode.

"Yes, I do. He wants to live again and I want my sister back. We both have something the other person needs. We'll come up with a plan and put it into action."

"Have me do it instead," David insisted. "If you can talk to him, then I probably can to."

"David, you can't do it, you have to go back to Samil. Even if you could communicate with him like I can, then Samil would use that to his advantage. We can't even flirt with the possibility that you and I are the same because nothing would stop him from killing you. I can't lose you. Not again."

David sighed in defeat and continued to eat his food and I did the same. As I'd predicted, he didn't like my plan, but he would have to live with it. It hurt me to see him so helpless. I was his daughter, and yet he was unable to protect me from the danger of possibly losing to Samil. The chances of my plan working were pretty slim, but I had to try.

Chapter Nine

David convinced me to take a few more days and think about my plan before acting on it. I kept protesting, but he was stubborn like me. I finally agreed and figured I owed Curtis an explanation for my mysterious disappearance anyway.

We pulled into Tampa around ten-thirty and I saw that there was still a light on in the house. I took my time walking up the steps but opened the door quickly, shutting it behind me. David wanted to give me a moment to talk to Curtis before coming in. Curtis was sitting silently on the couch and a lump formed in my throat. I went into the living room and sat next to him, but even then he didn't say anything.

"Hey," I said sheepishly. He didn't say anything but kept staring off into space with an angry expression. "I'm sorry I took off like that. I promise it was important and—"

"Lela, do you know how scared I was? Your parents were just killed and then you go missing with some stranger claiming to be your dad. It was like two thousand nine all over again. I thought you were gone for good!"

"I'm not! I came back. My dad...my real dad needed to help me. He had the same illness that I did and I was able to get treatment. Turns out it was a misdiagnosis. I don't have cancer."

He finally forced himself to look at me and I waited as he

assessed my appearance. I wasn't completely back to normal yet. I'd lost a considerable amount of weight over the past several weeks and blood couldn't fix that. But I knew that I looked healthier in color at least.

"You...look better. How is it possible? Just three days ago, you were practically on life support!"

"I told you, I found a new treatment."

He smiled lightly. "You're not dying then?"

"Nope. I'm going to be around for a long time, Curt. Thanks to my dad."

"Thank God!" He leaned in and kissed me and I kissed him back. I was glad that he didn't ask any more questions about what treatment I had or how I'd made such a speedy recovery.

That was when I remembered David was still outside. He'd probably met Curtis before, but I wanted to formally introduce them. David was just as important in my life as Curtis. I loved having the people from both worlds come together.

I opened the door and let David in. I wasn't worried about either one of them being unfriendly. Unless David decided to go into dad mode and interrogate him like he did Gallard and Tyler.

"It's a pleasure to meet you again," David said, shaking Curtis' hand. "Not to be creepy, but I've seen you before. Lela's mother sent me a picture from the Fourth of July about twelve years ago and I believe you were in it."

"Oh really?" Curtis said. "It's nice to meet you too, David. I see now where Lela gets her height from."

David and I laughed. This was a good start. I knew Curtis would warm up to David as quickly as I had. He even let David sleep on the couch, which I was grateful for. I only had a few more days with him and I wanted to keep him close by.

When I woke up the next morning, I found that David was gone. I worried for a moment, but Curtis said he'd gone to town for something and I relaxed. As long as he hadn't left in the middle of the night, I was okay with him running an errand. We still had so much to talk about.

Feeling better than ever, I made myself an egg white omelette with spinach, tomatoes, cheese, and mushrooms. I used about four eggs since I was so hungry. I offered to make Curtis one, but he wasn't as hungry as me.

"This is so strange," he said as he watched me eat. "The past month you've been like the walking dead and now you're all...bubbly."

"It's great being healthy again!" I said. "And I'm glad I get to see my father for a few days. I've missed him."

"I've missed *you*. The healthy you."

I kissed his cheek as I got up to put my plate in the sink. It was probably strange, but I missed my healthy self as well. I hadn't liked myself very much lately and curing my illness also cured my terrible attitude.

"Oh um...about what you asked. I know I kind of passed out a day before I was supposed to give you an answer. I've decided...to give us a chance."

He stood up really quickly and stared at me in surprise.

"Really? You've been through a lot this week, I didn't expect an answer so soon!" he paused for a moment. "What about Gallard?"

I'd checked my phone the night before as I was getting ready for bed and Curtis was the only one who'd called me. I couldn't decide if I was relieved or disappointed. Gallard didn't call, which I presumed meant he didn't feel the same way. This was a good thing, right? I finally knew and now I could go back to just being his friend.

"Gallard is my best friend. Nothing more. He said he wanted me to be happy, so I'm taking his advice." I turned around and looked at Curtis. "I can't promise you that this will work, but I'm willing to try."

There was a knock at the door and he left to answer it. I assumed it was David, back from his errand and when Curtis opened the door I saw that it was him but someone else was with him.

"Gabby, hey!" Curtis said, hugging his sister.

"Curt, the house looks awesome! What genius helped you decorate?" she asked. Before he answered she turned to me and put a hand on her heart. "Lela! You look wonderful as ever, how are you?"

"I'm doing better; how about you, miss bride to be?"

"I'm elated, ecstatic, and excited! They all mean the same thing, but there isn't a word that does all three of them justice." She glanced at David. "I found this man on the porch. Does he belong to you?"

"Yes, this is David. He's my...uncle on my mother's side."

David raised an eyebrow but didn't say anything and neither did Curtis. I wasn't really in the mood to go into the whole story about the affair and everything, so saying he was my uncle worked for the time being.

They walked away from the door and the four of us sat in the living room. Gabby had changed a lot since I'd last seen her. She used to have a lot of piercings, but now she had a single stud in her nose. Her hair was back to its natural color as well; auburn.

"Where's your fiancé?" I asked her.

"He's lost in some art gallery in town. We probably won't see him for several hours."

"We missed you at Christmas," Curtis said. "But we understood that you're saving your money for your honeymoon. Two trips from New York within four weeks would be spendy."

"Spendy indeed. I've missed you bro, which is why I'm here to convince the two of you...now the three of you, to come with Edison and me to Miami a few days early."

"Sorry, Gab, but I can't get off work until Friday."

Gabby pouted then turned to me. "You and your uncle can come with me, can't you?"

"Oh, I don't want to crash your wedding," David insisted.

"Nonsense! You're Lela's family and any family member of Lela's is a friend of mine."

"Then we'd love to," I said. "When are you leaving?"

"Tonight. Edison prefers to drive at night instead of the day, so we're chillin' in the city for a few hours." She stood up taking my hand. "Now, Curt, you go off and do your ortho thing. I'm taking these two shopping."

• • •

Gabby's wedding was going to be at my church. Her family wasn't Catholic, but I learned that my mother convinced the priest to let them use the church for free. Apparently she'd planned to go as well, which made me sad. I wished she could have gone. She loved weddings.

When I walked in, I was taken aback by how beautiful the sanctuary looked. All of the Christmas decorations had been replaced by gorgeous lavender, purple, and white flowers. Some were clumped together in tiny bouquets and fastened to the end of each pew with white satin draped underneath. It was elegant, but simple at the same time.

Her parents, who had been talking with Father Thomas, each greeted me with a hug then her mother joined the bridesmaids to continue decorating. I wanted to help, but Gabby insisted that I just visit with her fiancé. David wasn't there since he wanted to go and visit my mother's grave, so I didn't have him to help me talk to Edison.

"Are you sure? I have to do something to help," I insisted.

"You would be helping by keeping Edison occupied. His family isn't here yet, so he's super bored."

I wished that Curtis was here to entertain him instead, but he wouldn't get into town for another two hours. The entire way back to Miami, Edison had talked about art and famous artists from the eighteen hundreds that I'd never heard of. I learned that his real name was Dudley, which he hated so he went by his last name instead. I had no idea what we would talk about since we had nothing in common.

I sat next to him in the pew, looking everywhere but at his face. I hoped that he would initiate conversation so that I would be saved from embarrassing myself by saying something corny.

Five minutes passed and we still hadn't exchanged so much as a nod, and I took it upon myself to speak first.

"Where do you plan to go on your honeymoon?" I asked.

"We're going to Spain. There's so much art there that I've only read about in books, and we've wanted to travel there since we started art school. I want to paint. The scenery options are endless."

Edison was a slightly nerdy guy with his pencil mustache and disheveled brown hair. His personality was a tad dry, but there had to be some quality to his character or else Gabby wouldn't be here getting ready to marry him.

"Your last name is Sharmentino. Are you Italian?" he asked.

"My adopted father was, but my real father isn't. I'm not sure what I am, exactly."

"I wonder if you are of Dutch descent. You are very tall, and your blonde hair and blue eyes are common features of that race as well."

David never talked about his family much when we'd lived together. He'd kept to himself about a lot of things in his life for reasons that I'd only recently learned. I wanted to get to know him again, not as the friend I'd known and loved, but as the man who was my father.

"I really admire your features," Edison said, "To capture your figure on a canvas would be most enjoyable."

I scoffed at his bold request. This man was about to marry an old friend, and he was asking me to pose for him. I would have punched him if we were in a different location.

"You're joking, right? You're getting married, and you're asking if I'll let you sketch me?"

"Why not? I've sketched all of Gabriella's friends. She knows that it's purely for artistic purposes."

"You sketched her friends? What were they doing…what were they wearing?"

"Nothing, of course. The human body is a beautiful thing and you shouldn't be ashamed of it."

At this point, I'd had enough of Edison's company. He was a creep, and I didn't care that Gabby was fine with him doing nude paintings of her friends but I wasn't going to be one of them.

"I think I'm going to pass," I said. I left the pew without another word and began to wander around the church.

I hadn't been upstairs since I was a child, so I made my way up the spiraling staircase to get a higher view of the sanctuary. The stained-glass windows were more beautiful than I remembered, each one telling a different story from the Old Testament. I was in awe as I quietly looked around since there were people praying in some of the rooms.

I came across a confessional and peeked behind the curtain to see if a priest was there. It was vacant, so I went into the other side and sat down, leaning my head against the wall with my eyes closed. I'd been in one before when I was eleven, but it was only because I'd wanted to see what it was like. Aaron and I turned it into a joke with him pretending to be the priest and me a cheating wife. That was before I'd known I was the product of my mother's infidelity.

You should get out of there, Lucian said. *Churches make me…uncomfortable.*

Oh great, you're still hanging around. That means you know my plan.

David insulted me and your conversation was dull. Are you going to help me or not?

I am helping you. You want your body back, don't you?

Two must die, Lela. Who of your friends are you willing to sacrifice?

I'd forgotten to take into account that his coming back required a bloodletting. How was I supposed to ensure Robin's return by helping Lucian while protecting my friends at the same time? There was no easy way to do this.

Maybe the gypsy was exaggerating, I suggested. *What if you only need a little bit of blood? Each person doesn't have to give their entire supply, do they?*

I would not know, ask Solomon.

Solomon won't tell me squat. He's just as set on keeping you hidden as Samil is finding you.

This all seemed so hopeless. No matter who found Lucian's body first, Robin's release wouldn't be assured until Lucian was alive and breathing. All for some stupid day-walking secret.

How did you walk in the day, Lucian?

I assume the one who turned me would know that. Too bad I know not who he is.

You mean you don't know!

Bad news. Exactly what I didn't want to hear. Samil was doing all of this to learn Lucian's secret and Lucian didn't even know the answer, himself. If Samil found out, he would probably flip out and kill everyone, regardless a deal.

What Samil does not know will not hurt him, Lucian said. *If you bring me back, I swear to you that I will kill him.*

You would really do that? There has to be a catch to this.

Yes. Two will still have to die Lela. But at least to return the favor, your sister will be alive.

Since when do you care about my sister?

I do not. But it would not be honorable of me if I accepted your help without returning the favor.

188

"There you are!" I heard someone say. Curtis came walking towards me and I stood up. "Gabby said that you wandered up here." He reached down and warily took my hand. "Is this okay?"

Say no, Lucian said.

Shut up.

"Of course." I said.

I gave Curtis' hand a quick squeeze before we headed back down to the sanctuary. While we walked, I thought about Lucian's offer. If I helped him come back, Robin would be safe from Samil. How could I pass that up? The how and when could be worried about later. For now, I needed to find my friends and find his body first.

I snapped out of my daydream when I heard the wedding party let out a long *aww* as Gabby kissed Edison. Curtis let go of my hand and we clapped with them.

"You're cheating! You're supposed to wait until the real wedding!" her mother said.

"All right, all right," Gabby said, rolling her eyes. "Let's get to the restaurant, I'm starving!"

The rehearsal dinner was at Joe's Crab Shack; a sea food place, and Edison's parents were paying for everyone. I stayed silent while I listened to the random outbursts of laughter from the table; something that happened quite often. Curtis' family was known for being a bunch of clowns, most of who laughed at their own cheesy jokes. One couldn't help but laugh with them because of how utterly stupid the jokes were.

I noticed that Gabby was trying to catch my attention so I looked over at her just as she got up from her seat and left the table. I followed her to the back of restaurant into the bathroom. She was splashing water on her face as she leaned over the sink.

"Are you okay?" I asked. I rolled down some paper towels then handed them to her. She took them and patted her face.

"No, I'm trying not to throw up," she said. She took a deep breath and massaged her temples with her fingers. "I thought morning sickness was supposed to be in the morning."

I was shocked at what I was hearing. Gabby didn't look pregnant at all. She was super thin, maybe too thin.

"How…how far along are you?" I asked. I didn't know what else to say, I was still surprised.

"Ten weeks. I'm at the point where I'm nauseous all the time." She took some gum out of her purse and began to chew it.

"Does Edison know about the baby?" I asked. She nodded then she started to cry.

"Yeah, he knows. The catch is that it isn't his."

This conversation was taking a weird turn. I'd gone into the bathroom thinking that she just wanted someone to go with her like most girls did, but now she was pouring her heart out to me.

This is why I like you, Lucian said. *You do not get yourself into these situations.*

Lucian, I'm starting to think you don't like women.

Very few. The ones in my life have always let me down. Accept for you, perhaps.

Why, because I'm still a virgin? Your views are very outdated.

I merely believe that involving yourself with anyone in that way proves as a distraction. Besides, they will only leave you once they get what they want.

"Whose is it then?" I asked, tired of Lucian's weird conversation. I handed her some more paper towels and she lightly dabbed her eyes.

"My ex Spencer Hendrickson. We were together for almost two years. I was in love with him but then I found out what a creep he was. He was part of some cult and tried to get me to join. Edison was in my circle of friends and when he found out my situation, he offered to marry me. I accepted his proposal because I had no other choice. My parents would have killed me; they would have stopped paying for my tuition and I wouldn't be able to finish school."

"So instead you're marrying a man that you don't love?" I asked, baffled by her logic.

"Edison is okay. He loves me and that's all that matters. He'll be a good husband and I'm going to try to be a good wife in return." She looked at me. "I still love Spencer, but he's not good for me so I'm just taking care of myself. What would you do in my situation?"

I had no idea how to answer that. Talking to her made me realize that I *was* in her situation. I'd agreed to go out with Curtis because the man I loved didn't feel the same way. Was I settling like Gabby? I hated thinking about it that way.

How about you get rid of both men, Lucian asked. *Tis the easier choice.*

Or I could get rid of you. I'm trying to have a conversation here.

Part of me wanted to tell her to not go through with it; to wait until another guy came along that she truly loved instead of trapping herself in a loveless marriage like my mother had. She may have loved Mark at one point, but she'd cheated with David, which meant she wasn't madly in love with him like a wife should be with her husband. Could I really stand by and let Gabby make the same mistakes?

"I would do whatever I thought was best for me," I finally said. "And if marrying Edison is the right choice for you, then I'm not going to talk you out of it."

She hugged me then we left the bathroom to rejoin the party. Gabby entered the conversation with her family without missing a beat. The laughter continued, and I finished eating my crab legs and pasta. I wish I had said more to her, but love was not a subject I was good at giving advice for. I would have to hope that my advice was enough.

Chapter Ten

I admired the new dress I'd picked for the wedding ceremony in the mirror. It was a deep purple with one shoulder and had a flower on the strap. I preferred the original one I'd chosen but it no longer fit. I was about fifteen pounds lighter since I'd gotten it three weeks before, and it hung very loosely. Gabby insisted that I buy another and I did.

As I did my hair, I talked to David. He had to leave that night, and I was spending every moment that I could with him. I'd decided to keep my deal with Lucian a secret for the time being. I didn't need him to have more to worry about.

I set my flat iron on the counter and turned it off. I was tired of straightening my hair, and it looked fine to me. I wanted to spend more time relaxing before the wedding.

"You look so much older, how did you do that; control your age?" I asked David.

"It depends on how much blood I drink. The more I have, the younger I look. If I drink regularly, I can keep my youthfulness. If I space out the time between, I look how I do now. But if I stop completely, I'll age until I die."

"You should drink it more often, you're starting to look like an old geezer," I joked.

He laughed. I carefully lay on my bed so that I wouldn't

wrinkle the dress and closed my eyes. I didn't want to sleep; I just wanted to stretch out.

"Speaking of old geezers, how's Gallard? I haven't seen him in ages."

"I wouldn't know. He apparently has forgotten how to use a phone."

My voice had more hostility than I'd intended. David was bound to notice.

"Wow. Are you two at odds? I can't imagine you and Gallard being mad at each other."

"I'm not mad I'm...I don't know what I am."

David gave a half smile then moved closer to me.

"Don't tell him I told you this, but after you and Tyler broke up, he seemed...grateful. After that, I would sometimes catch him looking at you when you weren't paying attention. At first I was leery about it but then I gave it some thought. He's a respectable and honorable person. He's done so many selfless things for you and he's never overstepped any boundaries. He doesn't just care about you, he loves you. And I know you feel the same way."

David was right; Gallard was a great person and proved to be the most trustworthy man in my life. He hadn't overstepped any boundaries until New Years; we both had. But after he'd avoided my calls and pushed me to be in a relationship with Curtis. I'd decided to take the hint.

"He doesn't want me, David. I asked him to be honest with me and his silence gave me my answer." I put on my diamond stud earrings then applied a small amount of lip gloss. "I'm with Curtis now."

"I don't believe that, Lela. Gallard looks at you the way I used to look at your mother. Either he's afraid to tell you, or he doesn't think *you* feel the same way."

Someone knocked at the door and I was relieved. I wasn't ready to have this conversation with David, especially upon learning about our family relations.

I opened the door and found Curtis standing there. He was all dressed up in his black tux and plum colored cummerbund with a matching tie. He was a last-minute groomsman, and Gabby had to do an emergency trip to the tux place so he could match the other men in the wedding party.

"Hey! Is it time to go to the church yet?" I asked.

"Just about." He looked at what I was wearing. "You're beautiful."

"Thank you sir. You look dashing, yourself!"

He leaned in to kiss me but I stopped him, nodding my head towards the room and he understood. It was bad enough that David wasn't on board with our relationship, which was to be expected, so I didn't want him to witness any PDA.

I sat between David and Curtis' mom, Terry, during the ceremony. Apparently I'd been listed as family at the last minute, so I got to be in the front row. It was weird being in front since the last time I'd been there was for my parents' funeral. It was easy not to think about that though. I had David back and my good friend from childhood was getting married. I still thought her fiancé was a bit of a creep, but she'd said that he was good to her. That was all that mattered.

When the priest pronounced them man and wife, my mind went back to a year ago. If I'd kept my mouth shut, Tyler and I might have had our own wedding by now. In a way, I was glad as well. If I'd gone through with the wedding without telling him the truth, he would have eventually found out and our marriage probably would have ended. A divorce would have been more difficult to get over than a breakup. It just wasn't meant to be.

The usher held his arm out to Gabby's mother and she slipped her arm through so he could lead her down the aisle. David and I followed her until we got to the room where the reception was going to be. We sat at our assigned table and I people watched as the room filled with all the guests.

I ate a full plate of chicken fettuccini. It was the best fettuccini I'd had in a long while; better than my simple recipe. I needed something to wash it down with so when one of the servers walked by with a tray of champagne, I grabbed a glass.

"Finally, some real beverages," I said. I was about to drink it when David took it away.

"If I can recall, you're not twenty-one."

He took a sip. I grabbed it back and took a sip as well.

"I've killed people, and you're worried about my underage drinking?"

"I'm trying to keep you as uncorrupted as possible," he

insisted.

I gave him a sneaky look then downed the rest of the champagne.

"What is it with you and Lucian trying to protect my innocence? It doesn't need protecting, I've done just fine on my own, thank you."

"Is Lucian still talking to you?"

I nodded as I grabbed another glass from the passing waiter. I didn't mind David's lectures because he was my friend and father, but Lucian was infuriating.

I guzzled the second glass and David waved a condescending finger at me. "If your grandfather knew I let you drink, he would kill me."

"Why, was he a rally leader for the prohibition?" I asked. David pursed his lips and I laughed. "No way, I was right!"

"He was a strong Christian, but he wasn't convicted about anything more than the ban of alcohol. My brother came home drunk once and he nearly disowned him."

"That's so interesting. So when were you born anyway?"

"Nineteen-twelve. That makes me one hundred and two years old."

"Wow. You're a baby compared to Gallard, aren't you?"

"Speaking of Gallard, does he know about you and Curtis?" He was using his signature interrogational tone.

"It was his idea, believe it or not. If he had feelings for me, why would he push me to be with Curtis?"

"Maybe he's still trying to be the good guy and keep things platonic with you so you don't ruin your friendship."

"Didn't feel platonic to me when we fooled around in my parents' bed."

This was the alcohol talking. It had to be. Either that or I was officially crazy. I'd forgotten for a moment that David was my father and not just my friend. The look on his face was of pure mortification.

"Are you serious?" he asked, trying not to raise his voice.

"Can we forget I said anything?"

"Gladly." He shook his head then took my half-glass of champagne away. "You're just like me; a lightweight and an unfiltered drunk. No more for you, missy."

Someone clinked on a glass and the whole room fell silent. It was time for speeches, and the maid of honor and best man were standing next to the wedding party table with microphones. Both speeches were very touching, causing most of the people in the room to cry. Afterwards, the bride and groom cut the cake and shoved it into each other's faces.

The dancing began directly after the cake, and everyone watched as Gabby and Edison slow danced to Elton John's *Can You Feel the Love Tonight*. The fast music began almost immediately after the money dance. All of the couple's friends and family really got into the music while the parents and older people stayed seated.

David then smiled and stood up, extending his hand to me. "Dance with me."

"You're not going to sing are you?" I asked as I took his hand and walked with him.

"I promise I won't sing...for now."

We got to the middle of the room and began slow dancing to *Butterfly Kisses*. Dancing with him brought back memories from Texas and I longed for those days when everything was simple. I also wished that he could meet Lydian and Jordan. He would like Jordan since they both had great cooking skills, and I had a feeling that Lydian would drive him as crazy as she did me.

"Remember winter formal?" David asked. I smiled at the memory.

"I remember you freaking out when Tyler asked me."

"I'm sorry I was such a dad. Tyler was a great guy, considering. It broke my heart to see you so sad when he broke off the engagement. But between you and me, I like Gallard better, though your little revelation made him lose a few points in my book."

"It takes two to tango, Dave. I was just as much responsible for what happened."

While we were dancing, Curtis approached us and we stopped moving.

"Would you mind if I cut in? I'd love to dance with your daughter," he said to David.

David looked at me and raised an eyebrow.

"I don't mind at all as long as she doesn't," he said. I lightly squeezed David's hand before he went back to his seat and I switched to dancing with Curtis.

We swayed slowly to the music and I actually got into it. Unlike the last time we'd danced, we were completely sober, or at least more sober, so it was a more enjoyable experience.

"I can tell he's your dad," he said. "You look like him. More than your mom except for your hair color."

"I guess I do, huh?"

I suddenly remembered the picture we'd taken before winter formal. Gallard had pointed out that David and I looked like twins. I'd just thought it was because of David's hair, but now that I knew we were related, it made complete sense. David and I shared more facial characteristics than Kevin and I did.

I looked over at David while we danced. He'd struck up a conversation with Curtis' dad and I wondered what they were talking about. Mark had been pretty good friends with Curtis' dad in the past, and David's existence sort of made everything awkward. But Curtis' family treated him so kindly that I didn't worry about it.

"You know, we make pretty good dance partners," Curtis said.

"Yeah, you're all right; as long as you don't try to cop a feel again."

He hung his head. "I feel bad about that. I was drunk, high, and stupid. There's no good excuse for what I did."

"What hurt even more was your reaction when you found out how old I was. You acted as if you found out you just kissed your sister."

"You were fourteen! I was just scared that I was going to get in trouble. I could have gotten arrested."

"Well, I'm not fourteen anymore."

"No. Not anymore."

He lightly pressed his lips to mine then pulled back. There was something different about it this time. It didn't feel like he was trying to steal a kiss. It felt like goodbye.

We danced in silence for a bit and I glanced over at Gabby who was dancing with Edison. She had a faraway look in her eyes as if her mind was elsewhere. She looked content, but not like she was completely happy like a bride should. My heart went out to her, and I hoped that she'd done the right thing by getting married.

I checked the time and realized that I had to leave. David's plane was due to depart in two hours and I needed to drop him off at the airport. I let Curtis know then went over to Gabby to give her a hug since I hadn't had the chance yet. I even hugged Edison to be polite.

While we drove, David played the weirdest music. It didn't seem like his type, though I didn't mind it. I was suspicious because all the songs were about cheating or loving someone who didn't love the person back or pretending not to have feelings for someone. I started noticing the pattern.

"You're not tricking me with subliminal messages, Dave. I see what you're trying to do here."

"I'm not doing anything," he claimed with a mischievous

smile.

"Playing these songs isn't going to change my mind. Gallard and I are friends and that's how it's always going to be."

"And yet you hooked up with him." His expression softened. "Look, I only want the best for you. Every father dreams of their daughter marrying a good guy and just because you're mixed up with vampires doesn't mean you have to skip out on that. I won't bother you anymore, but do what makes you happy, okay?"

"Thank you. Dad."

I found a close parking spot and I was trying not to cry. It had been wonderful seeing him again, especially since I'd thought he was dead for the past year. I didn't want him to go back to that monster that killed my parents but he'd made a deal; get back by Saturday or Robin would be killed.

He dug in his jacket pocket until he pulled out something silver, about four inches. It looked old, very antique. He handed it to me and I realized that it was a pocketknife. I questioned him with my eyes and he explained.

"Your grandfather gave this to me on my fifteenth birthday just two months before I turned." He smiled as if to reminisce on the memory. "I want you to have it. You need some sort of weapon to protect yourself, especially now that you're somewhat mortal. It may not stop a vampire, but it's better than nothing."

"Thank you, I'll keep this always."

We both got out of the car and he gave me a tight hug. I hated saying goodbye, it wasn't getting any easier. I had to hold onto the hope that I would see him again; that he would survive this and we would both be free from all threats against us.

"I love you, sweetheart," he said, still hanging onto me. "Despite the fact that you drink and get yourself into dangerous situations." He released me from the hug and said, "Just remember that if you drink four ounces of blood every ten days or so, you'll stay healthy. You don't have to be over-dependant on it. You *can* have a somewhat normal life."

"I'll remember that," I said. "Now get out of here before I try to make you stay longer."

He smiled then walked off through the parking lot and I kept my eyes on him until he disappeared through the doors. He'd been right about the blood increasing my ability to feel the pull. It was faint at first, but the further he got away from me, the stronger it became.

On a whim, I decided to take a drive up to Orlando and see Bodoway. David and I never went since he'd saved me in time while on our way there. I wanted to get a small supply of blood from him for future use as well as talk for a bit. I hadn't seen him since Gallard and I first left for Texas.

I pulled into Orlando about an hour and a half later. I drove around until I found a dark place to park then continued towards the bar. I had only been there twice, so it took a few sweeps around town before I found it. The sun had gone down, which didn't make it any easier to spot the exact location.

The area looked just as I remembered. There was a drug

store across the street and the door on the front was chained up, with the windows painted black. A few people were hanging around the front, but I couldn't tell if they were immortal or not. By the way they were acting they seemed like a bunch of wannabes. A bouncer was standing by the door, trying to get the group of guys to leave. He was a giant; probably seven feet tall, and his long, black hair was pulled back into a low ponytail.

I parked on the street nearby and put money in the meter. I wanted to be close in case a quick getaway was needed. I was sure that I would be fine, maybe a bit too sure. I'd already made the mistake of trusting one vampire, and that had almost gotten ugly. I had to remind myself to be cautious and think before I acted.

I walked into the alley until I found the door and knocked three times then waited for someone to answer. The door was different than it was when I was last there. There was a new sign above the entrance, and there hadn't been one before.

The door opened and the same guy from last time stood before me. He was even wearing the same pants, looking as grouchy as ever.

"Donations are on Fridays," he snapped.

"What? Oh, no. I'm not here to give blood," I explained. "I'm here to see Bodoway."

He narrowed his eyes at me as if to try to remember where he'd seen me before. I wouldn't blame him if he didn't recognize me. I was four years older and blonder than when he'd last seen me. And it wasn't as if we'd talked to each other. Our first meeting had been brief.

"Who are you?" he asked. "Bodoway doesn't have mortal friends."

"I'm a friend of Gallard's," I said. "I came here with him four years ago, remember? You asked me for I.D."

He smirked and I frowned in confusion. Why would that seem strange to him? Was it that farfetched that Gallard actually had friends?

"He told me to watch out for a beautiful blonde girl," he said, giving me an amused smile. "He also told me not to let you in."

I felt myself blushing and tried to get myself together. This wasn't the time to be getting flustered over a flattering comment. But I was more surprised that Gallard had predicted that I might show up. I'd promised him that I wouldn't find someone to turn me back. Did he not trust me? Or was he just making sure I didn't try to find him, which was exactly what I was doing there.

"What can I do to convince you to let me in?" I asked, now annoyed that it was taking so long to get in the door. He didn't answer me, but I wasn't going to budge."

"How about a little taste? Then maybe I might reconsider."

"Like hell!" I said, stepping forward in a defensive manor. The man chuckled, causing me to be even more irked. I was afraid that he was going to try and start a fight. David had said that drinking blood made us stronger, but not enough to take on a vampire. I didn't want to find out.

"No sample, no entrance. It's your choice, baby."

Now I was frustrated. I needed to get in, and he wasn't any help. Without giving it thought, I pushed him out of the way and walked by. He hadn't been prepared for it, so he wasn't able to stop me until I was already inside. He grabbed my arm, jerking me back towards the door and I kicked him in the shin, causing him to grunt. David was right; I was stronger. I'd been able to inflict pain on this guy.

I turned around to see everyone staring at us and I was suddenly embarrassed by the attention. I hadn't planned to cause a scene, especially when there were over twenty vampires around. They could rip me apart any second if they wanted to. Thankfully, the bar's main rule was that violence wasn't tolerated. This also meant that I was breaking the rules and could easily be kicked out.

"All right, show's over," the guy said to the others in the bar. He was probably even more embarrassed than I was about the whole ordeal. Without another word, I walked away through the group of people.

I found an open seat at the counter and sat in it. I didn't see Bodoway anywhere, but Gallard had told me that he was always there so I waited for him to show. I had to ignore the hungry looks I was getting from everyone. The lighting was very dim, making it hard to see around the room. It was probably just fine for vampire eyes, but mine were normal. I could barely even read the different posters that were on the wall. The décor was that of a bit of everything from each century. There were old, Victorian paintings as well as a movie poster for *Easy Rider* and a mural of George Washington on the ship with his soldiers holding the tattered American flag.

I turned around after admiring the pictures and saw Bodoway come up to the counter.

"How can I help you?" he asked.

I smiled and said, "Hey, Bodoway, long time no see!"

He stared at me for a moment then let out a chuckle. "Well isn't it the shark wrestler? Look at you! You're a woman now! I didn't recognize you. I guess I still have the young girl in my mind. How have you been?"

"I almost died the other day, but other than that, I'm all right."

"Messed with the wrong shark eh?"

"You have no idea."

"Does Gallard know you're here?"

"Nope, but I was hoping that you knew where *he* was. I can't sit around while my friends do all the hard work."

Bodoway sighed and scratched his head. "He would kill me if I told you. He specifically said not to let you in here, so I'm already breaking the rules by talking to you."

"I need to tell him something important," I said.

I didn't need to just find my friends. I also needed to tell him and the others about Lucian. The fact that I'd been able to contact him was an interesting twist in the situation, and I thought we could use it to our advantage as Lucian suggested.

I was about to elaborate when a young woman came up next to me and sat on the counter, crossing her legs. It wasn't normal behavior for a restaurant, but I was amused by her boldness and obvious aversion to common courtesy. She looked extremely young; maybe fourteen or fifteen.

"Get off my counter, Emiline," Bodoway said. She smiled and ruffled his hair. Ignoring his remark, she shifted around until she was comfortable.

"I heard you guys talking about Gallard. I just couldn't help myself but join in."

I raised an eyebrow. This Emiline was definitely an interesting character. She was wearing really short jean cutoffs and a graphic t-shirt that was two sizes too small, stopping at her midriff. Her eyes were like that of a cat, most likely from contact lenses. Her hair was extremely long; longer than mine, hanging down to the table and draping over the edge.

"You a friend of his?" I asked. She giggled and started twirling her hair while looking off in the distance.

"We went out about a hundred years ago. But we weren't doing much *going out*, if you know what I mean."

She started giggling again. For some reason, I'd never been able to picture Gallard with a girlfriend, especially one as odd as Emiline. I'd known about his fiancé, Bodoway's sister, but besides her, he hadn't really talked about anyone that had been in his life.

I was willing to brush off her comment until she spoke again and said, "In fact, we had ourselves a little fun when he was here a few weeks ago."

Bodoway glared at her and said, "You're so full of it, Em. You were all over him when he was here, and he practically had to use violence to get you to leave him alone."

She huffed and gave him a childish pout. "Well if he'd been in his right mind we could have had a good time. I wonder if he still has that exotic bird tattoo on his chest," she said, that faraway look returning. I grew annoyed, and I felt my blood beginning to boil. I was not usually a jealous person. There was no need to be jealous. He was doing his thing and I was doing mine.

"He doesn't have a tattoo," I said. Bodoway gave me a suspicious look and I wanted to melt into the floor.

This was enough chit chat. I wanted to buy the blood, get my information, and get out of there so I could start heading back to Miami. I wasn't sure when I planned to find everyone or what I would tell Curtis I was doing. My group could still be in England, but I didn't want to travel all the way there to learn that they'd moved on.

"Bodoway, if you tell me where he is, I promise I won't bring your name up."

He looked down and folded his arms as he thought while I waited expectantly for his answer. I was also thinking myself about how I would explain my need for blood. I didn't really want to go into detail about everything that had happened. That would take all night.

"He called me a week ago. He said they were headed to

India. I guess Samil resides there quite often since it's his home land. I think he said Goa was the city they were aiming for."

"He called you? I called him twice and he didn't answer! He is so dead when I see him. If he calls you again, you tell him that!"

Bodoway laughed. He seemed amused by my annoyance but he wasn't the one who was getting ignored. I was pissed.

"Oh! And I found that blonde guy you saw in your vision. My guess was only half right; he was attractive, but he wasn't important. Other than break my heart, he didn't do anything extraordinary."

Bodoway gave me a sympathetic look. "Then maybe it wasn't the same guy."

"Huh. Let's find out." I extended my hand to him. "Wanna try again?"

"Ooh, I love it when he does this," Emiline said, moving closer to us.

Bodoway warily took my hand then closed his eyes as he had four years ago. My stomach began to knot as I worried that he would see something pertaining to my sister. As far as I knew, she was still alive a week ago.

Finally, Bodoway let go and his expression became pleasant once more.

"I still see him. And this time…you were with him."

"Seriously? What were we doing? No, don't tell me. I'd rather not know."

Bodoway laughed.

"Whoever he is, you care about him. I can feel it when I see the vision."

"I guess I walked into that, right? I asked you to tell me my future."

I gave a brief explanation for why I needed blood bags then I paid for them with my card. I even had a small glass to drink since I was paranoid that I would get sick again. David assured me that the affects of the blood would last for at least ten days before I would need more, but I wanted to be prepared.

Emiline remained sitting on the counter the entire time I was there. I didn't really want her listening to our conversation, but she seemed harmless. To me she was just some lonely and slightly immature girl who was stuck forever in the mindset of a teenager. I felt a tad bit sorry for her. Her child-like mentality made it hard to be harsh with her.

"Are you seriously going to chase him all the way to India? And I thought I was desperate."

I could have made a snappy remark, but I chose not to. Instead, I decided to just be honest. I'd already survived harassment from Lydian, and Emmeline's remark was child's play compared to the things that Lydian had come up with.

"No, I'm not chasing him. I'm doing this to get my sister back. In fact, if you want him, you can have him!"

She just stared at me in silence as I took the sack of blood bags and hopped down from the bar stool then Bodoway hugged me. When he released me from the hug he said, "You know he loves you, Lela."

"That's what everyone says. We're just friends, Bodoway. And though I'm pissed at him right now, I miss him."

"Give it more time. He's probably afraid of losing you. When Dyani died, it nearly killed him. I didn't think he'd ever recover. Now imagine if Samil killed you as well." His somber expression lightened a bit. "Plus, he's a D'Aubigne. They don't say how they feel, they show you. Trust me when I say that I've witnessed this from the three that I've known in my life. You just need to force it out of him."

Chapter Eleven

I turned the cruise control on and coasted down I-95. I thought about stopping at a motel, but I didn't want to make any more unnecessary stops than I had to. I needed to find a way to explain to Curtis why I was leaving without giving away specific details. I didn't want to lie to him anymore, but I didn't want to tell him anything that would freak him out either. He'd been more than good to me over the past months, and I owed him an explanation.

Every song on the stupid radio was about love or loving someone the person couldn't have. I got sick of it, so I switched it to Classic Rock and an AC/DC song started playing. I couldn't believe it and I got so frustrated that I changed it to an instrumental station. And that only reminded me of the joke I made about Gallard going to Beethoven concerts. I finally gave up and settle for the Spanish station.

I notice that the gaslight was on, so I stopped at the first gas station I came across. I was only thirty minutes outside of Miami, but I didn't want to risk it and get stranded. There was a warm wind blowing and I took off the jacket I'd been wearing. The air felt nice against my face and arms. I tossed the jacket onto the back seat then proceeded to put gas in the tank.

I put the nozzle on the automatic setting then went into the store. It was one of those all-night stations, so I was able to find a proper storage unit for the blood bags. I picked a medium sized blue and white cooler as well as ice packs then paid the man before returning to my car.

As I pulled the nozzle out, I got the sudden feeling that a set of eyes were on me and I looked around to see if anyone was there. Other than a man filling his Jetta and some teenager getting a soda from one of the machines, there was no one else in the parking lot. Neither of them had been looking at me when I glanced in their direction, so I brushed it off as paranoia. I hung the nozzle back on the gas pump then got back into the car.

I'd texted Curtis earlier to see if he was still at the hotel, and he was. He planned to fly with me back to Tampa Friday afternoon; about ten hours from now. It was nearly one a.m. by the time I pulled into the parking lot of the hotel. By then, I was exhausted, having been up for nearly twenty-four hours. I could barely keep my eyes open as I walked into the lobby.

I took the elevator up to the third floor then walked down to room number three fifty-three. Curtis said that he would be awake, so I knocked on the door. I would have stayed in my own room, but I didn't feel like being alone.

Curtis opened the door and I gave him a silent greeting before going into the room. He turned on one of the lamps and I sat at the edge of the bed that hadn't been slept in. He looked as tired as I felt. He yawned and ran his hands through his hair before smiling at me.

"Your trip go all right?" he asked.

"Yeah. It was bittersweet. I liked driving with my dad, but I'll miss him."

"Well, you didn't miss much at the reception. Riley got wasted, as usual, and...oh! I caught the garter."

He found it on the dresser and tossed it to me.

"Why do I have a feeling you *really* made an effort to get this?" I asked.

"You have great intuition."

He sat next to me and I felt moved to hug him. He was so good to me. Better than I deserved. He probably thought he was getting a drama free roommate and he had to deal with my occasional emotional breakdown, binge drinking, E.R. trips, and indecisiveness.

I got up for a second and went into the bathroom to change out of my clothes and into some sweats before returning to the room. Curtis had moved back over to the bed he'd slept in the previous night and I found myself trying to make a decision. Stay in the other one, or maybe try and get closer to him.

I chose the second decision and crawled under the covers next to him. He looked confused for a moment then his expression looked hesitant. I didn't understand his reaction. I thought this was what he wanted. Unless he was more like Tyler than I thought.

"Lela, we have to talk," he said.

"Am I moving too fast? I'm sorry, I'm really out of practice when it comes to this. I can back off if you—"

"I think we should break up."

I stared at him, puzzled because that was the last thing I'd expected him to say. He'd been the one who asked me out in the first place. He'd claimed he never got over me and he'd made the first move when we'd kissed in the kitchen. Men were confusing.

"Wha...why? We've only been dating for two days."

"And I never should have asked you out in the first place."

"Curtis, I'm lost. Please elaborate."

He sat up straighter then locked eyes with me, his gaze filled with a sadness I couldn't read.

"When I said Gallard talked to me about taking care of you...I sort of lied. He told me about your boyfriend and how you gave up on dating. And he asked me to try and change your mind. At first I was more than happy to make a pass at you, but deep down I knew that the two of you were closer than either of you were willing to let on."

I was even more annoyed than ever. Gallard was trying to play matchmaker behind my back? Why was it that everyone in the whole world wanted us to be together except for Gallard and me?

"Be honest with me, okay?" Curtis continued. "Do you or do you not love Gallard?"

"It's not that simple, Curt. It's complicated." It was a cliché answer, but the best I could come up with.

"Try me. Maybe I can give you some advice."

"He's my best friend, and I would do anything for him, and he for me." I fought back the tears as I continued. "I...I love him, Curtis. So much that it hurts."

He grew quiet again and we lay there in silence. Admitting it out loud had been difficult and I was terrified that I would regret it.

Tears filled my eyes and I looked down to hide them. Curtis lifted my chin up with his finger and wiped away the tears with some tissues from the night stand.

"Don't be afraid to love," he said. These words were the same that David had said before he'd gone unconscious. I'd been too distraught by the fact that I thought he was dying that I hadn't paid attention. It finally made sense to me now.

"Gallard. What kind of a name is that?" he asked, clearly trying to lighten the mood. "If you ask me, his brother got the better deal with Jordan."

I burst out laughing. "It's French. It's better than Gaylord, though, right?"

Curtis shrugged. "Gallard, Gaylord; either way, I'm not sure why you're still here with me. Go talk to him and take a chance. I am about five hundred percent sure he feels the same way."

"Maybe someday I will." I finished drying my eyes then tossed the tissues in the trash. "For now, I want to sleep. If you don't mind if I stay here."

"Not at all. I am an involuntary cuddler, though. Don't be surprised if I invade your personal space."

I kissed his cheek before shifting into a comfortable position.

"I can't believe you broke up with me after just two days!" I said in a joking manor. We started laughing again then went into a lighter conversation. We talked until we were both tired and Curtis fell asleep first.

One man down. One to go, Lucian said.

I'm so tired of men. I think I'll become a nun. I am Catholic, after all.

Smart idea. But first you have to bring me back and —

I know I know. Goodnight, creep.

A few hours later, I heard a loud clicking noise and groaned in annoyance. I was still tired and wanted to sleep some more. The last thing I wanted was to have to block out irritating sounds. I tried to turn over, but was constricted by someone's arm around me. I realized that Curtis was lying extremely close to me. He hadn't been kidding when he said he was a cuddler.

I gently moved his arm then shifted back into my spot, adjusting from being jerked out of sleep. Then I realized that I felt exposed, so I looked down to see why. I gasped when I found that I was wearing nothing but my underwear. I looked around and saw my shirt and sweats on the edge of the bed.

"What the..." I whispered to myself. None of it made sense. I couldn't remember undressing myself. I glanced over at him and froze when I saw that his shirt was off and he was in nothing but boxers.

That was when I noticed that he looked different, colorless and he was colder. I reached out to touch his face and pulled my hand back when I felt a warm liquid. It was dark in the room, but I didn't have to see it to know what it was; blood.

"Curtis?" I said, my voice cracking from fear. I shook him violently, but he didn't wake up. "Curtis, wake up!"

I sat up and turned his head towards me. On his neck was a distinct bite mark; a mark that I knew all too well and had one of my own. I put my head to his chest and listened for any signs of life. I began to cry when I heard a faint, but present heart beat and fumbled for the phone. I picked it up and started to dial, but nothing happened. There wasn't even a dial tone. I sensed the same feeling of being watched and goosebumps crept up my spine. Just as I was about to turn on the light, I heard the clicking noise again, followed by a familiar giggle.

"Sorry, phone's not working!" the intruder said. I jumped then scrambled to turn on the light. Emiline was standing in the corner of the room, taking pictures with my cell phone. My instinct told me to run, but my brain reminded me that it would be pointless. She was faster than me and would get to the door before I even took a step.

"What are you doing here?" I asked in a low voice.

She snapped the phone shut and put it into her back pocket. She began to twirl her hair again as she walked towards me. "I had to keep him quiet. Feeding on him was my best option." She stopped in front of the bed closest to the window then sat on it, crossing her legs. "I hope you don't mind, but I did a little photo shoot."

I swallowed hard, but didn't move. I had no idea what her state of mind was and didn't want to risk pushing her to the deep end by making any sudden attempt to escape.

"What photo shoot?" I asked, keeping my voice calm. I didn't want her to know just how terrified I really was.

"The one of you and Curtis! I thought it was so cute how the two of you were cuddling in your sleep, and I thought, you know who else would think this was cute? Gallard."

Now my stomach was really turning. She wasn't just crazy; she was the jealous kind of crazy. The kind of crazy that made front page news. I'd thought Lydian was jealous, but Emiline was taking it to a whole new level.

"I think he would *love* to see these pictures, don't you?" she continued. "They're just so adorable that I can't stand it!" She came towards me in one swift move and grabbed my hand, leading me over to the other bed. I didn't fight her. Cooperation was probably the only thing that would save my life. She grabbed my clothes off the bed then tossed them at me. "Put them on, I got what I needed."

I obeyed, eager to cover up as if my clothes would erase whatever had happened while I was out of it. She pulled the phone out of her pocket and opened it, clicking a few buttons to get to the pictures. I became sick with dread as I waited to see what kind of pictures she'd taken.

She clicked on the first one and I held back a groan. Somehow she'd moved the unconscious Curtis next to me into poses that looked very intimate. Each one she scrolled through was worse than the last. I was mortified. How had I managed to sleep through all of this? I must have been so exhausted that the outside world had been dead to me for those few hours.

"Curtis woke up before I could start taking pictures, so I had to take care of him first. You, on the other hand, were fast asleep. I didn't want to risk waking you as well, so I injected you with a little something to keep you unconscious." She scooted closer to me so that I could see the phone screen. "What do you think? Should I text them to him? I think he'd be interested to know that the girl he loves has been screwing around while he was away, don't you think?"

"What are you, twelve? This is so juvenile."

She gave a nervous laugh, twirling her hair as she did. I could not believe this girl. It was almost like she'd stepped out of an episode of *Wicked Attraction*. "I turned when I was ten," she explained. "My mother did it, but her boyfriend didn't like having me around. He saw me a nuisance. I woke up one day and they were both gone. I was on my own for nearly fifty years before Gallard found me. He was the first man that didn't treat me like a child. I'm *not* a child. I'm a hundred and thirty years old!"

She was starting to raise her voice now. I was afraid at any moment she was going to snap my neck, but I held my ground. I was determined to somehow talk some sense into her. But I had to think of the right thing to say to calm her down. I decided it would be best not to speak unless she asked me a question.

"He likes them young, you know," she said, her voice softer now. "That's the only reason he paid any attention to you. He made me believe that he loved me, and then he left me." She giggled again then looked at me. "You're too old now. That's why he left you. He probably wanted you when you looked as young as me, but now you're just old and mortal. In a few years, you'll be senile and wrinkled; hideous."

Who is this broad? Lucian asked.

Gallard's ex apparently. I doubt it, though.

Hah! Shows his taste in women.

I wanted to roll my eyes, but was afraid it would provoke her. I didn't know why she was doing this. I'd told her she could take a pass at Gallard if she wanted to. Curtis may have broken up with me with the idea that I was going to run off to Gallard and profess my love, but that wasn't on my agenda. I was going to find him, but for another reason.

"It makes sense now, doesn't it; why he left you," Emiline continued. "Don't you think it's odd that just when you turned mortal, he decided to take off?"

I never thought about it that way. He'd left because he wanted me to be safe while they were off trying to find a way to stop Samil. He'd promised that he would come back; he never broke his promises. So what if he hadn't answered my phone call. My mortality had nothing to do with it.

"Think about it, Lola. You fell for the same French charm that he used on me. He looked at you like you were the most wonderful thing in the world, he flirted with you, but never acted on his feelings." She looked me in the eye and asked, "Am I right?"

I am starting to like this girl. She has some good points, Lucian said.

She's going to kill me and you're agreeing with her crazy theories? You don't believe her?

She was so spot on that I wanted to vomit. She was winning. She was getting inside my head and causing me to doubt everything that I thought I knew. A second ago, I was ready to go off on her, but I had to admit she was getting to me.

"I know I'm right," she continued. "The only difference between you and me is that he and I, well...we've already been through this. That is, unless you already have. I doubt it though, you seem like too much of a prude to me."

I thought of New Years and smirked to myself. We may not have gone as far as he and Emiline had, if she wasn't just full of it, but I was no prude.

"After you send the pictures then what?" I asked, breaking my rule not to speak. "What are you going to do to me?"

She threw her head back and laughed, causing me to jump from her sudden outburst.

"I just want to see the look on your face when he leaves *you* for *me*." She shifted on the bed so that she was on her hands and knees, her face inches away from my ear. "And then, after you've experienced the rejection, I'm going to eat you."

At this point, I was done listening to her crazy ramblings. I needed to drink some more blood so that I could have a better chance of fighting her. I remembered that I'd put the cooler of blood bags in the bathroom. If I could get her to let me go in there, I would be able to drink. If I couldn't overpower her, then I would at least want to get out of the room and get help. Curtis was dying and needed a hospital soon.

"I need to pee," I finally said. I stood up but she grabbed my arm before I could walk away.

How can you relieve yourself at a time like this? Lucian asked.

It's a diversion, genius!

"Let me walk you to the bathroom," she said, linking her arm with mine. Her demeanor was suddenly friendly. She walked me as she said she would and let go of my arm before I closed the door behind me.

I lifted the toilet seat, letting it clink against the tank so that she wouldn't think I had an ulterior motive then pulled the cooler from underneath my back pack. I clicked it open then took one of the bags out, taking the top off as quickly as I could. Tilting it back, I guzzled down about half of it.

I could feel the strength of the blood already coursing through me as I recapped the bag. I put it back into the cooler, contemplating what my next move would be. I happened to put my hands in my pockets and was startled when I found something in it, restricting my hand. I pulled out the object and smiled when I discovered what it was; the pocket knife David had given me.

Perfect! Lucian said. *Now when you go out there, stab her in the neck!*

It's a wonder that I didn't turn into a serial killer because of you.

"Hurry up!" Emiline shouted through the door. "I'm not done talking with you yet!"

I flushed the toilet then put the knife back in my pocket, pulling my shirt down further to hide it and opened the door. She yanked me out of the bathroom and led me across the room before forcing me to sit on the bed once more.

She smiled at me, flipping the phone open and said, "I want you to watch me as I hit send. And then I'm going to send the next picture, and the next picture. There are about six of them. He should be thrilled to see your extracurricular activities."

I sucked in an angry breath through my nose. I was almost at my breaking point. If she said another word, I was going to explode with rage.

"You should be thanking me," she said. "I'm only helping you show him that he's lost his chance. And when he's heartbroken, I'll be the one there to comfort him." She clicked a button and my hand flew up to grab the phone from her, but she was faster. She grabbed my arm and twisted it, dislocating my shoulder then threw me on the floor. I yelled in pain and glared at
her as she hit send over and over, giggling as she did it.

I'd had it. I was done cooperating, so I lunged at her, catching her off guard and pushing her off the bed. The fury that I was feeling overpowered the pain in my shoulder. She threw me off of her and I collided with the dresser. The blow knocked the wind out of me, and I gasped for air. Before I could recover, she grabbed me by the throat and started strangling me. I tried to pull her hands off, but she was too strong. She was focused on my face, so I pulled the knife from my pocket, flipped it open, and stabbed her in the stomach. She let out a horrified shriek as she dropped me to the ground.

"Now you've made me *very* angry!" she yelled. She shoved me against the wall then pulled the knife out, holding it to my throat. I tensed up, preparing myself for the inevitable throat-slicing that she had in store for me, but she did nothing. She just held it there, her lip quivering. Tears began to stream out of her eyes and I stared at her in confusion. I never knew what to expect from her. She went from being giddy to angry to hysterical within a few minutes. She was psychotic!

"There's no need to get violent, Lola!" she said, wiping the tears away with the back of her hand.

"It's *Lela*," I snarled at her. She giggled again, her happy mood seeming to return. My eyes darted around as I tried to get a sense of where I was. She had me against the wall just underneath the window. The curtain rod had somehow been loosened during the struggle, and I could see sunlight peeking from behind it.

"It's too late. I've already sent the pictures. You're wasting your energy fighting me."

She moved the knife from my throat to my stomach and my eyes widened. I don't know what would have been worse, a stab to the gut or a slit in my throat. Either one would hurt.

"Go to hell," I said. She gave me a horrified look, as if I'd just insulted her mother. She took the knife and plunged it into me, just under my ribcage. I choked on a scream, the pain in my side stinging. I began to sweat as I fought through it. I needed to stay conscious and lucid if I were to follow through with my plan. I then somehow found the strength to grab onto the curtain and yank it down. The sunlight poured into the room and Emiline let out a blood-curdling screech. I watched as she burst into flames, the fire consuming her entire body. It took only a few moments before she was nothing but a pile of ash on the carpet.

Ashes to ashes, Lucian said.

Dust to dust.

I sat on the floor for a bit, still in a daze over what had just happened. I'd thought that Samil had been insane, but Emiline was a new level of crazy. The fact that Gallard had dated her only made it worse. Why would he have been with someone like her? I'd thought he was a man of sound judgment and better taste. Then again, Lydian had dated some whacks before she met Jordan.

The pain in my side reminded me that she'd stuck me with a knife and I pulled it out. I lifted my shirt to assess the damage and watched in amazement as the wound began to heal. It wasn't as quickly as when I'd been a vampire, but it was fast enough that I could find the energy to stand. I hurried over to Curtis to check his pulse. He was still alive.

I spotted my phone on the floor next to the bed and quickly dialed 911. I did my best to explain the situation without mentioning the involvement of my recently desiccated attacker.

After I hung up, I sat on the bed next to Curtis, hoping that he would stay alive long enough for help to arrive.

I'd been wrong about being able to have a normal life. I was mortal, yes, but that didn't mean that I could be an ordinary person. Like it or not, I was forever part of the immortal world. No matter how hard I'd tried they'd still managed to be a threat, and Curtis might be paying the price for that. Whether it was Samil, Lucian, or crazy exes; my life would always be dangerous because of who I was.

• • •

I sat next to Curtis' hospital bed with his parents as we waited for him to wake up. He'd gone into shock from the loss of blood, but the doctors were able to stabilize him. For now, he was going to be okay; he just needed to wake up so that I could believe that.

Having forgotten for a few hours about the pictures Emiline had taken, I looked through my recently sent messages. She hadn't been lying when she'd said that she'd sent them. All six of them had been successfully sent to Gallard's phone. He hadn't replied, but I couldn't help but imagine what he was thinking if he'd seen them. But then again, he hadn't replied to the other messages. Hopefully he wouldn't see these either.

Curtis began to stir and his parents rushed to his side. I remained seated since I wanted them to talk with him first. I wasn't sure how much he'd seen or experienced, but I doubted he would say anything to his parents about a vampire. They weren't the most religious people but enough to not believe such a notion.

His parents asked him a few questions, which he vaguely answered. I was right; he hadn't seen much. He only remembered that a woman had broken in and attacked him. I locked eyes with him for a second and he smiled before saying to his parents, "Could you give us a minute?" His parent agreed then his mom kissed his forehead before they both left. I moved my chair next to the bed and took his hand.

"How did you manage to get away barely unscathed?" he asked.

"I didn't. You just can't see my scrapes."

This wasn't a lie. The stab wound on my side was still healing and I'd needed several stitches. The blood had saved me from suffering major damage, but not from being left with a gaping hole. It would take more time to heal. One of the doctors had put my shoulder back into place, so I had my arm in a sling. I also had several bruises on my back, arms and legs. Without my clothes, I would have looked like I'd been hit by a car. I had to wear jeans and a long-sleeve shirt to cover up my injuries.

"What happened back there? That girl was so strong; she overpowered me in a second."

"She hurt me as well. If it weren't for the pocketknife David had given me, I wouldn't have been able to fight her off. I stabbed her and she ran away."

He whistled in amazement. "Damn, I wouldn't want to

mess with you."

I smiled and kissed his hand. "You won't have to. I'm leaving soon, and you won't be put in danger anymore."

The smile left his face. "What do you mean put me in danger? Was our attack not random?"

I shook my head as I looked down. "Curtis I have…enemies. I made a few while I was away, and I told myself that by returning, I could forget about them and go back to the life that I'd left behind when I was fourteen."

"Well, then I'll protect you. We can get the police involved and they can make sure they don't find you."

I gave him a half smile. It was thoughtful of him to want to protect me, but in reality, he was the one that needed protecting. As long as I was around, he would be in danger. I hadn't learned that lesson from what had happened to my parents, but it was becoming clearer now.

"It's not that easy. Almost everyone that I care about has been hurt by these enemies; my mom, my dad; and they almost killed you. They aren't going to just go away." I paused before saying, "Not unless I go away first."

A mournful look crossed his face and he leaned back against the pillow.

"I had a feeling you weren't going to stay for long. Are you going to join your brothers and Gallard in their search for Robin?"

"Yes, I am. I thought living with you would keep me hidden, but I was wrong. I'm done hiding, and I'm ready to start fighting."

I took both of his hands in mine and stared at him until he made eye contact with me. "Since I saved your life, I want to ask you a favor," I said with a jocular tone. But I was serious about the favor.

"Name it and I'll do it," he said. This was the hard part. When I'd said goodbye to my life in Florida the first time, I'd done it with the intention of it being temporary. But this time, it had to be for good. My brothers were planning to leave, and I realized that the best thing was for me to do the same.

"Forget that you ever knew the Sharmentino family," I said. "Pretend that you had a bunch of friends when you were young; that you had an awesome childhood, but forget that Aaron was your best friend.

"Forget that you and I danced at that party, and that you kissed me. Forget that I moved in with you and for a while we played house. Forget that…" At this point I was crying and so was he. My voice was cracking from the sobs I was trying to fight. "Forget that we dated for two days and that I saved you at the hotel, and live your life as if I died there while you survived; as if the woman had killed me then tried to kill you but failed."

"How can I do that?" he asked. "Your family is a huge part of my life; they saved me from my heroin addiction. Aaron is like a brother to me and you —" he lost his voice.

I hadn't expected our parting to be so emotional. Curtis had been a big part of my childhood, and we'd reconnected over that month we'd been roommates. Nostalgia was likely the factor in this. He symbolized my old life and how simple and uncomplicated it used to be. He was the one person I was sure I could save, and I was determined to do it.

"Goodbye, Curtis. Have an amazing life. I wish you all the joy in the world."

I let go of his hand then forced myself to walk out of the room. I closed the door behind me and headed down the hall, into the elevator, and down to the first floor. By the time I was in the car, I was sobbing uncontrollably. I leaned against the steering wheel and let myself release all the frustration I'd felt about everything in my life; my mortality, my recent brushes with death, my leaving my old life behind. I had to get it all out before I went against Samil. I couldn't have any bottled up emotions getting in the way.

Chapter Twelve

I stopped at the house in Tampa to pack some clean clothes before heading to the airport. I had to buy a ticket there instead of online in fear that Curtis would arrive before I left. I couldn't run into him again. I said goodbye, and the only reason I would return to Florida would be to pick up the rest of my things and move on.

I was on auto pilot as I went through security. I had one goal, and that goal was to get to India and help get Robin back. I was on a mission and determined not to let anything get in my way. I'd struggled with so many emotions over the past several days, but I had a whole new outlook now. I'd been hopeless Lela, confident Lela. Now I was angry Lela. Emiline had been the last straw, and I was tired of being messed with. I was tired of my family and friends being in danger

I got on the plane and ignored everyone for the entire flight. I didn't even amuse myself with one of the free movies they offered. I refused to eat or drink anything…anything but blood. I'd said before that I didn't want to become dependent on it; that I wanted to live as normally as I could, but everything was different now. I needed to be as strong as possible so that I wouldn't be overpowered again. If it weren't for the blood, Emiline would have stabbed me to death, and I would be on my way into the ground instead of on a plane to India.

While I'd stopped in Tampa, I'd put myself on a new phone plan as well as bought an iPhone. The one we had in Las Vegas didn't have good service, and I also wanted a phone that I could put a pass-code on. There was no way I was going to put myself in a situation where someone could take photos of me again. Deleting them wasn't even enough to rid my mind of them.

The only ticket I could get on short notice took me to Mumbai. When the plane landed, I grabbed my luggage than preceded into town to find a car rental service. There were no buses that traveled to Goa, so I would have to drive. It was a nine and a half hour trip, but even though I hadn't slept on the plane, I was full of energy.

So, are you telling your friends about our deal? Lucian asked.

Hell no! Gallard would give himself up and I can't have that. I know I can't talk David out of it and Lydian made it clear that she's not offering…so that leaves me.

No! Lela, you cannot be one of the donors!

Why not? If it means my sister will live, then I'll do it.

I had to use the GPS app on my phone to find my way. India traffic was extremely different than in the states. There seemed to be hardly any traffic signs, and I had to often slam on my breaks to keep from hitting someone who came out of nowhere. Cars were constantly changing directions without warning, and I was having mini heart-attacks from all the near misses I had. It didn't help that people on bikes or on foot would randomly walk into the road, causing traffic to slow down significantly.

After a few hours, I started to get the hang of it, and it almost became natural. Still, I would never complain about the traffic in Florida again. It also helped that when it got dark, the streets were practically clear and I was finally able to just coast down the road.

As I drove, I thought about what I would say upon seeing Gallard again. If he had seen the pictures, I was obligated to give him an explanation. It would be weird to let something as blatant as that go unmentioned. I may have been frustrated about the unanswered calls, but he was still my best friend. That wasn't going to change. I was just surprised that after two phone calls and six text messages, he still hadn't replied to any of them. No one was replying to me, and I found it a bit annoying. Had they made a pact to ignore me? The suspense of the progress of their mission was killing me, and I hoped that they'd just been too busy to bother returning a call.

I arrived in Goa around nine o'clock that night. The city was crawling with tourists, and there were more of them than Indians. There was a parade going on in the area, so I had to take a detour around to get to the city. The music was so loud that it radiated throughout the car. Unsure of where to go next, I pulled over on the side of the road next to a restaurant then looked at the GPS to find a better place to stop. I'd heard that the beach was something no one should miss seeing when visiting Goa, so I downloaded directions and headed there.

There was a crowd of people at the beach, so I had to drive

around for about ten minutes before finding a spot. I popped open the cooler and took a few sips from one of the bags before getting out. I was probably drinking more than necessary, but I didn't like the weak feeling that I had when I was off it. I didn't want to find myself in another situation where I was helpless.

I made my way onto the sand and a huge concert came into view. There was a massive stage set up on the beach and about two hundred people were dancing in front of it. Green and blue lights flashed everywhere as the performer sang something in Punjabi. I didn't recognize the singer, but whoever he was, he was good. But I wasn't in the mood for loud music and dancing, so I wandered off in the opposite direction, finding a quieter spot and put my feet in the water. It was warm and soothing as the waves rolled up against my ankles, getting higher and higher each time. The ocean was beautiful; maybe even more beautiful than South Beach. I couldn't believe that I was on the other side of the world.

I was getting distracted. I wasn't here for vacation time, I was here on business. I reluctantly pulled myself away from the tempting waters, dialing Lydian's number as I walked back towards my car. It rang a few times then went to voicemail. Determined to get her to answer me, I called her again. I got the same results, so I redialed without giving it a second thought. Lydian wasn't the most patient person the world and was bound to get annoyed at some point.

She answered the seventh call and I smiled to myself over my victory.

"For all that is holy, will you *stop* calling me?" she yelled. "One message would have sufficed!"

"Sufficed? That's a big word, coming from you."

She scoffed at me then asked, "Where are you? Why do I hear ocean?"

I put my shoes back on as I came up to the pavement then sat on one of the log benches. "I'll give you three guesses. If you fail, you have to tell me where *you* are."

"Like I'd tell you! It's supposed to be a secret. We don't want Samil torturing you until you give us up!"

She grew silent. I wasn't worried that she would hang up, she was too curious to pass up on my little game. It was only a matter of time before she would give in. I had nothing but time, so I waited to see what would happen.

"All right, fine. I'll try to guess. Hmm…Los Angeles?"

"Nope, two more guesses."

She groaned and I listened as she hummed while she thought. She must have moved to a different location because I suddenly heard music in the background. It almost sounded like the music at the concert. I felt the familiar tug and wondered if she was in the same place as me.

"How about the Bahamas?" she finally asked.

"Wrong again! One more guess."

She groaned again in frustration, but didn't back out of the game. I was sensing that she was bored or else she wouldn't have been so compliant.

"Oh, I get it!" she said, chuckling. "This is a joke. You're at South Beach. Am I right?"

"Sorry, but you're wrong; you're very wrong, now you have to tell me where you are."

The tug was weaker now and I was certain that she was at the concert. I got up from the bench and started making my way back in that direction. I hadn't expected it to be so easy to find them and I was relieved that I wouldn't have to waste time chasing them all over the Middle East.

"How's the concert?" I asked with a hint of cockiness.

"How did you know I was at a concert?" she asked, trying to hide the shock in her voice. "Oh my lord, you're here in Goa aren't you?"

I found the party again and started searching the crowd of dancing people to see if I could spot her. The music was deafening, so I said, "I can't hear you anymore, text me your location and I'll come find you."

I hung up and continued to scan the crowd while I waited for her text. I wondered if she was there with Jordan or if my brothers were with her. It wasn't really Gallard's kind of thing, so I didn't expect to run into him. I wasn't ready to see him anyway despite the several weeks we'd been apart.

My phone buzzed and I read her message. *Don't find me, I'll find you.* I rolled my eyes and put my phone back in my pocket. She could never do anything the easy way. But since she was willing to meet up, I chose to stay where I was and wait for her to make an appearance.

I didn't want anyone asking questions about how I'd hurt my arm, so I took off the sling and threw it away in the nearest trash can. I rolled my shoulder a tad and winced as pain shot through it. I was still pretty banged up despite the amount of blood I'd had. I was glad that the bruises were beginning to fade at least, but it still hurt to bend over with the cut on my side.

Oddly enough, I spotted Lydian before she spotted me. She was slightly swaying to the music while she looked around and I decided to scare her. I skirted the crowd so that I was behind her then began dancing suggestively against her.

"What the hell!" she shouted, turning around. When she saw me she laughed. "I thought you were some pervert. You're lucky I didn't clock you."

"Miss me?" I asked.

"No, you're going to get me in big trouble!" she said. "If Gallard knew you were here, he would think I blabbed." She folded her arms and sighed. "But maybe it's a good thing you're here. He's been super cranky for the past few days and I don't know why."

I stopped breathing. The pictures; it had to be about the pictures. It was too much of a coincidence that they'd been sent only three days ago simultaneously to his apparent mood change. I had to play dumb for just a little longer so I asked, "Why is that do you think?"

She shrugged. "Who knows? One day, he was just super unpleasant and he even snapped at Jordan. *Jordan*! The sweetest guy in the world. And then Jordan snapped back and then they yelled at each other in French. It was kind of sexy and kind of scary at the same time. Whatever they were talking about, Gallard apologized for yelling, but he's still not his normal self."

Now I was even more nervous about talking to him. If he was mad about the pictures, he might not even want to see me. But at the same time, I felt like I didn't really have any explaining to do. He'd encouraged me to go out with Curtis. He'd even joked about me marrying Curtis.

"You should take me to him. Maybe I can figure out what's up," I said.

"Only if you drive us. I don't want to walk all the way back."

I nodded then we started walking towards the parking lot. While we were walking, I noticed she was looking me up and down. I knew my injuries were covered up, so it couldn't be that.

"What are you staring at?" I asked.

"You! You're all…can I be honest with you?"

"You always are anyway, what about?"

"Lela, you look anorexic. You're crazy thin and you were already a great size before. Did they run out of food in America or something?"

"I lost a few pounds. I'm fine though, really."

We found my car and she got into the passenger seat. I winced from the soreness as I got in the driver's seat then started the motor. I half wished that I'd kept the sling, but I had to put up a tough front. If I showed any sign of weakness, there would be no stopping them from putting me on a plane and sending me back to Tampa.

She gave me the directions to where they were staying and I was able to find it easily with her guidance. I parked in the driveway and stared in awe at the beautiful house. It was three stories high and had a large colorful drape over the entrance. The roof was rounded and made of clay. There were huge palm trees on the porch and the door was covered in intricate gold-plated designs.

"How did you manage to score this house?" I asked.

She jiggled on the door and found that it was locked so she knocked.

"It's Samil's. Gallard said he has vacation homes all over the world, and this is one of them. We had to convince his house keeper that we were friends of his so that he would let us in."

I was about to ask how long they'd been crashing there when the door opened and Jordan stood in the doorway.

"Look who I just happened to run into," Lydian said, trying to expel any guilt. Jordan smiled and gave me a hug. It hurt, but I did my best not to show it. I'd missed Jordan. I couldn't tell if it was just his tank top or if he'd gained muscle because I could have sworn he was larger than when I'd last seen him.

"How did you find us?" he asked. "Doesn't matter, I'm glad you're here. I don't think we can take Gallard's mood for much longer."

"That bad huh?" I asked. He nodded and stepped out of the way to let me in. I then realized that I'd been in somewhat of a funk as well. Maybe our bond consisted of sharing moods as well. I did tend to be happier when he was happy and sad if he was sad.

I checked out the house as I walked in. The décor on the inside was even more impressive than the outside. The walls were painted yellow, and there were real trees in each room. The couches were made of expensive silk and there was a huge flat screen TV in the living room. Lydian informed me that in addition to what I saw, there were six bedrooms, each with a king-sized bed and an adjoining bathroom. Every room had a different color scheme, and a door leading to a deck next to an in-ground pool. I had to admit, Samil had good. Then again, so did Patrick Bateman in *American Psycho*.

"Where are my brothers?" I asked Jordan.

"They're out feeding. They left about an hour ago, so they shouldn't be long. I'm sure they'll be happy to see you."

"I doubt it. Aaron's probably going to be pissed that Curtis even let me leave. I was given strict orders not to follow you, and here I am." I hadn't intended to bring up Curtis and now that I had, the look on his face when I'd left flooded my memory. I couldn't let it get to me; I had to stay emotionally sound.

"I got your message, by the way," Jordan said with a smirk. "What did you say again? 'Heeeeeey. I looove yooou!'"

I groaned in embarrassment. It had slipped my mind because I'd been extremely drunk at the time of the call and then rushed to the E.R. for an iron overdose.

"That message was for Aaron, by the way."

"You meant to drunk dial your brother? You Sharmentinos are weird."

"Why did you come looking for us?" Lydian asked, changing the subject. I sank into the cushion on the fancy couch, eager to get off of my feet. This was my first chance to relax in the past few days and was going on ninety-six hours without sleep. The human part of me was beginning to crash while the semi-vampire part of me worked hard to keep me awake.

"It's kind of a long story. I would rather wait until everyone's here so I can tell it just once."

"Fine by me," Jordan said. "Why don't you go see Gallard. He's in the room at the end of the hall. I think he said he was taking a shower, so you might be able to surprise him."

Lydian laughed and said, "Oh, she would *love* to catch him getting out of the shower, wouldn't you, Lela?"

A breathy laugh escaped my lips and I got up from the couch. Oddly enough, I found Lydian's inappropriate remarks refreshing. There wasn't anything vindictive behind them unlike Emmeline's, and she was actually of sound mind, for the most part.

I went down the hall and found the room Jordan directed me to. The door was cracked so I slowly pushed it open. Gallard wasn't anywhere to be seen, but I could hear the water running in the bathroom. I wandered over to the bed and lay down on it, closing my eyes.

The truth was that I was afraid to sleep. The past few times that I'd allowed myself to, I'd had nightmares about Robin and I'd been drugged then forced into taking racy pictures. Sleep was becoming a vulnerable state for me, and I wanted to avoid it for as long as I could.

My eyes flew open when I heard the water shut off. I prepared myself for what he would say upon seeing me. Would he be angry? Would he throw me out of the house and make me go to back to Florida? He had never been the type of guy to fly off the handle, but according to Lydian and Jordan he hadn't been himself lately. If he was angry enough to yell at Jordan, there was nothing stopping him from yelling at me. And I was prepared to yell back if needed.

He came out of the bathroom wearing just a pair of black jeans and my heart raced. For a second I forgot that I was mad at him. Why did he have to have this affect on me?

When he saw me, he stopped and stared as if he were trying to figure out if what he was seeing was real or not. I swung my legs over the side of the bed and stood up, slowly walking towards him. I hadn't planned on what I would say to him upon seeing him for the first time.

"You...you're here," he said almost silently. "You're all right?"

I was confused by his question. There was no way he could have known I'd been sick or injured. All I could do was nod and he let out a sigh of relief, which confused me even more. What would he be relieved about?

"You shouldn't have come here," he said coldly. "You should be in Florida with Curtis where it's safe."

This wasn't like him. He was never this cold with me before, and I didn't like it. I didn't want to admit that his words hurt so I decided to be equally as harsh towards him.

"Well, I was safe up until I ran into your ex," I snapped. This wasn't part of my strategy. I wasn't going to bring up Emiline until later on, but his attitude was causing me to start blabbing.

"What ex?" he asked as he pulled on a shirt. I crossed my arms and forced a frown on my face.

"Emiline, the one that looked like she was twelve. The one with psychotic tendencies."

"Emiline? How did she find you?" he asked, suddenly sounding very concerned.

"It was a chance encounter," I lied. "She told me about all the fun times you used to have way back when. That was before she nearly killed Curtis then tried to kill me. Luckily I caught her off guard and exposed her to the sunlight. Now she's history."

"Lela, I'm so sorry! I hadn't seen her in years before we ran into each other at the blood bar in Orlando. She was a very sick person. I never imagined that she would approach you."

He looked so guilty as if he'd been the one that sent her after me. I wanted to abandon my interrogation all together, but I needed to know the truth. He was the only person I could get the real story from.

"In case you were wondering, she was the mastermind behind the pictures. It was juvenile of her to send them, but I just wanted you to know that they weren't intended for you to receive."

Now he was frowning and he asked, "What pictures?"

I scoffed then sat on the bed again. I couldn't tell if he was genuinely uninformed or if he was pretending not to know.

"Come on, you're telling me that you didn't get those six text messages with the pictures of Curtis and me?" I asked, hostility filling my tone.

"Pictures of you and Curtis doing what?" he asked. This took me by surprise. He was more curious about the pictures than the fact that he hadn't received them. I detected that same hint of jealously he'd had when he first found out Curtis had asked me to move in.

"Lela, I honestly have no idea what you're talking about. I lost my phone in Bradford two weeks ago. I accidently left it in the hotel and realized it by the time we were already out of the country."

I could feel the knot in my stomach unraveling by the second. He hadn't seen the pictures. He probably hadn't gotten my ultimatum about his feelings either. I thought he was being cold because he was mad about the texts when in fact he hadn't even gotten them.

"Well this is awkward," I said, wanting to crawl under a rock. I wished that I'd asked if he'd received the texts first before even hinting about what they were. Now he knew that there were pictures that I didn't want him to see, and he was probably going crazy with curiosity. "Can we pretend like the past five minutes of our conversation didn't happen?"

His expression softened then he pulled me into one of his hugs that I'd missed terribly. In that moment, I forgot about all the anger and frustrations I'd had. I'd missed my friend and two and a half months was a long time to be away from him.

"You really shouldn't be here," he whispered into my hair. "But I'm glad that you are."

I pulled back enough to look at his face but still had my arms around his waist.

"I have to ask…did you really use to be in a relationship with her? " I asked. "The way she talked made it sound like the two of you were…pretty serious."

"Hell no!" he said chuckling. "I helped her out because she was living in the streets. It only took me two weeks to realize how crazy she was and I high-tailed it out of there."

I gave him an unabashed smile of relief. I suddenly felt stupid for ever considering that she had been telling the truth. I'd allowed myself to be jealous of a crazy fifteen year old-she was obviously older but didn't act her age.

"Now that I've explained my history with the schizoid girl, are you going to tell me what these pictures were about?" he asked.

"It's nothing interesting," I said quickly. "Long story short, Emiline drugged me, she took provocative pictures, which she then sent to your phone, and now they're ancient history. I would like nothing but to forget it ever happened."

As the minutes passed, I could feel all the angst I had over the past few days fading away. I was still on a mission to tell everyone my plan as soon as possible, but I wasn't as angry as I'd been before. I wondered if this had to do with the fact that I hadn't had any blood in a few hours. I hadn't noticed before, but I found that whenever I was drinking it, it made me grouchy and somewhat passive. David had said that I only needed four ounces every once in a while, and I'd all but exceeded that limit. I was getting too dependent on it like I'd feared.

"Why are you here?" Gallard asked. "Is it because you missed me or…because you missed Jordan. Rumor has it that you, quote, *looooove* him."

"He told you about that?" I asked in horror. I should have known he couldn't keep it to himself.

"Miss Sharmentino, I never would have thought you would drunk dial someone. You have to know you're never living that down."

"Yeah, I figured." I forced a glare. "You're in trouble, by the way. Curtis told me you tried to set us up. It didn't work. We lasted all of two days."

His eyes widened and he looked away.

"I should have known it wouldn't work," he said. "Now I don't have an excuse."

I turned his face to mine, forcing him to look at me.

"An excuse for what?"

I heard several voices in the front of the house and figured my brothers had showed up, so the two of us went out to greet them. I was glad we'd cleared everything up about Emiline, but something was still bothering me. I was planning behind his back to resurrect Lucian and that meant there was a chance I might die.

I couldn't admit my feelings for him now and I prayed to God that he wouldn't say anything either. If we were just friend, he would take my death easier. I hated doing this to him, but I had to put my sister first, no matter what the cost.

You're really going to die with things unresolved? Lucian asked.

You must have had someone you would die for, right?

I did. But she was taken from me anyway. I suppose making this easier for him is the civil thing to do.

Well, there you go. It's what I have to do.

Chapter Thirteen

Seeing my brothers again was the icing on top of the whole trip. I didn't realize how much I'd missed them until I was in the arms of both of them at the same time. Kevin was a lot stronger than he'd been when he left and his eyes and hair had changed completely. Other than that, he was the same old Kevin. Aaron wasn't any different though. I'd hoped that somehow the old Aaron would make an appearance, but I'd gotten my hopes up for nothing. He was changed for good, and I doubted that he would ever be the brother I grew up with again.

    We did some catching up on what we did over the past month and a half before we'd parted, but I left out the gory details. I would go into that later once I got to the part about my plan. Despite the several hints that I'd driven for almost ten hours, no one let me to go bed. It was like everyone forgot that I was human because they were all eager to know more about my sudden appearance. I wanted nothing more than to sleep, but I forced myself to stay awake just a little bit longer in fear that they would die from suspense.

    We gathered in the living room with my brothers on either side of me on the couch, Lydian in Jordan's lap on the love seat, and Gallard standing by the fire place.

    "So, little sister, what caused you to ruin our plan to keep you hidden and follow us to our impending doom?" Aaron asked me.

"Many things transpired while you guys were away, and they've all culminated into my coming up with a way that won't end this mission with doom. I have a plan and I think it just might be the thing that will get Robin and David back," I explained.

"What sort of things are you talking about?" Gallard asked.

I decided to tell them everything, minus the awkward photo shoot and my encounter with the vampire at the bar. Those events weren't pertinent to my plan. I watched as their expressions changed from concern to horror to curiosity as my tale unfolded. I told them about how I'd been given a death sentence by the doctor and how I'd planned to let it run its course until David showed up and helped me get better with the blood. I also told them about the dreams I'd had and the voice I'd heard.

When I was finished, I waited to see what they had to say about everything they'd just heard. The room was nearly silent, and I began to feel nervous. I'd left out the part where Lucian and I could speak to each other; I wanted to save that as part of the punch line.

"You were dying and you didn't tell us?" Aaron asked.

"Well it wasn't like you were answering my calls. I called you twice and you didn't answer."

"You could have called someone else," Kevin said. "There are three cell phones among us."

"Do you think I didn't? I called Jordan and Gallard. Plus I

had to call Lydian seven times straight before she answered me tonight. Besides, no one was calling *me* to see how *I* was!" I didn't want to argue about this anymore. "But that isn't the point. I'm better now. However something did happen."

"Well, spill it, Lela. We're on the edge of our seats!" Lydian insisted. The room went silent once more and I took a deep breath before finishing what I had to say.

"I told Gallard this before, but when I was still human five years ago, I heard a voice speaking to me. We lost connection when I turned, but when I changed back, the voice came back as well. I soon figured out that the voice is Lucian Christophe.

"This whole thing is creepy but it got me thinking. Samil has been searching for Lucian's body and hasn't gotten any closer to finding it. I realized that we now have something that he doesn't; a direct line of communication to Lucian. Here's what I figured. If I could somehow contact him again, then maybe he could tell us where his body is and use it as a trade; his body for David and Robin."

That was not your plan! Lucian said. *You said you were bringing me back!*

I know. And I will. Just trust me on this.

"And you plan to do this how?" Gallard asked, sounding more wary than before. I already knew what he was going to say about my plan, but I had to make it sound as rational as possible.

If they didn't agree to go along with it, I may have to take matters into my own hands. It was a drastic resort, but I had my sister to think about.

"I can speak with him whenever I want. We just have to find Solomon, get the body, and make a trade."

"Samil needs Lucian alive, Lela."

"I know, but...we could use it as a diversion. We'll meet Samil for the trade then you guys can attack or whatever." No one spoke, so I said, "What other options do we have? You've been running all over Europe for weeks, and you still haven't gotten close to finding Solomon. If we had something that Samil wants, he won't be able to resist but make a deal."

I looked at the others to see if anyone else would be on my side. If I could get at least one other person to be on board, then I wouldn't have to be alone in this.

"I think it's the best idea I've heard," Lydian said, breaking the silence. "I'm game, and so is Jordan, aren't you Jordan?" she nudged him with her elbow and he furrowed his eyebrows in concern. He didn't seem to want to side with me, but Lydian had a strong gift of persuasion when it came to him. Jordan was the most compliant person that I knew, and though he looked tough on the outside, he had the biggest heart.

"Yeah, I guess I'm game as well," he said reluctantly. Lydian smiled enthusiastically. Gallard did not look pleased but he didn't say anything. I looked at Kevin and pleaded to him with my eyes. But it was Aaron who spoke first.

"Me too, I'm in," he said. So it was four against two. Kevin and Gallard were the only ones who didn't want to go along with it. I could live with that. Once my plan was put into action, I was sure that they would see that I'd been right. The only problem was somehow resurrecting Lucian behind their backs.

Gallard said that I could crash in his room, so I took him up on his offer. I could hear the bed calling my name, and after getting my bag out of the car, I changed into some athletic shorts and a tank top then tied my hair up. The house was pretty quiet save for the low hum of the voices in the living room. They were somewhat soothing since I'd missed everyone so much.

I heard the door open and shut quietly. I looked over to see Gallard walking in and he sat on the couch that was adjacent to the bed.

"Are you mad?" I asked in a soft voice. He looked at me for a second then returned his gaze to the opposite wall. His non answer told me that he was. He mumbled something that sounded French and I couldn't help but smile. I walked over and sat next to him on the couch.

"I never got to tell you before, but I've missed you," I said in an attempt to put him in a better mood. He chuckled then pulled me close to him, giving me another hug.

"It's impossible to stay mad at you," he said. "But I do think your idea is too dangerous. If anything were to go wrong and Samil demanded two donors—"

"We're going to be fine. We've survived this far. I'm pretty sure we can handle anything at this point."

I shifted my weight and grunted a bit when I moved my

shoulder wrong, so I rolled it to give it some relief.

"Are you okay?" he asked.

"Emiline dislocated my shoulder. Still hasn't healed yet."

He stroked my shoulder with the tips of his fingers and my heart rate quickened. I wasn't use to his touch making me react the way it did. When I was a vampire and had no heartbeat or changing body temperature, it was easier to hide it.

As he started to kiss my shoulder, the coldness of his lips soothed the throbbing pain better than any pain killer.

"What else did she do to you?" he asked.

"If I tell you, you're just going to worry."

"Too late, I'm already worried."

I lifted my shirt to show him the stab wound on my rib cage. It still had the stitches in it, so it probably looked revolting. He reached over and traced the wound gently and it made me shiver. He then found every bruise that I had on my arms and shoulders then lightly pressed his lips to each one.

"I'll let you sleep. You're probably exhausted."

"Wait, I wanted to say something first."

I stood up, unsure of what it was exactly that I wanted to say. I couldn't give any hints that I was trying to say goodbye, but I at least wanted him to know how appreciative I was for having him in my life.

"I'm just so grateful to you for everything," I continued. "From the very beginning, you've done so much for me. You've spent the past month trying to save my sister and I don't know anyone who would do that so selflessly."

"Lela, you don't have to—"

"No, I really do. I don't thank you enough, so I am making sure you know."

"You know I would do anything for you, Lela. From day one, I've never regretted bringing you along. I never once saw my looking out for you as a burden. Even when I was arrested. I wouldn't trade these past four years for anything."

He smiled at me and I became even more nervous. It was so hard keeping secrets from him; about my plan and about my feelings. He'd never broken any of his promises and he'd stuck by me through everything, all my tragedies, all my embarrassing moments, going to parent teacher conferences when I was in school. Not once did he complain or express that he wanted out.

I couldn't be honest with words, so instead I took his face in my hands and kissed him, this time following through unlike my first embarrassing attempt in Las Vegas. At first he didn't move, but then he stood up and tightened his grip around me and returned it. His lips were so soft against mine, like he was unsure if I was comfortable with it, so I kissed him harder to show him that it was okay then his intensity matched mine and it was somewhat intoxicating.

There was a knock on the door and we reluctantly pushed away from each other only moments before Lydian opened the door and poked her head in.

"Hey. Jordan wants to know if you're coming with us to

feed."

"Yeah um…I'm coming," He looked at me for a second. "Lydian, would you mind sticking around? I'd rather not leave this trouble maker alone."

"Sure thing, captain. I guess I could always snack on her if I get too hungry."

He gave me a weak smile before following her out the door and I crawled under the covers on the bed. The kiss hadn't lasted as long as I wanted it to, but one thing was certain. I was definitely in love with him and I wished more than anything that I had the courage to say it.

• • •

I wandered around the house the next day to see what everyone was doing. Gallard had gone into town, probably to clear his head and I wanted someone to talk to. Earlier that morning, we'd discussed the different strategies for finding Solomon. They still had the address I gave to Jordan, but they wanted more to go on.

My brothers and Jordan were talking in the kitchen and their conversation didn't sound interesting so I went to the back of the house onto the balcony. I found Lydian lying in the sun in her bikini and sunglasses on a lawn chair. I sat in the one next to her and soaked in the rays as well. I didn't understand why *she* was doing it. It wasn't like she could tan.

She didn't acknowledge me for a while, but when she did,
She didn't acknowledge me for a while, but when she did,
she took off her sunglasses and tossed them onto the chair next to her feet.

"I'm so jealous," she said. "You got so tan. It ain't fair."

I looked down at my brown arms. I hadn't realized how much darker I'd gotten over the past month. I'd spent some time outside, so I wasn't as pale as I had been before.

"Look on the bright side; you can't get skin cancer and I can."

She pouted and put her glasses back on. "I would rather have skin cancer and a tan than be pasty."

I reached over and stole her sunglasses. She didn't protest though. I needed them more than her.

"So what went down with Gallard last night?" she asked. "When I came to get him it looked as if I were interrupting something."

"You're always interrupting something," I said. "But to answer your question, I…kissed him."

Lydian sat up, her eyes wild with excitement. She almost seemed happier than *I* was about it.

"No way! So it finally happened! I'm impressed!" I laughed and took off the sunglasses. She scooted her chair closer to mine, eager to hear more. "Well, tell me. How was it?"

"It was…amazing. It was well worth the wait."

"Oh I bet it was," she said. "There's nothing like being

Frenched by a French guy, am I right or am I right?"

I couldn't believe I was having this conversation with her. Normally I would have just kept everything to myself, but she was easier to talk to for some reason. Maybe it was because I was so glad to be reunited with everyone. Her company was refreshing.

"I wouldn't know…he didn't…we didn't." I suddenly felt very lame. No matter how bold I got, there was always something Lydian would bring up that I should have done, or even should have done better.

"Really? Well why the hell not?" she asked. Her extreme outrage made me laugh.

"I don't know, maybe he was trying to be a gentleman."

She huffed then returned to her reclined position on the chair. "This is not the time to be a gentleman. We're about to go on a suicide mission and he wants to be a gentleman?"

I sighed and twisted my mouth in thought. Tyler had always been so proper and never let us get too carried away whenever we were alone together. At least not until the night he'd proposed. But he never kissed me the way Lydian was talking about and neither had Curtis or Gallard.

"Or," Lydian said. "Or maybe he doesn't know how. He is pretty old. That technique probably didn't exist back then."

I scoffed at this ridiculous notion. "It's not rocket science. I'm sure anyone could figure it out if they don't live under a rock."

Lydian laughed. "Oh no it's not. Trust me, I'm older and wiser. I know these things. Jordan is a master at kissing. If you want, you can practice on him. I'm sure he wouldn't mind. Spend a few minutes macking on him and he could make you a pro. You have my permission because your love life depends on it."

I stared at her with my mouth agape. I couldn't believe what she was saying. I was wrong. She *was* crazy.

"Thanks but no thanks," I finally replied. "Did it ever occur to you that Jordan inherited his skills? He had to get them somewhere."

Lydian grew quiet for a moment then smiled. "Touché. I never thought of that."

She stopped talking and focused her attention on the ocean. It was in plain view from the back of the house and was a beautiful sight to see, even better in the daylight. I had a fleeting notion that for some reason moments like these wouldn't come too often. I didn't want to, but I had to prepare myself for the possibility that I would die.

Lydian's phone buzzed, breaking my train of thought and she looked at her phone before texting the person back. I figured she was texting Jordan since he was inside and couldn't join us in the wonderful sunshine. I hoped that she wasn't asking him to give me any kissing lessons. I wouldn't give in to that. But her facial expression went from content to morose after she put her phone on the table, so I relaxed a little.

"So, you really hear Lucian in your head?" she asked.
"Going on twenty years now. Minus the four I was a vampire Trust me when I say it's getting very old."

Come off it, you know you like my company, Lucian said.

"What kind of things does he say? Does he whisper naughty things to you with his sexy British accent?"

You think British accents are sexy? I did not know this.

Don't even start, Lucian. I mean it. I'll change my mind about bringing you back.

"He mostly berates me about my relationships," I said. "In other words, he doesn't want me to be in one."

"He wants you all to himself then?"

"I never thought about it that way....He does act like a jealous boyfriend. Do you know how hard it is to talk to any guys with him in the back of my head, saying —" I put on my best British accent—"'Lela, you should not be talking to this man. He only wants to steal your virtue.'"

Lydian laughed. "Steal your virtue? I thought after New Years there was nothing left to be stolen."

"We didn't go that far!"

We went back inside after sitting for about fifteen more minutes and joined my brothers and Jordan. Lydian was still looking a bit down, and I wished that I'd asked her what had caused her mood to change. If the text had been from Jordan, then she wouldn't have been sad. Jordan was always the person to make her happy. He brought out the best in her. Just like Gallard brought out the best in me, usually.

Gallard returned to the house around three in the after—noon. I'd decided to go through with the plan that evening so I could take some time to mull through everything. I felt extremely guilty for hiding the truth from my friends, but it was the only way I could keep them from stopping it.

I ate India's version of McDonalds for dinner that night. It was strange, but edible. I didn't feel like eating, but I needed something in my stomach other than blood. I hadn't had any in a while, yet the energy I'd gotten from it was still there. It was like this weird high, minus the mind altering affects. Almost as if I'd had several Red Bulls but wasn't suffering from the affects.

Each tick of the clock made me even more anxious to get everything over with. I was nervous about speaking to Solomon again. He'd taken off the last time we spoke, and he was probably still adamant about hiding Lucian's body. There had to be some way to convince him to help. It was his descendant that was in danger, after all.

I threw my trash away then walked into the living room and found the card that Father Frederick had left. There was an address as well as a phone number written on it and I knew I was taking a chance calling it. What could I say that would convince him to help me talk with Solomon?

"Hello?" a familiar voice said. I was stunned at first because I'd expected Father Frederick to answer, but it was Solomon on the other line.

"Hi! This is Lela...Sharmentino? Your uh...friend gave me your number."

"Lela! It is wonderful to hear from you. Are you doing all

right?"

His kind voice made it hard to be angry at him. It sounded sage-like and peaceful. Could this man really have murdered Lucian's family?

Do not let him fool you. He let my daughters die and then he killed me. He is nothing but a hypocrite and a coward.

Wait, he let them die? I thought he killed them.

They did not die by his hand...but that does not make him any less responsible.

"I am doing better, thank you," I finally answered. "I...I'm calling because I want to take you up on your offer. I was attacked by an enemy recently and my friend nearly died in the process. It will be safer for him if I go away."

"That is a wise decision. I can keep you safe for as long as necessary."

I wasn't usually a deceptive person, and it was hard enough lying to my friend without trying to trick Solomon. He was obviously no dummy since he'd eluded Samil for so long. I was afraid that he would find me out by just listening to my voice and nothing could calm my nerves.

"Um...how soon can I come to you?" I asked.

"How about two days? That will give me some time to prepare for your arrival and I can meet you in London. You still have the address I presume?"

"Yes I do. Thank you Solomon. I really appreciate your doing this for me."

"I would do anything for my family. I will see you Wednesday then."

"Yeah, I'll see you. Goodbye Solomon."

I hung up and I couldn't stop the smile that was forming on my face. I had a legitimate meeting with Solomon, which meant we were one step closer to getting my sister back. Solomon seemed like a reasonable person. If he knew the gravity of the situation, maybe he would be more willing to help. I had a feeling he would.

I was still feeling slightly nervous, so I decided to take a hot bath. I hadn't done that in a while and since everyone but Kevin had gone out to feed, I had some alone time. This would give me a chance to regroup with Lucian and get some advice on how to approach Solomon. Lucian knew him better than anyone, so his tips might be useful for a change.

I sat on the edge of the tub and watched as the water began to rise. I thought back to the day my lungs had filled up with blood to the point where I couldn't breathe. I never wanted to experience that again nor did I wish it on anyone. Except maybe for Samil and Matthew and the rest of his psychotic posse.

I heard footsteps and smiled when I saw Gallard walk in. He was just the person that I wanted to see and it was almost like he read my mind.

"Do we have good news?" he asked.

"We do. Solomon plans to meet me in London two days from now."

"That's great. If only we'd gotten your call sooner, maybe

we could have met up with him last week."

"That's okay. He probably wouldn't have listened to you anyway. He's very selective with whom he talks to. From what I've heard."

He took one of my hands in his and kissed it. I thought back to what Lydian had said earlier and contemplated whether I should take her advice. She was right; we could die, and I needed to spend as much time with him as possible just in case.

"I have to admit that I'm warming up to your idea," Gallard said. "We had something similar planned, but nowhere to start. Your arrival gave us hope."

"I think that the odds are on our side," I assured him. "And if Solomon doesn't comply, we'll tie him up and threaten to pull his teeth out with old, rusty pliers."

"Mon ange des ténèbres." He pushed a lock of my hair behind my ear.

Listen to him, trying to seduce you with his French words, Lucian muttered.

Well, it's working.

Please. I have been around long enough to know the way into a woman's heart. Trust me.

Really? Because nothing you have said so far has impressed me. You're too creepy.

Or you are too particular.

No. Just in love with someone else.

I smiled at Gallard until a grin formed on his face as well. I was waiting expectantly for him to make a move, and contemplated making one myself.

"So...about last night. I hope I didn't scare you," I said.

"Yes, you're a terrifying person, Miss Sharmentino." He stroked my hand with his thumb. "I guess I should have seen it coming since I was all over you on New Year's."

"It's finally happened, hasn't it? We're turning into friends with benefits."

He laughed and I suddenly forgot what I was going to say. I shouldn't have wanted him to kiss me again. It would only make it harder to do what I had to do. I at least wanted to kiss him once, but it only left me wanting more. We didn't have much time and I wanted to make the most of it.

I felt my pants grow damp and I jumped up when I realized that the tub had overflowed. Gallard chuckled as I reached over to turn the faucet off. I groaned when I looked at my pants and saw that it looked as if I'd had an accident.

"Why didn't you warn me about the water?" I asked, grabbing a towel and wiping up the water. He put his arm into the tub and lifted the stopper a bit until the water level went down then reinserted it.

"I'm sorry," he said. "I was...distracted."

"Yeah, you were, old man."

"Well, I won't keep you from your bath. I'll let the others know about our plans."

He left the bathroom and my heart sank. Nothing had

changed since we'd kissed. He was still treating me like he had when I was fourteen. I thought kissing him would validate his feelings for me, but just like New Years, he was avoiding talking about it. Maybe it was better this way.

I had another vivid dream that night. This one was by far more terrifying than any I ever had. I was in a house I'd never seen before and by the length of the hall, I could tell it was very massive. I heard voices coming from downstairs, so I walked over to the staircase and slowly went down.

When I got to the bottom, I saw that some people dressed in fifteenth century servant's garb were bustling back and forth from one room to another, carrying plates and silverware. They must have been cleaning up after a meal. By the lighting from the windows, I guessed it was mid morning.

The servants stopped arriving, so I wandered into another room that looked like a parlor. There were antique couches there as well as a coffee table. Not long after I entered, four people joined me and on instinct, I hid in the corner so they wouldn't see me. I studied the people from afar; there were three men and one woman. The woman was quite small and had black hair while the man next to her was tall and had blonde hair and baby blue eyes. The second man was a priest, about the same age as Father Frederick.

But the third man I recognized. It was impossible not to miss his red hair and otherworldly blue eyes. He looked a lot younger, but it was Lucian without a doubt. He was dressed in an expensive tailored suit, but by the circles under his eyes, I could see that he was ill. He looked like how I used to look before I'd gotten better.

The priest performed Mass, which I found slightly creepy because of the message behind it then the maid left and closed all the windows. The priest then began telling Lucian a story. I became enthralled by it and how interesting it was. Was this a dream? Or was I accessing his memories like he did mine?

After the priest finished the story, I noticed that the blonde man was holding something behind his back. I moved around the room so I could see it. I gasped in horror when I discovered what it was; a wooden stake. Didn't he know a stake couldn't kill a vampire? Only sunlight, draining their blood, or decapitating them would work.

Without warning, the man lunged at Lucian, plunging the stake into his chest. I watched Lucian fall to the floor, writhing in pain.

"No stop!" I shouted to the people. I didn't know why I was trying to save him. Pity maybe? I knew what it was like to feel helpless and overpowered and I hated to see other people experience that.

"You cannot save me, darling."

I turned to see another Lucian, the one from my other dream, standing next to me.

"Tis but a memory," he continued. "And I lived to talk about it."

I watched as the younger Lucian attacked his parents and when I tried to scream, the present Lucian covered my mouth. I could feel his touch as vividly as when I was dying. I felt a tear trickle down my face as the younger Lucian dropped his parents' bodies to the ground and stood over them. I didn't know how I should feel about what I was witnessing. He had acted in self defense, yet I couldn't imagine taking the life of my own parents.

"I learned that day that I cannot trust anyone." He removed his hand from my mouth and started stroking my hair. "But you are different. You've made an impression on me, darling. Can I trust you?"

I woke up before I could answer that. Witnessing Lucian being attacked by his own father made me feel sorry for him. Pity wasn't an emotion I thought I could feel towards him. Mostly it was annoyance and revile. This glimpse of his past broke my heart and also made me curious. What had he done that caused so many to want him assassinated? I dreaded what the answer would be.

Chapter Fourteen

I wasn't tired anymore, so I went into the bathroom to get a drink. I was still trying to process what I'd seen. I couldn't figure out how Lucian was able to manipulate my dreams. Maybe he was more a part of me than I wanted to believe. He'd said that I'd made an impression on him, and that made my stomach turn. I didn't want to imagine what he would be like if he was returned to his body. The gypsies had put him down for a reason, and it was probably a good one.

All but Gallard and Jordan left the house to check out some parade downtown. I wished that I could have gone so I could get my mind off of the dream. I also wanted to take a shower since I'd woken up all sweaty. I hated that Lucian had touched me, even if it wasn't real. He had his moments where I could tolerate him, but he was extremely controlling and manipulative.

When I finished washing off, I sat on the floor of the shower and hugged my knees to my chest. I was starting to question my deal that I made with him. Could I in good conscience let him roam the earth again, considering how dangerous he might be? Even if it was for my sister's sake, how many would die because of it?

I stood up and turned the water off. I was starting to prune and it wasn't good for my stitches to get wet. I had to move around gingerly because of my old wounds as well as the new ones. I had some blood to speed up the healing process, but this time I didn't drink as much. I'd gone nearly twenty-four hours without it and felt just fine. I was treating it like I needed it for sustenance when really I didn't need it in the quantities I'd been consuming it in.

After I dried off, I put on some clothes. I chose a t-shirt and denim shorts. My clothes were still light enough to not be too warm. The weather in India was amazing, but at night it was scorching hot. If it weren't for the air conditioner, I would probably have died from heat exhaustion.

I opened the door to let the steam out then started brushing my hair. It was a difficult process since I couldn't lift my arm up all the way. I then tossed my brush into my bag and prepared to leave the bathroom but flinched when I saw Gallard standing in the doorway. I'd been so deep in thought that I hadn't even heard him come in.

"I thought you'd still be asleep," he said. "Nightmare?"

"Yeah, something like that." I forced a smile. "Why don't we join the others in town? I'm not really up for sleeping and I'd like some fresh air."

He had a sad expression on his face and he acted like he was trying to avoid eye contact with me. Something was bothering him and I wanted to know what it was.

"Why the long face?" I asked. "We got a new lead, and we're in one of the best vacations spots in the world."

"It's just…there's something you should know, and I feel guilty that I kept it from you."

I leaned against the counter to convey to him that I had his full attention. I had to pretend that I wasn't anxious to hear what he had to say.

"When I found out that you were losing your immortality, I had to make sure you would be okay. Since David found a way to stay alive, I thought you would be fine. While we were searching for Solomon, we ran into a few immortals along the way and I asked them if they knew more about the whole family blood thing. They said that no matter who drank it, ancient or new, the vampire would die.

"That's why I've been so upset lately. I was trying to cope with the fact that you weren't going to live very long. I wanted to find David and save him, but mostly because I wanted to know how he stayed alive. But we had no leads and everything was starting to look hopeless. Even still, I couldn't go back to you. I couldn't watch you die."

"You would have rather left me behind to die then spend the little time you had left with me? Thanks a lot. That makes me feel great." I grabbed my bag and walked passed him. I was done with this emotional rollercoaster. I dropped the bag next to the dresser and was about to leave the room when he spoke up again.

"It was selfish of me, I know. But if I'd returned, I wouldn't have been able to stop myself from turning you back."

"Well you *should* have turned me back," I snapped. "Because I tried to live a normal life. For five weeks I did normal people things. I went shopping, developed new hobbies, I even made some friends. But no matter how many human things I did, the vampire world still crept up on me. I ran into two of them and both tried to kill me. I'm used to having attempts made on my life, but when you're human it's kind of an inconvenience that you can't defend yourself."

He didn't respond to me. He kept his gaze cast down to the floor. I wasn't finished with my ranting yet. There was a whole lot more that I wanted to say. This time I wasn't going to hold anything back. I needed to get everything off of my chest so I could finally put all of my focus into more serious problems.

"What are we even doing? This whole thing between us; it's confusing. One second I think you're interested and the next you treat me like you always have since we met."

Finally he looked up at me. I was surprised that he hadn't said anything yet in his defense. He was just letting me ramble on.

"None of this has been easy," he said. "Leaving you there with Curtis, knowing I might never see you again. It was hard. But seeing how excited you were when you and Lydian talked about your new life, it helped me leave knowing I'd made the right decision. I wanted you to have your life back. That's why I never called."

"I understand that, but the reality is that my old life nearly ended when Emiline tried to kill Curtis. I may have longed for how things used to be and I know that every now and then I will. But the reality is that you need me on this mission and you know it."

I bit my lip before continuing.

"I've been plotting behind your back with Lucian." I stared at him to see how he would react. "I'm going to resurrect him in exchange for his saving my sister."

"Lela!" Gallard's expression looked more horrified than when I'd told him I met with Samil without him. "You know two have to die to resurrect him. What were you…no. Don't tell me you were going to sacrifice yourself."

"That's the plan." Gallard groaned in disgust and I continued, "David already told Samil he was going to do it, and I'm going to be the other. You've already spent almost three hundred years running from Samil and I won't let you be the other donor."

"You're not resurrecting Lucian," he said firmly. "You found a way to stay alive, and I don't care how long it takes, but I'm going to make sure that you're safe from all of this. For good this time."

I let out an exasperated sigh. We'd already been through this. I couldn't have a normal life. As long as I would need blood to stay alive and breathing, I wouldn't be normal. I didn't even know the meaning of that word anymore.

"I'm doing this for my sister and for you. Lucian promised he would destroy Samil if I brought him back. You'll finally be free of him. I'm doing this and you can't stop me."

"Oh yes I can and will! I can't lose you, Lela, I…I—"

"You what?"

"*Parce que je t'aime!*" he said suddenly shouting. I was stunned by his raised voice.

"What?" I asked, hoping that this time he would translate. He came closer to me until he was standing directly in front of me.

"Because I love you. I said it at the airport, I said it on New Years, and I said it again before I left. Human or vampire, that's never going to change."

"Wha...why didn't you say something before?"

"Because you'd already had your heart broken. Because the last man that said those words to you left you behind. I knew that you were hurting and you said you were finished with relationships. I couldn't tell you then. I had to wait until you had healed so that when I finally said it, you would know that I meant it." He locked eyes with me. "And I was afraid I would lose you. That if I admitted out loud that I loved you, it would be a death sentence. It's been difficult not acting on my feelings, but I can't let fear hold me back anymore."

Suddenly, everything made so much more sense to me. I'd always wondered why he'd flirted but never went any further than that. He loved me so much that he waited for me to break down my wall and learn to trust again and he stayed silent as a way to protect himself from being hurt as well. We were more similar than I ever thought we were.

"Well it would have been nice to know that your flirting was genuine all this time. When you started hitting on me, I didn't know what to think," I said, my frustration disappearing almost instantly.

"You think *I* started it?" he asked. "I beg to differ, Miss

Sharmentino. *You* started it."

I scoffed and asked, "Oh really? How did I start it?"

"I remember the exact moment. It was back in Texas. You were playing with my hair and gazing at me. Trying to charm me with your feminine wiles."

I started laughing. I remembered that day. I had been determined to prove to David that I could cut hair, and as I cut Gallard's, something had come over me. I wasn't usually a presumptuous person, but for some reason I hadn't be able to resist running my fingers through this hair.

"Feminine wiles? You're dating yourself, old man," I said grinning up at him. I reached my hand up and began playing with his hair as I did before. It was longer than when I'd last seen him. Probably because I wasn't around to cut it for him. I then took his face in my hands and said, "I love you too."

He then pulled me closer to him and his lips came down on mine. At first he was kissing me lightly as before, but then it changed. It was different than the last time; more passionate. I lost myself in the moment and I could feel my body temperature rising. I was no longer in control over what I was doing. Soon I realized we were on the bed and Gallard's shirt was off then he started to remove mine as he went from kissing my lips to my neck.

We were almost completely undressed when suddenly, a warning signal went off and I became overwhelmed with the feeling that we should stop. I wasn't sure why. Here I was with the man that I loved and he wanted to be with me and I with him but something was telling me that this wasn't the time or place for this. I was normally good at listening to my conscience. So as much as I didn't want to, I had to say something.

"Gallard, wait," I said calmly. He stopped kissing me then gave me a puzzled look and I continued saying, "I can't do this. Not right now. We're both caught up in the moment from professing our love, but this isn't how this should happen."

He looked away from me for a few seconds. "I'm sorry," he said while turning his eyes to mine. "I just...I thought...didn't you and Tyler?"

"No. We almost did, but...it never happened."

"I...I shouldn't have assumed. I apologize."

"Don't be sorry. It's just that...I want it to be when it's our choice and we're not acting on our irresistible desires. But please know that I do love you and I want you to be the one I do *this* with."

The expression on his face made me want to hug him. I felt bad like I'd led him on and wanted to apologize as well. "Gallard," I whispered, unsure of what to say after. He opened his mouth to speak but was interrupted when we heard the front door open followed by Lydian's voice saying, "Jeeze Louise, that parade was super pathetic!"

We quickly got up and scrambled to get decent before leaving the room to speak with them. Gallard went out first and I took a minute to take in all that had just happened. I leaned against the wall and exhaled deeply.

While it had ended abruptly, every second until then had

been perfect. I finally knew that he loved me, and nothing could ruin that. Even still, I was glad that I'd gone with my gut and suggested that we wait to take things further, and for the first time, I thought to myself, *Thank God for Lydian*. Her unexpected return had saved us from rushing into something prematurely, and I was grateful for that.

The group decided to spend the evening watching a movie to make up for the lame parade. Surprisingly, they hadn't tried out the huge entertainment center yet. Kevin picked some Indian movie and the entire time, Lydian and Aaron made fun of the bad English dubbing, which was a few seconds off.

For a few hours, I was able to forget my worries about Lucian and Samil. I was enjoying my time since I was with almost all of the people I cared about. All that was missing was David and Robin. If they had been there, I would have been completely content. I knew they were all right, though. David was safe as long as they didn't have Lucian's body and he was taking care of Robin. The rest was up to me and my group. They were counting on us to pull through, and I was going to do whatever it took, even if it killed me. If I couldn't save David, I would at least save my sister.

I'd been curled up next to Gallard on the couch when I felt myself drifting off. I could hear the movie going, yet I wasn't completely conscious. Eventually, the sound faded out and I listened as everyone stood up. From the brief conversation they had, I discerned that they were going off to feed and I heard Jordan whisper, "Are you coming Gallard?" to which he replied, "Yeah, go on. I'll be out shortly."

I felt myself being lifted off the couch and carried away. This was the first time that Gallard had ever carried me, and it felt good. I felt safe in his arms, like nothing could touch me. Not even Lucian who was lurking in the recesses of my consciousness could frighten me now.

Gallard pulled the covers back then lay me on the bed before pulling them up to my shoulders. He started to walk away when I reached out and grabbed his hand to stop him. I wasn't ready to be left on my own. With him around, I could be sure that I wouldn't have nightmares. His presence seemed to keep them at bay.

"Don't go out tonight. Please? I don't want to be alone," I said softly. He smiled then slid under the covers, wrapping his arms around me. At last, I was at peace and was able to drift off.

• • •

I awoke the next morning to find him gone, but smiled when I heard his voice somewhere in the house. I looked at the clock and saw that it was still early. When I sat up, I found that the pain in my collarbone was nearly non-existent and my shoulder had healed completely. I felt better physically than I had in weeks. I hopped out of the bed and changed into some capris and a t-shirt before tying my hair back.

I left the room, making my way to the kitchen. I found

Jordan in the kitchen with headphones on and he was dancing while he was cooking something at the stove. Jordan wasn't wearing a shirt, and I wondered why that was so. That was when I noticed the several scars on his back. They were very light and I probably wouldn't have noticed if I wasn't standing so close. They weren't small though. They were long, wide and some stretched from his shoulder blade all the way to his waistline.

I refrained from ask him about them. I had a feeling the story behind them wasn't pleasant and I wanted to keep good mood. Optimism was the key to succeeding in our mission and unnecessary sadness would put our optimism in jeopardy.

"Good morning," I shouted. He quickly turned around and laughed when he realized I'd seen everything. He then took his ear buds out.

"I hope you don't mind curry powder in your eggs. I couldn't find salt."

"You didn't have to cook for me," I said, standing next to him and admiring the food.

"It's the least I can do since you looooove me."

"And I'm going to tell everyone you dance while you cook. I am not kidding."

"You should be dancing too. We have a new lead and we're on our way to winning this war."

He put his ear buds back in and started dancing around me. Gallard walked in not long after and stared at Jordan as he continued to dance. Gallard once hinted that he knew how to tango, but I'd never seen him try to attempt modern dancing.

"Is this guy really my nephew?" Gallard asked.

"You're just jealous because you wish you were this sexy," Jordan said while nudging him.

Gallard laughed then leaned against the counter next to me. He was smiling at me and I couldn't stop myself from grinning. At the same time, I didn't know how to act around him. I wasn't sure if we should get all cozy like how Jordan and Lydian were always standing incredibly close to each other or holding hands. I then realized that we'd acted more like a couple when we weren't together than now when we were.

Lydian came into the kitchen and I raised an eyebrow at her attire. She was wearing Jordan's shirt and probably nothing else. The mystery of Jordan's missing shirt was solved. He'd returned to the stove and she hugged him around his waist from behind then yanked her arms back, gasping in pain.

"Frickin A! Burned my arm on the stove!" she said, examining the red mark on her forearm that was slowly disappearing. Jordan turned around and kissed her wound.

"I've already been popped a few times. I could have avoided the pain if I'd had my shirt."

"Oh, I'm sorry. Why don't I give it back?" she said. Without warning she pulled off the shirt. Gallard and I groaned in disgust, looking away while Jordan swiftly tried to cover her up. He wrapped the shirt around her then carried her out, mumbling something about getting her some real clothes and Gallard took his spot at the stove, stirring the eggs.

"Well that was a lot more nudity than I wanted to see today," I said, shuddering at the memory. Where she got her inhibition from, I had no clue. Just when I thought she couldn't surprise me with her actions anymore, she would do something even more impudent. I somewhat envied her confidence, but only to a point. I would never be that bold.

Gallard scooped the cooked eggs as well as a piece of naan bread covered in butter onto a plate then handed it to me with a fork. I thanked him then we sat at the table.

"Where are my brothers?" I asked while I ate.

"They've been on the phone with your aunt and uncle. They're telling them that the police have new leads. It's not the complete truth, but I think they're confident your plan will work."

"That reminds me, I have more information I got from Lucian." I stabbed a bite of eggs with my fork then put it in my mouth. "He showed me something from his past. Apparently when he was younger, his parents tried to kill him. But this is the interesting part. He was adopted and his birth father tried to murder him and his mother while she was still pregnant with him. Some guy with white hair and green eyes saved her."

"That's extraordinary. How did he save her?"

"Here's where it gets weird. According to witnesses, she gave birth not long after she recovered from her wounds and Lucian was stillborn. But! He came back to life about twenty minutes after he was born. I guess the man touched him and he came to life."

"You're kidding! So this mysterious man resurrected him from the dead?"

"Appears so." I took another bite of food. "Gallard...after Lucian's adopted father tried to murder him Lucian fought back and killed him. He killed his mother as well. Isn't that tragic?"

"That's terrible. I couldn't imagine going through that." He looked at me warily. "You're not feeling sorry for him, are you?"

I didn't answer.

"I did promise him I would bring him back. I guess...I sort of do."

"Don't feel sorry for him, Lela. That douche has been manipulating you for your entire life. He was the one that convinced you to drink the blood that turned you. I could kill that guy."

I stood up and put my plate in the sink, running the water over it to rinse it off. I shared his feelings toward Lucian. He was a creep; a manipulative creep. He wasn't going to help me because he cared. It was because he knew that I was the only one who would protect the information he had to get him back into his own body.

"You would have to kill me too," I muttered as I shut off the water. "Until his consciousness is put back in the right place, Lucian and I are stuck with each other. If he dies, I die."

Gallard stood up as well and turned me around to face him.

"You're right. This whole thing is completely bizarre. It's just that...I hate thinking of him using you. Not on my watch."

I smiled and pulled him closer to me by his belt loops. "How about you kiss me? I'm sure you'll feel better."

He rested his hands on either side of me on the counter and took my suggestion. I was glad that he wasn't too much taller than me. The way we were standing put us at just the right level.

As he kissed me, I thought about what Lydian had said. I was curious to know if her theory about French guys was true since I still hadn't found out for myself. If she was right, Gallard had been holding out on me.

When my tongue found his, I was surprised when he didn't draw back. He kissed me back the same way and I finally realized what Lydian was talking about. It was beyond amazing. Since he was colder than me, I compared it to having an ice cube on my tongue, which made it numb, but not enough that I couldn't feel anything.

We made out for another thirty seconds before I felt eyes on us. I opened mine and saw Aaron staring at us with his mouth open so I stopped kissing Gallard.

"What's up, bro?" I asked, trying to act nonchalant. He looked at Gallard and then back at me.

"Uh...I came to ask when we planned to leave," he said. "But if you're busy—"

"No, we're not busy," Gallard said, moving away from me. Aaron turned around and we followed him out of the kitchen. My heart was still racing, so I had to try and calm down for our serious conversation.

"I think that's all the information we need," Gallard said once we'd gathered in the living room. "We'll head out of here tonight and fly back to England. We know the location where Solomon plans to meet Lela, so we're all set."

"I'm so glad we're getting out of India!" Aaron said, leaning back on the couch and stretching. He then stood up and asked, "What time do we take flight?"

"Sundown would be best," Gallard said. "That should be about six-thirty. We'll leave then, and not a second later. We have a little girl and an old friend that are counting on us."

"Houston, we have a problem," Jordan pointed out. "Lela can't fly with us."

Gallard folded his arms and shifted his eyes in thought. I already knew the solution to my problem. I could fly there by plane. It might take longer than it would for them to get there, but I wasn't about to separate from the group again.

"I think it would be best if she went back to Tampa," He finally said, "It would be safer there."

I frowned in protest. I'd been left-behind girl before, and I didn't like that title. I couldn't believe after everything I'd just told him about it not being any safer back home he was still trying to get me to go back.

"No! No, no, no! I am *not* going back to Florida!" I said, standing up.

"Lela, not to sound like Lydian, but you *are* as good as dead if you came with us."

"I was as good as dead in Florida too! Hello; evil, psychotic Emiline, remember? Plus, you might need me. Solomon might bail if he sees I'm not there."

Gallard walked up to me and gave me a firm stare. "You're not going."

I put my hands on my hips. "Yes I am! And you're going to have to drag me yourself if you want me to go back to Florida."

"Uh oh, lover's spat," Lydian said, trying to sneak off with Jordan. I shot her a glare that warned her not to leave the room and they sat back down. There was no way I was losing this battle. Even if he did force me to go to Florida, there was no way he could stop me from leaving there and going to England. I had nothing but time and I had the money to make such a trip.

"I'm stronger now, Gallard. I healed from a stab wound in three days and my collarbone healed overnight. As long as I drink blood, I can withstand almost any injury. And I don't even need to be there when you go against Samil. I just want to go with you to find Solomon, not fist fight with the undead. I know that they can rip me apart. Just don't leave me behind again."

Gallard gave me a half smile. "I'll make that compromise. You come with us to London, but you won't go near Samil."

I smiled back, proud of myself for yet another victory. As for the compromise, I would have to work on that later. I wanted to help retrieve Robin as well. I wouldn't be able to rest assuredly until she was in my arms, healthy and alive.

Gallard was still being overly protective, so he insisted that

Lydian go with me on the plane. She complained since she didn't want to be separated from Jordan, but eventually gave in. I'd never seen a girl as attached to a guy as she was. I could swear that she would drop dead if he were more than a mile away. She spent the rest of the day with him, either sitting in his lap while he played cards with my brothers or off in their room, and I didn't have to guess what they were up to.

I started getting bored of being indoors and wanted to go back to the beach. Since Lydian was otherwise occupied and Gallard was the only other person who could go outside, he went with me. We had plenty of time before they were leaving, so we walked there. It wasn't that long of a walk since there was a trail from the house to the beach.

The area we went to was somewhat secluded and only a few other vacationers were there, most of who were surfing. I would have worn my swimsuit, but I still had an ugly scar from the knife wound and my bruises hadn't healed yet. Lydian cut the stitches out earlier since it was well enough, and it left weird little holes where the thread used to be. I didn't want that abomination of a sight to be seen by anyone.

I walked into the water knee deep and took in the beauty. It was late in the afternoon, so the sun was shining just above the edge of the horizon. I wanted to dive in and explore the wonders underneath the surface just as I had nearly four years ago, but I couldn't. I didn't have the ability to do so anymore.

"Looking for a shark to wrestle?" Gallard asked me.

"Nah. I've moved on to wrestling whales. They're more of a challenge."

"I pity any animal that dares to anger *you*. Why did you kill the shark anyway?"

"There was a girl who was night-swimming. She cut her foot on some coral and the shark and I both had the same idea. He wouldn't relent, so I got rid of the competition. I fed on him and afterwards I wasn't hungry anymore. Thanks to him, I didn't take that girl's life."

We walked out of the water and sat on the sand with me leaning against him. The sun was now beginning to set and the surfers had moved on, probably to some party happening down the beach. I enjoyed listening to just the sounds of the water and a few birds. It was relaxing. I had a feeling that there weren't going to be many more opportunities to relax. There was quite a bit of danger ahead of us that I didn't want to think about.

"What's going through that head of yours?" Gallard asked, nearly whispering.

"Samil is never going to take Lucian's body without any donors. David already promised to be one in exchange for my immunity and—"

"It won't come to that. We'll distract Samil with the trade and we'll kill him and his followers if he tries to stop us from taking David and Robin back."

I sighed then sat up to look at him. "And what about Lucian? I made a promise to him and now I'm breaking it. I don't like breaking promises."

"It wouldn't be breaking it if I physically stopped you from following through. That way he can blame me."

I bit my lip then leaned against him again. He was right. There was nothing I could do in return that wouldn't cost someone their life. I hated that he'd made me feel a little bit sorry for him, despite his creepiness. He'd had his family taken away from him just as I did, and evil person or not, that was a tragedy.

"What if I just kept him company every once in a while? We used to talk often but now that I'm older we don't get along so well." I wasn't serious, but I wanted to see what Gallard would say to my idea. It was a bad attempt at making light of our situation.

"You are something else, Miss Sharmentino," he said, squeezing me tightly. "You have such a big heart. Maybe too big sometimes. That lunatic doesn't want company, he wants to come back and wreak havoc in everybody's lives."

"Or," I pointed a thoughtful finger at him. "I could try to reform him. Give him a lesson in social skills. Anger Management 101: How *Not* To Piss People Off."

"Lela—"

My mind suddenly started racing with ideas. The gypsy said that in order to bring him back, two of us needed to be completely drained of blood. What we hadn't realized was that there was a loop hole.

"I have an even better idea," I said. "What if the four of us each gave half of our blood? That way, no one would have to die and I wouldn't be breaking my promise."

He let out an exasperated groan. "I can't win, can I?" he asked.

I swung my leg around so that I was sitting in his lap facing him.

"You won *me*. The rest is just a bonus."

He started kissing me and he hugged me closer to him as we fell back against the sand. We rolled to the side and he ended up on top of me. It wasn't a very graceful move, and he was just dead weight. I tried not to laughed, but I couldn't hold it in.

"I'm sorry, am I squishing you?" he asked, not making any effort to move.

"A little. You're getting fat, old man. Am I going to have to put you on a diet?"

He kissed me again before sitting up, pulling me with him. "Why don't we exercise right now? We still have an hour before we take off."

"And how will we do that, exactly?"

He smiled then removed his shoes and socks before taking off his shirt and pants. He was only wearing his boxers now. For a moment I just stared at him, growing redder by the second and he laughed when he saw my expression.

"What's wrong?" he asked.

"Nothing! It's just…do you really want to do this here? What if someone shows up or—"

He smiled and leaned close so that his lips practically

touched my ear.

"As much as I would love to, I don't think skinny dipping is the best idea right now," he said.

He then backed away from me and dove into the water. Judging by his speed, I figured he'd already made it about fifty feet from the shore. I had to contemplate what I was going to do. Swim in my underwear, or turn back into shy, uncomfortable Lela and swim in my clothes. I didn't want to waste time that I could be spending with him on going back to the house to get my swimsuit.

I made my decision. I took a quick glance around before slipping out of my capris and shirt before quickly wading out into the water until I couldn't touch anymore. It seemed like forever since I'd gone swimming. The last time was probably when we'd still lived in Las Vegas. It felt good to glide through the water. It was so clear and I could almost see to the bottom.

I came back to the surface and scanned the area for Gallard. He'd been under for a solid five minutes, but I wasn't worried. He didn't need to breathe. So while I waited for him, I floated on my back and watched the other vacationers as they surfed and rode in their boats.

I almost lost myself in a daydream when I felt two arms slide around my waist, followed by a kiss on the side of my neck. I smiled, glad that Gallard had finally made an appearance. I hadn't minded waiting for him, but I liked having him with me.

"Sorry I took so long," he said. "It's beautiful down there. I wish you could see it."

"Did you see any mermaids?" I joked.

"No, just a blonde siren. I tried to ignore her, but I couldn't."

I turned around, hanging onto him by putting my arms around his neck and kissed him. His hands rested on my hips, pulling me against him then slid down the sides of my legs and I crossed them around his waist. This was probably dangerous territory, but I didn't care.

"You're making it very hard to resist you, Miss Sharmentino," he said.

I stared into his eyes for a moment. I was feeling the same way, being so close to him and because he looked really sexy when he was wet. What made this more enjoyable was that I didn't have Lucian scolding me in my head. He'd gone silent since the nightmare I'd had.

"Then don't," I finally said, nearly whispering. He chuckled then began caressing my legs again.

"What happened to waiting? Did you change your mind overnight?"

"Well, we seem to be in control now. Besides, we've done a whole year of waiting; waiting for the other person to speak of first. And though I've spent the past several months battling my emotions, I've come to the conclusion that you're it for me. I'm never going to love anyone else like I love you. I want all of you and I want to give you all of me in return. I'm all yours, Mr. D'Aubigne."

He looked over towards the beach then sighed. I looked too

and saw that Lydian and Jordan were walking around, appearing as though they were searching for something.

Gallard mumbled something in French then said, "Always an interruption."

He then ducked under water, holding on to me and supporting me so that my head stayed above the surface. We weren't that far from the shore, so they were bound to see me eventually. When they were facing my direction I waved to get their attention.

"Lela? What are you doing out there?" Lydian asked.

"I'm baking a cake," I said sarcastically. "What does it look like I'm doing?"

"Have you seen Gallard?" Jordan asked. "He's not in his room and he never mentioned leaving the house."

I opened my mouth to speak, but was distracted when I felt Gallard's lips press against my skin and he started making a trail of kisses up my spine.

"Um...no. I'm out here alone. No company whatsoever. All by myself."

"Okay, well...be careful out here," Jordan said. "He would kill me if I let you get pulled under by a rip tide."

Jordan took Lydian's hand and I watched them walk back up the trail and disappear around the cliff towards the house. Gallard must have heard that they were gone because he popped back up and chuckled.

"You're good," he said. "You're starting to be a good

enough liar to fool me."

"Why did we lie, exactly?"

"Because the last thing we need is Lydian making some obscene joke about us." He kissed my cheek and smiled. "So where were we?"

"We were discussing taking the next step in our relationship."

"Right." He pushed my hair away from my face. "Lela, I do want to be with you. But not in this moment. I want us to be at least ten thousand miles away from Jordan and Lydian because if they interrupt us one more time, I swear I'm going to find a coffin and seal her into it."

I laughed and he laughed with me. It was true, though. Lydian had a knack for showing up at wrong time. It was probably her fault that it took us so long to finally kiss and even then she'd interrupted us.

"We should get back at them." I thought for a moment. "Oh, I know! We should fool around in their bed. Show them how it feels."

"Who knew you could be so naughty? We should probably get back, though. They're going to figure it out eventually."

I nodded then he put me onto his back and swam at lightning speed toward the shore. We got dressed in silence then hiked up the trial. I could sense him going into worry mode. Whenever he did, he would either get really affectionate or just more quiet than usual. Right now he was being a mixture of both.

He didn't say a word the entire way up the trail, but stood really close to me as we walked. I was starting to think that maybe I wasn't worrying enough.

We walked through the door just as everyone had gathered in the foyer. The sun was down, with just a hint of light struggling to shine so it was safe for my brothers and Jordan to go outside. By the expressions on Jordan and Lydian's faces, they knew they'd been duped.

I hugged my brothers first, hanging on to each of them for about thirty seconds. I wasn't usually so sappy, but goodbyes were getting harder and harder for me, though I was sure it was only temporary. I would see them in a few, short hours.

I hugged Jordan and he surprised me with a peck on my forehead.

"What was that for?" I asked.

"For taking care of my girl while I'm away."

"Hey, *I'm* the one doing the babysitting, remember?" Lydian said, defending herself. He started covering her face in kisses and I laughed then turned to Gallard, who was still looking very worried. He was not happy about my tagging along, but even his morose expression wasn't going to convince me otherwise. While he embraced me, he slightly lifted me up until my feet were barely touching the ground. When he set me down, he tilted my head up by my chin and gave me a soft kiss.

"I love you," he said, nearly whispering. "I don't care how, or what it takes. I will save your father and sister, I promise you that. And I promise you that no matter what happens, we'll find our way back to each other. We always do, right?"

"You're getting all sappy on me, old man. We'll see each other in five hours."

He rolled his eyes. "Lydian, guard her with your life," he said, not looking away from me. Lydian did a corny salute to him and said, "Yes, captain!"

All the guys left the foyer in somewhat of a line behind Gallard with Lydian and I following close behind. We watched as one by one they transformed and flew off into the sky. I kind of missed flying, though I was the clumsiest flyer there was. It was a faster and more convenient way of travel. Knowing that I would never fly again caused me to wish I'd done it more often and appreciated the ability.

Chapter Fifteen

Lydian and I stood in silence for a while. We'd locked up the house and I already had my luggage in the car, so there wasn't much we could do. Our plane wasn't due to leave for another hour and forty-five minutes.

"Well, I'm officially bored," she said. "What are we going to do?"

I thought for a moment. "Hmm…you could take me to dinner! I'm starving, and I haven't had any real Indian food yet."

"I'm not taking you to dinner. You can get something at the drive-through."

"I don't want fast food. I want to sit down somewhere."

"And what am I supposed to do?"

"You can watch me eat."

We got into the car and I drove towards the airport to find a restaurant nearby. Most of them looked expensive and posh and seemed like tourist attractions rather than authentic Indian eateries. They were somewhat Americanized and I wanted a cultural experience. I finally settled for a small place with a name I couldn't pronounce and parked. It was very quaint inside and one of those seat-yourself set ups. We picked a booth close to the door and began looking at the menus.

"Man, I would have killed for some of this food back in the

day. Now it all just looks disgustin'," she said. I couldn't read half of what they were serving and I had to pick something based on how good the picture looked. I settled for a dish that had a coconut curry sauce and chicken over rice.

"Blood, food; both taste good to me," I said. "Though I prefer food. Blood just has one flavor and food has more variety."

Lydian sighed as she closed the menu and set it on the edge of the table.

"You and Gallard seem pretty cozy," she said. "Did anything else happen between you two?"

I avoided the question by talking about the menu some more. It wasn't that I didn't want to share. I was doing it on purpose.

"I think I might order dessert. The options look really tasty."

"Lela, you're not getting out of this. I won't stop asking until you give me some juicy details."

I pretended to ignore her and she yanked the menu from my fingers. "If you don't start talking, I'm going to resort to violence!"

"All right already!" I said. I took a sip of water as a pause for affect. "We...had a moment."

Lydian smacked the table with her hand and I jumped. "I knew it!" she shouted. "You two did it in the ocean! That sly dog! I *knew* something was going down in that water!"

You did what! Lucian said.

Your judgmental comments were amusing but now they're just annoying.

He defiled you in the water? Does he not respect you at all?

Would you listen to yourself? If I didn't know any better, I would think you're jealous.

Lucian went silent and I suddenly got paranoid. He wasn't jealous, right? He was just a sexist pig who thought non-virgins were trashy. I hoped that was it.

I couldn't think about it anymore, so I said, "Sorry, but no. Last night we…started to, but we decided to wait. I do know that he loves me though. He finally admitted it."

So nothing happened. Why did you let me believe it?

Go away, Lucian! I'm with Gallard whether you like it or not. It's none of your business and your opinion doesn't matter to me.

I studied Lydian's face and she didn't look impressed. "Really, that's it? I love you, you love me; we're a happy family? That's so lame, Lela, there has to be more to this super lame story. Unless I was right and you are just the lamest person ever. At least tell me you got to third base."

"Oh yeah…well, wait what's the difference between second and third base?"

Lydian rolled her eyes. "If you have to ask that question, then you definitely didn't get to third base."

The waitress came to our table and I ordered my food. By then I was extremely hungry and since there were hardly any customers in there with us, my order came back in a little over fifteen minutes. I attacked my plate with earnest and ate most of it in fifteen minutes.

"Out of curiosity, I've noticed that you've stopped accusing me of trying to steal Jordan. Did you finally come to your senses or did something change?" I asked. She scooted to the corner of the booth and rested her legs on the bench. Her demeanor changed again, like it had when we were by the pool. Something was off with her.

"This whole situation has just inspired me to realize I should appreciate what I have. If Jordan says that he loves me, then I'm going to believe him. I want to enjoy that while I can."

"While you can? Do you think he'll stop loving you for some reason?" She avoided eye contact and that gave me my answer. "Why?"

"He may love me despite my craziness…but there are some things that are…unforgivable."

I stopped chewing and set my fork down.

"Lydian, you're scaring me. What's going on with you? Look, we may have clashing personalities and fight all the time, but I still think of you as family. You've become like a sister to me, and I actually don't mind your company. You are very eccentric, that is true. But eccentric Lydian is the Lydian I've grown to love. And if *I* can love you unconditionally, then Jordan can as well. He's never going to stop loving you. He's your D'Aubigne, as you so lovingly called him before." I laughed. "Wouldn't it be awesome if we ended up as in-laws?"

She sucked in her breath and shuddered a bit. If she was about to cry, she was having a difficult time fighting the tears.

"Lela, I have to—" she began to speak, but her phone buzzed and she pulled it out of her pocket. If it was Jordan texting her, they'd gotten to England a lot faster than I'd thought. They would have to be flying at an amazing speed to fly four thousand miles in less than an hour. "It's my alarm," she explained. "We should go if we want to get through security and all that crap."

I took one more bite of food before going up to pay. I was still hungry, but the food wasn't on my mind. I was curious to know what Lydian had been about to say before her phone had interrupted her.

We walked out to the car and I got in the driver's seat. I put the key in the ignition and turned it, but it just made a sputtering noise. I tried it again but got the same results.

"That's strange," I said. "It's gassed up and we didn't leave any doors open."

Lydian got out and I popped the hood so she could check it out. For being a very girly girl, she was quite knowledgeable when it came to cars. She once told me that her dad had taught her about auto repair so she could help herself if her car ever broke down in the middle of nowhere.

"The battery is dead," she deduced. "I'll go inside and see if someone will give us a jump."

"Well, *that's* not appropriate. We're both in relationships," I joked. She rolled her eyes. "What? I can't make dirty jokes too?"

She started to go into the restaurant but turned around and hugged me. I was confused, but hugged her back. As long as we'd known each other, she'd never hugged me, not genuinely anyway.

When she let go she said, "I'll go see about that help," then continued through the door. I leaned against the car while I waited for her. There was a van parked next to me that was playing very loud music and I found it strange that the driver was just sitting in the car instead of going in to eat. The person in the passenger seat kept glancing at me every now and then, making me feel uneasy. It was dark since there were hardly any lights in the parking lot. I suddenly wished that I'd gone in with Lydian.

Three minutes passed then five and she still wasn't back. It shouldn't have been that hard to find someone to jumpstart our car. There were only six other people in the restaurant, for crying out loud. I was about to go in when the guy in the van got out and started talking to me.

"Are you having car trouble?" he asked. He wasn't Indian. He had a foreign accent, though.

"Uh, yeah, but my friend is getting help," I replied. I wished that he would go away. He gave me the creeps.

"She's been gone a while. A girl like you shouldn't be left out here in the dark. It's dangerous."

He stepped closer to me. My gut told me that I should run and I started to, but he caught up with me, pulling a bag over my head. I kicked and yelled, hoping that someone would hear me, but it was a pointless effort. I heard him open the door to his van and he tossed me in. I rolled a few times before hitting the door on the other side.

The van started and he drove away while I tried to pull the bag off. He'd tied it on pretty tight, so I crawled along the floor until I got to the back and attempted to kick out the tail light. It was a harder feat than I thought and didn't get any results after about ten tries. I couldn't believe this was happening. A million ideas kept running through my head about why he had taken me. Was he a serial rapist? A sex trafficker? Neither of those sounded better than the other. Either way, I knew that I was in a very bad situation.

I felt for my phone in my pocket but it was gone. It must have fallen out during the struggle. I hoped that Lydian had at least seen the van take off so she could chase after it. If she did manage to catch up with it, I couldn't wait to see what she would do to him. I'd never seen her fight, but the man wouldn't stand a chance against her.

The van finally stopped after what felt like forever and I listened as he got out of the driver seat and walked around to the side. The door opened then he grabbed my arm, yanking me out. He walked rather quickly, so my feet were practically dragging across the dirt as I tried to keep up with his pace.

He opened another door and I was forced inside a dank smelling room. I came upon some steps unexpectedly, nearly tripping, but the man caught me. I didn't know if I should be grateful or wish that he hadn't caught me. Death by stairs sounded like a good way to die compared to what he probably had in store for me.

We got to the bottom and he pushed me across the room then sat me in a chair before tying me to it. I could sense that there were others there with me. There was a lot of movement and I could feel a hundred eyes on me. I hated the silence, so I decided to break it.

"If you guys are trying to sell me, you won't get much. I have Gonorrhea, Herpes, and all sorts of nasty diseases."

"I'm afraid you are wrong about who you are dealing with," said a man's voice. My sarcastic grin turned into a look of dread and my stomach became sour. I knew that voice. I hadn't heard it in weeks, but it was distinct enough to invoke fear in me.

"Samil," I said. He chuckled then someone pulled the bag off my head.

"Ding, ding, ding, and we have a winner!" another man shouted. It was Matthew. The rest of the group laughed in amusement, but I gave him a fierce look.

"It's so wonderful to see you again, Lela," Matthew continued. "Love the hair, by the way. But I'm surprised that you aren't, well…dead!"

"Yeah, I guess it takes more than a few bullets and a switch to mortality to stop me. Sorry to disappoint."

Samil walked up to me and knelt down in front of my chair. The very sight of him filled me with rage as I thought of how he'd ordered Mark and my mother to be killed without hesitation. I hated him. I wanted to burn him alive, over and over until he couldn't bear the pain anymore and then burn him again.

"It's been fun watching your friends running around, trying to find Solomon. I've been in India for quite some time now. We thought about closing in on you at my vacation home, which you have all so easily made yourselves comfortable in. That was until we learned of your new...ability."

I forced myself to look at him. "And what ability is that?"

He stood up and started pacing the room. "I heard from a reliable source that *you* are able to communicate with Lucian Christophe."

I didn't change my expression. How he'd come across this fact was beyond me, unless David had said something. But he wouldn't do that. Not if he wanted to protect me.

"I wouldn't really call it communicating. More like fighting and arguing."

"So it's true. You have no idea how much easier you are making this for me!" Samil looked behind me and smiled. "Thank you, Miss Powell. You've done well. As promised, you are free to go. And also as I promised, Jordan will remain unharmed."

I frowned then turned around to see who he was talking to. I felt tears burning in my eyes when I made the connection. "Lydian?" I said as she stepped out from behind the large group. She didn't look at me but passed by my chair, stopping next to Samil.

"*And* Robin. You promised I could take her with me," she said to him.

"Right! I almost forgot. Thank you for reminding me. Matthew?"

Matthew left the room and disappeared behind a door down the hall. I tried to get Lydian to look at me, but she wouldn't. I was reeling from her unexpected betrayal. The whole time I thought she was just having mood swings she'd been secretly plotting to hand me over to Samil.

"Why?" I asked her. "How could you do this? You were my friend, I *trusted* you!"

Matthew came back and I forced a smile when I saw that Robin was with him. She looked fine, only really sad. She'd been taken care of, just as David had promised. When she saw me as well, she let go of his hand and ran over to me, hopping into my lap.

"Lela! I missed you!" she said, hugging me around my neck. I wanted so badly to hug her back, but my hands were tied to the chair. I kissed the side of her head.

"I missed you too! Are you okay?"

She nodded and said, "These men are mean. David was nice though. He didn't let them be mean to me."

Samil sighed from impatience then lifted her out of my lap. "Come on, Robin, It's time to leave with Auntie Lydian. I've got work to do."

She started screaming and hitting him, trying to get him to put her down. I held my breath as I waited for him to hurt her. If he did, I would probably find some inner strength to free myself from the chair and maim him.

"Samil, let me talk to her for a second. Please!" I begged. He hesitated then let go of her and she ran back to me. "Robin, I love you. And I need you to do something for me, okay." She wiped away her tears and nodded. I hated seeing her so afraid. She was so young and innocent. I didn't want her to lose her innocence as I had. "You need to go with Lydian, sweetheart. If you do, she will take you to Aaron and Kevin. You want to see them right?"

"Yes. I miss my brothers," she said, her lip quivering. "Are you coming with me?"

I looked over at Samil. If he was telling the truth and Lydian had informed him about my direct link to Lucian then he was probably planning on using me to talk with him. The problem was neither I nor Lucian had the information Samil wanted. And he probably wouldn't believe me if I told him.

It hit me like a swift kick to the gut. I was going to die. Unless Gallard and the others found a way to get to me, Samil was going to do whatever it took to get me to talk to Lucian. He would probably try to torture the information out of me and then kill me when he realized I was useless to him.

Of all the times I'd been attacked, shot, sick, or stabbed, the realization that my time was up had never frightened me as much.

"I don't know, Robin. There's a chance that this is the last time you'll see me."

She started bawling and I felt the tears coming as well. "Give me a hug before you go, all right! And tell our brothers that...I said hi," I instructed her. "And...there's a man with them. He's tall and has long, black hair. His name is Gallard. Tell him...tell him that I love him and not to be sad. You can trust him okay. He'll make sure you're safe."

She squeezed me around the neck once more then Lydian picked her up.

"Lela, I'm really—"

"Don't," I said. "Just leave. Get my sister back to her brothers."

She wiped away a tear then walked through the door and up the stairs. Once I couldn't see her anymore, I struggled to pull myself together. Whatever Samil had in store for me was going to be hell, and I needed to save my energy for it. It would be painful, but not as painful as Lydian's betrayal. It hurt more than any knife ever could.

"Matthew, untie her," Samil commanded.

He came over to me and cut the ropes with a knife. I massaged my wrists, glad to have my hands free, but the comfort didn't last long. Samil pulled me out of the chair by my hair and dragged me across the floor. "Now, we can do this easily or with difficulty. Ask Lucian about his day-walking ability. If you give me what I ask, I may let you live.

"Just listening to your voice makes me want to die," I snarled at him. "Keep talking, maybe it will work."

He glared then threw me against the wall. I hit my head pretty hard and I became disoriented. I didn't even try to get away from him. It was a pointless fight. There were about ten other vampires in the room. I didn't have a chance.

Samil grabbed my hair again and tossed me aside in another direction. This time, I felt a rib crack, knocking the wind out of me. It hadn't punctured my lung, but it hurt miserably.

"Come on! Just talk to him and the pain will stop," Samil whined. He picked me up by my throat and began to squeeze. Between the struggle to breathe and the pain in my rib, I was in agony. I should have been used to it by now. I'd been subject to a lot of maiming in a short period of time. "You know, the sooner you talk to him, the sooner I can let you go! If he can tell me how he walks in the sun, I won't need to bring him back."

"What...do you...mean?" I asked, gasping for air. "I thought...you wanted him...alive."

He dropped me to the floor and I coughed.

"Of course not! I don't want that pompous idiot walking around. I only wish to know how he can be out in the day."

I used a nearby chair to help me stand up, wincing as I did. "Why didn't you say so in the first place? We could have come to you and made a trade; Lucian's secret for David and Robin. You didn't have to kidnap me or turn my own friend against me."

He shrugged. "Well, partly I wanted to make Gallard suffer. He made me rather angry when he killed my other followers. And I won't stop until I've had the last move. Since he's in love with you, I get to use you to hurt him. The fact that you can speak with Lucian, well...that makes this a win-win deal."

He stepped toward me and I flinched. He grinned, pleased that he'd invoked fear in me.

"Lucian Christophe is not someone you want to let loose on this earth," he said, standing over me. "If you think *I'm* cruel, you have another thing coming. He has no limits. No line he won't cross. I spoke with a few immortals that had the unwanted privilege of meeting him. One of them even claimed that he'd had an affair with his own daughter."

Lies! All lies! Lucian bellowed.

"That's a bit far....fetched don't you think?" I struggled to speak through the pain. "Besides...I thought...his daughters were children when...they were killed."

Samil shook his head. "I don't know where you got that impression. They were young women when Solomon Sharmentino murdered them. Close to your age, I presume. Doesn't make it any less sick. Lucian is a twisted fellow. He didn't deserve to have the power that he did."

"And *you* do?" I snarled. Provoking Samil probably wasn't the best idea, but I wanted him to just knock me out already so I couldn't feel any more pain. I'd consumed so much blood over the past week that my body was more resilient than usual.

He pushed me backwards with full force and I landed on a glass table, shattering it on impact. By then I was too tired to move, even as I felt the glass shards penetrating my arms and back. He picked up one of the broken shards of glass and traced the tip of it with his finger then dug it into his skin. "It's sharp. And very small, so it wouldn't damage any organs. It would just make you bleed enough to lose consciousness." He looked down at me. "But I think you've been through enough for now. Matthew. Put her in one of the rooms. Maybe her untreated injuries will encourage her to talk. We'll check on her in the morning."

Matthew pulled me up by my arm, dragging me across the floor. He took me to one of the rooms down the hall and tossed me onto a foam mattress before closing the door behind him. I was about to sit up and try to pull some of the glass out of my skin when someone spoke up.

"Lela! What have they done to you?" It was David. I was so happy to see him that I couldn't even express it. He'd moved from across the room to my side and was gently stroking my hair.

"You're here," I said, reaching out to touch him. He took my hand and kissed it.

"He promised me that you would have immunity. He swore to me that no harm would come to you! Why does he have you here?" I was about to answer when he stopped me. "No, don't speak. You need to rest. More importantly we need to get this glass out so you can heal." He examined my wounds and started with my arm first. I whimpered with each tug of the be tough in front of David.

It took about thirty minutes for him to get it all out, but I felt so much better afterwards. The pain was subsiding as each cut healed, leaving tiny scabs all over me. I turned over to my side and smiled at him in thanks. He looked even older than when I'd seen him only a week before. The grey had spread throughout his beard and started to show on his sideburns.

"Why is it that whenever we see each other, one of us is hurt?" I asked. He chuckled.

"I guess it's our lot in life." He sighed and leaned against the wall next to the mattress. "I promised your mother I would watch out for you. I assured her that I would make sure you were safe. I failed her."

I shook my head. "Don't blame yourself for what happens to me. There are some things that are just out of our control."

"You're so smart. Your mother was smart too. You didn't get that from me. I'm just book smart." He forced a smile. "How did you end up here?"

"I found Gallard and the others and told them my plan. Turns out you were right about him loving me. I'm glad we were able to clear that up before…however this ends."

"You're going to see him again, Lela. Though, as your father, I shouldn't encourage you to have a relationship with a man so much older than you, Gallard is an exception. He's the one person I can trust to take care of you. If you would stop trying to be such a hero all the time, maybe you wouldn't be hurt as much."

"You and I both know I'm not the damsel in distress type."

I shifted so that I could get somewhat comfortable. The mattress was so old and had no support, which was what I needed. The hard floor only made the pain of my injuries less bearable. I needed something to distract me; to get my mind off of my aching body.

"Tell me about yourself. Since everything I know about you is a lie, I would like to know the truth."

"Is this to make up for all the years I didn't read to you at night?"

"Sure, why not?"

He told me everything; how he'd been born in Virginia and grew up with seven siblings and how his father was a welder and his mother was a housewife. He revealed that he'd turned at fifteen after being given the blood as a joke by one of his coworkers. His family believed he was dead and when he showed up after being gone for several days, they'd turned him away in fear.

He'd later enlisted into the army and served WWII. He even saved his brother's troops when they'd been trapped for days in an abandoned house. They were surrounded by enemies and were dying of starvation. He earned a medal of honor for his heroic act and also gained back the respect of his father.

He met my mother fifty years after that and his tone became somber as he described their brief romance. A month after David turned mortal again, Mark made my mother choose between losing custody of Aaron and being with David and David didn't give her the choice of giving up her children, so she'd returned to Mark.

He finished the tale by telling me about the first time he'd met me in Orlando and how he'd spent the week with my mother and me. Apparently she'd sent pictures from each of my birthdays, including the sonograms she'd gotten before I was born.

His story moved me to hug him, despite my injuries and I held onto him for quite a while. There was so much love in his embrace and I never felt more at home than in the arms of my real father. Nineteen years was worth the wait to meet him.

I heard someone yell David's name and he groaned before standing up. I didn't want him to go. I didn't want to be alone in that cold room on that itchy mattress.

"They always need something. I'm not sure if they'll let me see you again anytime soon, so hang in there, all right! I love you."

"Love you too, dad," I said. "Can I call you that, or is it weird?"

"I've waited almost twenty years to hear you call me that." He kissed my forehead before reluctantly walking out the door.

• • •

I lay on the mattress, waiting for Samil to return and continue his torture session. My cuts from the glass may have been healing, but my rib was still broken and my head throbbed. I never thought I'd say this, but I was hoping that Lucian would make an appearance. It would make my predicament so much easier if I could get the interrogation over with. At least when I was unconscious, I didn't feel any pain. I would take Lucian's company over a broken rib and concussion any day.

As I turned over, I felt something hard in my pocket and reached in to see what it was. My heart leapt a bit when I realized I still had David's knife. Ever since he'd given it to me, I made sure to keep in nearby or on my person. I didn't know when, but I planned to use it at some point. It wouldn't inflict as much damage as I wanted, but it could be enough to incapacitate someone when stabbed in the right place.

Hours passed when I heard someone at the door and I quickly shoved the knife back into my pocket. It was Matthew. The last person I wanted to see. He had an arrogant smile on his face and it made me want to stab him right then and there. I hated that he was able to gloat. I'd started to kick the crap out of him almost six months ago in Vegas, but now I wasn't as strong anymore. He was enjoying my weakness.

"Samil had to step away. He told me to take over for him, so you get to spend the next hour or so with me." He reached down next to his ankle and pulled a knife out, one that was much, *much* longer than mine. "Welcome to sixty minutes in hell."

I started scooting away, but he was at my side in one swift move with the knife to my cheek.

"You know what. I think you're too pretty. Why don't we do something about that?" He sliced my face and I winced.

"What the hell? I thought you were here to help me contact Lucian, not play plastic surgeon!" I yelled at him. He held the tip of the knife just above my navel and pressed hard enough to make it sting.

"Samil didn't give me any specific orders. He just said to get the job done." He pressed harder and I gritted my teeth. "You're going to wish that you'd killed me in Vegas when I'm through with you."

The pain in my head worsened and my vision blurred. I was starting to think that the injury to my head was worse than I thought. I could barely even see Matthew's face and he was a foot away from me. I felt myself falling over until I was lying down once more.

"You know, you could have been an amazing immortal. You were strong. You could walk in the day. If you asked, I would have gladly joined your side. But instead you chose to spend your time going to high school and working at a bowling alley. Such a waste of power."

I didn't reply. I just wanted him to shut up because his voice wasn't making the pain in my head any less unbearable. I looked past him and slightly raised my head. Someone was standing just behind him, but he didn't seem to notice. My vision cleared a bit and I was able to make out the person's features.

"Lucian?" I whispered. He smirked at me then knelt down beside Matthew.

Are you really going to let him mess with you like that? Get up and fight him! He taunted.

"Easy for you to say."

Matthew looked around the room. "Is he here? Is Lucian making contact?"

Beat him while you still can, Lucian continued. *His voice is annoying me too.*

Matthew forced me to sit up again. "Answer me, is he here?"

"Screw you," I said. "Samil wanted the information, and he's the only one I'll talk to, not his pathetic middle man!"

He slapped me across the face and it stung on impact. Feeling rather bold, I balled up my fist and slugged him back with the same force that he'd used.

I'm surprised you're even talking to me after I snapped at you, I said.

I should ignore you. Tis what you wanted right?

Then why are you here?

Lucian chewed on the inside of his mouth then looked away. He never gave me an answer and I thought back to my previous suspicion. He'd been relentless with his jealous comments. Could he possibly want me for himself? Was that why he didn't want me in any relationships? That possibility freaked me out.

Matthew leaned over me, a frightening look on his face. Something in eyes had changed. He'd snapped, and now there was no telling what he was capable of.

"I think that your being able to talk to Lucian is a bunch of crock," Matthew sneered. "You're playing Samil like a fool. He's just too obsessed with the prospect of walking in the day to realize that." He stroked my cheek with the back of his hand. "But at least you're good for one thing." He started sliding the knife up my shirt and I began to panic. I'd thought they'd done everything horrible to me that was possible. But this was ten times worse.

"No, don't! I'll talk to him! I'll ask him anything you—"

He covered my mouth.

"If you scream, I'll do more than just cut your face, little girl."

He jerked the knife up, ripping my shirt. I used all my strength to try and push him away, but he straddled me so that I couldn't kick him. The only thing that was free was my right hand and I felt around for the knife in my pocket. Matthew's knee was in the same spot, so I couldn't reach it. I began to cry. I cried because nothing would be more shameful than what he was about to do to me. I'd never felt so helpless in my life.

I prayed that I would black out. I didn't want to be conscious for this. The pain in my head was growing worse and worse, giving me some hope that I would get my wish. I continued trying to grab a hold of the knife despite the small chance that I had. If Matthew would just shift a little bit, I would
be able to get to it.

"Gallard's not going to be happy if he knew that I got to you first," Matthew jeered. "Unless he already has. Guess I'll just have to find out."

Finally, his leg moved back as he was unbuckling his pants and I grabbed the knife with the tips of my fingers. He was distracted, so he didn't even see me flip it open.

What are you waiting for? Lucian asked. *Stab him!*

It was strange thinking that Lucian was on my side, and

even stranger that I found his presence comforting. I found my target then stabbed Matthew as hard as I could in the stomach, just above his groin then ripped out the knife in an upward motion. He let out a blood-curdling yell and moved away from me, falling backwards on the floor. Finding a new sense of empowerment, I got up and leaned over him, plunging the knife into his chest over and over.

I could feel Lucian's hand on my shoulder as I continued stabbing Matthew. I must have been lingering between life and death if I was still able to see and feel him.

Good, he said. *Kill him! Teach that pervert a lesson.*

You think every man besides yourself is a pervert!

Well, I was wrong. Curtis and Gallard are more honorable than this man. You need to kill him before he does this to someone else.

I held the knife in the air, ready to bring it down again, but something stopped me. I felt sick, but not because I was ill. It was an entirely different cause; guilt. In just a few minutes, I'd turned into a blood-thirsty killer. I enjoyed inflicting pain on Matthew, not because of what he'd almost done to me, but because I wanted to hurt him. This wasn't me. I wasn't this person that I was acting like in this moment. Lucian's influence was getting stronger and stronger by the minute.

"No," I said to Lucian. "I can't."

Why not? He tried to rape you. He deserves to die!

I dropped my arm and backed away. "I'm not going to stoop down to his level. If I do, it will make me no better than him."

I glanced over at Matthew who was still lying incapacitated on the ground moaning in pain. He was bleeding quite a bit, so I had time to prepare for his retaliation. If I was lucky, someone would come in to see what was wrong, unless Samil had taken everyone with him.

The door flew open and Samil stormed in. I flipped the knife closed, hiding it behind my back. I was somewhat grateful that he'd arrived when he did. I'd rather be a punching bag than Matthew's sex toy.

"What happened here?" he demanded. I smirked then kicked Matthew's foot with my own.

"He got a taste of what it's like to cross me. The bastard tried to force himself on me so I stabbed him. Seems like a fair case, don't you?" I was trying to act like I wasn't afraid, but the whole thing had shaken me up. The thought of what he'd almost done to me made me cringe with fear.

Samil groaned then called for two of his followers. They came into the room and lifted Matthew off the floor, helping him out the door. He then turned his attention to me.

"Did he at least make any progress? Did you speak with Lucian?"

I was mortified that he'd written off Matthew's attempt as a minor thing. He really didn't care what happened to me as long as he got what he wanted.

"Lucian was turned by a man with white hair and green eyes," I said.

"That is not enough. I need a name."

"He doesn't know, Samil."

"Ask him again! Be persuasive!"

"He. Doesn't. Know."

Samil grabbed me by the throat. "You're lying. This whole time, you've made me look like a fool! You can't really talk to Lucian, can you? This was just a trick, a distraction so that Gallard could find us! Where is he, Lela? Is he somewhere gloating? Is he biding his time, laughing at me while we try and contact a dead man?"

"I'm not lying. After everything you've done to me, why would I lie? You've beaten me, tortured me, and had one of your followers try to assault me. You think that I like this? You think I get off on pain? Well I don't!"

He squeezed my neck even harder. "I don't have time for this. You are of no use to me."

Lela, what are you doing? Fight him! Lucian said.

I can't. I'm too tired. You're going to have to find your body without me.

Samil let go of my neck, grabbing either side of my head. Time seemed to slow down at that point. I thought back to when Gallard and I had parted and what we'd promised each other: that we would find our way back to one another no matter what happened. It was the only thing I could hang onto. I didn't know how, but I was determined to follow through.

"I promise," I uttered out loud.

With one flick of his wrists, Samil twisted my neck to the side, breaking it instantly. I felt the pain for a short second, but not for long. Everything went dark before I even hit the ground.

Chapter Sixteen

•••Lucian•••

I'd forgotten what it was like to be alive. To breathe. To touch. For so long, I'd been in darkness, waiting for something. Anything that would bring me back. My body coursed with blood, the warmth overhwelming me like a hot bath. The very beating of my heart felt foreign. I became aware of every part of me. My lungs, my fingers, the nerves and tendons. Too much time had passed since I'd been corporeal.

My memories came after the shock of being alive. They flooded my mind, over and over, each point in time becoming clearer as they replayed. It was almost as if I were present in different time periods all at once. Finally, it came to a stop. Right where I had my earliest memory.

I hung onto it, not wanting to let go. Part of me wanted to wake up; to use the body that I had waited so long to get a hold of, but another wanted to stay and see everything that had happened. To cling to the times before everything I'd worked for shattered in an instant. The moment Cherish was born.

My memory began to have gaps after that. I couldn't remember what happened after that. It turned back to the night I killed my parents, only this time there was another girl there. I knew who she was, but my mind refused to put a name to her face. Then it jumped to a place I didn't know and I saw the same girl, killing some man. Then I was in a strange room. Each time, I would see her and soon I saw several faces I could not recognize. I had memories that weren't my own. I didn't want to see them, so I tried to go back to my last moments I had been alive.

I remembered hearing screams from somwhere in the house. I remembered Florence wailing in agony. I remembered Solomon being in my room and the flash of a knife and how it had severed the nerves in my neck, causing me to be paralized from the shoulders down. I remembered being dragged through my house, unable to fight him off. I remembered the anguish seeing my two daughters lying dead on the floor in their bedroom. I remembered being hung upside down and Solomon slitting my throat, draining my blood into a bucket below me. I remembered him cutting me down and placing me into a box, sealing me in.

I heard voices and was brought back to the present. Something inside of me was saying that I needed to open my eyes. I didn't know why, but the will was so strong that I couldn't fight it. Then it came to me. I recalled the moments prior to my period of remininsce. I had been speaking with the girl, Lela. The one that reminded me of my daughter, Cherish. The one I'd been able to speak too since she was a child. She had been in danger and I had tried to help her. But I had not been able to save her. The dark one, Samil had killed her. Something had happened the moment she died. I had lost my train of thought and it took me a while to comprehend what had happened. She had lost the fight for her life and now I was in control of her body.

• • •

I lay on the floor, taking in my surroundings. I rememered where I was, but I wanted my next move to be just right. Samil had left Lela's body in the room so I was alone for the time being. I craned my hearing to take in the voices that were outside the door. I distinguished two of them, one being Samil's and the other Matthew's. He was berating him about his carelessness and demeaning him for his inablitlity to think outside of his pants, or something along those lines. That's when I recalled the incident that had happened only ten minutes before. Men like him disgusted me and I looked forward to teaching him a lesson.

"Get rid of the body," I heard Samil say. "Unless you're not competent enough to do so."

I heard footsteps coming towards the door and I shut my eyes to feign death. I lay completely still as Matthew walked up to me then stopped. He nudged me with his foot and I could sense the smirk on his face, like he'd been the one that was responsible for her demise.

"Poor, poor Lela. Thought you had the last laugh, didn't you?" he taunted. He knelt down and took the knife out of her pocket, or rather mine. It was confusing to me where the line was drawn between her and me. "I didn't appreciate your stabbing me. Doesn't matter anymore, though. You're dead. You can't fight anymore."

I had a bad feeling about where this was going. I could almost smell the perverseness that radiated from him when he spoke. I felt him tug on the top of her jeans and I swiftly grabbed his hand, twisting it and breaking his wrist.

"I am sorry, what were you saying?" I retorted. I stood up and kicked him across the room. He tried to run away, but I beat him to the door and shoved him backwards again. He fell to the floor and began trying to scoot away.

"You're alive? How? I watched him kill you!" he sputtered. I sauntered over to him then picked the knife up from the floor. It was still covered in his blood from Lela's attack on him earlier.

"It takes more than a broken neck to stop me." I rammed the knife into his femur and he shouted in pain. I wanted him to be quiet so I pulled the knife out then cut out his tongue. "She was right, you know. Tis quite annoying to hear you speak."

He moaned and I stared at him, watching as he slowly began to give up. I hadn't had this much fun since I'd partied with Solomon in Italy before he'd gone soft on me. Before he'd become my enemy. But I was tired of Matthew and his sadistic ways. The sooner he was dead, the sooner I could move on and find Lela's lover. The one I was sure would help me get my real body back.

"Goodbye, Matthew. Tis been a pleasure…well…not really. Honestly, I rather despise you," I said. He tried to beg for his life, struggling to speak but I stopped him short by tearing his head from his shoulders, tossing it to the side. Seconds later, Samil burst into the room and I stepped aside to let him admire my work.

"What is this?" he asked. "It's not possible! You are dead!"

"Am I? You never learn, do you, Samil? How many times have you tried to kill me, two; three times? I cannot be killed. Tis time that you accept that."

I stopped next to him in front of the door. I hoped that he would let me leave without causing any trouble. I didn't want to kill him. Out of courteousy, I was willing to save him for someone else. Someone who had more of a reason to end his life than me.

"I am leaving now. Do not try to stop me," I said. I began to walk out of the room, but he grabbed my arm. Annoyed, I stuck the knife in his side. "Let. Go," I commanded. He groaned as he obeyed. Before I left, I asked, "Who is the pompous idiot now?" then I continued out of the room and into a different part of the building.

There were about a dozen other immortals in the next room, all who were staring at me. Most of them were men and about a fourth were women. They looked terrified, probably because I was covered in blood. Or because they'd been informed that Lela was dead.

One in particular looked familiar. The man in the back. He wasn't pale like the rest of them and I could hear his heartbeat. He was human.

"Lela?" he asked. He stepped away from the group and came towards me. No one else dared to move, not even to stop him. "What are you doing? Is Samil letting you go?"

"Aw yes," I said. "David." I looked around the room and found a partially opened door that revealed a staircase behind it. My instinct told me that it was an exit so I did my best to put on an act. I had to act as if I were Lela in order for him to trust me. I took his hand in mine, pulling him behind me. "We are leaving."

"Wait, what? We're leaving? Just like that. Samil is okay with this?" he questioned as we made our way up the stairs.

"Samil has no say in the matter. I am leaving and you are coming with me."

He didn't say a word as we got to the top then opened another door, sunlight pouring into the room. I took in the fresh air, the warmth on my face. It had been too long since I had seen the sun. The sky. The clouds. I couldn't get enough of it.

But the appreciation of life would have to wait. I had an agenda, and I needed to get away from wherever I was.

"I need you to procure us a means of transportation," I ordered. "Anything will do."

"Uh…all right. I suppose I could hotwire the van. Where do you want to go?"

"London. Where Gallard is," I paused to think for a moment. What would Lela say that would convince David that I was her? "He would want to know that we are safe."

David opened the right door to the black vehicle then adjusted a few wires just below the seat. The vehicle sputtered then the engine roared to life and I walked around to the other side and got in. I had never ridden in a car before. I only knew what they were from Lela's memories. When I had been alive last, we still had horse-driven carriages.

He pulled out of the lot then started driving down the road. As we drove, I observed what I was wearing. My clothes were covered in blood, Lela's as well as Matthew's and I wanted to get out of them and into something clean. Not more than a day could have gone by since Lela was taken, and I hoped that her car was still at the restaruant. If only I remembered what it was called.

"What happened to your shirt?" David asked quietly.

"This little gift is from Matthew. He tried to assualt me and your knife saved my life…again."

"No! He tried to…" David slammed on the breaks. "I'm going to kill him. I don't care if I die trying, but I—"

"It is too late. I already killed him shortly before we left. I believe that is why Samil let us go. He's afraid of me. I showed him that I can't be underestimated."

David took one hand off the steering wheel and put his arm around me in a comforting embrace. I almost pulled away but remembered I had to keep acting in order to maintain his cooperation.

He drove with no real destination in mind while I tried to access her memories. It wasn't as easy as when she'd been alive. Before, I had been able to learn things because she used her brain. When she thought about things, I had the ability to retain her thoughts.

"Come on, girl. What's the restaurant's name?" I whispered

outloud, unintentionally.

"What did you say?" David asked.

"Nothing. I am trying to remember..." I found it. The sign written in red and yellow. It was a name I couldn't pronounce for I didn't know Punjabi. "I need paper and something to write with."

"Check the glove box."

"The what?" Did people have a special box for gloves? I didn't think anyone wore gloves that often in this day and age, let alone had boxes for them in their vehicles. David pointed to the compartment in front of me and I pulled the tab, opening it with curiosity. I was slightly disappointed that there were no gloves, but I dug around until I found yellow, lined paper and a pen. I wrote down the name then showed it to him.

"Do you know this place?" I asked. David glanced at the paper and nodded.

"Sure. I've passed by there a few times. Are you hungry or something?"

"No, her...my car is there. I would like to retrieve my belongings."

David changed the direction he was driving and I assumed he was headed to the restaurant. So far, he didn't seem to be suspicious of who I was. It helped that I wasn't saying much. The less I spoke, the better.

He pulled into the parking lot and I was pleased to see the silver car still sitting in the same spot as the day before. He parked next to it and I got out to look through the window to see if it was still unlocked. Thankfully, it was and I opened the back door to grab the suitcase and cooler of blood bags.

"If you do not mind, I would also like to stop by the vacation house to clean up. I do not wish to be in these torn clothes any longer."

"Whatever you need, Lela. You've been through a lot. You should take some time to rest before we leave."

I tossed the bags and cooler into the back of the van then we took off. David knew which vacation house I was speaking of, so we were able to get there within ten minutes. The traffic was astonishing and I hadn't seen so much chaos in my life. I'd lived in a part of London that wasn't riddled with people in the streets, unlike other areas where the alleys were full of beggars and lunatics.

We got to the door and David began looking for a key. It was a very nice house, unlike any I'd ever seen. The design wasn't traditional as I was used to. Then I remembered that I had seen it before, just not with my own eyes. Lela's memories were starting to get clearer and clearer as time went on.

"I can't seem to find a key. Do you remember if Gallard put it somewhere?" David asked. I thought back to the time before everyone had left the house. Lela had said goodbye to him last, but she hadn't been paying attention to the keys.

"Sorry. I did not notice. Gallard and I were...distracted. The keys were the last thing on my mind."

David raised an eyebrow then continued searching. "I know

I said I don't mind your seeing Gallard, but the less I know about what you two do, the better. There's only so much a father can handle."

I smirked. "You do not have to worry, David. We have not done anything...yet."

"Okay, now we're done with this discussion. Let's keep looking for the key."

I smiled to myself as we continued searching. It didn't appear that we were going to find it so I walked up to the door. "We may need to force our way in, David. The key is not here." I turned the doorknob and to my spurprise, it opened on the first try. "Well, well. it seems that someone forgot to lock it."

"Or someone else is already here," David nearly whispered. He went in first and I followed, walking as quietly as possible. The house was silent, but I could sense that someone was there. David went out back and I looked in the living room then edged my way to the kitchen. The stove was on. I stood in front of it touching the top with my hand and pulled it back. It was still very hot. Someone definitely had been there not too long ago.

I heard movment behind me and I turned around to fight off my potential attacker. I grabbed them, swung them around, then pressed the person's face to the burner. The girl yelled then swore at me and I let go of her.

"You! Why did you not identify yourself?" I asked upon releasing her. Lydian held her hand to her face as it slowly healed.

"I'm sorry I...they told me you...how are you here?"

"What is it that you mean?"

"Edgar called...he's the middleman that passed my messages to Samil. He said that you were dead. That he'd killed you!"

"He was mistaken. I was only injured and was able to get away. Not so much get away as kindly persuade him to not interfere. We have come to an understanding."

"Lela, why are you talking like that? You sound like a horrible immitation of Data on *Star Trek*."

I didn't understand her analogy, so I brushed it off as some twenty-first century joke.

"Well this is just great," she continued. "You know, I already called Gallard to give him the news. He's devastated. I've never heard him so upset. It sounded like he was dying. I even...I don't know how to explain it, but I felt it when you died." She suddenly glanced at my clothes. "Lela...what did they do to you?"

"Think of the worst thing you can imagine and they probably did it." I got close to her face as her expression filled with horror. "Now wallow in your guilt."

David entered the kitchen at the time and he was holding the hand of a little girl. Her eyes brightened when she saw me and she ran, leaping into my arms.

"Lela, you're back!" she said, hugging me around my neck. It had been a while since I'd held a child. She was as small as Cherish had been at her age. To keep up the façade, I would have to play the part of the loving sister.

"Yes, I am back, darling. Are you well?"

"I don't like McDonalds here. It's gross," she said, pouting. "Lydian said you were gone like mommy and daddy and couldn't come back. Are you an angel?"

David frowned and looked at Lydian. "What are you saying? You assumed Lela was dead?"

Lydian shook her head. "No, I didn't assume, I was told by a reliable source that she'd been killed by Samil. He even saw her body himself."

They both turned to me and I froze as I held the little girl in my arms. My trick was failing.

"Well clearly I was just unconscious," I insisted. "The blood healed my broken neck and I awoke a few hours later."

"It doesn't work like that, Lela," David said. "The blood can make us stronger and heal faster, but there's no way it could heal an injury as severe as a broken neck in just a few minutes. We're human and a broken neck is fatal to us in almost every case."

I was running out of excuses and theories to throw out. Eventually I would have to tell them the truth about what really happened but I wanted more time.

"While I would love to sit around and chat about my mistaken death, I want to clean up." I handed Robin back to Lydian. "I should not be long."

I went into the first room I came across and made my way to the bathroom. I was looking forward to using a shower for the first time. It was a much more convenient way of cleaning than taking a bath in a wooden basin. The water would come out a huge spout and there was no filling or dumping of it afterwards. The used water simply went down the drain.

I spent more time in the bathroom than I planned to. I was curious about the new body I inhabited. I would have prefered to possess a man, but she would have to do for the time being. She was tall and had beautiful hair. Her legs were strong, like she'd used them quite a bit. I remembered she was a runner when she was younger. But what I was most impressed with were her scars. She had so many that I couldn't even count. Scars on her back, some she'd gotten from the table and some that had been healed from a while ago. Several on her front that resembled the ones on her back along with a long, diagnal one under her ribs, just below where Samil had broken one. A bite mark on her neck, probably from the vampire she'd run into while in Florida. There was a fresh cut on her face and one above her navel where Matthew had left his mark. This girl had been through a lot, and she'd survived that long.

After I chose some clothes from her bag, I stared at her facial features in the mirror. Her eyes were blue, but not as blue as mine had been. Her hair was as long as Cherish's had been when she died. I wondered what Lela would look like with red hair. Would she look like her? Would she look like my daughter?

As I was thinking this, the reflection in the mirror began to change. I moved back, startled by it at first, but then I realized what was going on. Somehow, by thinking it, I had caused her hair to go from blonde to crimson and her eyes grew a shade darker. I'd nearly forgotten that I had this ability. I had used it to change my appearance a few times when I wanted to hide that I was different. Whenever I came across night-walkers, I would darken them to grey. I had done this to avoid the questions, or fanatics like that of Samil who wanted to know my secret. The truth was, I didn't know why I was different. I never found the man who had been responsible for turning me.

I loved this new look on her. I knew that David and Lydian were already doubting me, so I decided to keep it and tell them the truth. They deserved to know that their friend was dead. I could only pretend to be her for so long before they found out anyway.

I opened the cooler and drank one of the blood bags. I prefered it fresh from the vein, but it would have to do for now. The blood healed her wounds faster than they had when she was alive. The broken rib and the bruise it had left on her skin became nonexistent and the cut on her face disapeared in seconds. My abilities were starting to take over her as well as my consciousness. Her body was definitely stronger than it used to be.

I found David and Lydian talking in the living room. They were speaking in hushed tones, but instantly went silent upon my entrance. I wasn't sure if it was because of Lela's new hair or the fact that they had been talking about me.

"Please tell me that isn't permanent," Lydian said. "You know what they say about gingers. No soul."

"Oh, Lydian, darling. I could say so many things about

traitors and the consequenses of treason, but I will hold my tongue since I have no desire to have this conversation with you. I am saving it for someone to whom it truly belongs."

"Lela, we've been talking," David said, changing the subject. "You've experienced so much this past month; loss, sickness, torture. After so much, it's going to start taking a toll on you. We think that—"

"Basicaly, we think you're going crazy," Lydian said. "You're strangely aloof and you're acting as if you just got done spending the day at a theme park instead of being roughed up by vampires. And your hair...I'm not even going to start with your hair."

"What Lydian is trying to say is that we're worried about you," David finished. "And I agree. Your hair...that's a drastic change."

I chuckled as I sat in the chair across from them. I had another memory flash of Lela's, probably from two days before. She'd watched Lydian and Jordan as they'd sat in this chair and wished that she could have that kind of relationship with Gallard. It must have been before he'd professed his love to her.

"Have you ever considered that it is not me that is different, but that I am not even who you think I am?" I asked. They both looked confused, so I waited for them to figure it out for themselves. They didn't seem to have any idea what I was hinting at. I was hoping that my hair would help them out, but I'd been wrong. "Bloody hell, you two. How can you not know when you are not talking to your friend? I thought you knew her better!"

David closed his eyes and hung his head. "Lucian. Of course, why didn't I see it before?"

"Lucian?" Lydian said. "No, it can't be Lucian! If that's Lucian then that means Lela is—"

"Dead," I said. "Unfortunately your source was correct. Samil broke her neck and within seconds, she died and I took over. I am sorry for your loss."

I hadn't sounded as sincere as I'd tried. I was never good at comforting others or being sympathetic. I'd been that way towards Lela when I was inside of her head, but not now. Not when I had an agenda.

Lydian burst into tears and David fought to hold back his. I couldn't remember the last time I cried. It had to have been when I was a child. I never even had a chance to cry when Cherish died. I'd been killed soon after. After all these years, all I had left was rage. Solomon would pay and pay dearly.

"I do not mean to sound inconsiderate, but I would appreciate if we could begin our journey to London as soon as possible. Solomon has my body and I would very much like to get back in it."

"We're not doing *anything* for you!" David shouted. "You've done enough. The only thing we're going to do is leave you here and hope that we never lay eyes on you again!"

He got up to leave the room and I tried to stop him, but he shoved me away, angering me and I retaliated by twisting his arm.

He punched me in the stomach, knocking the wind out of me and I slammed him to the ground. He kicked me in the leg, bringing me to the floor then grabbed Lela's knife that he'd taken from me and held it to my throat.

Ow! Quit it! I heard a voice say.

"Don't think I won't hurt you, Lucian," he said. "You may be in her body, but you're *not* her. I'll kill you if you cross me again!"

I laughed as his boldness. I'd underestimated him. I knew that he'd been drinking blood, and it had made him quite strong. I was stronger. Even still, I let him have his little victory. He deserved it since he'd just lost a daughter.

"I will let this slide for now. Call it a grace period. But if you try to fight me, you will lose," I snarled.

He gave me an icy glare as he stood up then kicked me, hard, in the side before leaving the room.

I said stop! The voice said again. I looked over at Lydian to see if she'd spoken, but she was still crying on the couch. I was sure at this point that I hadn't thought it. I began to recover from David's maiming and got up from the floor. I didn't want to read too much into it. My memories were clashing with Lela's.

And I was tired. It was funny since I'd spent the last five centures sleeping, yet I wanted nothing more than to shut my eyes and rest. I went back to the room where I had showered and lay on the bed. It was a huge bed. Bigger than the one I had shared with Florence. She never slept after I turned her. She was always out, feeding or whoring around with other nightwalkers. We'd stopped being intimate after Cherish was born. I'd assured her that after she'd turned, she couldn't have children anymore, but she didn't believe me. So instead, she got her pleasures elsewhere from men she was sure couldn't impregnate her like I could. I didn't care. I didn't love her anyway. She'd gotten what she wanted from me, and I from her. She had her immortality and I had Cherish.

I'd turned a blind eye to her infidelity until she'd brought one of her lovers home. I'd specifically told her to keep her indiscretions away from our children, but she broke the rule. Upon discovering them, I went after the immortal in a rage and cut him in half with one of my father's swords.

Unfortunately, Cherish saw the whole thing and she ran away, screaming. Her cries made me forget my anger towards Florence and I went after her. She'd locked herself in her room and I spent the rest of the day coaxing her out. She eventually came out and let me hold her. She was never the same after that. Her innocence was gone, and I didn't know how to give it back to her.

I heard the door open and I looked up to see who had come into the room. It was Robin and she looked like she'd been crying. She didn't say a word but curled up next to me on the bed.

"What is it, Robin?" I asked her. She wiped her red eyes and burried her face in my hair.

"I had a bad dream. I dreamed that Samil came back and got me!"

I forced a smile and patted her arm. "It twas just a dream,

darling. You can sleep now."

She sniffed then started twirling my hair around her finger. She was so young. Lela had mentioned once that she was only five. The same age I had been when I was adopted by the Christophes.

"Your hair is different, Lela. You look like Ariel!"

"Who?"

"*The Little Mermaid*. The princess that has a pretty voice."

I had no idea what she was talking about. There was still so much I had to learn about the times I was now living in. So much had changed since I'd been alive. The technology had advanced beyond my wildest dreams and the social norms were quite radical compared to what I was used to. It would take quite a bit of learning, but I was determined to adapt quickly after I got my body back.

"Sing me a song, Lela. Mommy used to sing to me whenever I had a nightmare," she said.

I panicked. I wasn't a singer, and I didn't know any songs that she would know. I had memorized some hymms while living at the convent, but that was centuries ago. I thought hard to see if Lela had any songs in her mind. She'd had to know one, maybe her favorite or even Gallard's favorite. One in particular stood out, so I began to sing *Highway to Hell* to Robin.

"Lela, that's a terrible song," she said. "Daddy said that hell is a bad place and we shouldn't talk about it."

"He was probably right. I could stop if you like."

She shook her head. "That's okay. I like to hear you sing.

Keep going."

I was hoping that she would have said otherwise, but there was no stopping now. Whatever this song was, I was stuck singing it to her. I didn't get to finish because David came into the room, interupting me. The expression on his face could have ended me where I lay.

"Robin, you need to come with me," he said.

"Aww, but Lela was singing to me!" she whined.

"Please come with me, sweetheart. I will sing to you in the other room."

She reluctantly left my side and followed him out the door. I was mildly disappointed that I hadn't been able to finish the song. I was just starting to get into it. I hadn't done anything wrong by her, really. He should have been thanking me for making things easier on the child. Sooner or later she would have to be told the truth, but I was going to leave that to her brothers. I had no responsibility for her.

I closed my eyes and attempted to fall asleep again. I was worn out from all the events of the day. Coming back to life was an exhausting experience, especially the adjustment to a woman's body. I secretly wished that I would wake up the next day and find that it had all been a dream. That I would be myself again and Solomon hadn't killed me. But this was a fools wish. This wasn't a dream, and I was trapped in this shell of a person that many people had loved.

Hello? Lucian, can hear me?

My eyes flew open. There was that voice again. The urgency of it was eerie and I recognized it. I'd heard this voice before. I'd spoken to this voice. And I'd been positive that this voice was never going to utter another word again. That only meant one thing. Lela was still alive. And if she was alive, her friends would want to do everything they could to get her back, even if it meant bringing *me* back.

"Thank you, darling. You have just made my plan so much easier," I said aloud. I then closed my eyes once more and drifted off to sleep.

Chapter Seventeen

I rose from the bed in the evening. I'd planned to sleep until morning, but I wasn't tired anymore. The house was quiet and I worried that they'd left like they'd said they were going to. If they had, I would be left to look for Solomon on my own. I hated to admit it, but I needed them. They had crucial information that would get me closer to being back in my own body. Without them, my search would last weeks, if not months.

I walked throught the house, searching for any signs of life. I checked the other bedrooms and let out a sigh of relief when I found Robin asleep in one of them. They wouldn't have left without her. That meant they were still somehwere in the house.

David and Lydian were in the living room talking. I hoped that they hadn't been talking the entire time. I'd been asleep for a good six hours. They had to have done something besides converse. If David was still in as horrible of a mood as before, it would be difficult to get him to believe my news about Lela.

"Good evening, you two. Still hanging around I see," I said, standing next to the fire place.

"Not for long. I contacted the others and they're on their way as we speak. They're coming to pick up Robin and then we're going back to the states," David said.

"And where does that leave me? Are you going to

abandon me here in this foreign country?"

"I think you'll survive," Lydian jabbed. "So if you could leave…like right now, that would be appreciated."

I rolled my eyes. She was clearly in denial over what she had done. I would be shocked if her friends didn't treat her like a pariah after what she'd done to Lela. Unless she hadn't told them. She had to have been honest.

"I have something that you would be interested to know," I assured them. "Tis about your friend, Lela."

"We don't want to hear anymore of your lies, Lucian. Get out!" David shouted.

There was so much animosity in his voice. I was sure he would all but throw me out physically. He wouldn't try to come after me again, unless he was a fool.

"She is alive," I said flatly. I didn't want to try and get them to listen anymore. I was done with polite conversation. If they were going to hear me out, I was going to have to force them to. "I have been hearing her voice in my head. At first I thought I was imagining things, but I am possitive that it is her."

"If this is some trick to get us to help you, it's not going to work," Lydian. said "We know B.S. when we hear it."

This wasn't going as planned. They were more hopeless than I'd thought. If I was going to convince them, I would have to lie. While I couldn't talk directly to Lela, I could still use her memories to prove she was in fact still in my head.

"I will prove it to you. Ask me something that only she

would know and I will answer it."

They looked hesitant and I could tell they were growing more and more exasperated with me by the minute. I was running out of time and I needed them on my side before the others arrived. Gallard would never listen to me. He would probably attempt to flay me alive upon seeing me.

"Okay, let's see if you're pulling our leg," Lydian said. "Who's the King of England?"

"Henry the Eighth," I stated proudly. She scoffed and my smile turned to a frown.

"Wrong! There is no king of England! The *queen* is Elizabeth the Second!"

David pinched the bridge of his nose and sighed. "That wasn't an adequate question. Ask him something that pertains to Lela's life."

Lydian twisted her mouth in thought, looking up at the ceiling and I tapped my foot impatiently. I didn't realize how hard of a task this was. How difficult could it be to ask a simple question?

"All right...how did Jordan and I meet?"

I closed my eyes to try and focus. This memory was from before she'd turned mortal, so I would have to go way back. The images flashed in my head until I got to the moment I was looking for.

"You met at some bar called Mist...Lela was dancing with him first, but you cut in. Called him a Gallard clone."

Lydian folded her arms. "I'm impressed! But I think we

need a few more questions. David, you ask him something."

"I'd rather not."

"Come on! If Lela is really still in there, then we can't risk turning him away and having her trapped forever!"

"Fine. Uh...back in Texas when we lived in Arlington. Lela made fun of me for liking a certain book. What was it?"

This was an even tougher one. This was almost five years ago. "J...*Jane Eyre*?" I asked.

David looked up at me and I knew that I'd been right. He looked more convinced than ever.

"You like *Jane Eyre*? Really?" Lydian asked David. "You are definitely her dad. You both like the weirdest things." She curled her legs underneath her on the couch. "Okay, one more question. This is going to be a tricky one. Gallard is a recovering addict of something. What is it?"

"So, Mr. D'Aubigne *does* have a flaw," I said. "Hmm..."

"Maybe we should wait for Gallard to come and ask his own questions," David suggested. "After all, he's the main one that's going to need convincing aside from her brothers."

"Do you believe me, David?" I asked. "You are her father. Yours should be the final say."

"They won't be here until around two in the morning. Give me some time to think and maybe...*maybe* I'll let you meet them and help them decide for themselves."

I was willing to agree to this. It wasn't like I had much of a choice. I either agreed to their terms or went off on my own. The latter wouldn't be beneficial for me.

I stayed away from David and Lyidan for the rest of the night. I could sense that they didn't like me and my presence was a painful reminder of Lela. But I was growing restless as the time passed. I had no one to talk to, not even her voice in my head.

I sat on the back porch and watched as several people swam or lounged on the beach. They were enjoying themselves more than I was. Soon, I could no longer watch and decided to make my way down there and see what people did for passtimes these days. I went through the gate at the end of the deck and followed the trail. It took me less than two minutes to get to my destination.

I found an area that was the least populated and planted myself on the sand. Those who were nearby were either eating food while sitting on a blanket or screaming and running through the water. The women were very exposed, hardly wearing anything and their attire surprised me. In my day, women were looked down upon if even their legs were ever uncovered, but the women now were pushing the limits.

Another memory flashed in my mind. It had to have been from the day before because Lela was wearing the same clothes as I had been when I'd woken up for the first time. She'd been sitting almost in the same spot as I was, only Gallard was with her.

"What if I just kept him company every once in a while? We used to talk often but now we don't get along so well," she'd said to him. I didn't understand where she'd gotten the idea that I was lonely

And reform me? I didn't need to be reformed, and I definitely didn't need a lesson in humanity. I'd seen both sides of humanity, the light and the dark. I'd just decided that there wasn't enough of the light to have hope in it. I didn't belong with the rest of humanity. I'd had a taste of evil and was content with it.

"You know, your new hair makes it easier to spot you," I heard someone say. I turned to find Lydian coming up behind me and she sat down about four feet away. She was a very interesting girl. She was petit like my mother had been. And her accent was very odd. I'd never heard one like it before.

"Lydian Powell. The promiscuous friend of Lela's. You remind me of my late wife," I said.

"Was she hot and super awesome?" she asked. I blinked, unsure of how to reply to her.

"She was a nag and a whore. You were most like the latter until you met Jordan, am I right? Somehow, he made you monogamous."

"My private life is none of your business. Besides, I doubt that *you* were so virtuous."

I couldn't argue with her. I had been unfaithful to Florence after she'd begun to cheat on me. At first it was only to get back at her. To show her how it felt, but once I realized that she didn't care, I just had other women on the side for pleasure.

"Touche," I finally said. "The only virtuous person in our midst at this time is Lela."

"Very true. And you better make sure it stays that way. Just because you're in her body doesn't give you permission to start sluttin' it up around here. If she *is* still in there, I want her to be the same as the way we left her."

"*If?* You still doubt that I am telling you the truth? I have answered several of your questions; displayed more knowledge that only she could have. What more proof do you need?"

She groaned then stood up, brushing the sand off of the back of her pants. I'd upset her. But I had a right to be frustrated. For my sake and for Lela's, everyone needed to be convinced that she was alive.

"I believe you," she said. "I have to. She's my friend, and if there's any hope that she's still alive, I'll jump at it. And maybe Jordan will be able to forgive me for what I've done."

She started heading back to the house when I asked, "Why did you betray her?"

She stopped then sighed before turning around and sitting by me once more.

"I was scared. He threatened Jordan, and I acted out of fear. When Samil asked me to help them get to Lela, I thought that they were only going to get information. Samil had promised David that she wouldn't be harmed, and he broke that promise." She looked at me with tears in her eyes. "Lela, if you're in there, I was going to come back and get you. I told myself that you were going to be fine. You're tough. You can handle anything. I was stupid enough to trust that Samil wouldn't kill you."

She burst into tears and covered her face with her arms, her knees tucked close to her chest. There was no way to tell if Lela had heard her. Not until this was all over and she was awake again.

"Yes, she is tough. By rights, she should have been dead long ago. She is a fighter. I have not seen a woman as…resiliant as Lela."

Lydian raised an eyebrow. "Careful, Lucian. It almost sounds like you like her."

"What do you…oh, I see. No, I do not care that way about Lela. I stopped attaching myself to people long ago. Love is a pointless emotion. Everyone just betrays you in the end. But you know that, right?"

I heard voices from up at the house and we both stood up. I assumed that the group had arrived from London earlier than planned. It was only eleven o'clock. They were probably eager to pick up Robin and leave so they could grieve.

Lydian and I hiked back up the trail and got back to the house just as David was about to answer the door and told Robin to go find us, maybe since he wasn't sure who was there. Samil was still in town as far as we knew, and if it was him, it was best to be cautious, though I could just kill him if he caused us any trouble.

Robin obediently ran to me and I picked her up without giving it any thought. She hadn't heard the conversation about my not really being her sister so she still believed that I was Lela. The three of us stayed hidden and listened as David opened the door.

"David?" I heard a man say. I recognized the voice as

Gallard's. "Look at you! You look older than me."

"It's been too long, Gallard. It's good to see you again."

The rest of the group came inside and Gallard introduced David to them. Lydian was wringing her hands, trying to build up the courage to go out and talk with them. I had no words of encouragement that would help, so I remained silent. What they would do to her couldn't be as bad as what they would want to to do me. Finally, she took Robin from me and left my side, walking into the living room, She was using her as a shield. As long as the little girl was at her side, no one would attempt to harm her.

I moved closer to the corner so I could see what was going on. Robin let go of Lydian's hand, running to Kevin who picked her up and hugged her. Some words were exhanged between the group, but I didn't pay attention to a thing anyone said until Gallard spoke again.

"Kevin, take Robin into the other room."

"What for?"

"Please, just do it."

Without another word, Kevin obeyed and I watched him leave with Robin and go into the kitchen. I heard the back door open and I assumed he was taking her down to the beach.

I was shocked by Gallard's next move. I saw his eyes fill with rage as he lunged at Lydian and threw her backwards and her impact broke the front door and she landed on the porch. I couldn't see what else he was doing since they'd gone outside, but by the sounds I heard, it must have been brutal.

Curiosity caused me to run out to the back and around to the side to see what else he planned to do. She was trying to get away, but he latched his fingers onto her neck and began to squeeze. He was squeezing so hard that I feared her head would pop off if he did not release his grip. I knew that it would kill her, and it would hurt like hell.

"Is this how she suffered? Huh? Is this what she felt before she died?" he yelled at her.

"I'm so sorry, Gallard. I didn't mean—"

"How could you do that to her? She cared about you, and you left her to die!"

He looked like he wanted to kill her. Like he wanted to rip her to shreds and decimate all the pieces, but before he could act, he was pulled away by Jordan, Aaron, and David.

"Gallard, stop!" Jordan said. "This won't bring her back! Think of Lela, she wouldn't want you to do this!"

He didn't fight them. Probably because he knew deep down that they were right. His battle was not with her. It was with Samil. And what he had planned for him was most likely ten times worse than what he'd planned to do to Lydian.

"You're right. She deserves to live with what she's done," he said. They slowly let go of him and he glowered at her. "Get out of here. I never want to see your face again because if I do see you, I won't hestitate killing you."

He turned and walked back in the house. David and Aaron followed, but Jordan remained outside. I stood still, and I listened as he began to speak to Lydian.

"How could you do this, Lydian?" he asked.

"I don't know. I keep asking myself that! The second I left her alone, I felt extremelly guilty, and I went back to get her, but the van took off just as I'd returned. I wanted to go after them, but I couldn't stand a chance against all his followers. Jordan, you have to believe me when I say I honestly thought they were just going to get information from her. Samil promised that he wouldn't kill her. I was naïve and stupid, and I will regret that for the rest of my life."

"I feel the same way that Gallard does. I don't think I can ever look at you again without being reminded of your betrayal."

Lydian began to sob again. "What about us? I love you, Jordan! What can I do to fix this?"

He looked extremelly torn. I almost felt bad for her. This girl was suffering rejection after rejection.

"Thanks to you, there is no *us*, Lydian. Don't make this harder than it is. Please, just leave."

And with that, she ran off into the night and Jordan went back into the house. I let out a strong exhale since I had hardly breathed for the past ten minutes. I was afraid that my presence would be given away with any small sound. The whole scene I'd just witnessed had been so intense.

Now it was my turn to face the jury. I was at the mercy of four angry vampires who were all ready to blame someone for

Lela's death. I wasn't looking forward to playing a guessing game with Gallard, let alone being in the same room as him.

I went into the house through the back. I was headed to the living room when I stopped in front of a mirror. I was debating whether I should change my hair back to blonde or keep it red. It would be a bit dramatic to make an appearance with my natural color than if I had Lela's color.

In the end, I chose to make it blonde again. If I was going to try and get sympathy from them, I would have to look as much like Lela as possible. That meant changing her eyes as well.

I wanted to get it over with, so I remained around the corner as I listened to them talk, waiting for the right moment to make an appearance.

"What do you mean Lucian is alive?" I heard Gallard ask.

"It was...unintentional. Samil didn't know it was going to happen, but now we're kind of stuck with him. You see...the thing is—"

"Stuck with him, how?" Aaron asked. "You mean he's *here*?"

The room went silent and I heard someone walking towards me. "Where is that creep?" It was Aaron still. "I wanna talk to him and kick his scrawny little—" He stopped in front of me and his eyes widened in fear.

"Hello, Aaron," I said. "I suggest that you think before you try and kick anything of mine because I will only kick back."

He didn't say a word, but backed away from me and I

followed him out into the living room. Kevin had returned with Robin and everyone's eyes fell on me. They had the same expression as Aaron. I looked at each of their faces, stopping at Gallard's who acted as if he were about to crumble to the floor.

"No," he said. "How…what is going on?"

"He took over her body when she…." David put a hand on his shoulder. "But I have reason to believe that she's still alive."

Gallard moved to fold his arms and I flinched. He was a bit intimidating to me, like my father had been up until the day I'd killed him. He was taller than I had been as a man, and his grey eyes were intense. Full of grief and a silent fury. He'd never looked at Lela this way, but he was giving this stare to me. I'd been convinced by the memories she had of him that he was this kind, pacifistic man who was slow to anger and wouldn't hurt a fly. But after what I'd seen him do to Lydian, I was proved wrong. He was like a wild animal that had been messed with too many times. He'd finally snapped.

"How?" he asked, with no real interest in his voice. He kept his eyes fixed on me.

"I have heard her speak," I said, talking to him for the first time. "I hear her voice in my head. And she tells me things…things that only she could know."

"Elaborate, please. I'm just dying to know what sort of proof you have! And make it fast so I can decide whether or not I'm going to kill you," he said with exasperation.

Like an alpha dog that had been challenged, I clenched my

fists and glared back at him. In the reflection on the window, I could see that my hair was turning black as well as my eyes. This had only happened twice before, when I'd nearly strangled the boy at the convent and when I'd killed Florence's immortal lover.

I wasn't really angry now. I wanted to show him just how dangerous I was.

"You want proof? I will give you proof! But do *not* threaten me, D'Aubigne!"

My voice had changed as well. It became not only Lela's but a combination of both of our voices. I was surprising myself. This whole possessing a body ordeal was not something I'd experienced before, and I kept discovering new abilities. This was the most shocking of them all.

He stood firm where he was, showing no sign of being frightened or swayed. If possible, he looked even angrier.

"You know things that only she would know?" Aaron asked. "Then what is her—"

"No, I do not want *you* to ask the questions. I have already been through this with David and Lydian. You need to ask me something personal. Not about birthdays or who the government leader is. It should be something I cannot be correct on by chance."

"Then *I'll* ask the question," Gallard said. "What is my nickname for her?"

"Still speaking in the present tense, I see," I jeered. "To answer your question, you have four. Which would you like me to name?"

He shrugged. "Either would do, but let's go with all of them. That would impress me."

"Shark wrestler. Angel of Darkness, or if you prefer the French translation, *Mon ange de ténèbres*. Sometimes you call her a siren. And last, but not least, Miss Sharmentino. I like that last one. It's very…polite."

He sighed then sat on the couch. I'd finally evoked an emotion besides anger in him and I was proud of myself. I'd answered his question correctly and I hoped it was enough. Any more trivia games and I was going to walk out and get my own help.

"So, did you find ol' Solomon yet?" I asked. "I am ready to get going. Tis not enjoyable being a woman."

Gallard stood up again and walked towards me. My hair was blonde again since my temper had cooled. He stared deep into my eyes as if he were looking for something. A sign maybe, that she was still there.

"Rot in hell, Lucian. Go find him yourself." He said before leaving the room. No one else said anything.

David broke the silence after a few moments. "We'll continue this discussion in the morning once everyone has had a chance to cool off. For now, it may be best that you…stay away from us. Your presence is putting people on edge."

"Fine by me," I said, leaving the room as well. I wasn't tired, and didn't feel like being in the bedroom any longer, so I lay on the sofa in a room next to the living room. It wasn't the wisest choice of location. Being anywhere in the back of the house would chance me running into Gallard again. I didn't want to admit that he made me nervous. He was one of my creations after all. That meant that he was stronger than Samil and Matthew. He would be even more of a challenge to best in a fight.

Unintentionally, I fell asleep. It was a strange sleep, though. I lingered between being awake and being unconscious. I could hear everything around me, though the sounds were distorted and I heard someone coming and I wasn't in the mood for another confrontation, since I'd had about three in one day. Sooner or later, people were going to see how foolish it was to challenge me. I could only take so many threats before I would start inflicting harm.

The person stopped in front of me and I continued to try and rest. For being the least liked person in the house, everyone sure kept seeking out my company. First Lydian and now Gallard. I knew it was him because of how he smelled. Lela liked how he smelled so it was burned into her memory. He did smell quite pleasant. Like a mixture of rain and peppermint. There wasn't a scent like that for people to wear in my day.

"Look at you, laying there like you're so innocent. You have her face, her hair and her eyes, but you're not her." His voice sounded distorted since I wasn't fully awake. "You know things about her. So what? You probably just have her memories. She's not really in there. You've just been inside of her head for too long."

I heard him walk away, but he didn't leave the room. I then heard the sound of metal sliding past metal, like a sword being removed from its sheath. Still, I didn't move, even if he was going to try and kill me. I didn't think he would be able to do it.

Lela, say something. Anything! He needs to be convinced or he is going to kill us, I thought to myself. It was a stretch trying to communicate with her, but this may be my last chance to show I wasn't lying.

Gallard must have had some sort of sword in his hand because he touched the tip of it to my throat and I felt the coolness of the steel. It then moved away and my heart raced as I prepared for him to drive it into me.

Suddenly, I heard something drop the ground with a thud followed by Gallard making a noise. He was crying, but it sounded more like tears of joy than of sorrow. I was confused since I thought he'd been about to kill me and I had no idea what had stopped him.

He went silent after a few moments and I heard him stand up. I thought he was going leave, but then I felt his lips gently press against mine. I'd never been kissed by a man before and it was so strange and awkward. It almost woke me up.

"I'm going to bring you back," he said. "I promise you, Lela. I will bring you back." And then he got up and left the room. I admired his courage kissing me like that when I could easily have woken up at any second. He must have really loved her. Enough to take such a risk. And for a moment, I almost envied him for being able to love in such a way that I never had the ability to.

Chapter Eighteen

I remained on that same sofa for the rest of the night. I awoke the next morning feeling more refreshed than ever and even more confident that they were going to help me. If Gallard had been genuine when he'd said he was going to bring her back, he'd probably convinced the others to help as well.

I went back into the living room to find them talking amongst themselves. Upon seeing me, they stopped and Gallard stood up.

"Good morning, Lucian," he said with genuine kindness. He was being significantly nicer than the night before. In fact, Jordan was looking at me with more enmity than anyone, though I didn't know why. Maybe he was still upset about his lover betraying his friend.

I sat in the same chair as I'd sat in the day before. I knew that it was probably a good idea to remain civil with them, though I wasn't used to being civil. It was already a lot of work for me to be pleasant. I wasn't looking for friends, just allies.

"Did you all decide that you believe me, or am I going to have to do everything on my own?" I asked.

"Yes, we are now convinced. And we've decided to help you after all," Gallard said. Their expressions ranged from skepticism to hopefulness but no one looked angry or hostile as they had the night before.

"So, to England we will go, then?"

"No, that's the only set back. Lela was supposed to meet Solomon there yesterday, but we were turned around because of...recent events. If we're going to find him, you're going to have to contact him again and request a meeting."

"You want me to call Solomon?"

"Yes. You're the only one he'll speak to, so it's our only chance."

I really didn't want to do this. I hated Solomon more than anyone for his betrayal and now I had to call him and act all civil? This would be difficult. But if it meant we could get to him sooner, I was willing to cooperate.

"All right, I need a phone."

Gallard handed me his phone along with the paper containing Solomon's number. He must have known I had no idea how to use a cell phone because he dialed it before showing me how to hold it. I held it to my ear and listened as it rang.

"Hello?" I heard Solomon say. It took everything in me to not go off on him and accuse him of being a traitor.

"Solomon. This is...Lela."

"Thank the Lord you are safe! When you didn't show up, I was worried!"

He was worried? Had he really attached himself to Lela like he had my daughters? It wouldn't be surprising if he did.

"I apologize. My trip was infiltrated and we had to lay low

in case we were being followed. Is there any way we can still meet?"

"Of course! To take precautions, why don't we meet somewhere else? I am currently at the Vatican, so you can come here any time you want. I go to Saint Martha's Square every afternoon to pray. We can meet there if you like."

"I will. Thank you again, Solomon. I will see you in a few days."

I hung up, grateful to get that call over with. It had been almost too easy to imitate Lela. It helped that I knew her so well; her thought process, her voice. I knew her as well as I knew myself.

"Well?" David asked.

"He said to meet him at the Vatican in Saint Martha's Square. He is expecting us within the week."

"Perfect," Gallard said. "Before we go, I would like to take care of something. Samil may still be in town and I need to speak with him."

I sighed with exasperation. I was hoping we were finished with that imbecile. He'd insulted me and made disgusting accusations about me. But Gallard wanted his revenge, no doubt. If he wanted to kill him, I wanted to be there to watch.

"David and I know where he is," I said. "We should go there soon if we are to catch him before he leaves." I stood up from the seat. "I am going to have some blood then change into more appropriate attire and we can be on our way."

"Hold on!" Kevin shouted. "You're going to *change*? No, not going to happen. Not while you're in my sister's body."

I smirked and folded my arms. "If you are trying to protect her privacy, you are too late. I have already showered. You are just going to have to deal with this inconvenient situation."

Gallard looked like he wanted to rip my throat out, but remained calm. I decided not to taunt him since I'd gotten him on my side. We needed each other. We both had something the other person wanted.

"Just…be quick," he said. "You and I are the only ones who are going to meet Samil and I don't want to waste any time."

I went back to the bedroom to find her bag. She'd packed heavily, so I had many clothes to choose from. I decided to go with the white shirt with really tiny straps and the frayed, denim shorts. This shirt was probably meant to be worn under something, but I was trying to wear the most shocking thing I could find.

I then drank one of the blood bags and went into the bathroom to see the final product. She probably wouldn't have picked this outfit, but I couldn't deny that she looked good in it. It was a cross between sexy and simple.

I stared at her reflection a little longer before leaving. It was strange seeing her outside of her memories. I'd been inside of her head since her infancy and now she was a woman. She'd grown to be beautiful, though I would never say it out loud for fear of being accused of having feelings for her. I didn't. I couldn't. I just found her fascinating as a person. She was everything that I'd wanted my Cherish to be and everything that Florence was not; strong and brave, but also pure and good.

Finishing off the outfit with socks and a pair of white shoes, I left the room, guzzling down the second bag. I hoped that we could get our information from Samil without getting into a fight. But if we needed to resort to violence, I was willing.

I found Gallard in the foyer next to the door and he froze upon seeing me. To poke fun, I turned around as if to model for him. Florence always had Melody do that whenever she tried on a new dress.

"Do you like what you see?" I asked with a smirk on my lips.

"Maybe you should put a shirt on over that. It's a bit…revealing."

"It is okay if you find me attractive, D'Aubigne. Tis not my body, after all."

He rolled his eyes and opened the door. "Let's just get this over with."

Before we could leave, Robin came into the room and starting running towards us. I thought she was coming to me, but was surprised when she passed by and headed for Gallard. He had to pick her up before she would collide with him and he held her in his arms.

"Gallard! Where are going with my sister?" she asked. He looked at me then back at the girl.

"We're just running an errand, little one. We'll be back soon."

"Are you guys still fighting? Mommy and daddy used to

fight and then daddy left. You aren't leaving Lela are you?"

"Never. I promise I will always be around to take care of her and you."

Robin smiled then her eyes brightened.

"Oh! I was supposed to tell you something!" she said.

"And what is that?"

"Lela told me to tell you she loves you and she doesn't want you to be sad." She looked at me and smiled. "Did you still want me to tell him that?"

I opened my mouth to answer, but I didn't have a clue what I would say. I didn't have it in me to reply to that. Lela had asked her sister to deliver this message thinking she wouldn't live and she'd been right. Now we were trying to reverse whatever happened and I hoped Robin's message would inspire Gallard to work harder.

"Thank you, Robin," Gallard finally said. I could tell he'd been moved by what she'd said. "I love her too. And I'll try my best not to be sad if you promise me you won't be sad either."

She nodded then he kissed her forehead before setting her down and telling her to stay with her brothers until we got back. She obeyed and after she left the room, we continued on our way. I went out first and he shut the door behind us. We took the van since neither of us felt like running the entire way there. The warehouse Samil had taken her to was a long distance from the house. About a fifteen minute trip, not including the traffic.

He didn't speak to me the whole way there, only to ask me

for directions. He didn't seem angry, just quiet. He probably missed the woman whom I inhabited. If anything, he was anticipating getting his revenge on Samil. I felt the same away towards Solomon, and it would take everything in me not to kill him until after I was successfully returned to my body.

We finally pulled into the parking lot of the warehouse twenty minutes later and got out. It looked different than I remembered, probably because I hadn't been paying attention. The pathway up to the door was gravel and the outside looked worn, with unpatched holes in the wood and shingles falling off of the roof. The wood, itself was very faded from the sun and showed signs of water damage. The door looked as if it were barely hanging onto its hinges.

Gallard turned the knob and opened it cautiously. There was no telling how many vampires were down there and it wouldn't be wise to barge in. He went in with me following close behind. The room smelled dank and musty as if no one had cleaned in years. It was dark, but not hard for me to see. Gallard found the stairs and began descending them. I waited until he got halfway before going down, just in case someone decided to make a surprise appearance at the bottom.

He put his ear to the door, listening for any movement then opened it.

"Hello?" he called out.

"Hello? Is that the best you could come up with? You might as well ask if we can join them for tea as well."

He ignored me and went into the room. The light was on, but there was no one in sight. If anyone had been there, they'd cleared out hours ago. They hadn't even cleaned the glass from the broken table.

"What happened here?" he asked. I picked up one of the shards. It still had blood on it. Her blood.

"Do you really want to know?" I closed my eyes and thought back to everything she'd gone through. Samil had beaten her so badly that she was close enough to death for me to feel it. I'd felt everything, and it was not a pleasant experience.

I wandered over to the wall where he'd first thrown her and saw the dent where she'd hit her head. There was blood on it as well.

"Yes, I do," Gallard answered, breaking the silence.

"He threw her here, first. She did not know it, but the blow caused hemorrhaging to her brain. Also, she had a broken rib." I turned around and walked back to the broken table. "After he strangled her, he tossed her onto the table. She had several pieces of glass imbedded in her arms and back. But she was a fighter. She did not lose consciousness, so he had Matthew drag her into another room."

I went down the hall and opened the first door on the right The only light was from a part of the window that hadn't been completely covered. I ripped off the rest of the boards and the sun flooded in, illuminating everything. I then examined my surroundings. The mattress was still on the floor, also covered in her blood and the floor was smeared with Matthew's from when she'd stabbed him multiple times.

Gallard stood in the doorway, staring at the mattress as well.

"David was already here when they locked her in," I continued. "He helped her get the glass out and nursed her wounds. They did not let him stay for long. She was left here alone for several hours." I shifted my eyes, trying to remember what happened next. "Matthew came in. He said that Samil put him in charge of finishing the job. He told her that she was too pretty and cut her face. She talked back to him and he started pricking her abdomen with the knife." The rest of what happened was the clearest of all because that was when I'd made my appearance. By then, her head injuries were fatal. "She made him mad and that was when he—"

"What?" Gallard asked, his voice cracking.

"He held her down and—"

"No!" he yelled, punching the wall. "Not again. Please not again!" I saw the same rage in his eyes that I'd seen the night before. He was going to lose it if I didn't say something quick.

"She's been assaulted before?" I asked him. I thought I would have remembered this. Unless it happened when she was a vampire. I hadn't been able to access her memories over the past four years until recently.

He took a second to compose himself then shook his head. "Not her. It was someone else from my past."

"Gallard, he did not…he never got that far. Lela had a knife of her own. She overpowered him and stabbed him. He was incapacitated for several minutes and by then Samil came in and one of his followers dragged Matthew out of there." I smiled as I remembered how good it felt to kill him. "That man…I have never known anyone to be so…twisted. He even went for her after she was dead. I had taken over by then. Do not worry. He got what was coming to him. Cut out his tongue, I did. That was before I ripped off his head."

Gallard started to calm down, but he was still very angry.

"She could see me by then," I continued, "Samil asked her to ask me how I could walk in the day. She told the truth of course; that I only had a description of the man and nothing more. Samil did not believe her. That was when he snapped her neck and I took over."

We heard someone come out of the room next to us and we ran out to catch the person before they could try to get away. Gallard grabbed the man and shoved him against the wall.

"Who are you?" Gallard asked. The man looked terrified, an emotion I always loved to see from the weaker ones. I didn't recognize him, but he was a follower of Samil, no doubt.

"My name is Edgar. Samil recruited me twenty years ago."

"And where is he now?"

"I…I don't know. After…after the girl left with her father, everyone cleared out. He was afraid that you would come after him so he left. He asked me to stay behind so I could spy."

I remembered Lydian mentioning an Edgar being her middle man to Samil. This must be the same man. He didn't appear to be menacing enough to work for Samil; not like Matthew had. He had too much heart, too much empathy in his eyes.

Lela's memories began to form in my mind once more and it went back to the night Samil killed her parents. The faces of those who were there flashed by until the memory focused on one. Edgar's. He was holding on to Mark, drinking his blood then he dragged him outside. Shortly after, a loud sound echoed then the memory ended.

"You're the one who killed her…my father," I said. Edgar looked at me and I realized it was not empathy that was in his eyes; it was pure and untainted fear. He knew what he'd done and he was afraid that we would find out, which we had.

"Please, don't hurt me. I only did was I was commanded. Samil never said we were going to kill anyone, we were just supposed to—"

Gallard rammed his hand into Edgar's chest, squeezing his heart and Edgar cried out in pain. Ripping out his heart wouldn't kill him, but it would hurt like hell.

"I don't give a damn about why you did it!" Gallard shouted. "Just tell me what I want to know!"

"All right! I'll tell you." Edgar grimaced and cleared his throat. "Samil went to Italy. He's looking for Solomon. He's a Cardinal at the Vatican. Been there for the past three hundred years. He learned this recently after her father gave us his name."

Gallard released his heart, wiping the bloody onto Edgar's shirt and Edgar leaned over, clutching at his chest. I didn't know how he planned to kill him, but I was eager to get everything going, so I took out the knife David had given Lela from my back pocket and handed it to Gallard.

"Do it. It will bring you great pleasure to see him dead," I said.

"Wait!" Edgar pleaded. "I have more information."

"About what?" Gallard asked.

"Samil is not the only one I'm working for. I've been acting as a double agent. Someone in your group is on my side as well."

I sighed in exasperation. "We already know about Lydian, you idiot. I was present after all."

"No, I'm not talking about Lydian. There is someone else. That is all I can tell you. Except...I must tell you that what happened the night your parents were killed...not all was what it seemed."

Gallard looked at the knife then back at Edgar. He then plunged it into the man's torso, slicing him upwards until Edgar bled out and fell to the floor in a heap. He then handed the knife back to me and we exited the building, leaving Edgar lying in a pool of blood.

"Revenge is sweet, is it not?" I asked, once we'd started driving down the road. Gallard wouldn't say it out loud, but I knew that he was relishing in what he'd done.

"I suppose."

"You suppose? Tis the best feeling in the world; watching the surprised look in their eyes when you kill them. Then you can carry on with your life without having to think about them anymore." I paused for a second. "What do you think Edgar was talking about? Do you believe him when he said someone among us is lying? And what about his cryptic message about her parents' murders?"

"I think he was trying to buy himself some time. He gave us no reason to trust him, so I am not going to listen to anything he said."

Gallard didn't speak for a while and I wondered if he was feeling guilty. Why would he? He'd avenged the murder of Lela's family. He should be glad that the imp of an immortal was dead.

Finally he spoke again.

"When Lydian called and told me that Lela was dead, I...I lost it," he said. "Never in my life have I felt the way that I did in that moment. I had a glimpse of what it was like to die. I...somehow I knew before I even got the call. I felt it; I felt her disappear, like the bond between us was broken. To try and numb myself from the pain, I fed during the day. I haven't done that in years, and I lost myself for a few hours. I don't know how many
people I killed, but the body count was pretty high."

This man wasn't as self righteous as I'd thought he was. He too knew what it felt like to be filled with a red hot rage that could not be controlled. He didn't even try to justify his actions.

"You know, Lela would not kill Matthew, even after what

he had tried to do. Why is that, do you think?"

Gallard sighed and switched hands on the steering wheel.

"Because she's better than us, Lucian. She refuses to lose her humanity despite everything she's done. She's taken lives just like any other immortal, but she doesn't let it change her. She recognizes that it's a tragedy and she feels remorse. That's not something you can learn. You have to already be that way."

It was hard for me to understand this. I hadn't felt remorse for taking a life since the peasant girl I first fed on. After that, I killed for survival and I didn't think twice about it. Though I didn't kill indiscriminately like Florence had, it never bothered me. My parents' attempt to kill me destroyed what sympathy for humanity that I had left. It opened my eyes to how the world was. Either kill, or be killed.

"Well, we know where Solomon is. As soon as I am back in my body, you will get her back and all will be right with the world."

Gallard scoffed. "Really? How does your being let loose again make everything right?"

"Oh, come off it, I was not *that* horrible!"

"Then why did Solomon kill you?"

I opened my mouth then shut it. I hadn't spoken of this with anyone but Solomon. His reasoning for ending my life was something I'd promised myself I would take to my grave. My final grave, anyway.

"That does not concern you, D'Aubigne."

He didn't speak anymore after that. I knew he was

probably angry that he'd had to kill one of Samil's followers and not Samil himself. He would find him eventually, though. Just like how I would find Solomon and do to him exactly what he'd done to me, only I would make sure he was dead and not just locked in a box for eternity.

Chapter Nineteen

Before we left, the group agreed that it would be best for Robin to be sent back to the states. They didn't want to have to explain her mysterious reappearance to her aunt and uncle, so David offered for her to stay with a relative in Virginia; Declan Shepherd. David explained that he was the grandson of his oldest brother. Another reminder that he was a rather unique individual. Though David was human, he preserved his life by drinking blood. He was like me, only a weaker version.

His relative arrived in Goa about a day later and after Robin was successfully handed over to him, we were able to go on our way.

Italy was over a thousand miles away from India, so getting there would not be simple. Since two of us could not fly there, we were forced to take an airplane most of the way. When I learned we would be over thirty thousand feet in the air, I was very concerned. I was not afraid of heights, but after they informed me we would be inside of a closed off capsule, I hated the idea even more. Gallard and Jordan had to practically drag me onto the plane and once I was seated- we were in the middle row, thankfully- I clung to the armrest so hard that there were hand prints indented in them. The group made no attempt to hold back any insults. They made fun of me the entire way there.

We had to stop in Greece since some in the group were getting anxious to feed. We remained there for half a day and then traveled up to Albania where we purchased tickets to a ferry that would take us the rest of the way to Italy.

The seats weren't very comfortable, so I got up and wandered around for a few hours. I went to the top and looked over the edge at the water. It had been ages since I'd been on a boat, and it hadn't been nearly as advanced as the ferry we were currently riding. I liked the sound of the water going through the propellers. It was soothing and rid me of the tension I'd been feeling.

Being in Lela's body was getting more and more uncomfortable, as if it was aware I wasn't supposed to be there. I hadn't heard her voice in days and was beginning to wonder if she was still there. She wouldn't have given up that easily. She was either being patient or just had nothing to say.

When I found a decent spot to linger, I watched as different people walked back and forth down the hall. A few men smiled or winked at me, which made me uncomfortable, but as I began to get hungry, I realized that I could use it to my advantage.

One man started making conversation with me, and I did my best to flirt back. I had been an expert at flirting with women back in my day, and I figured that I could be equally as alluring to men. It felt strange, but I knew it was the best way to get blood. I pulled him into an empty compartment and he tried to kiss me, but I snapped his neck before he could. I didn't want to feed on him while he was still alive because I knew that he would draw too much attention to us.

When I was finished, I hid him in one of the utility closets then joined the others in the seating area. The sun was still up, so Aaron, Kevin, and Jordan had to stay in an area with the least amount of sun exposure.

"Lucian, did you feed?" Gallard asked.

"How did you come to that assumption?"

"I could smell the blood from all the way down the corridor. You can't feed here, it's too obvious!"

"I'm a very conspicuous man, Mr. D'Aubigne. I do not do subtlety."

"Even after all these years, you still haven't learned have you?" Aaron said.

"Says the one who dumped three bodies in a hotel bathtub," I said. I opened the window shade next to his seat and smirked as he yelled from the burn of the sunlight and then pulled it back down again. "Do not judge my actions again, or next time I'll throw you out of the window."

I could tell that my presence was not wanted in the room any longer, so I went back out to look at the water.

We arrived in Bari, Italy around eight o'clock that night. After everyone had fed, we stole a car and drove the rest of the way to the Vatican City. It was nearly a five hour drive and we pulled in a little before two in the morning.

There weren't any hotels that were open for booking quite yet, forcing me to have to sleep in the car. It wasn't comfortable since we were crammed so tightly. Aaron, who had been driving, parked somewhere the car wouldn't be exposed to the sun and we remained there for the rest of the night.

I didn't realize I'd fallen asleep until a loud horn blasted, waking me up prematurely. Everyone accept Gallard laughed at me and I groaned, frustrated that I was still the butt of everyone's jokes. They were obviously not afraid of me anymore or they wouldn't be testing my wrath.

"Good morning, Lucian. Did you sleep well?" Jordan asked.

I leaned forward to stretch my back then cracked my neck. I'd spent the night sandwiched in between Gallard and Jordan, both of whom were broad-shouldered men. Apparently they didn't trust me and wanted to keep any eye on me. Most likely, they wanted to make sure I was taking care of Lela's body.

"Had the bloody best night's sleep in my life," I answered sarcastically. "I just love being smashed between you apes."

"Well, I'm glad you're awake," Jordan continued. "You kept feeling me up in your sleep."

"You lie!" I protested. Never in my life had I been told that I moved in my sleep. In fact, Florence told me on our honeymoon that she was afraid that I was dead I lay so still.

"Honest to God. You talk in your sleep too."

"Clearly it was Lela and not I. I neither move, nor speak while I am asleep."

"Lela doesn't talk in her sleep either," Gallard said. Everyone turned to look at him and he said, "What? Lela and I have slept in the same bed on more than one occasion. No need to act surprised."

He seemed angry about something, but I doubted it was because of their silent judging expressions. He then got out of the car without saying another word and neither did the rest of the group.

After he got out, David and I joined him as well since the rest couldn't be out and about. It was nine-thirty, just the right time to start our next mission; finding Solomon before Samil did.

We left the other three gentlemen in the car and took a taxi to our destination. Italy was beautiful, but my mind was not on the scenery. I would have to enjoy it later when everything was said and done. We got to the Vatican just when they were opening. The entry fee was a bit expensive, but we had Aaron's card, which we used a machine to convert the money into Euros.

Instead of signing up for a tour, we began wandering around looking for someone who we thought would know where we could find Solomon. Not many of the clergymen were around, but instead tourists littered the entire city. I'd only been to The Vatican once when I was alive, so I had no idea where to go first.

David suggested that we start with the Sistine Chapel and we headed there first. I wanted to start looking around for anyone who could help, but David and Gallard kept stopping to look at the paintings. I couldn't get annoyed with them since I was equally as mesmerized by its beauty, though I didn't care to admit it. The Chapel was practically empty since almost all of the tourists were attending the Mass, as we'd been informed by the man at the door. It was very quiet, but in a peaceful way.

We walked around and around for over three hours before we finally decided to ask someone if they knew the directions to Saint Martha's Square. I found a Bishop and caught up with him before he walked into one of the prayer rooms

"Excuse me, father, I do not mean to keep you from your engagement, but my companions and I are looking for a one Solomon Sharmentino. Do you have the knowledge of his location?" I asked.

"Oh, you must mean Cardinal Solomon. Yes, I know where he is, Miss. He's always praying in Saint Martha's Square this time of day. He usually attends the Mass, but he has been more reserved lately. I feel that he is troubled in spirit, but he will not say why."

Probably because Samil had been hounding him about my body, I thought to myself.

The priest gave me the directions to the square and I thanked him before he went on his way. I jogged back to where the other two were. I found Gallard and David waiting for me at the bottom of the stairs.

"I have directions to his whereabouts. If we leave now, we may be able to catch him."

Quickly, we found the exit and started heading to Saint Martha's Square. It was a twenty minute walk from the Sistine Chapel, but we went at a quick pace to cut our time down by at least five minutes.

As we walked, Gallard started asking me questions. I actually didn't mind speaking with him as much as the rest of the group. He was the only one who didn't taunt me or treat me like an idiot. Jordan was the worst of all of them. He was relentless with his jokes and demeaning.

"You and Solomon were enemies, yet you created him. Were you friends before that?" Gallard asked.

"We were good friends, yes. He amused me and I gave him the gift of immortality. When we were out feeding, I was able to forget my troubles at home. But after my second daughter was born, things changed."

I'd nearly forgotten what had originally caused the rift between us. Cherish's birth marked the days when I spent more time at home and less time running around causing chaos with him. He didn't seem to mind, though. He'd adored Melody and Cherish. He spoiled them with gifts and took them on picnics, and in return, they treated him with the same adoration. But of the two girls, he favored my Cherish the most, just as I did.

When they were older, sixteen and twenty-two respectively, he left London to return to Italy and re-evaluate his life. He'd claimed that God was convicting him to turn away from his old lifestyle and begin to take his life as a priest seriously. He was gone for nearly five years before I saw him again. By then,
Cherish had grown into a beautiful woman, and he'd noticed.

Florence insisted that we give her a party to celebrate her twenty-first birthday since we'd done the same for Melody, and I'd allowed it. Florence wanted it to act as a coming out party as well since Cherish was not yet married, but I didn't want Cherish to meet anyone. I had plans for her future, and a husband would ruin them, especially since she'd already been scorned by one man.

It was during the party that I noticed Solomon couldn't keep his eyes off of her. He even danced with her, despite the nasty rumors that were bound to arise from it. Most saw it as innocent since he was known to be close with my family, but I knew better. I knew what he'd been like before and just because he'd claimed to be a changed man didn't mean that I believed him. I'd taken him aside later that night and warned him to stay away from her. He assured me that he was done with the promiscuous lifestyle and that he renewed his vows, planning to hold to his promise from then on, yet I threatened him anyway.

After that, he spent less and less time at the Christophe house, only visiting when the girls were not around. Our meetings were a bit awkward, but he came anyway. He didn't have anyone else, really, since his son had left the country with his mother and her new husband. And when the incident occurred for which he killed me, our friendship had ended for good.

"Solomon was in love with your daughter?" Gallard asked, bringing me out of my daydream.

"Yes, he was. And I resented him for that."

"Of course you did," David chimed in. "She was your baby. You didn't want some old man coming along and taking her away. I understand because I'm a father as well."

"I'm guessing that *old man* was directed at me?" Gallard asked, smiling.

"It was. But I'm okay with you and Lela being together. I spent three years making sure you were good enough for her and you passed the test. So, you have my blessing."

"Thank you, David."

When we were getting closer, we slowed down since David was getting winded. I noticed over the past week that he was starting to look different. His hair was showing signs of grey and there were slight wrinkles forming on his face. He had managed to age at least thirty years in the past five days.

"You are looking a bit aged lately, why are you not feeding?" I asked.

"I don't see the point. I'm not going to live for very much longer anyway."

Gallard stopped walking and I reluctantly stopped as well. "What are you talking about?" he asked.

"You know what the gypsy said about Lucian. To bring him back, he must feed from two of those who drank his blood. I am to be one of them."

"You don't have to do this. We can find another way. That can't be the only option."

"I'm not changing my mind. I'm doing this for my daughter."

Since I really couldn't care less about their discussion, I walked ahead as they continued their conversation so that I could get a head start on finding Solomon. I figured that his red robes would be easy to spot, and I knew that I would be able to approach him since he wouldn't recognize me.

I found him sitting underneath a tree on a stone bench reading a book. He looked exactly the same as when I'd last seem him nearly half a millennium ago. His black hair was cut short under his red cap and his grey eyes had a far-off look as if his mind wasn't on the pages he was reading. I never noticed before, but he looked quite a lot like a slightly older version of Aaron. In fact, Aaron was more like him in personality and looks than I had realized.

I spent about a minute preparing what I would say. I had planned for years to murder him the second I laid eyes on him, but I didn't want to do it in one of the holiest cities in the world. I also needed him to tell me where he was hiding my body.

"Solomon?" I said, using the best impression of Lela's voice as I could. He looked up and gave me the friendliest smile I'd ever seen. It was the same way he used to smile at my daughters when they were young.

"Lela! I am so glad you made it here safely."

He set his book down and walked over to me, taking my hands in his. He studied my face for a few moments and I wandered what he was looking for. Maybe some indication that she was in fact related to him, which she wasn't. I doubted Solomon knew her true origins.

While still holding one of my hands, he linked arms with

me and began walking out of the Square. He then asked, "Did you have a good trip?"

"Not exactly. Spending the night squished between two Frenchmen is not my ideal way of travel."

Solomon laughed. "I see. Plane rides can be quite a bother. I thought of getting my own private jet, but I do not travel enough to need it. Besides, as a cardinal, I'm supposed to be frugal. That has probably been the most difficult struggle in the church."

"Is that why you gave your money to Mark?"

"Partially. And because he'd contacted me several years ago. He wanted my help to get your mother and brother out of the neighborhood they were living in, so I sent him enough money to put a down payment on a house."

"That liar!" I was suddenly shouting. "Mark said you contacted him first and that he didn't want the money. All this time, he was acting all humble when he was too proud to admit he had asked for help."

Before he could say more, David and Gallard arrived. Solomon let go of me, and I moved over to the other men.

"Is this him?" Gallard asked me.

"Yes, this is Solomon."

"Cardinal Solomon, officially," Solomon said, shaking Gallard's hand. "Lela never mentioned having companions. To whom do I owe the pleasure?"

"I am David Shepherd. Lela's biological father. And this is Gallard D'Aubigne, her—"

"We're lovers," I said, taking Gallard's hand. He stared at me in shock and so did David. Unbeknownst to them, I had decided in the past few moments not to reveal myself. I didn't want to until I was back in my own body for a confrontation.

"Could...could I talk to her for just a moment?" Gallard asked.

Solomon nodded then Gallard dragged me quite a ways away from the two men. I had to admit that it was kind of fun pretending to be Lela. I was excelling until I'd revealed myself David and Lydian. Gallard figured it out the moment he'd laid eyes on me, but Solomon was convinced.

"What the hell are you doing?" Gallard asked in a hushed tone.

"He will never give me my body if he knows I am back. We have to make him think Samil still wants it in exchange for Robin and he will cooperate better."

"So you want to lie to him? He seems like a very intelligent guy; he's going to figure it out eventually. All it will take is for you to make one snide remark and he'll know it's you."

"I fooled David for hours into thinking I was Lela. I have been inside of her head for nearly twenty years. I know her better than you think."

Gallard grew quiet for a moment and I waited to see if he would go along with my plan. He didn't seem like a deceptive kind of guy, so lying to Solomon might be difficult for him.

"I don't feel comfortable lying to a priest," he said.

"Especially since he was so kind as to letting Lela come here for protection."

"Do not let his title fool you. He is the most hypocritical bugger in Eastern Europe." He didn't speak so I said. "Do you want Lela back or not?"

"It isn't a matter of getting her back, but giving her life back to her. Two have to die Lucian, and I think we both know which two that's going to be."

I hadn't thought about that. Since Lydian had been banished from the group, the only two donors left were Gallard and David. I couldn't donate because that would risk killing her. Gallard was right; he wouldn't get her back because he will have died.

"All right," he said. "We'll do it your way, I suppose. If he figures it out, it's on you."

I let Gallard and David tell most of the story since I knew practically nothing. There were parts of my story that I didn't even know that they had learned from the gypsy's descendants, and I was fascinated by everything they talked about. They answered many questions about the vampire lifestyle that I never knew existed. I hadn't had time to ask any questions since we had been so focused on reversing what had happened to me.

Eventually, the sun started going down, and Solomon agreed to continue the conversation at the place where the others were waiting. When we got back, everyone was introduced, and he seemed more than happy to meet Aaron and Kevin. He hadn't seen any of his relatives in years, and I could tell that knowing his bloodline was still continuing gave him peace of mind. He had kept tabs on all of his family members, but never got around to seeing them face to face. He didn't want them to know what he really was.

I envied him. His family was able to grow, and mine had ended the moment he'd murdered my daughters. I was being civil with him since he was still of use, but I knew that the second I was back in my body, he was going to pay somehow for what he'd done.

He spoke with us for several hours, but still didn't reveal the location of my body. He was purposefully stalling because he didn't want to help us, really. He kept trying to suggest other ways we could rescue Robin, though we kept reminding him that we had no idea where Samil was. He was just as stubborn as he was five hundred years ago.

Finally, I took him aside to talk with him alone. If the others couldn't appeal to him, then maybe Lela could. If I made him empathize with her the way he had Melody and Cherish, maybe he would be more likely to cooperate.

"What are you doing, Solomon? If you were not going to aid us, then why take the time to speak with us?"

"This is not a decision that can be made lightly, Lela. I ended Lucian for a reason and a damn good one. I can't just hand over the body, knowing what he's capable of."

I could feel the anger rising again, but I didn't lose control. I was still weaker than I used to be and he could easily hurt me if I tried to fight him. Besides, I needed to keep up the façade for a while longer. Gallard was right. He was bound to get suspicious soon, but until then I was going to play along.

"Why did you kill him? No one seems to know the exact reason."

"He was a heartless killer. I just wish that…that I hadn't been so foolish as to believing he had boundaries. But he crossed a line that I could not ignore."

"Do not speak to me of boundaries. You didn't have boundaries when it came to my daughter!"

He stopped walking and turned his head towards me, fear flashing in his eyes. I was angry at myself for letting that slip and now my plan was ruined. Gallard was right about my mouth eventually blowing my cover.

He grabbed me by the shoulders and glared at me. "You deceitful little bastard! How are you here? How are you in Lela's body?"

"I know not myself, Solomon. We are stuck in the same body and I am here to reverse it. The only way to do so is by bringing me back."

"So all of this; the begging to save Robin's life, was all a lie to get me to help you?"

"I am afraid so. Robin was rescued a week ago. Now all we want is to give Lela her body back and put me into mine."

"When did this happen? Have you been the one contacting me this entire time?"

"No, I have not. She called the first time but then she was

captured by Samil. He killed her when she would not give her the information he wanted, but somehow I took over her body. I hear her inside of my head and I know she is still alive."

"Your word is not good enough. Her loved ones may believe you, but I know you. I know you do whatever it takes to get what you want!"

"You are nothing but a coward, Sharmentino. A coward and a hypocrite. My Cherish is dead because of you and now I am trapped in this girl's body. A girl that is associated with *your* descendants. If you do not give her release, then you are just as evil as I am."

"Since when do you care about what happens to others? I thought you would be happy to be alive again." He stared at me for a bit then scoffed. "Oh, I see how it is now. You care about Lela, don't you?"

I held my head high in pride. "She is nothing but a person to me. A vessel. Once I am in my own body, then what happens to her is not my concern."

Solomon stood up and straightened his robes. "You're right. If I don't help you, then this poor girl is going to be trapped inside your mind. There's a whole group of people counting on me to bring her back, and I will." He walked up to me, stopping a few feet away. "But you have to prove to me that you deserve this."

"Bloody hell, Solomon. Nothing is ever simple with you, is it?" I folded my arms. "What proof do you want?"

"Show me that you have some humanity; that you're not a

complete menace to society, and I will give you what you want."

I chewed on the inside of my mouth and glared. Of course he would make it that complex. Knowing him, the humanity he wanted to see would take weeks to achieve. I didn't want to wait that long. I would have to come up with something sooner. Proof that I cared about something; anything at all. Even Lela.

I did care. I tried not to, but the more time I spent inside her head, the more I found her fascinating. That was the word I kept using when it came to her. Because I didn't want to admit that she had a way about her that drew her to me. Maybe it was her audacity to challenge me, or the way she didn't let anyone dishonor her. Yes. I cared. And I hated that I did.

"She reminds me of Cherish," I finally said. This wasn't a complete lie. With red hair, she could easily pass for my daughter, but it wasn't what I originally found interesting about her. "She's been tortured, maimed, killed and still life wasn't done with her. I possessed her body and she's trapped inside her own mind while I'm in control. I tried to help her for as long as I could, but after she died, I took over. She was just trying to save her sister and father. Just like…"

"Just like Cherish," Solomon finished. "She died protecting her family. And unlike Cherish, she still has a chance to live." He touched my arm as if to ask me to follow him and began walking back to where the group was. "All right, you win. I'll tell you where your body is."

Chapter Twenty

When he finally revealed the location of my body, I was stunned. He had hidden it under the bench which he had been sitting on in Saint Martha's Square. I nearly lost my temper. We were right where we needed to be the entire time, and he had stalled instead of just telling us where it was. I wanted to grab some shovels and go dig it up myself, but he warned me that the Vatican City was under tight surveillance. He attempted to explain to me what cameras and video footage was, but I brushed him off and assured him that I took his word for it. He had buried it there in nineteen-forty during the Second World War, and he hadn't planned on ever digging it up, so security was never a problem for him.

Solomon's plan for us was easier than I had thought it would be. It was almost too simple that it was hard to believe we could pull it off. Honestly, I didn't care how we would do it because it meant we were closer to getting my body back. Each moment that passed caused me to become even more and more impatient, but I didn't let it show.

Two of us were going to pose as plumbers and Solomon was going to inform the city council that work was needed to be done on some pipes in the Square. In order to do this, we had to steal a van from a local plumbing company. David had to be the one to hotwire it, but we didn't ask him to help us with the rest. He was growing weaker each day and seemed to age more rapidly as time passed. We would have to work quickly since he was running out of time.

It wasn't until a week later that Solomon finally contacted us and gave us instructions on where to enter the city. We had been staying at the Vatican Bed and Breakfast, which Solomon had generously arranged for, since it was closer to the Square than where we originally had been staying. We acquired jumpsuits in order to be more convincing about our profession.

Gallard drove us into the city and went straight to our destination. He and I were the only ones who were able to work since we had to go during the day, so we planned on getting as much done in one day as possible. To our surprise, the area had already been roped off and the roads blocked for maintenance. He parked the van and we both grabbed our shovels from the back.

"So how are we going to get through the concrete?" I asked.

"Solomon is going to have someone bring a jackhammer. There was already an air compressor in the back, we just need the tool."

I grew silent and stared at the bench under which my body was hidden. I wondered what kind of shape it was in. If it was decomposed beyond recognition; if I had been chewed at by the creatures of the earth. For weeks I'd lay in the darkness, hoping for some relief of my hunger and waiting for the day when I would see the sun again. The more I thought about it, the more I grew anxious to use that body to get my revenge.

"I thought you would have started digging with your bare hands by now," he said.

"Oh believe me I am eager! I am just thinking of who I am going to kill afterwards."

"Seriously? You are getting excited thinking about your future killing sprees?"

"Oh, stop judging me, D'Aubigne. You are the last person to be lecturing me on the value of human life. I know what you did in London, how you killed all those people in a violent rage. Now enough talking, let's start digging, shall we?"

The entire process didn't take long. The jackhammer came about twenty minutes after we arrived, and with my help, Gallard was able to rip the concrete bench off of the ground in one try. The actual jack hammering part was an interesting experience. He nearly lost control of it since he was unprepared for the force, but once he'd worked with it for about ten minutes, he was nearly a pro.

"How long is this going to take?" I asked in an annoyed tone.

"Most of the day, I would assume. It would probably take a normal person a lot longer since they would have to take breaks, but I can go for hours."

"So when will we be able to start digging?"

"Not until tomorrow. We can't stay all night since we have to operate according to the company's advertised business hours. We'll probably be able to get the slab all broken up today and we'll dig tomorrow."

"I am not going to wait another day. If we get it broken up by tonight, we are going to stay if I have to get my body out myself!"

"And risk being seen by the security cameras? I don't think so. We'll come back together and get it tomorrow."

"You just love to watch me squirm, is that it?"

"No, I am just trying to be reasonable. We can't be drawing any unnecessary attention to ourselves."

I wasn't in the mood to be reasonable. I'd spent a total of ten days in her body, and I didn't want to be in it a second longer. He needed motivation, and I didn't care how I would do it.

I took the knife from the pocket of my jumpsuit and stabbed myself with it. It stung terribly, but I was trying to get a point across. Gallard was so stunned that he dropped the jackhammer on his foot. It probably hurt, but he was more focused on me than his injured foot.

"She can probably feel this," I said through clenched teeth.

"Are you insane? What are you doing?"

I stabbed myself again and I said, "She can probably feel this too!"

"Enough Lucian!"

"We will work on *my* terms, D'Aubigne. The moment that this concrete is all broken up, we are going to start digging. I care not what time of day it is. Any failure to comply and I will do more than just poke holes into this body. I will take off fingers, then toes, and maybe even gouge out an eye. None of it matters to me since I will be in a new body very soon."

He nodded and I smirked at him before putting the knife back in my pocket. I was trying to hide it, but I was in pain.

Gallard finished breaking up the concrete around five-thirty just as the others arrived. He wasn't tired from the process but claimed that his hands tingled from the long-term vibration of the hammer. It had taken eight hours to complete, but it had felt like eight years. I sensed that he didn't want me to know, but my little stunt with the knife had alarmed him and caused him to be more urgent with his work. It was finally time to dig, and this part would take no time at all.

Solomon joined us as well, but admitted that he wasn't quite sure where the coffin was exactly. He'd buried it so long ago before the park had even been built in the Square, so we would have to dig in various areas. I didn't think it would take us long since there were six of us.

As I was working off by myself, I listened as Gallard struck up a conversation with Solomon.

"The Bishop who told us where to find you mentioned that you come to this park quite often. Why is that?"

"You must be wondering why I would visit the place of Lucian's burial. It's a valid question. I would wonder myself if I were in your place. The fact of the matter is that I am struggling with my repentance. When I helped slaughter Lucian and his wife many centuries ago, something inside of me changed forever. I'd done horrible things before, but I had made peace with God about them. This was different, though. While I was taking care of Lucian and his wife, two gypsy men came in and slit the throats of Lucian's daughters. I didn't know that they'd planned to do it, and I hated myself for not protecting them. I come here to pray in hopes that one day, I may forgive myself."

I kept my comments to myself, but I wanted to slit my own throat listening to him. He wasn't sorry. He knew very well what those gypsies were planning or else he would have gotten them out of the house before he killed Florence and me. I didn't believe a word he said.

"I think I found something!" Aaron shouted.

We all hurried over to where he was digging and he showed us by striking the ground with the shovel, which made a thud, and it didn't sound like that of a rock. We all bent down and started digging. A few moments later, we were starting to see the top of a flat surface, and I took the shovel to make the edges wider. Soon, we were able to reach down the sides, so we each took a corner and lifted the box out of the hole.

We stood back and just stared at it unsure of what to do next. We'd found it so easily that we couldn't comprehend it. I was the first to move and I pushed them out of my way to look for the latch. I tugged at the lid, but it wouldn't open and I started to get frustrated.

"How do you open the bloody lid, Solomon?" I yelled.

"I'll show you in time, Lucian, but we won't do it here. Let's put it in the van and go somewhere else."

"What are we waiting for? We have the blood and we have the body, now let's finish this!"

Solomon suddenly got very angry. "We're on sacred ground, Lucian. This is the Vatican City; the Catholic capital. I wouldn't have agreed to help in the first place if it wasn't for you possessing my descendent. I will not let this ritual be performed here!"

We loaded the coffin into the van along with our tools and drove out of the city. I had no idea where Solomon wanted us to go. Gallard drove back to the bed and breakfast to pick up David. The others stayed in the car, and he asked that I go with him since he was afraid I would try and drive off without him.

He opened the door and the room was very dark.

"David, are you here?" Gallard asked.

"I'm here, Gallard," said an unfamiliar voice.

We walked into the bedroom and I turned on a light. I was speechless when I saw the man lying on the bed. David no longer looked like himself, but he was replaced by an old man with snow white hair, deep set wrinkles, and translucent skin. His voice had baffled me as well since it was low and raspy. The young vibrant boy whom Lela had first known was now aged and looked old enough to be a grandfather.

"Why are you doing this to yourself?" Gallard finally asked after a long pause.

"It's my choice, Gallard. I've relied on blood for too long.

It's time to let nature run its course."

He struggled to sit up on the bed, and Gallard helped him by using a pillow to support his back.

"Did...did you find his body?" David asked.

"Yes, Aaron found it," I explained. "Solomon has some place in mind where we'll do the ritual, but I have no idea where. Are you ready?"

"Ready to die?" he asked smiling.

"Don't talk like that," Gallard said. "I hate that you have to be involved in this. But I'm glad that we're in this together. It's how it's always been, right? We'd both do anything for her."

"What do you mean *in this together*?"

I looked at Gallard and understood what he meant. It took David a second, but he figured it out too.

"No, Gallard. You can't do this!"

"I have to, David. It's our only option."

"There has to be another option! If we both die, Lela will be alone!"

"She won't be alone. She has her brothers and her sister. Besides, I have to be the other one to do it. If Lucian did it, then her body would die."

David covered his face in his hands and sighed.

"Why is it that there are no good options? No matter what we do, someone is going to get hurt."

"Lela will heal in time. It will be hard for her, but at least she'll be alive. She can move on with her life."

Just then, I felt my phone buzz in my pocket and I looked to see who texted me. I was glad that Lela's phone had been among her belongings so I could use it to contact people. It was Aaron asking if we were coming down or not. I texted him back and then let David know that the others were waiting.

"All right, let's go. You'll have to carry me though. I no longer have the strength walk."

Gallard lifted him off the bed. David looked very thin and frail in his arms and I was sure he would break. His clothes barely fit, and I watched him shiver, probably from a combination of Gallard's skin and the weather. Gallard wrapped a blanket around him then walked slowly as he carried him out the door and into the elevator.

When we got outside, Jordan got out and opened the door before taking David from Gallard and placing him on the seat.

"We're going to do the ritual at the Temple of Minerva. No one is there, and it's not a place of religious significance," Solomon said. He was now in the driver's seat. I got in on the passenger side and we drove off.

It was a fifteen minute drive to the temple, yet we got there in ten since there was hardly any traffic. When we got there, we parked the van in a discreet area before unloading the coffin from the back. Gallard held David while the others carried the coffin. We got to the center of the ruins and set it down. We hadn't uttered a single word the entire time, and even when we'd been
there for about ten more minutes, no one wanted to speak.

"Well, I suppose we should open it," Solomon finally said.

"It is about time! If we moved any slower, we'll be in the next century," I complained.

"You know, you're starting to sound like Florence, nagging us to get going. Silence, before I change my mind."

Solomon walked over to the coffin, and with one shove slid the lid off. We all took a quick step back not really knowing what to expect, and then we slowly walked towards it and peered in.

My body was just as I figured it would be. It looked like that of a mummy with the skin clinging tightly to the bones and the eyes sunken in. The hair was sparse, but what clumps there were hung to the shoulders and were dull orange. My body lay with arms at the sides, and was clothed in old, yet recognizable sixteenth century night garments that had several holes and was covered in dirt and cobwebs. I'd hoped that Solomon would think to put decent clothes on me before burying me away forever. But then again, he probably didn't plan.

"Kevin brought you something to change into for after. You're about his size. It wouldn't be decent of us to let you run around in these old rags," he said. I nodded in thanks. But I wasn't really concerned about clothes. I wanted to get this ritual going.

"David, you go first so we can see if this plan works." I suggested.

"If it's what you want, then I'll do it," he replied.

I watched as Solomon took a knife out of his pocket. Gallard still had David in his arms, and he looked sick. Sicker than David.

"It's all right, Gallard. I'm ready," David assured him.

He reluctantly set him on the ground. He looked up at us and to Aaron said, "I need to apologize to you and your brother."

"For what?" Kevin asked. "For giving us an amazing sister? I'm not sorry that she was born."

"Even still, what I did to your family was wrong. I loved your mother, but she was taken. I feel responsible for—"

"David, our parents' marriage would have imploded with or without you. They weren't happy together. You just brought their real problems to the surface. Just the same, we do forgive you, if that gives you peace of mind," Kevin said.

David then turned to Gallard and waved him over. Gallard knelt down beside him as David spoke.

"There's something you need to know and I want you to tell Lela and only her."

He then whispered something into Gallard's ear, but I couldn't hear it. By the look on Gallard's face, I knew it was something shocking. David smiled and I knew that he was finally ready to die.

Solomon knelt down beside him with the knife. We had decided that the fastest way to drain his blood was to sever the carotid artery, so David leaned close to the body's mouth, which we had to pull open. Then, with perfect precision, Solomon slit his throat.

David slightly grunted, but he didn't yell. He was probably too tired and weak to yell. Gallard walked away, unable to watch him struggle. I listened from a distance as his heart beat slowed until it stopped completely. It had only taken thirty seconds for him to die, but he remained in the same position until we were sure he had bled out almost completely.

Afterwards, Solomon wrapped David's body in the blanket we he had brought along. I wasn't sure what they had planned to do with the bodies once it was all over. I felt that they deserved a proper burial. I respected them for making such a sacrifice.

"Well, the body is already showing some improvement. The skin is starting to get color and the hair is getting thicker and darker," Solomon said, "Who is going to be the final donor?"

Gallard stepped forward and walked over to the coffin and knelt down next to it. I knew that the knife wouldn't do enough damage, so Solomon would have to cut the artery with his teeth. I sympathized with him. Having the entire body drained of its blood was not a pleasant thing to experience. I would describe it as being like starving to death, only in a few seconds instead of over several days.

Before Solomon did the deed, the rest of the group said their goodbyes to Gallard. It wasn't a tearful goodbye, for which I was grateful. The last thing I wanted to see was a bunch of crying men. They were very somber, but all eyes remained dry. Jordan was the most upset of the three, considering he was Gallard's relative.

"I'll take care of her," he said. I didn't have to ask who Jordan was speaking of.

"Thank you," Gallard said, closing his eyes. "All right,

Solomon, finish it."

He tilted his head to get a better angle for his bite and Solomon opened his mouth. When he bit into him, I cringed. I'd only been bitten once, by Solomon just to see what it was like. That, too, was unpleasant.

Only a minute passed before Gallard reached up to touch the wound then sighed.

"It healed," he said.

"I may have to hold the wound open with my hands," Solomon said, "Otherwise it's just going to keep closing up, and it will take a long time to drain."

"Whatever you have to do, do it," Gallard said, "let's try again."

Solomon bit him once more, this time trying out his plan. I could tell it was working because Gallard was getting progressively paler by the second.

A sound in the distance caught my attention and I looked around. Someone was lurking nearby and everyone else was too distracted to notice. I didn't hear a heartbeat, so I knew it was an immortal. I inhaled, trying to see if I could identify the person's scent. I recognized it. Roses.

"Stop! Gallard, don't do this!" Lydian shouted as she came running into the clearing. Solomon stepped away from him and Gallard looked up to face her. I held my breath, waiting to see if he would get up and maim her again. Surprisingly he didn't. He even looked a bit glad to see her.

"Gallard, are you an idiot? You can't die!" she said, now standing next to me.

He struggled to stand up and was stunned when she helped him. I was even more impressed with her bravery of being so close to him after what had happened the last time they were in the same vicinity. The others looked on edge as if they were afraid that he would do something rash.

"We don't have another choice," Gallard said. "I—"

"No, you have another option. Me."

I looked at her face to see if she was being serious. She seemed scared beyond her wits, but determined. It would be rather noble of her to die in his place.

"You would do this? Give up your life for Lela? Why?" he asked.

"Believe it or not, I care about Lela. I didn't realize how much until after everything happened. She's like my sister, and I owe her for betraying her. Besides, we both know that if your situations had been reversed, she would die in Jordan's place and you know it, Handsome."

Gallard seemed hesitant to agree. If our places were reversed, I would have gladly let her die instead. But he wasn't me. He was a gentleman. An honorable human being.

"Are you sure you want to do this?" he asked.

"Yes I am. And don't try and stop me because you're weaker than me right now and I could easily overpower you."

She began walking over to Solomon when Gallard gently

grabbed her arm.

"I just want to know why. Why you joined Samil, why you betrayed your best friend," he said.

"When Samil said that he was going to kill those close to you until you agreed to join him, I had to do something. The three of you were all I had, and I figured that if I could know what they were up to, I would be able to help protect you. I told Samil that I would alert him of your every move and in return he would spare Lela. When he told me that he planned on kidnapping her in order to get information from Lucian, I agreed. He wanted to know Lucian's secret to his ability to walk in the sun, and that would mean he wouldn't need to bring him back. Nobody would have to die. But I didn't know he was so erratic, and when I found out that he'd killed her, I was crushed. In exchange for my loyalty, he let me leave with Robin and promised to pardon Jordan for his impersonation stunt in Vegas."

"Why didn't you tell me that you were passing information? We could have helped you, and maybe even saved David sooner and none of this would have happened!"

"Don't you think I know that? I regret not speaking up every day, and I can't live with myself anymore. At least if I die, Lela can have another chance."

She took his place next to the coffin and waved Solomon over. He looked at Gallard as if to ask for his approval and he vaguely nodded. I knelt down next to her and smirked.

"I must say, Powell. I was wrong about you. You may still

be a harlot, but you are not like my wife as I assumed."

She put a hand on my shoulder and leaned close to my ear. "I'd keep your comments to yourself Lucy. That is, unless you want me to tell Gallard you have a thing for his girl."

I frowned then stood up. I was done dealing with these people and ready to move on. I had planning to do, and sitting around here wasn't getting me any closer to it.

"Wait!" Jordan shouted. He jogged over and knelt beside her, and gave her an adoring kiss while everyone just watched in surprise.

"Thank you. This is very selfless of you," he said.

"No problem, Jordan," she replied, lightly smiling. "I love you."

He kissed her one last time then said, "I love you too." He stood up and placed a reluctant hand on Solomon's shoulder to give him the okay.

Lydian's death took significantly longer than David's. Solomon's method worked on her just as it had on Gallard, and she was completely drained within about five minutes. Jordan then lifted her off of the ground and she shriveled down to nothing in his arms. It was amazing how life could suddenly. One second she'd been up and talking and then the next, she was gone.

Chapter Twenty-One

Soon my body was almost completely regenerated, and we watched in fascination as it changed before our eyes. The hair grew about two feet and darkened to a rich burgundy. The skin had more color but was still pale.

Something was wrong. The switch should have happened by now. We'd done what the gypsies said we were supposed to do and nothing had happened. Lela and I were still trapped in one body and I began to panic. What if they'd lied and there was no way to switch? What if my body could regenerate, but my mind could not?

"Why am I still in this body? Shouldn't the exchange have happened already?"

"I don't know Lucian. It's not like we've ever done this before!" Solomon said.

"Oh, sod off Solomon! The gypsies told you how I could be brought back, so you should know! How long is this supposed to take?"

"I told you, I don't know!"

I began to pace back and forth, struggling with anxiety. I started clawing at the skin on my arms and face. The anxiety was too much, and I felt very uncomfortable. The idea of being trapped in Lela's body forever was starting to drive me insane. I was losing my mind by the second.

"I can't be in this body anymore, I can't take it! There has to be something we missed!"

Solomon grabbed me by the arms before I could do any real damage to myself and shook me to try and snap me out of my state of panic. I was about to speak when I became aware of the presence of a human being in our midst. I'd smelled them before I heard their footsteps.

"What are you doing here?" the man asked in Italian. By the uniform he was wearing, I could tell he was a security guard. Gallard, who was probably extremely thirsty, was about to go after him when I raced ahead and grabbed the man by the throat dragging him back towards them.

"I figured out what we're missing!" I said.

"What?" They asked in unison.

"Human blood. I figured this out when I was observing you, D'Aubigne. I probably can't wake up in my body because it's too weak and needs to feed just like any other vampire."

Solomon folded his arms. "What makes you so sure that this is the answer?"

"Well no one else is coming up with any brilliant ideas. If you think of something else, by all means speak up."

No one moved a muscle as I dragged the man towards the coffin. They didn't say it, but they knew I was right; no one had any better ideas, so they didn't see the harm in experimenting.

The man started yelling for help, and then I snapped his

neck. I then ripped the man's throat open and held him next to the body.

After a few moments the body sat up in the coffin and bit onto the guard and I let go.

"See! I told that I—"

I was cut off by the sudden sensation that I was spinning. Everything around me swirled into a blur of color and then I fell to the ground. I'd experienced this before when Lela had died. I was sucked into a place void of light and my memories began to flash through my mind.

I saw my childhood. I saw Florence. I saw Cherish and Melody. I saw Lela. Then I saw Matthew and Samil. The flashes did a loop and I was back to my childhood. And then I saw people I barely recognized. A man and a woman; Lela's parents. Her memories were beginning to mesh with mine, only with each one I saw, they disappeared and were replaced with mine.

Faster and faster, they flashed in my mind until I couldn't even see anything clearly. I felt like I was being torn apart mentally, pulled into two places at once. The half that seemed furthest away longed to be united with the other half. I didn't know how, but I called for it, reached out for it. And as I'd hoped, it drew closer and closer before everything went dark.

For those few moments, I didn't feel solid, but slowly I began to feel the remnants of a body. It wasn't foreign like it had been when I woke up as Lela. This time, it felt right, as if I'd been fit into the correct glove.

I opened my eyes and the first thing I saw was Solomon standing over me. He didn't say a word and I began to crawl out of the coffin. My legs were stiff, so it was difficult to stand. I had to slowly push myself up.

Once I was standing, I looked down at my arms and hands. They were mine. I reached up and touched my hair and found it was longer than I remembered, but it was my hair, crimson and soft.

"Lucian?" Solomon asked.

I quickly turned my head in his direction. For some reason, my memories were hazy. I couldn't remember the last few hours. I couldn't even remember what had happened before I woke up.

"Where am I?" I asked.

"Do you remember anything? What's the last thing you remember?"

I walked a few paces forward and stopped.

"I remember...I remember you being in my house. I remember there was someone screaming. And then pain, terrible pain."

"What about the last few weeks?"

"The last few weeks? I was at a city council meeting. Someone died and...you thought I was responsible." I pressed my fingertips to my temple and closed my eyes, trying to bring back my memories. I was starting to remember. I was alive, but I was not myself. I was someone else. It was all so hazy, I couldn't piece everything together.

He'd killed me. That's why I was in pain. And the screaming; that had been my daughter; my Cherish. She'd needed me, but I couldn't help her. I couldn't even move.

And I'd come back. Lela; the young woman; I'd taken over her body. We were there to reverse what had happened. I turned and saw a man holding onto her. It took me a second to remember, but I knew who he was. Gallard. The one who loved her.

"Lela! Lela, can you hear me?" He pleaded.

She didn't move a muscle. I moved closer to him, curious to see what would happen. He lifted one of her eyelids and looked at her eyes. They were still blue but foggy. He put his head to her chest and listened for a heartbeat, but from where I was standing, heard none. This was a bad sign since she'd had a heartbeat even when I'd possessed her.

"Come on, Lela, you have to wake up!"

"What if she needs blood like Lucian did?" Jordan piped in.

Before Gallard could make a move, Jordan went over and grabbed the dead guard and brought him over to us. He tore open the man's wrist and held it to Lela's mouth. He opened it to let the blood drop in, and did so until it stopped flowing. Gallard looked in her mouth and found that the blood had just filled it up and wasn't even going down her throat.

"Lela!" Gallard shouted, tears streaming down his face. "Don't do this to me! I can't lose you! I can't!"

He held her in his arms and waited. Waited for any sign of life, for a miracle while I watched. She couldn't be dead. I would have known. I'd heard her speak in my head. The only reason they had helped me was because I'd convinced them that she was still here.

"She was never alive, was she?" Solomon asked, keeping his gaze on Gallard. He grabbed me; pulling the knife he'd used earlier from his pocket and held it to my throat. "You deceived them! You had them believing in a lie so that they would help you!

I pushed him away and he stumbled a bit. "I swear on my life, Sharmentino! I honestly thought that she was alive. Who else would have been in my head?"

"If she's dead, then Lydian died for nothing! And her own father…David…he died for nothing!" Jordan shouted.

Gallard shook his head saying, "They died for love. They died for hope. I would have gladly died too if there was hope that it would bring her back."

I looked down at the lovely girl in his arms. I was disappointed that she wasn't waking up. It was so unfair that she'd gone through so much; sacrificed so much, only to lose her life in the end. I'd known her for her whole life and just like Cherish, she'd been unjustly killed.

I picked up the clothes Solomon had given me and began to put them on. It was odd since I was so used to being in a smaller body, but it was refreshing to be a man again.

"Tis a shame that she had to die," I said, once I was dressed. "She was beautiful. Death is always wasted on the beautiful. Now if you'll excuse me, I have business elsewhere."

"What business? Where are you going?" Solomon asked.

"My memories are unclear, but they are coming back to me. I have unfinished business with a certain gypsy family. I think I'll pay each of them a visit."

I turned and started walking away but stopped and said, "Do not worry, Solomon. I have not forgotten you. I'm not going to let you off so easily. I am saving you for last. First, I'll kill that niece of yours, then Aaron, then Kevin. Robin I will spare because I made a promise to Lela and intend to keep it. And finally when you've watched everyone you love die, I'll rip out your heart."

I was about to run off when I heard more footsteps approaching the temple. First I heard one set, then two and several others joined until I was sure there were at least a dozen people approaching. The others noticed as well and looked around as immortals began to step out of the shadows from all corners of the temple.

One man in particular looked familiar; the hooded one with dark skin. Samil was in Italy as Edgar informed us. We were surrounded and definitely out numbered. This did not frighten me. There were three day-walkers on our side and they had none.

The others moved closer to me, with Gallard still holding Lela in his arms. I could tell Samil's followers were trying to look intimidating but I could see past their tough exterior. They were afraid and probably because of what we'd done to Matthew and Edgar.

"You brought back Lucian, I see!" Samil said. "Greetings,

Mr. Christophe. How does it feel to be back in your own body?"

"Peachy. Now if you will excuse me, I want to be on my way."

I started to move then Solomon grabbed onto the back of my shirt, restricting me from walking. I didn't want to stick around for this. Why did he want me to stay? If he thought I was going to fight with them, he was mistaken. Samil could slaughter the lot for all I cared. I had business to attend to.

Samil and his followers closed in on us, forming a circle so there was no way we could escape. There was no leaving now. I would have to help these people in order to help myself. As much as I hated it, I still needed them and they still needed me.

"What do you want, Samil?" I asked, speaking for the group. It was me he'd been looking for, after all.

"You know what I want, Lucian. Tell me how you walk in the day and we will let your friends go freely."

I laughed at him. Where did he come off threatening me after I'd already stabbed him and ripped apart his main man? He was either stupid or very desperate.

"You think these idiots are my friends? Quite the contrar—" I couldn't finish because Solomon had covered my mouth. He always used to do this whenever I was about to start a fight in a bar and it still infuriated me to this day.

"Lucian was born a vampire," Solomon answered for me. "The man responsible disappeared over almost six hundred years ago and no one has heard from him since. If you want answers, look for him."

"I've spent my whole life searching for answers!" Samil shouted. "I've had enough of this. Kill them! Kill all of them!"

The followers began moving closer and Solomon let go of me as we prepared to fight. He pulled me aside and began to speak quickly.

"I need you to clear the way for Kevin so he can take Lela and run," he said.

"You think I will save your descendant when you didn't save mine?"

"This isn't about him, Lucian. You care about Lela, right?"

Why did he have to ask this question now when the situation was stressful and dangerous? I had to answer quickly so I could take action, and I hated being honest, but honesty would get things moving faster.

"Yes, I care, all right!"

"Go then!"

I let out an annoyed sigh as I ran off towards Gallard. He looked confused when I approached him.

"Give her to me," I said.

He slowly turned his gaze from Lela to me. His eyes looked dead; soulless. I wouldn't want to be on his bad side anytime soon because he had nothing else to lose.

"D'Aubigne, they need you to fight," I said. "Kevin will take her to safety."

Kevin must have heard his name because he came running

over to us. Gallard appeared to be in shock, like he wasn't able to accept Lela was still lifeless. He didn't even protest when Kevin took her from him.

I found a gap in the group and motioned for Kevin to follow me. I ran for it and as I predicted, someone came at me. I knocked him over in one blow, then as another attacked, I grabbed his arms and tore them out of the sockets. No one else dared come near me after that, so I kept an eye on Kevin until I saw him put Lela in the van then drive away.

I then ran back into the temple and assessed what was going on. Most of them were holding their own, but I noticed Samil was still standing in the same place, watching from a distance. He looked afraid and about to make a run for it. I ran towards him just as he started to leave and slammed him onto the ground.

"Why are you going to kill me?" he asked.

"Because you annoy me. You wasted your life obsessing over me and my ability for the answer to a question I know not myself."

"You should thank me! I gave you life!"

"You gave me nothing. Lela was right. You should have your stupid head put in a blender. Immortals like you are a waste of space."

I lifted my hand, prepared to use my nails to tear open his throat when someone grabbed my arm to stop me. It was Gallard. "He's mine," he said, his eyes filled with more rage than ever. I nodded then stepped out of the way. He was right. Samil was not mine to kill. He deserved his chance at getting vengeance.

For several moments Gallard just stood over Samil, not saying a word. I remained close by, eager and curious to see how this would end. In a way I was taking mental notes for when I would exact my own revenge. Solomon's demise had to be just right; the perfect payment for his crime.

"Gallard, old friend. Couldn't we forgive and forget? We've both made mistakes in the past, and I believe—"

Before he could finish, Gallard kicked him in the face and without given Samil a moment to recover, kicked him in the side of the head as well. Samil tried to crawl away, but Gallard stepped on his back, pressing down as hard as he could and I heard Samil's spine make a sickening snap. His yells pierced the air and the rest of his followers that survived the fight took off running in every direction out of the temple.

Gallard removed his foot from Samil's back then used it to turn him over. By Samil's lack of movement, I knew that he'd been paralyzed, as I had the night Solomon killed me. How much pain he was in could range from none to severe. I'd only felt a sting for a second before I lost all feeling, but breaking the back was different.

"You've taken away everything I care about. Everything I love," Gallard said.

"What about *him*?" Samil nodded his head in my direction. "It was his blood that turned you. He's the reason you're doomed to live a life where everyone you love dies!"

Gallard picked him up by his jacket and glared at him.

"Lucian didn't kill Dyani! Lucian didn't kill Lela's family in front of her, torture her then murder her in cold blood. You did. And after all these years, I finally get to destroy you for good before you do this to anyone else."

Gallard grabbed Samil by his head and in one swift jerk separated it from his body before dropping both to the ground. A calm swept through everyone in the group; a sense of peace and relief. I couldn't imagine being harassed and beleaguered for over two hundred years. Then again, being trapped in a box for half a century was worse by far. I would have given anything to trade circumstances.

"Glad that is over with," I said. "Shall we—"

Gallard turned around and punched me in the mouth before I could finish. It had taken me off guard and he even caused my lip to bleed. His strength was definitely more massive than the immortals I'd just fought. He was more of an adequate fighting opponent than they had been.

"You should not have done that, D'Aubigne."

We lunged for each other and he shoved me to the ground. I quickly recovered then kicked him away, but he was more resilient than the night-walkers I'd just fought. He jumped back up and we were about to charge at one another when Solomon stopped me while Jordan held Gallard back. It was a struggle for both of them to keep us from tearing each other apart, but eventually I backed off and so did he.

"You've done enough here, Lucian. I think it would be best if you leave," Solomon said.

"You want *me* to leave? What have I done but help you and try to save this girl you all care about?"

"You lied to us!" Gallard shouted. "You made us think she was alive and she clearly is not. You've wasted our time and toyed with our emotions long enough!"

I smirked at him. At all of them. They were accusing me of such injustice when I'd stayed behind and helped fight when I easily could have run off.

"I saved your descendant, Sharmentino. Tis more than you have done for me." I jerked away from his grasp. "You will regret asking me for a favor. You will pay for it, as you will pay for what you did to me and my daughter."

I walked away from them, half expecting someone to try and stop me, but no one did. They were either too tired to fight me or they didn't take my threat seriously.

I had no idea where I would go or what I wanted to do. Solomon said that the gypsies were responsible for Cherish's death, so they would be the first to go. I would have to find them and make them wish they'd never heard the sound of my name.

As for Solomon, I wouldn't go after him right away. I needed to plan first, like I had when I plotted to kill Florence. Killing Solomon now would not give me enough satisfaction. He needed to suffer as I had. He needed everyone he loved to be ripped from him as he watched and only then would I take his life.

Chapter Twenty-Two

Gallard stood in the back of cemetery, keeping his distance while the group including Curtis and Gabriella Taylor gathered around the Sharmentino burial plot. It had been two weeks since they returned from Italy and Lela's brothers had already had her name engraved on the family headstone. They wanted a small ceremony for when it was finished.

Gallard didn't want to go and said that he wouldn't be there, yet here he was. The ceremony couldn't give him the closure he wanted. Her body wasn't even there. It was buried in a cemetery in Rome. He wished that he'd been able to bring her back so she could have a proper burial. She should have been put to rest alongside her parents.

It all seemed so surreal. He'd been to several funerals in his lifetime, yet this one felt like a dream. A horrible nightmare. All three of those who he'd been drawn to were dead, leaving him with a loneliness he never thought possible. He'd felt the pull almost his entire life and in the past, he used to wish it would stop. Now that he knew why he'd felt it, he would give anything to feel it again; to feel her again.

The moments up until he'd buried her had been strange. He'd had a bad feeling ever since Lucian was switched back and he couldn't explain it. He knew quite a bit about death and he was certain that rigor mortis was supposed to set in after at least six hours. They'd waited nearly ten to burry Lela and it never happened to her. She remained as though she were only asleep.

He'd laid her on the bed of the hotel and watched her for hours, waiting for some sign that she was alive. But her heart never beat again and she never opened her eyes. He finally listened to everyone's pleas to let her rest and that was when they'd taken her to the cemetery. They found an empty stone casket with an angel carved on top and decided it was perfect for her. He'd kissed her one last time before sealing her in.

The group started to break up and he hid himself more as the Taylor siblings passed by. Gallard glanced at Curtis' face and saw that it matched what he was feeling. He'd never thanked Curtis for watching over Lela those two months while they'd been searching for Solomon and Samil. It was obvious that Curtis had cared for her, but Curtis let her go so she could be with him.

The only ones left were Jordan and Lela's family. They were lingering a bit longer, taking their time leaving the cemetery. It was darker, making it less likely for him to be seen. He stepped out from behind the tree and prepared to leave. He was supposed to be waiting for them at the house and didn't want anyone to know that he'd caved and came anyway. They hadn't discussed the plan for avoiding Lucian and his plan for revenge. Everyone agreed that they needed time to mourn first.

As they walked by with Robin's hand in Kevin's, the little girl looked in Gallard's direction and he made eye contact with her.

There was no hiding now that she'd seen him. What surprised him more was that she let go of her brother's hand and came running in his direction. Kevin called to her, but she ignored him. She didn't slow down, even as she drew closer and he had to reach out and pick her up before she ran into him.

"Gallard! Why didn't you come? We missed you," she said. He smiled as he held her. She was a near replica of Lela, minus fifteen years and the curly hair. She was so trusting of others, growing comfortable with strangers more quickly than anyone should. He'd only been around her for a short time and she was already running to him like he was important in her life. Just as Lela had when they'd met in Orlando. She'd known him for a day before asking to tag along on his trip.

He then remembered what David had whispered into his ear the night he'd died. The secret he was supposed to pass on to Lela and never could. Samil had not only taken Robin as leverage against Lela, but also to ensure David's loyalty. Because the truth was, Robin had been David's daughter as well. Gallard decided that this secret wouldn't benefit anyone, so he would keep it to himself until maybe when Robin was older. She deserved to know the truth just as much as Lela had.

"I'm sorry, little one," Gallard said. "I was too sad to come. But I am here now."

"Lela said not to be sad. But it's so hard! I wish she could come back."

The others joined them and he let out a guilty sigh. He'd

hoped he could sneak out of there without their knowing, but he couldn't ignore the little girl.

"What are you doing skulking around here?" Jordan asked.

"I'm keeping an eye on everything. We don't want you-know-who making a surprise appearance."

"We'll be fine, Gallard," Kevin said. "Solomon is flying over here soon and he'll be around to look out for us."

"I guess that means Jordan and I can go back to Vegas then. I still don't have a phone, but if you need anything you can call him. Just because Lela is gone doesn't mean I don't care about her family."

Robin rested her head on his shoulder and he held her tighter, but not enough to hurt her; the same way he'd always held Lela.

"She gave her life so she could protect her sister. Take care of this little girl. Don't let it be in vain."

Epilogue

Evelyn McAlister stared at her brother's house as they pulled into the driveway. It looked nothing like the last time she'd been there, and it was almost as if it were a completely different home. The lawn looked extremely unkempt and the windows were all boarded up.

The house was supposed to have been sold by then, but after everything that had happened, Aaron decided to take it off the market. The house was filled with too many memories and her nephews didn't want to let go of it. She understood, and that was why she and her husband decided to move into it. For that reason and also to take care of her niece. She felt it was best that Robin not be dragged across the country away from her brothers. They were all she had left.

"Mark would have hated to see his lawn like this," she said to her husband Jeff. He took her hand and squeezed it.

"Are you all right? We don't have to go in now, we could grab dinner in the city first."

"No, I'll be okay. We have two nephews and a niece that need us to be there for them."

They got out of the car and walked up the steps to the door. Aaron and Kevin had said they were home, but there were no signs of life in the house. The lights were off, though it was only six-thirty and the curtains were closed. Jeff knocked on the door and they waited for an answer.

Not thirty seconds later, the door opened and Kevin stood in the doorway. It had only been a few months since she'd last seen her nephews when she'd been in town for her brother and sister in law's funeral. Kevin seemed to mature beyond his years overnight, and he looked even more solemn.

"Aunt Evie, it's so good to see you again," he said wrapping her in a tight hug. She tensed up a little in his embrace. The coldness of it shocked her as if she'd hugged pillar of ice.

"Kevin, sweetheart, it's good to see you too."

Kevin greeted Jeff as well before inviting them into the house. Evelyn was surprised that everything was so clean. The last time she'd been there, the house had still been messy from their stuff being moved in. Now, the floors looked like they had been waxed and the carpet recently vacuumed. There wasn't a speck of dust anywhere.

"The house looks nice," she said turning on the lamp to get a better look. Kevin nodded.

"I have been cleaning like crazy. I guess I wanted to get my mind off of everything."

As he finished speaking, Robin came down the stairs. The look on Robin's face broke Evelyn's heart, and she reached out to pick her up. She hadn't seen her since she was returned by her abductors and she longed to hold and comfort her niece.

"How are you doing, pumpkin?" she asked.

"I miss them," Robin replied, "I want my mommy and daddy. And I want Lela back!"

She started crying and Evelyn fought to keep her composure as she comforted the little girl. She couldn't imagine what it was like to lose both parents and a sibling at such a young age. She had to have been distraught and confused, more so than the rest of them.

"I know, baby. I miss them too."

"Where's your brother?" Jeff asked Kevin.

"Probably at his girlfriend's house. I've been taking care of Robin by myself since he moved to Orlando."

They all went into the living room to talk. Robin fell asleep in Evelyn's arms and Kevin took her upstairs to her room. No one knew exactly what to say, so they just sat in silence until Kevin returned to the living room.

"So, how's the search going?" Jeff asked. "Do they have any leads to where that Terrence Fox guy is?"

"We don't have a clue," Kevin said. "We haven't heard anything since we received the message that Lela was dead. We are just as much in the dark as you are."

"I still can't believe this is happening. How did Lela, my sweet innocent niece, get involved with such a dangerous group of people?" Evelyn asked.

"She wasn't involved. Terrence Fox was. She just got roped into his problems by association," Kevin explained. Evelyn watched as Kevin's expression became troubled. She started to get the feeling that he knew something but was holding back. Secrets were the last thing that she needed right now.

"What aren't you telling us?" she asked.

"Aunt Evelyn…there's something you should know about Terrence Fox," Kevin said. "Before Lela left four years ago, she learned from our mother that Mark wasn't her real father. That was why she left; to find out more information. It turned out her biological father was Timothy Fox and her half brother Terrence was the one she was living with all those years she was gone. And it was his enemies that came after our family. They found out that Lela came from good money and they killed our parents then took Robin to try and get her to give them ransom."

Evelyn gasped in shock. All this new information was almost too much for her. Sheila had had an affair and because of that affair almost her entire family was nearly killed by enemies associated with her lover. Evelyn felt as if the picture of her brother's perfect family that she'd always had in her mind was slowly being tarnished as skeletons started coming out of the closet.

"Excuse me, I need a minute," she said. Jeff started to follow her, but stopped at the last second. She was glad since she wanted some time alone, to wrap her head around everything. She found herself going up the stairs. She wanted to check on Robin and see if she was still asleep. She didn't like thinking of the little girl being alone with all that she was going through.

She slowly opened the door and quietly tiptoed towards the bed. She heard a slight whimper, and her heart broke all over again.

"Oh, sweetheart. It's going to be okay!" she said sitting next to Robin and wrapping her arms around her. "I promise you that you're going to be fine."

The little girl cried into her shoulder, convulsing as each sob wracked her body. Evelyn said a silent prayer for her as she attempted to sooth her. At this point, it seemed only God could take away her niece's suffering.

She jumped when she heard the doorbell, and wondered who would be stopping by at such a late hour. It was nearly ten-o'clock, and she was looking forward to taking a hot shower and going to bed. She kissed Robin's forehead before leaving the room and heading downstairs. She waited at the foot of the staircase as Kevin looked through the peephole.

"Who is it?" she asked. Without answering, he opened the door.

"Solomon, hey! You came just in time," he said to the visitor.

Evelyn watched as the man at the door came in. He was of average height and dressed in a polo and black slacks. He looked like he belonged to some sort of fancy corporation. But what puzzled her most was how much he resembled her brother, Mark. Besides his dark hair and eyes, he had the same strong jaw-line as her father had and his nose was eerily similar to hers.

"Aunt Evelyn, this is Solomon Sh…Schaech," Kevin said. "He's the private detective that's looking into our parent's and Lela's case."

Evelyn warily shook his hand. Jeff came into the foyer from the kitchen.

"Who's this?" Jeff asked. Kevin smiled and Jeff shook Solomon's hand.

"Jeff, Kevin said that this is a private detective," Evelyn explained. Jeff frowned, equally as confused as his wife.

"I didn't know we had one."

"Neither did I," Evelyn replied.

Solomon then went on to explain that he'd heard about the case and contacted the boys recently. He even showed Evelyn and Jeff his badge and driver's license, so she came to the conclusion that he was telling the truth.

Jeff invited him to sit down in the living room and everyone moved from the foyer to the couches. Evelyn offered Solomon some tea, but he assured her that he was all right, so she sat down next to her husband, resting her hand on his knee.

"So, what exactly will you be doing for us?" she asked.

"Whatever you need me for. I'm here to investigate the case as well as make sure you, your husband, and your brother's children are safe. I'll be on your case until it's solved, no matter how long it takes."

"How much is this going to cost?" Jeff asked.

"Don't worry about the cost. I'm not here to make money; I'm here to help your family."

Jeff suddenly tugged on Evelyn's arm and excused his wife and him from the group, pulling her off the couch and into the kitchen. She had a feeling that sooner or later her husband would want to discuss the whole Solomon thing. He'd given the impression early on that he was leery about the situation.

"Evelyn, are you sure you believe this guy?" he asked. She put a finger to her lips, hoping he would lower his voice.

"I think he's telling the truth. He seems credible, and Kevin trusts him."

"Just because Kevin believes everything he says doesn't mean he's genuine. He has a badge and dresses nice, so what? For all we know, he's just trying to scam us out of Mark's money."

Evelyn sighed and folded her arms. Her husband had a point. She would have to get to know him better before being quick to trusting his every word.

"What do you think we should do?" she asked Jeff.

"We could spend some time with him; look for any hints that he's a con man. I don't think it would be smart to start calling him out in his B.S. right away. He may be telling the truth."

Evelyn nodded then they both went back into the living room. By the look on everyone's face, Evelyn could tell that they'd walked in on an intense conversation.

"I hope we're not interrupting," she said sitting back down. Solomon's serious face became pleasant once more, making her feel comfortable speaking with him. "So, what information have you found so far?"

Coming soon…

The Resurrection

Part Three in the Day-Walker Saga